Caroline stood on the snowbank to see the new governor, Lord Elgin, ride into Montreal.

Against the background of the snow the sleek horses and their brilliantly arrayed riders made a brave sight.

Then Caroline let out a cry. The snow had moved most treacherously, and was carrying her on out into the road, in front of the plunging horses.

Suddenly there was someone there, arms about her steadying her. Caroline, shaking as those pawing hooves barely missed raking down her, looked up into Corbie Hannaker's face.

His eyes were like blue sparks of fire.

Caroline

André Norton
and Enid Cushing

TOR

A TOM DOHERTY ASSOCIATES BOOK

CAROLINE

Copyright © 1983 by André Norton

A Tor Book

Published by Tom Doherty Associates, 8-10 W. 36th St., New York City, N.Y. 10018

First printing, January 1983

ISBN: 0-523-48059-8

Printed in the United States of America

Distributed by Pinnacle Books, 1430 Broadway, New York, N.Y. 10018

Caroline

1

Caroline Warwick drew her shawl closer about her shoulders with an impatient jerk which made the long red braid of her hair swish across her back. She still hesitated, in spite of her need, for a moment or two before opening the too-long closed door of Richard's room. Of course it was opened weekly, for a good turn-out. Her mother would have allowed no room in the tall St. Gabriel Street house to escape that. However, with Richard gone so long overseas it was a dead room—if rooms could be considered dead—maybe better to think of it as sleeping. Caroline wrinkled her nose slightly as she slipped within and could catch the welcome, to her, scents of drugs and salves— even though it had been some years now since any box or jar of medication had been opened here.

Without any fire the room was doubly cold—the window panes near frosted over. The Warwicks' most elegant residence, as the saying went, might be one of the most desirable in the English section of Montreal, but that did not mean that fires were wasted upon empty chambers. Caroline ran her fingers along a line of somewhat shabby books on a nearby shelf, pulled free the volume she sought, to carry it closer to the window.

Doctors—real doctors—were supposed to learn more from observation than from books. But young ladies—even when they were doctor's daughters—were not encouraged into any such observations. Though Richard, before he had left for the special polishing the Scottish and European medical schools could promise, had always answered most of her questions fairly and completely. Of course she dealt with animals—not people. For three generations the Warwicks had been doctors in Montreal. Her father had taught in the newly opened medical school at McGill University, before his time had been absorbed by a large private practice. His patients came here for consultation; the whole house smelled sometimes of oil of peppermint. Caroline smiled—perhaps that remedy did make more palatable some of the more nasty doses one had to take.

She slipped hastily through the somewhat yellowed pages of the book, paused at one with a sketch very clearly shown. That was the way it went; she remembered it all even as Richard had first outlined the process for her.

And a cat's leg could not be too different from a human one—not for the treatment of a simple break. She could get the footman James to whittle two pieces of wood for a splint. Then Boots would walk about on four feet again—and straight, too, if she had any talent at all. Richard had always said she had.

Caroline set the book regretfully back in its place. If she had only been a son—instead of a daughter! Her brother Perry did not seem to care for medical learning at all, though he had Father's help. It was Richard Harvey (he was not a Warwick at all, although he had lived with them since his mother died when he was born and his father had gone west and died in the wilderness) who seemed to be the truly devoted doctor.

Even through the tightly closed windows Caroline caught a sound which startled her into going closer to the nearest and scraping a peep-hole in the frost.

It was—it truly was!

She headed for the door, Boots not forgotten, but the chance to see Corbie Hannakar's choice team was too imperative. Those matched greys were the envy of every young man, and a lot not so young, too, in the city—maybe even in the province. He was coming to pick up Priscilla, of course.

She must tell her sister he was here.

Only, as she reached to open the door, she heard voices beyond.

" 'Tis lazy in your very bones you are, m' girl. Miss Priscilla will take the rough side of her tongue to you and rightly this time. Touch up the lilac she was saying—give it a bit of the iron here and there. And what have you been doin' instead? Get to it, Jessie! Her young gentleman will be comin' and no dress for her back!"

"Dresses for her back, is it now?" came a sullen reply. "She has so many of those that the door of her wardrobe can't decently close on 'em. I had me polishing of the silver to do, and then cook sent me out for some spices. Lay an iron to her dress? Show me a free time I had for that—and it not even creased enough to matter!"

"Miss Priscilla is particular," that was Mollie, Caroline's own favorite downstairs. "Rightly so—don't she move like a princess herself with all the gentlemen a-sighing after her?"

"They do more than sigh, were it a time for truth tellin'. And Miss Priscilla, she ain't as mindful of bein' a lady as—"

Caroline stepped into the hall. Both girls, Jessie with her mouth half open, moved a step or so away, as if she had indeed caught them in some household dereliction of duty. Over Jessie's arm was folded the lilac silk in question. With only a half glance at Caroline the maid hurried past, but Mollie stood her ground.

" 'Tis Mr. Hannakar coming, Miss Caroline."

"I'll tell Miss Priscilla. You may go, Mollie—"

She was aware of the reluctance with which Mollie went. The Irish girl was fiercely loyal to all the doctor's family. Wasn't it now, as she often said, that the doctor his own self had had her off that immigrant boat where there was black trouble, and into his home quick as the flash of a gull's wing—and she no more idea where to lay her head come night, with her uncle Padric dead and all? He had been like an angel right out of heaven to bring her to this fine house where there was always good food on the table and the work not near as hard as in the fields to home—with wages in her hands, too, come the day for the paying of them. A fine man, the doctor, and she would like to see anyone in this whole city who could say no to that! Sure, the mistress had a keen eye for any wrongness about the house and why not? Was not it her own fine things to be guarded so? And Miss Priscilla, for all her flirting and play-acting before the gentlemen, was a beauty. Though for Mollie she could not touch the warm heart Miss Caroline had in her bosom, and her always remembering the ills and hurts of others, trying to make them the less. Like the doctor she was—only she had an eye for the ills of the heart like, and not just those of flesh and bones.

Caroline at that moment was very much aware of some ills—since those were being spoken clearly in her mother's voice and in a tone she had been only too often hearing herself from time to time.

"—Lieutenant Masterson—four dances—AND the

supper! This is NOT to happen again, Priscilla. Mrs. Mostrain was keeping count of your actions, and you know well how sharp her tongue can be. Let any young girl have her name mentioned too much in that quarter and she will suffer the consequences—Caroline!''

She had caught sight of her younger daughter in the mirror as Caroline hesitated just within the door.

''What is it now?'' Exasperation raised Mrs. Warwick's usually calm and well bred (the two faculties which were always paired, as every proper matron knew) voice several tones higher than usual.

Caroline was flurried, a condition to which her mother often reduced her.

''It's Mr. Hannakar—his sleigh is in the street.''

The sharp frown lines between her mother's brows smoothed a fraction. Corbie Hannakar was one of the catches of the tightly woven English society. Though Mrs. Warwick would not descend to such a vulgar statement before her daughters. Having spent two years in the west visiting the posts established by the family fur trade, he was a member of the very elite ''Beaver Club,'' also the master of a sizable estate in the country not too far from the city, and he was even a personable young man in his own right. So far he had chosen no permanent attachment among the young ladies of society. His house was ably presided over by the formidable Madam Hannakar, his mother, who went out little these days, but could still make her presence felt when she wished, or if her son desired. To be asked for a drive behind Corbie Hannakar's greys established one's daughter a fraction more securely.

''Hurry, Priscilla—Caroline, your father is in his office and cannot be disturbed; go down and make sure Mollie receives our guest properly. She is too apt to forget to take his hat or show him into the sitting room rather than the parlor.''

Caroline caught a last glimpse of her sister. Pris had not made any move at all, but was still sitting with both elbows planted on her dressing table, staring into the mirror, her lips tightly compressed together and that stubborn gleam in her eyes which, Caroline had noted, came more and more often nowadays.

What was wrong with Pris, she wondered as she hurried downstairs, her shawl loose and trailing behind her. Pris was so pretty—no, she was really beautiful! Her hair was not this horrid red but more like the first turn of the maple leaves in fall—all golden and rich—while her eyes were that shade of blue which can also seem violet upon occasion, not hazel like Caroline's own. She *did* look like a princess—walking as if all the world belonged to her. Nor was it true that because she was near twenty and had no ring in her finger she was going to be left an old maid! Priscilla an old maid! Caroline laughed out loud at that thought, then realized that a tall, very tall, man had turned to face her inquiringly. She blushed, feeling the heat of her own cheeks, and knew that she was acting just like a child again. She so often did, her mother was quick to tell her.

''Mr. Hannakar,'' she hurried on, for one could not very well curtsey properly while one was on the stairs, and he made her feel even more odd because he was bowing in the same way he might greet Priscilla. ''Pris—Priscilla—will be right down. Won't—won't you come into the parlor?''

He was smiling now, but he was so tall she had to look up quite a distance to make sure that he was not smiling *at* her but with her. There was a difference, but Caroline could only be truly sure of it with a few people. With Richard and, oddly enough, with this very fair, tall young man who, for all his size, moved so quietly and easily that Caroline wondered if he had learned that skill in the Indian country.

"Miss Caroline, I shall be delighted to step into your parlor." His voice was smiling, too, and her unease of moments earlier was quite gone.

"Please," she stopped beside the small hall table and jerked open a drawer, "could, could you give these to your horses? They are so—so very beautiful!"

He looked at the outspread palm of her hand, on which rested a pair of sugar lumps.

"So your hospitality extends outside the door also, Miss Caroline? Why not put on your bonnet and cloak and present your gifts yourself?"

For a moment she was eager—to be allowed to touch one of those peerless horses she had watched such a number of times these past few weeks. Then she remembered, and shook her head.

"Oh, I would like to so much, but there is Boots—and I have left him far too long. Cook said she would watch, but she has dinner to be thinking of and I must tend him as soon as I can."

"Boots?" Mr. Hannakar, standing by the marble mantelpiece, was looking at her almost as if he were really interested.

"He's a kitten. Tim found him. He has a broken leg, and he crawled into the stable yard. I will have to set the bone, then make sure he is comfortable. Richard had a drawing in his book I needed to see. Of course, a man's bones and Boots' may be different, but I think I can splint it."

"I am sure Boots is in the best of hands—My word, are you all doctors under this roof, Miss Caroline?"

This time her flush was even hotter, her chin came up determinedly and she was not afraid to look at him. Perry teased her, and sometimes Mama was really angry at her care for the lost animals and their hurts. Only Richard had somehow understood. Now this Mr. Hannakar, whom she had thought just a moment ago to be so pleasant, was using that same tone Perry did when he really wanted to make her angry.

"I do not like to see any creature in pain, sir," she said steadily, "if something can be done to help." Carefully she put the sugar lumps down on the table, which already bore two small figurines, a picture framed in carved oak, and a miniature vase on its brocade-covered surface. "My sister will be down shortly."

He took a single stride to come between her and the door.

"I'm sorry, Miss Caroline. My mother has said that I have a tongue I should watch at times. Your interest in this Boots and his troubles has everything to commend you. You admire the greys; I shall see they get their sweets." He turned and swept the sugar cubes into his own hand. "Not only that, I shall have them beg my pardon for me. Tomorrow I am coming in town to a meeting. Barney shall bring the greys around, and you will have your own ride behind them. Will that be atonement enough?"

Caroline drew a deep breath. He meant it, she was sure of that. He was not like those young gentlemen who made some careless promise in a moment and then forgot it.

"I would—it would be very kind of you, sir." She schooled her rising excitement to the proper level. "Oh, Priscilla is coming now. And—thank you so very much,

Mr. Hannakar.'' Now she had space and time to make the most proper of curtseys even as her sister, her face framed in a ravishing bonnet of fur, her fur-lined cloak wrapped well about her, appeared in the doorway.

She might have been sullen upstairs, but it was plain that Pris was now in the best of humors, and her beauty glowed under her warm greeting for Mr. Hannakar. Caroline was able to slip away without Pris noticing her.

However, she was not to reach the kitchen quarters and the waiting Boots without a further sign that all was not well in the household. The door of her father's office stood ajar, and she was stopped short by his voice raised in the same severe tone that her mother had been using with Priscilla. It would seem that both the twins were in disgrace today.

''I cannot understand you, Perry. Such a report concerning your lack of true interest—it is a disgrace!''

''I can't help it if old Howards has taken a dislike to me. I've been doing my best.'' Perry was petulant. Caroline need not see him to know that his rather full lips were shaping a pout to match any Pris could summon at will.

''*Dr.* Howards. You will be respectful in this house, Perry! Also I will accept no such excuses—they are unbecoming a Warwick.''

''Why didn't you try to make a doctor out of Archie? He's near pompous enough—''

Caroline drew a deep breath. Perry was going too far. How dare he talk to Papa in that fashion?

''We shall leave Archie out of this. And I shall expect a better report next time, Perry. You have no excuse—you are intelligent enough to master what you must learn. Richard—''

''Always Richard!'' Perry exploded. ''I'm sick and tired

of hearing about Richard— Let's just agree he's perfection itself and forget him—sir!'' That last word was in a slightly different tone, as if Perry realized he had gone too far. ''With your permission, sir,'' he added after a moment, ''I'll be on my way—to Dr. Howard's lecture, I assure you!''

''You may go.'' There was still that harsh tone in Papa's voice.

Caroline moved back just in time as Perry threw open the door. There were flaming red spots on each rounded cheek above the fringe of whisker he was so carefully encouraging, and he pushed past her without noticing her at all. Caroline drew a deep breath. This was no time for seeing Papa, even though she had wanted to beg some healing salve from his stores.

She drew her shawl once more about her and went on to the far back of the hall, pushing through the butler's pantry into the warm and busy kitchen beyond. Busy it was, for this was Friday and on Fridays Archie and Agatha came to dinner—a meal to which Caroline had only recently been promoted as a young lady, and from which she shrank when her elder brother and his wife were present.

Cook presided over the long table with a regular regiment of bowls, cups, and measures before her, and there was a glow from the big stove which made Caroline quickly shuck off her shawl and throw it over the back of the rocking chair where cook took her well-earned ease as she supervised the washing up later on. There was going to be a lot of that, Caroline thought, as she slipped by to kneel by the basket on the edge of the wide hearth.

A grey kitten raised its head and whimpered a very small mew as Caroline, having collected her supplies, went to work with the efficiency taught by other such episodes in the past. Twice tiny jaws closed on her fingers warningly, but, all in all, Boots was not hard to handle. He must somehow understand that she wanted to help. And when she was through, she held a saucer of warmed milk at which he lapped greedily, with more appetite than she had hoped for.

Orders and admonitions flew over and above her, all issuing from cook and intended for the two maids and the tweenie who had such lowly tasks as the scrubbing of vegetables and the washing of the pans.

Caroline, the kitten safely back in its basket bed, dared to sit in cook's chair and watch. Breakfast seemed very far away, and she munched on the bits of pie crust browned in the oven on a pan of their own, sprinkled with cinnamon and sugar, which cook made out of habit and the desire to see that nothing ever went to waste in *her* kitchen. Their light flakiness melted on the tongue as Caroline reluctantly started back to the forepart of the house. Mama would be hunting her sooner or later, and she had no excuse which would justify such a departure from a young lady's role.

The hall seemed doubly cold as she left the kitchen quarters, though there would be fires going now in all the rooms along it. She saw that her father's office door was closed. It was the hour for patients, and the family were supposed to stay in their own part of the house. Only Caroline ventured quickly to the front door and peered out.

Sleighs swung along and there were clouds darkening, maybe bringing more snow. Pris should be back soon; they would not go far with that threat of a new storm. Was it snowing in Scotland, too? That was a cold country from all she heard. Richard—when was Richard coming home?

"Caroline!"

She started, looked up the stairs over her shoulder. Mama had that sharp frown line showing again, and the lace lappets of her house cap lay askew on her shoulders, almost as if she had been whirled about by the same wind which was raising the snow outside.

"Coming, Mama." She licked her lips twice to make sure that none of the betraying sugar crystals still clung, and hurried up the stairs.

"Your practicing, Caroline. I do not understand why is it necessary for me to keep reminding you. Any young lady who has no accomplishments to interest company cannot be expected to become a welcome part of society. Pris should be an example to you, but one would think that your fingers were all thumbs! I declare I do not see what we shall do with you when it comes time for you to accept your proper station among our friends! Let me hear you try that piece Miss Watkins sent you."

Caroline slipped on into the upper sitting room where the somewhat shabby cottage piano stood. With a smothered sigh she adjusted the stool and obediently seated herself before the keyboard, wondering for perhaps the thousandth time why her fingers, which seemed to obey her so well in other pursuits, were so awkward when she strove to stretch them over these black-and-white oblongs. It was so true that Pris was as able to draw music from this instrument as she was to blush becomingly at will, use her fan with skill, and generally be a credit to all young ladyhood, while Caroline had never been able to catch up with that list of proper accomplishments.

Dutifully, she studied the piece and spread her fingers, wriggling them a little and hoping, as she always did, that this time she could be a credit to Mrs. Watkins' patient endeavors to make a musician out of her.

She was very much aware of Mama, *her* fingers busy with a new Berlin woolwork pattern, sitting there listening. That very fact made Caroline falter more than once. Mama's silence was worse than any rebuke could have been. Then the door opened and Papa's firm step was heard. Thankfully Caroline let her hands fall into her lap. Papa was notoriously tone deaf and had little liking for what he termed "that thumping."

"A letter from Richard," he announced. "He has been in London to observe the work of Liston. Such experiences are seldom given a student. It is very commendable that Richard makes every possible opportunity to avail himself of these chances to see the most competent of medical men at work. He has done very well—"

For a moment Papa paused, and Caroline guessed that he must be matching Richard against Perry. But was that quite fair? Richard had never wanted anything else but to be a doctor, while Perry—Perry was not like Richard, nor Papa. He was Pris' twin, and sometimes he was just as sure to want to go his own way as she was.

"He is hoping to return home, perhaps this summer."

"Richard is coming home!" Pris' voice came clear and excited from the hall. "Oh, that is good to hear! He's such fun!"

"Such fun!" That was Perry. "It's all right, Papa—I didn't slight any lecture this time." His voice sounded tight. "Dr. Howards is ill, and we were dismissed. There seems to be a new storm brewing. So Richard's coming back. You'll have him to twist around your finger again, won't you, Pris?"

"Perry! That's not so!"

Caroline had turned on the piano stool to see her sister

frown, a sign of rising temper.

"Richard was always just the same with all of us," she declared. "He listens to one and makes you feel as if he really hears what you have to say and—"

"Children!" Mama had laid her work on the tabor table; that warning note in her voice seemed to fall on deaf ears.

"Richard is *such* fun," Perry repeated in that taunting voice Caroline always hated to hear. "You've had plenty of fun with him gone—assemblies, dances, parties—I can't see that you've done much pining for his company, Miss, with all your admirers cluttering up the parlor. I declare I can't see what makes you so important. Your new beau—Corbie Hannakar—he's the prize so far, isn't he. Kind of old for you, though."

"He's not, and what business is it of yours anyway?" Pris had pulled off her bonnet and thrown it toward the nearest chair, but instead it had hit the floor. She did not even look to see its fate.

"Ten or eleven years—" Perry was pleased with her flare-up—"I'd call that a little old."

"He's not stupid. He can talk about things which matter—"

"Greasy Indians, the price of fur pelts—"

Pris grabbed for a cushion and Perry ducked, but Papa put an end to their bickering.

"I will have no more of this childish behavior. You will both go to your rooms!"

Pris, leaving her bonnet where it lay, her cheeks flaming with her quick anger, whirled about and went. Perry gave a quick bow in his mother's direction, but did not glance at his father. His face was sullen and his eyes seemed bloodshot. His hands shook a little as he followed his twin.

Caroline caught up the discarded bonnet and fled after.

She caught up with her sister at the door of the latter's bedroom.

"That—that Perry!" Pris jerked the door open. "He—he can't stand anybody saying anything good about Richard. He's jealous. And Corbie is a gentleman. He asked for the first waltz at the Bingham's party. Perry! I could—" She turned a stormy face to Caroline and snatched at the bonnet the other was holding. "Sometimes I wish I could just give Perry what he deserves!"

Caroline suddenly laughed. She knew well the signs of the clearing storm; Pris was working out of her temper fit. A moment later her sister's frown cleared, but she continued:

"Perry is going to go too far some day. Oh, not with me—just let Papa find out what he is doing. He doesn't go to more than half of those lectures, you know. And he's been playing cards with Walter Rush and that set."

Caroline was instantly sobered. "Pris, if that's true—"

"It is. I heard it from Sissy Rush herself. I think he's lost money in those games. Let Papa know that and Perry'll be in real trouble. I wish Richard would come home soon; he could help. Yes," she turned her back on Caroline and went to the window, where she stood drawing the tip of her finger up and down the cold pane. "I do wish Richard was home."

"We all do." Caroline pulled at her shawl. If this was true about Perry—surely Sissy Rush must have been exaggerating! Perry could not be going with those young men who had such tastes. Papa would be so angry!

"Oh, well," Pris turned away from the window. "He *is* coming home. Then a lot of things will go better."

The small clock on the mantel chimed and both girls

started. The Warwick house ran on strict adherence to time, and even a family dinner was an occasion for promptness.

Caroline scurried to her own room where Mollie had brought up a tall copper can of hot water, set out the cake of sweet lavender soap, and had Caroline's dark green woolen dress ready for her. Washed, brushed, and in her second best gown, Caroline studied herself in the glass while she rebraided her hair. She had not grown too much since Richard had left, nor did she look, she decided a little forlornly, much like the young lady she was supposed to be—or almost to be.

Mr. Hannakar must have thought she was a child today. The greys—her thoughts leaped on to his promise—she was going to have a ride behind those tomorrow! Surely Mama would not mind if she went. Mollie could go with her for proprieties' sake, and they would not be gone long.

If only the storm would not render such an expedition impossible. She went to the window but the early winter twilight had already closed in. There was a hissing of snow flakes against the pane—she hoped that those would not go on falling long.

From the downstairs sounded the gong one of Papa's patients, Colonel Hughes, had brought from India. It had a queer, heavy sound which echoed through the house in a hollow way Caroline had never liked. She started downstairs to face another dinner with Archie and Agatha, wondering just how long it would be before Agatha made one of her flattening remarks to Pris, and whether her sister would hold her temper successfully or not. What would it be like if everyone in the family really, truly liked each other?

She had tried for four years, ever since Archie had made

his very solid and suitable marriage alliance with Agatha Holmes, to truly like her sister-in-law. Caroline sighed. In this respect she seemed woefully devoid of Christian charity.

2

"Good evening, Caroline." Archie stood with his back to the fireplace—a large, square back, which could be and was this evening an effective firescreen. Since Papa and Mama were not there, he attempted to dominate the room as he had for more years than Caroline was aware of. Agatha was not present, probably up in Mama's room laying aside her bonnet and furred cloak.

Caroline gave an inner sigh. By all the signs, Archie was not only well pleased with himself (which was usual) but also wanted to discuss something—or rather state an opinion as firm and as heavy as he himself had become.

She seated herself on a chair which was as far from Archie as she could get without freezing in the draft from the hall. She resented that critical stare which swept from her feet to her head and back again—but that was Archie, and one had to put up with it.

"Has Perry come in?"

"Yes," she made her answer as short as possible. So it was Perry Archie was going to fulminate about. She wished she had been a little more tardy.

"He had a lecture today, I believe?"

"They were dismissed early. Dr. Howards is ill."

Archie looked a little taken back, but before he could ask whatever question he had in mind, Caroline dared to turn the subject:

"Papa has had a letter from Richard. He is coming home."

"It is about time! All this traveling about will never establish any profitable practice. No, it will not. He should be well settled and at service here where he belongs."

Caroline wanted to say that Richard had certainly not been wasting his time, at least from the accounts he had written to Papa, but there was no arguing with Archie. It was better simply to keep an interested expression on one's face and allow one's thoughts to drift in more pleasant and profitable directions—such as whether the snow would stop in time for her promised outing tomorrow.

"Caroline, my dear. Archie—"

Shaken out of her own thoughts, she smiled up at Papa as he passed by her chair. The smell of medicine was faint in the air. Mama always declared that no amount of airing or cleaning could *ever* get Papa free of that. But there was something safe and solid about it, just as Papa's kind face (even if it often seemed that he, too, were elsewhere in his thoughts) could give one the feeling that he was safety itself.

Archie reluctantly left the fire rug, but he did not seat himself. Instead he waited with visible impatience before he said:

"Papa, Perry is indeed becoming a problem!"

"Oh? And in what way, Archie?"

"Agatha witnessed him coming out of Slaters two evenings ago. He requires disciplining. To frequent such a place is beyond a boyish prank. Besides, Perry is no longer a boy. Agatha was most embarrassed. She was with the

Wittenburs, and—''

Caroline wondered if she should excuse herself now. All Papa's usual good humor was fast fading. Surely Archie should know by now that Papa would not be pleased by—

''I believe that Perry may well have an explanation. This is no time for such a discussion anyway.''

Archie shrugged his heavy shoulders. His superior expression made him look nearly twice his years, Caroline decided, especially since Archie had put on so much weight that his brocaded waistcoat was now straining far too visibly at the buttonholes.

''Agatha is right. You are always ready to excuse Perry for any outrageous actions, just as you do Priscilla.''

''Agatha's opinion always seems quotable, doesn't it?'' That was Papa's smoothest voice, the one which meant he was reining in anger.

Archie could not be called stupid, Caroline supposed. Certainly he was shrewd at business and had made a great deal of money—a fact Agatha was always ready to hint about. But he never seemed to know people—as beings who had feelings and thoughts and were more real than the matters he controlled.

His pompous always-being-right had grown as fast as his affairs—ever since he had married Agatha, one of the four Miss Holmes. All of those had been raised to believe that duty and obedience were prime requisites in both a daughter and a wife. Though, of course, a wife might now and then point out deficiencies—in anyone but her lord and master. Sympathy, understanding, and kindness were weaknesses of the type one vanquishes first and most firmly.

''Perry's behavior is fast becoming the talk of the town,'' Archie sailed on into what was going to be a very stormy sea. "And Priscilla flirts in so forward a manner that Agatha has said many times she does not know where to look when they are in company together."

Papa said nothing. Perhaps that silence spurred Archie on to the last recklessness.

"Indeed, Papa, Agatha has said, very unhappily to be sure, that she does not altogether believe Mama is doing her duty in allowing Priscilla to—"

The storm broke.

"Archibald," Papa was speaking softly, "have you anything more to add to this discussion of our private affairs?"

Archie neither shrank nor colored. Instead he drew himself up with the self-satisfaction of the truly righteous:

"I would consider that *I* was doing less than *my* duty if I did not bring such matters to your notice, Papa. It is a difficult thing, yes, but one cannot allow one's family to be talked about generally."

"And you do not consider it disrespectful for your wife to speak critically of your mother?"

Archie's mouth opened and then closed again. Caroline thought that no one could have an answer to that.

"Agatha has been most upset. She has heard the most unpleasant talk; she has seen Perry's foolishness as well as witnessed Priscilla's behavior in company."

"This is not the first time you have quoted Agatha to me. In this house you have no right to speak so of your mother, and, of course, indirectly of me, as to the management of our affairs. Thus you are better in your own home, learning how to control your wife's tongue. I have no doubt that she takes interest in repeating gossip to others as well as to you."

Archie was flushed now, his beginning jowls flaming.

"That is an entirely unprovoked insult to my wife!" he said. "We have both wished only the best for this family! I think that you and Mama would welcome our warnings—"

"I am quite certain that I and my wife, who is also your mother, though you seem able to forget your duty to *her* at times, are completely capable of moulding the characters of your brother and sister. I suggest that you now collect Agatha and return home until you understand just how impertinent you have been. I shall expect an apology from you both when that wisdom is vouchsafed you."

"If that is how you see the concern I hold for my brother and sister's welfare, I promise you we shall not accept any hospitality in this house again!"

Caroline was alarmed at the deep shade of red of Archie's full face. He had raised a hand and was digging a finger between his tight cravat and his thick neck.

"I will not soon forget this, sir." He turned and made for the door, fumbling at the latch as if for a moment he could not even see it. Then he was gone, and Caroline could hear the heavy tramp of his feet on the stairs— going up to claim Agatha, she supposed.

"Caroline!"

She squirmed in her chair. Papa was looking at her as if she had suddenly appeared out of the air itself. She stammered a little:

"I—I did not mean to listen, Papa. I was just here and Archie started in at once and—"

"It has been an unfortunate scene, child. Better that it not be discussed." He frowned now, and added, as if to himself, "though I am afraid that it may be in some quarters. I must go to your mother." He left almost as abruptly as had Archie, and Caroline wondered just what was going to happen to Friday night dinner. In spite of cook's earlier tidbits in the kitchen she was uncommonly hungry. Archie had always been a trial, but now perhaps they would be spared him—and Agatha—for a while at least.

Dinner was a quiet affair, though Mama attempted to keep a certain neutral flow of remarks going. Papa seemed to have withdrawn into his own world. Perry chewed and swallowed with his eyes on his plate as if he, instead of Caroline, had been the witness to the scene in the parlor. Pris acted as if she felt nothing strained in the atmosphere, but answered Mama's questions about her afternoon drive and chattered about tomorrow's party and whether her new gown would need an extra tuck at the bottom.

Caroline suddenly wondered, as she glanced from face to face, what would happen if they all spoke their thoughts aloud instead of conversing politely. Perhaps it would make family dinner even more of a disaster than this one was. No one had mentioned the absence of Archie and his wife. Perhaps their names would be erased from all family tongues and remain so.

When she went up to the small "school room" shared by her and Priscilla while Miss Wylie had had the task of their education, Caroline was still thinking of the snow. This room was hers now—the ink-stained table, the chairs with their shabby cushions, the shelves of books (some of her own choosing)—was precious because it *was* hers. She moved the lamp a little closer as she drew out her ledger and began carefully to add her account of Boot's treatment to the "case records" she kept. She had visited the patient in his hearthside basket and found him asleep, having, as cook had said, filled himself up for sure. In fact, his middle section had looked quite round. The splinted leg was stiff, but his head rested on it, and he had contrived, Caroline believed, a measure of content. In other words, Boots was "resting comfortably"—an expression she was very familiar with.

Caroline had not prayed for the end of the snow—one did not dare to so meddle with Divine Providence, as Miss Wylie had often pointed out to her charges. But in the morning the drifts were not so high that a gentleman of such a sporting nature as Mr. Hannakar would choose to stay at home. The day held a promise of sun to turn the upper layer of snow into diamond sparkles.

It was after breakfast, while Mama was washing the best teacups herself in the bowl of warm water Mollie had brought in and Caroline was dutifully wiping them with all the care necessary to such a delicate task, that she dared speak of the invitation.

The suggestion of a frown returned to Mama's brow. Then after a moment came her answer:

"Mr. Hannaker is a very pleasant young man, but often a person can make an offer which does not linger long in his mind. Do not be disappointed if you hear no more of this, Caroline. Of course, perhaps he would like to give you pleasure, since you are Pris' sister and young enough to seem a child to him. Yes, if you take Mollie with you, I see no harm in a short ride."

"Pris' sister"—that was what was important to Mama. Caroline was quick enough to understand that. If Mr. Hannakar wished to find favor with a family, he might do such a thing for a younger sister. Mama was pleased, really.

Caroline set a cup very carefully on its saucer and inwardly sighed with relief. Her highest barrier had been crossed successfully—unless Pris might object. Pris was often a little contrary.

Anyway, she would find Mollie and tell her to be ready, see that her own cloak and bonnet, muff and boots, were duly waiting. Which she did before settling down to battle her excitement into seemliness as she stitched away at a shirt for Perry, trying very hard to make those seams even and near invisible. Mama's eye was sharp.

It was after the light luncheon which the three Warwick ladies shared in the morning room that Caroline's faith in Mr. Hannakar was sustained. The smart sleigh and greys appeared before the Warwick house. Pris was far too interested in the coming of Mrs. Riddle for the last view of her new ball gown to pay any attention, but Caroline and Mollie (breathing hard with excitement) were installed in the sleigh by its master himself. He took up seat beside the coachman, and they stopped only to drop him at his destination before being whirled off for a journey along the streets, the snow making a squeaking noise under the runners and the warm breath of the greys puffing a cloud into the air.

" 'Tis like flying, Miss Caroline.'' Mollie's knitted hood was pulled down, and a scarf wound up about her chin, until very little of her face showed at all, but her eyes shone at the unexpected treat.

Caroline snuggled blissfully under the fur robe Mr. Hannakar himself had carefully tucked about them.

"They're grand,'' she broke out. "I've heard Perry say that there isn't another pair in Montreal that can touch them. I wonder if Mr. Hannakar ever tried racing with them. I should think they would win.''

"He's a fine gentleman, that one is, Miss Caroline. So polite, and yet he sees you and don't think you are just a part of the wood wall.''

Caroline was startled by Mollie's comment. It was true

that their host had asked Mollie if she were warm enough, just as he had Caroline. And he had moved the heated soapstones so that both of them had warmth for their feet. At the time it had seemed only natural to Caroline that he do this. Mollie was her friend—a friend, she realized suddenly now, in some ways closer than any other girl she knew. Mama was not one to encourage close friendships outside the family, and Caroline's friends were mostly acquaintances, with formal visits tying them very loosely into the social rounds of the tightly woven English society.

"Do people do that, Mollie?" she asked now. "Make you feel as if you are not a person?"

"Not everybody, Miss Caroline. Not you, nor the Doctor—that good-hearted man—nor the Missus either. But mostly we're hands and feet and not faces. Some has it a lot worse. We got it good, cook always tells us that. And it's the truth, too. I think Mr. Hannakar's people must be happy, too."

"He lives with his mother. People say she's grand and proud, but nobody seems to know her well. She doesn't come into the city much—"

"Oh, but she's a good lady, Miss Caroline! Indeed she is. Cook has a friend who works out at Ste. Catherine's and, though it's a grand place, near like a castle, they are easy with their people. The Madam—they call her that— she is a proper one for seein' as how all goes smoothly, but she is the first to go to if one is needin' anything. They have a nearby village, and the Madam, she keeps an eye and sees no one wants for aught. If they be sick there's the doctor and good food. And the children, they have a school of their own and a man teaches them.

"He has only one arm—from the west, he is. The young master brought him back. Hurt he was, and no job for him as he had had before, but he now keeps track of all the spendin' and the sellin', and teaches the school besides.''

Caroline had long known that gossip spread swiftly from one kitchen to another, but that Mollie was so much aware of the life at Ste. Catherine's surprised her all the same. It did sound as if Mr. Hannakar came by his care for people naturally and as if his was a happy place. Maybe a happier place than the Warwicks' house right now. Perry, and Pris, and Archie—it seemed as if there was just one prickly happening after another. Maybe when Richard came home it would be better. Richard had always had the ability to smooth up and over the rougher places in life. Meanwhile, she had this—this blissful ''flying,'' as Mollie so aptly termed it—and she was going to hold on tight to every moment of it to remember after. It was the best thing that had happened to her for a long, long time. Pris might be all in a froth over tonight's dancing, but she had this special ride all for herself—and Mollie, of course.

It was childish to hope that one could just go on and on with any pleasure. Caroline realized that. But why did the pleasant things or times in life seem to fly by all too fast? She climbed the stairs slowly an hour later, holding to her the memory of that fine dash along the snow-covered streets. Pris was so lucky—Caroline did not doubt that the sleigh and the greys would be often at her sister's beck and call if she expressed a desire. Mr. Hannakar certainly was ''catched'' by Pris. Caroline smiled at her thought—Mollie's way of expressing herself was catching, too.

Hearing her mother's voice from the sewing room, Caroline went in that direction to dutifully report her safe return. Mrs. Warwick was supervising the final fitting of Pris' new ball gown, intended to outshine as far as possible all others on the night of the Charitable Soirée. It was rumored that even the new governor general—Lord Elgin —would attend, and Papa had been coaxed into providing this splendor since the cause would add to the funds of the University wing in the hospital.

Pris herself stood before the long cheval glass, a critical look in her eyes as she surveyed her reflection. Mrs. Riddle, a pincushion fastened to her wrist, more pins between her pursed lips, knelt to one side, an entirely appropriate worshiper at the shrine of fashion.

"A fraction, just a fraction more on that side, I believe. Please hold still, Priscilla. When you move, it makes it difficult to be sure the skirt is exactly even."

Her mother pointed out a dip to Mrs. Riddle who obediently jerked two pins from her mouth and set them into place with exactitude before sitting back on her heels.

Pris slowly turned to display her new glory. But she kept her eyes as much as possible on her reflection. The pale blue of the rustling taffeta set off to perfection her maple-gold hair. The bodice had been cut low, but not as low as fashion dictated. Folds of the material, artfully set in by Mrs. Riddle, molded her breasts, displaying with a demure promise the swelling ripeness of her figure. Her slender waist was also artfully displayed by the draping of a long spray of crystal-beaded flowers which arose to the shoulder on one side and dipped to the skirt on the other.

Caroline drew a deep breath as she viewed this splendor. It seemed that Pris could never be less than a fairy-tale princess, whatever she chose to wear, but sometimes her appearance was especially overwhelming. She pulled off her bonnet, settled down in a small sewing rocker, and laid down her muff.

"Quite attractive indeed, my dear."

They were all a little startled as Papa appeared in the

doorway. He seldom intruded into this wholly feminine territory. "But is it not a little—a little low on the shoulders?" There was an odd note in his voice, as if he hesitated between a rebuke of sorts and the knowledge that he was venturing on a subject where the judgment of a man did *not* carry full weight and prestige.

Pris frowned. "Don't be old-fashioned, Papa. This is not nearly as low as those Edith Barnard wears all the time. Miss Stoner's was lower, too, at the last assembly. Mama says that this is right, so I suppose it will have to—"

The Doctor shook his head. "Your mother, my dear, is perfectly correct. Young ladies who make displays of themselves are not in the best of taste at any time. Mrs. Warwick," he turned to his wife, "have you seen the *Gazette*? I do think this household would be more considerate of the paper, when all know that I have not yet had a chance to peruse it—"

Mama caught up the scattered newsprint from the other chair and quickly put the pages in order.

"I am very sorry, Doctor. We were reading about the arrival of the new governor."

"Yes," Pris nodded at her reflection. "And it is most tiresome. Lady Elgin is not coming after all, not until spring. While we have been looking forward to real parties at Monklands all winter. I do think it is too bad for her to so disppoint us all!"

The Doctor was already reading: "Well, at least he is on his way. 'Lord Bruse'," he read aloud, "'and a party of gentlemen are to proceed across the river to meet His Excellency and his entourage in St. John and escort them into Montreal.'"

"It is unfortunate he had to come by the way of Boston," Mrs. Warwick commented.

"With the roads in such condition he could do little else. We should have communication with Halifax winter and summer."

"Perhaps, having suffered from the inconvenience himself," the Doctor's wife returned, "the governor will be moved to remedy affairs."

Dr. Warwick snorted. "He will have no say. That is a matter for the government. And politics are in as much a mess as usual."

"The government perhaps will suffer a little also," his wife commented, and reached forward to twitch again at Pris' skirt.

Papa laughed as he tucked the paper under his arm. He seemed then to sight Caroline for the first time.

"Have you been out, my dear? It is far too cold to venture far."

"Mr. Hannakar sent his sleigh—for me to ride," she returned eagerly.

"Corbie asked me to go again," Pris broke in. "I said no—it was too cold. I hope that he does not think I'm impressed enough to do just as *he* wishes all the time."

"Priscilla, you are not to refer to Mr. Hannakar in that common and familiar fashion!" Mrs. Warwick was sharp.

"Mama, you know he's an old friend of Richard's. The way he used to come here when Richard was home—why, I've known him most of my life!"

"That is no excuse, now that you are a young lady. Mr. Hannakar is a fine young man. I trust that you are not leading him on in any light fashion. You rode with him the other day without taking Jessie as I ordered. A young lady does not go out alone—"

Pris turned around from the glass, a gleam in her eyes now which Caroline watched apprehensively. More and more Pris was losing her temper these days. A spat with Perry, words with Caroline—those might be overlooked. But one did *not* speak with the same freedom to Mama.

"Mama, lots of girls go sleighing without a sniffling little scarecrow of a maid bunching herself in where she isn't wanted!"

"Priscilla," Doctor Warwick eyed his daughter quellingly, "your mother is entirely right. You will not drive out with Mr. Hannakar, nor any other gentleman, alone. There are loose tongues in this town, and no member of my family is going to set them a-wagging. Do you understand?"

"Yes, Papa," Pris began sullenly, and then suddenly she was all smiles and brightness again. "No lone gentleman—does that mean you, too, Papa—or Perry?"

As usual, Pris' smile coaxed one from him in return. "Do not try to practice your wiles on me, young lady. You know perfectly well what I mean."

He left, and Pris began the delicate operation of getting out of her gown without disturbing any of the pins about the hem.

Caroline went on to her own chamber, standing for a moment before a glass which was not as large as Pris' and certainly did not reflect such an exciting picture as a princess in pale blue. She pulled her braid up on the top of her head and wondered just how many pins she would have to use to keep its heavy length in place when Mama deemed it was time for her to "come out." Parties might be fun, but right now Caroline doubted that.

Every one would, she was sure, compare her with Pris, and she would not be able to match her sister either in looks or "accomplishments." Pris seemed to know by instinct just what to do and say. Sometimes it seemed to

Caroline that those who were "out" had an entirely different language they used in company—a language she
feared she would never be able to learn.

She let the braid fall and headed for the back stairs and
the kitchen. Boots was doing very well. Cook had taken a
liking to him—saying he was "no more trouble than most
animals around a kitchen" which Caroline was able to
translate (as she could not society chatter) into the accep-
tance of her patient for the rest of his life—always supposing he did his duty and kept down the mouse popula-
tion.

In fact, he was resting, splinted leg and all, on cook's
well-upholstered lap as she took her own tea, stewed nearly
black and with at least four spoons of sugar, strengthening
herself for another bout with pots and pans, while she kept
an eye on those lesser jobs which her underlings had been
set.

There was the jangle of a bell and Mollie, whose turn it
was to answer, jerked off the coarser apron she had tied on
over the finer stuff of a parlor maid's, wiped her hands on
it, and set off in a hurry for the front door. Caroline was a
little surprised at the arrival of any visitor now. Papa's
office had a separate bell; those who would come to the
main door on this very cold, late afternoon would be few.
Probably just a message.

Mollie came hurrying back.

"Oh, Miss Caroline, he says he is Dr. Richard! But
Missus never—"

"Richard!" Caroline was bewildered. Papa had just had
that letter; how could Richard be here so soon? She looked
quickly at Mollie. "Tell Mama—and Papa, too—"

"Missus was in the parlor when I showed him in. I'll tell
the Doctor directly."

She headed back to tap at the study door as Caroline swept by her, with more speed than a young lady should ever show, and flung open the parlor door.

"Richard!" she cried out. "Oh, Richard!"

Arms were about her with strength enough to swing her off her feet as she looked up at a brown face with dark eyes, near as bright as Pris', and a curving mouth which always had showed more smiles than the sullen, pouting Perry ever turned on the world.

3

"You've grown up, Pusskins. You're far more of an armload these days." He gave her a quick, cold kiss (for the Arctic air of the outer world still clung to his lips) and set her down. Caroline, blinking with a kind of faintness from her excitement, could only hold onto his sleeve and repeat, "Richard!"

"Caroline, do control yourself, child." There was happiness in Mama's voice, too, and very little sharpness. "You have indeed given us a surprise, my dear boy. No notice of your coming and—"

The parlor door flew open with unusual force. Pris, her hair loose about her shoulders, looking as if she had hardly stopped to button her wrapper, flung herself directly at the tall young man.

"Richard! Richard, darling, you've come home!"

Caroline, who was now subsiding into a chair, stared at her sister. That expression on Pris' face—she had never seen her sister wearing it before. And Pris sounded as if she were going to cry.

"I saw you from the window, and I could hardly believe my eyes. Richard, dear—to have you here again! Why did you not let us know you were coming?"

"You didn't get my London letter, then? But wait—I have some one else for you to meet. Just wait—"

He had not taken off his coat, where the powdering of snow flakes had turned into small drops of moisture. Now he caught up his hat from the table by the door and was gone as if he had been a dream.

They heard the door without open and shut, then open again with vigor. Richard had certainly wasted no time. He came back to the parlor with the same speed, ushering before him a small person well bundled up in furs, behind him a tall man none of the Warwicks had ever seen before.

Richard led the befurred girl directly to Mrs. Warwick.

"Mother, this is Althea, my wife!"

Perhaps only Caroline heard that gasp, saw Pris sway a fraction. Her hand went out, but her sister was already standing straight again. Her bright color was gone; her eyes looked very wide and yet strangely empty, as if they saw nothing before them at all. For a moment Pris stood just like that, and then she was smiling, as if her teeth had not caught at her lower lip.

Mrs. Warwick was on her feet, her hands out to the girl.

"My dear, you must forgive our seeming astonishment. This bad boy gave us no preparation for such a delightful surprise. Welcome home, my dear, for this will be your home as it has always been Richard's. No one could ask for a better son—and now he has brought us a truly lovely new daughter!"

Richard was beaming at them both, his delight plain to see. "We came with Lord Elgin's party—it was an excellent chance. Though it was thought that Lady Elgin would come, too. She is Althea's godmother, you see. But even though those plans were changed, Althea insisted that we come along now. She knew how much I was missing you all—so here we are!''

His smile grew tender as it swept from Mrs. Warwick to
the small girl whose blonde curls framed a delicate face.
She looked almost like one of Mama's cherished porcelain
ladies, Caroline thought, her skin so very fair, her features
so fine. It was true: Richard's new wife was indeed lovely.

"Thank you." Althea's voice sounded particularly soft
after Richard's hearty tone. "I have heard so much about
you—all of you." Her glance swept from Mrs. Warwick on
to Pris, then to Caroline, and her smile was perhaps a little
timid, as if she were indeed asking for their approval. "I
am sorry that you did not get Richard's letter—that you
did not know. To descend upon you in this fashion is a
matter of—"

"Of nothing but welcome, my dear." Mama drew the
little figure closer to the fire. "On such a day you must be
half frozen. Caroline, ring at once for tea. And Papa—
where is Papa?"

"I told Mollie to fetch him," Caroline went to the bell
rope, passing Pris as she went. Her sister's smile seemed
fixed, and her eyelids were half lowered. Could Pris be
fighting now for control over *tears*?

"Oh, I am forgetting my manners sadly." Richard, still
exuberant, swung about to bring forward the man by the
door. "Mother, may I also present Captain the Honorable
Alexander Carruthers, of Her Majesty's Twenty-Third
Regiment, at present on duty as aide-de-camp to Lord
Elgin. Also he is Althea's brother. My mother, Mrs. Warwick. And this is Miss Priscilla Warwick, my elder sister,
and Miss Caroline, the younger daughter of the house."

"Richard, my boy!" Papa had entered with more speed
than dignity, his hand outstretched to take Richard's.

There were more explanations to be made then, during

which Pris escaped, probably suddenly aware of the disarray of her clothing. When she returned, wearing her lilac silk, her curls in perfect order, she was a Pris at ease. Caroline, seated on a low chair, was somewhat removed from the main party. Mrs. Warwick had installed Richard's wife at the tea table near the fire, her bonnet now removed, her furs laid aside to show an even smaller and more fragile-looking person.

Althea, it seemed, was really the Lady Althea, a daughter of an Earl. That information seemed to remove her even farther from their own world. Caroline wondered, having heard the gossip of English-born Montreal for years, the accent placed on birth and breeding, how Richard, a mere Mr. Harvey, and a doctor, had met such an exalted being, and, having met her, how he had been able to carry her off in marriage.

Yet it was evident that Lady Althea was in love with Richard—the way she looked at him from time to time could not be misunderstood. Richard's wife plainly meant to make his life and family hers. She had spoken to them like a child asking for approval, and not at all like a haughty lady.

Captain Carruthers was not in the least talkative. He stood watching Pris like one bemused. Caroline smiled in spite of herself. She had witnessed the same reaction to her sister from many gentlemen before. Pris had plainly charmed a new admirer, though she had not sent any binding glance in his direction at all.

Richard, still beaming at the group close to the fire, had taken a step or two backwards, closer to Captain Carruthers, who started as if awakened from a short dream. Caroline was sure she was the only one who caught the somewhat drawling speech of the newcomer.

"Gad, Richard, that sister of yours—she's a beauty!"

Richard's smile grew wider. "So you admit it! I told you Canadian ladies were a fit match for any London Incomparable."

The Captain was shaking his head. "How do they stand up to this damnable weather? I haven't been warm since we took ship."

"Not a good crossing, eh?" Papa had come up to them now and Caroline wondered if he had caught the Captain's remark about Priscilla. He did not look cross as if he thought that comment far too free.

"It was a damned awful one, sir. That blasted boat couldn't keep an even keel for twenty seconds." The Captain spoke with feeling.

"It *was* pretty bad," Richard agreed. "Even the captain admitted it. Lord Elgin kept remarking that he was glad his lady had decided not to come. I would have been happier if Althea had not chosen to. She stood up to it, though—she's much stronger than she looks, sir."

"Lord, yes. Looks like she'd snap right between a man's fingers, doesn't she?" Her brother almost sounded, Caroline thought, as if he had some old grievance. "Not a bit of it—mind of her own. Not right—females shouldn't be so emphatic. You married her—never could understand how you two took to each other so fast. Now—Miss Priscilla," his eyes had gone back to the girl, shaking her head at some question, her curls falling back into place in the most bewitching fashion, as if the gesture were one long practiced into a state of perfection. "Now there's a sweet little thing. I'll wager she has none of Althea's 'I'm right about this' in her at all."

Caroline bit hard upon her lower lip. It was plain that this rather lank and wispy young man, who was not her idea of a soldier, really meant that. Well, if he came to know Priscilla better, and she was sure that he was determined to do so, he would discover how very wrong he was.

But it was Richard who laughed, and there was even a small smile about her father's lips. However, the Captain pulled out a watch, and a shadow of consternation crossed his face. Caroline found him not only lacking in the vigorous good looks she would have expected in Althea's brother, but also slightly vacant in expression.

"Gad! Look at the time! I've got to get to where His Nibs is holing in. Woodfield—something of that name. Not too far, is it?" His look was now anxious.

"Monklands," Dr. Warwick answered. "That is about eight miles from here. You have something of a ride yet. I shall see that you have a carriage—or do you have one?"

"Got a feller waitin', yes. Thank you, sir. Got to be on duty at six. Richard, my regrets to your mother—sure she'll understand—duty—I'll pay m' respects as soon as I can."

Richard moved to the door with him. Dr. Warwick looked at the two, shrugged his wide shoulders, and went back to the fire. Caroline realized that the cup of tea she was holding was cold and undrinkable now. She arose from her shadowed seat and took it back to the table, to be drawn into the conversation there—though her own remarks were apt to be drowned out by Priscilla's quick, easy flow of speech—faster and more excited now than Caroline had heard it before. Nor did she see her sister ever look directly at Althea. It was almost as if Priscilla was trying to hold at bay some unpleasantness, putting off some reckoning. That was a trick from their days in the school room when Priscilla had failed in some set task and was staving off the moment when she must confess.

Richard did not return, and after a moment her father
also excused himself and went out, to have his own private
time with Richard, Caroline knew. She wondered what it
would be like to come home like Richard—knowing so
much, ready to help Papa and be of some use in the world.
Of course, Mama always proclaimed that there was
nothing better for any lady than to be able to run a house
usefully and well, to support and comfort her husband, to
raise her children properly, to—well, to be just like Mama
herself.

Caroline helped herself to one of the sandwiches cut so
thin that it was already curling a little as it dried out. She
bit into the fine bread without tasting it, her thoughts still
busy with a rush of things which she had no time now to
sort out, or which she somehow shrank from examining
too closely. It was as if there was something she did *not*
want to know.

Mama herself took Lady Althea up to the chamber
which had been hastily made ready. Not Richard's old
room, which Caroline had always found so welcoming, but
the large "company" chamber with the fine curtained bed
and the best carpet. There a middle-aged woman with a
closed-in, disapproving face busied herself unpacking.

Priscilla had excused herself and gone into her own
chamber, but Caroline had followed, carrying, indeed,
Lady Althea's muff and listening to her light and charming voice as she talked with Mama and then introduced her
maid—the dour-looking Skinner, who seemed to have no
other name at all, or was determined to keep it a secret.

Skinner was sweeping a froth of dresses away to the
wardrobe. They seemed to Caroline's dazzled eyes like the
rainbow lights one saw sprinkled across the snow under the

sun. Then Mama favored Caroline with one of her "speaking looks," so the girl excused herself and made for her own chamber at the end of the hallway.

The winter twilight was already drawing closely in. Althea—that was an unusual name. Just as Richard's choice of wife seemed still so surprising to Caroline that she could not be quite sure, now that she was away from the newcomer, that she existed at all. She sat down before her mirror and shoved her comb and brush back and forth, feeling a little lost and strange. People did marry—everyone did in time. The trouble was that she kept thinking of Richard as he had been—hardly more than a boy when he went away—not a man and married. Would they continue to live here? Richard was intended to be Papa's partner— to share the practice with Perry when Papa retired. They had known that ever since Richard first said that he wanted to study to be a doctor.

Now there was Lady Althea, and she might well want a house of her own. No house could have two mistresses— Mama had often said that. Archie had set up his own establishment. She thought of Agatha and Mama under the same roof, and that made her give a small chuckle. Althea was not Agatha, though.

She was young; she could not be any older than Pris. Maybe girls in England married younger. Caroline planted her elbows on the dressing table and settled her chin on her clasped hands, looking into the mirror before her but not seeing anything reflected there. What would it be like to be married?

If someone had a husband as good, as nice as Richard— yes, maybe that would be a pleasant way of life. Richard knew so much, and he was kind. He would listen to one. Then there was Mr. Hannakar; he was kind too. Though of course he was older, and very grand. Though if Pris married him Caroline believed he would be nearly as kind and pleasant to have about as Richard. He certainly would not be sullen and snappish as Perry sometimes was. At least she thought he wouldn't. Mollie had said he looked at people as if they were people. It had been a queer thing to say, but one Caroline understood.

There was the ball—would Althea be going? Which of those lovely gowns would she wear? She was an Earl's daughter. Caroline was not quite sure just what that might mean, but she had visions of jewels and velvets. Then she laughed at her own thoughts, gave herself a little shake and got up to change for dinner. It was only the past year —the fourth since Richard had been gone—that she had been considered old enough to dine with the family. She had better put on her best manners now so that she would seem to be grown up—or at least partly that.

"Caroline!" She was struggling with the last of her bodice buttons when Pris swept in. "How *could* he do this?"

She took an impatient step forward and then swung around a little so that her sister could no longer see her face. "Why didn't he tell us about her? To be married and we never told—!" That breathless note was back in Pris' voice. Her hands were so tightly clasped about her fan that Caroline half expected to see it snap in her grip.

"Maybe it happened so fast because they wanted to come with Lord Elgin's party—"

"She—she'll think that we're not good enough for her, that we're coarse and common and colonial—"

"Pris!" Caroline caught at her sister's arm. "Pris, you know that can't be true! She's not like that at all! She's kind and sweet. And, Pris," Caroline smiled a little as she thought of it, "her brother called you a beauty! You are, you know." Caroline spoke honestly. She perhaps envied Pris a little from time to time, but she could never deny that her sister was—what had Richard said? Yes, an "Incomparable."

For a moment Pris stood, her face still turned away so that her curls fell far enough forward to hide her expression. Then she laughed and tossed her head, looked about.

"So Captain the Honorable Carruthers thinks I'm a beauty?" There was a dancing light in her eyes, a slight curl to her lips.

"He said so to Richard," Caroline assured her.

"And Richard?"

Caroline smiled in relief. "Well, he agreed. He said he had told the Captain so—"

"Good for Richard! Then he hasn't forgotten old friends after all!"

Caroline could not quite follow Pris, but she felt a little of that odd shadow she had sensed earlier lift from her. Pris was back—the old Pris. She was sparkling and alive and all was well again. Now she swept out an arm and brought it about Caroline's waist.

"Come on, slowpoke, we Canadian beauties will have to make a good entrance and uphold all Richard has said about us." Her laugh arose as she brought Caroline with her into the hallway.

They were passing the door of the guest room when the note of the gong sounded from below. Pris had been in a hurry, drawing Caroline on to match her pace; now she slowed as the door opened and Richard appeared, holding it open for Althea. She had changed into a velvet gown of a deep blue, over which the fine lace of a knitted shawl showed like a spider's dew-jeweled web. Pris was all brilliance and fire, life. Althea was quietness and something of a shadow, until you saw her eyes, the lift of her small chin. She was one of Mama's porcelain ladies—but Caroline thought she had more strength within her.

Richard's face was flushed. He looked—angry? Althea had laid her hand upon his fine black coat sleeve, as if she were trying to give him comfort, or to warn him. But surely there was no trouble between the two? Even at that moment Caroline was aware of something invisible which bound them together, kept the rest of the world outside.

"Times have changed, Richard." Pris gave a little jerk forward so that Caroline was now nearly between them. "Little Carrie is with us now! Even though she does have a liking for the kitchen still."

Caroline bit her lip. This sudden turn on her—why was Pris doing this? It was as if she was just there to be used. She did not know why she felt that, but she was certain it was true.

"My sister is an odd one, you know?" Pris had dropped her hold now, but Caroline could not escape. "She haunts your old room, Richard—hunts up remedies for her animals in your books. If you find jam smeared on a page now and then, you will know the reason. Why, the child would rather doctor a sick cat than go to a party, I truly believe. It's a pity that she and Perry can't change places."

"Pris!" Caroline could feel the hot blood which must be making her face as red as if she were disgracefully rouged. Why was her sister doing this?

Richard looked at them both in open surprise, and then quickly he gave a little laugh and smiled at Caroline, then at Althea, his hand coming up to cover hers where it lay upon his arm.

"Caroline has always had a feeling for hurt things. And she is a surprisingly good nurse, even if her patients have been all furred or feathered. As for hunting remedies among my old books—well, if she can find the knowledge she needs there, she is very welcome to it. Knowledge," he had sobered again, "is never rightly denied. We live in an age of new discoveries, and we must learn to reach out for them, use them properly. Pris," he smiled again now, "you grow more beautiful with the years." He was being tactful, deliberately forcing a change of subject. Caroline was grateful to Richard as she had been many times, but the new pain of what Pris had done—and the need to know why her sister had lashed out at her—was at the fore of her mind.

"With the years," Pris repeated. "La, sir," she put bold affectation in her speech, "how you do go on! One would think I was nearing the shelf rather than still a proper partner for a gallop on the floor! Perhaps it is you who have aged. You must see, Althea, that he buys a gold-headed cane like Papa's, and wears a sober coat to suit this new dignity."

"Priscilla," Mrs. Warwick had come from her chamber, "you are letting your tongue run. It is time for dinner, we must not keep Papa waiting."

As if they were all obedient children again, she swept them before her down the staircase. But her mouth pursed a little, Caroline noticed, whenever her eyes touched Pris. Mama was not pleased, and trouble might lie ahead for Pris. She felt cold and a lump moved into her throat. Last night they had had the gloom over Archie's bad behavior —what might happen tonight if Mama was displeased?

Perry was waiting with Papa and had to be made known to his new sister. Then they were all at the table, and

Caroline found that she was hungry enough after all to eat the soup set before her.

If Pris had sensed Mama's displeasure, she showed no sign of it. Instead she was full of conversation and many questions directed to Lady Althea, mainly about society and London and the world overseas. Papa appeared to be thinking his own thoughts—perhaps it was some serious case, Caroline thought. But she was a little surprised that he allowed the flow of light chatter, which in the past he had often put an end to decisively.

Caroline saw Perry glance apprehensively at him once or twice, as if he were expecting some verbal missile. And Richard was very quiet, too, seeming to be aroused out of thought when Pris threw some question deliberately in his direction.

When Mama gave the signal to rise and the ladies went out, leaving the three gentlemen alone behind them, Caroline glanced back. Papa—what was wrong with Papa? He had waited so long for Richard to come home. Was it something new about Perry? A case—yes, it must be a case.

The parlor was warm enough about the fire, but the outer edges of the room were cold enough to make one glad of a shawl. Caroline was happy she did not have to linger long. She was not expected to keep the same late hours as Pris.

Now she murmured her goodnights, received Mama's kiss on her forehead, and was glad to return upstairs into the warmth of her own small room. She sat by the fire, her ledger for treatment on her knee, thinking about the day and trying to sort out feelings from thoughts. When she had been very little, she had once heard old nurse say that that little Miss Carrie was a strange one. Seemed as if she always knew when there was trouble brewing, even if she had no finger in it herself. When she got too quiet, then you were ready for some kind of misbehaving.

In a way it was true—she *could* feel it when people were unhappy and troubled; she *did* know when storms of some kind lay ahead. It was not a happy circumstance, but she had no choice—it just was. Richard had been happy when he came home, warm and loving just as he had always been. Now there was a difference; there was trouble. And it had come upon him between leaving the parlor and bringing Althea down for dinner. She did not believe Althea was a part of it. No, Althea's attitude had been one of reassurance—of loving support.

Caroline rested her head against the shabby cushion of the chair. She hated—she even feared—these feelings. However, when they came she had learned she must allow them freedom. If one sensed trouble strongly enough, one was sometimes better prepared to face it when it came into the open. There was no trouble between Althea and Richard. When she looked at them together she had felt only a warm goodness inside. Then—was it Perry? Perry had always been slightly jealous of Richard, she realized now that she was older. But he had not been home—he had not even seen Richard until the trouble had begun.

Pris? She did not want to think of Pris—to remember that look on her face when Richard had spoken of "his wife." Could Pris have—did Pris love Richard—not as a brother but in that special way which was still a mystery to Caroline? If that were true, then she could understand a lot of things. Except—no, she did not believe that Richard was aware of any such feeling.

Caroline did not try to enter any notes in her ledger. Sighing, she put it back in the drawer of the table, and began undoing the long line of bodice buttons. It was there somewhere—the trouble—but she could see nothing that she could do about it. So often her fears for the family ended in just such a helplessness, and it always hurt. They were a true family as families should be—loving and caring for each other.

Why could not it be like that always? But if Pris had— did—love Richard, then how dreadful she must feel now! She would have to see him and Althea every day, always pretending not to mind, to be happy because they were happy. Perhaps—there was that Captain; he had plainly been taken by Pris. And there must be other young men with Lord Elgin's party, young men who were not married, or engaged, who were free to court a girl.

She did not believe that the dashing Captain Carruthers, for all his being an Honorable, could stand at Richard's side and show up very well. But there were others, and Pris might well find someone who would come to mean as much to her as Richard had. There was Mr. Hannakar, for instance; he was like Richard, for all his being older and in society. He was kind and warm, only it did not show as much with him. But it was there underneath.

Caroline thought of all Mollie had said about the Hannakars. Old Madam—she was a very great lady, of course, but Pris was a lady too, and she was sweet and dear —mostly. She was so lovely that surely Corbie Hannakar's mother could not help loving her if Corbie wanted her for a wife.

It would be nice to have a new brother like Mr. Hannakar. He was the sort one could trust to help when there was trouble over some patient such as Boots. He liked horses, and his house was in the country—there would be room there for animals.

Caroline unbraided her hair and dutifully began the nightly brushing of its long strands, coming closer to the fire as she drew the brush down again and again. She put aside her uneasiness, remembering instead that joyous ride behind the greys. Yes, Mr. Hannakar was a kind and thoughtful person.

4

Sunday followed the usual pattern of the Warwick household. There were morning prayers led by Papa, with cook breathing heavily right behind Caroline's chair and her corset creaking a little as she knelt, the maids flanking her, James and Edward right by the door. Mama, in her grey woolen, had her prayerbook to hand, and even Pris and Perry were properly respectful and ready with responses. Althea and Richard had been prompt, and Althea also held a prayerbook. Her lace-capped head drooped a little forward, so that all Caroline could see were ends of pale curls and a small portion of fair cheek.

Papa had chosen one of the cheerful psalms today, and Caroline relaxed. Whatever shadow had lain across them all last night was gone now. It was going to be a happy day. She listened to Papa's prayer, which was one of decorous thanksgiving that those gone had returned safely and that the family were united in the eyes of the ever-watchful Lord.

Breakfast was warming, and the dishes were plentiful. Caroline relished hot muffins and ate with a hearty appetite. Maybe a full stomach, along with the well-heated footstove, would make church going tolerable, in spite of the bite of the cold. She wished that she could get over her own shivers, and she hoped that she would not catch her usual winter cold. She had managed to escape it so far this year.

Pris excused herself first and was gone, but Caroline arose at the same time as Althea, and Richard's wife smiled at her. Oh, she did like Althea! Not only because she was so pretty and soft-spoken, and plainly loved dear Richard so very much, but also because she was herself. Of course, she was a married lady and in society. She would be going to the balls and parties with Pris. Still, she might spare a little time for Caroline, too. It would be nice to have someone to talk to. Pris' world was so very different, and Caroline felt totally lost when her sister talked about it.

Caroline smiled back now. As they came into the hall, Althea spoke:

"I hear that you have a patient of your own just now, Caroline."

For a moment Caroline was disconcerted, but there was no teasing note in Althea's voice, so she answered shyly:

"Just a kitten. Its leg was broken, but I looked in one of Richard's books and then I set it. I think," she frowned a little without realizing it, "he will be all right. Cook likes him, too, which means he can stay. I call him Boots. He is grey with white feet—"

She stopped because Perry came out then, and Pris was coming downstairs again. Her Sunday best gown of a lovely shade of violet fitted well her slender waist, her full, arching breasts. There were bands of velvet ribbon three shades darker about the skirt, outlining the shoulder seams and set in artfully to make her waist seem even smaller. A ruching of wider velvet framed her neck artfully to make her skin appear even whiter.

"Aren't we fine, sister mine!" Perry did not seem to see Althea and Caroline where they had withdrawn a little to the rear of the wide hall. There was a look of mischief about him. Caroline's happiness dimmed. Perry was in one of his moods—and when he chose to tease Pris there was often an answering flare-up which made trouble. "Who is the cavalier to be overcome by violet eyes under a fetching bonnet this fine and frosty morning?"

Priscilla flushed. "I am going to church, not to a party, Perry."

"And since when did all the gentlemen lose their eyesight in church?" he asked with that same baiting smile. "Sometimes I worry about you, Silly—after all, mind you, you're my sister. A feller takes an interest in his female relations. You're getting along, m'girl. Don't want to be left on the shelf, you know."

That was insufferable of Perry! Caroline forgot herself and took two steps forward, her hand going out to the newel post of the stair. Calling Pris by that old name "Silly" which she hated so, and making mock of her before Althea, too. Pris—Pris might do something very—

"I hardly think that Pris will ever lack for an escort."

Caroline had not had time to interfere after all. Richard had come out and closed the door so quietly behind him she had not been aware of his arrival until he spoke.

"Yes, I can imagine that Pris holds her own very well in any company," he continued.

"You don't know the half of it, Richard," Perry snickered. "Out near every night—beaux enough to sweep off the step with the last snow. Pris is a real flirt. But she'd better take care and make the most of her chances while she can."

Pris had flushed a deeper red now which contrasted poorly with the ruffle about her throat. She was keeping control only with an effort. Perry to say that before Richard! Caroline's half-knowledge made her want to throw her arms about Pris, stand between her and Perry. Sometimes one could nearly hate Perry! He had a sly streak in him which made him want to hurt. Caroline had to admit that to herself now.

Richard was frowning. "Come, Perry, that's a bit sharp, isn't it? Pris has always been popular, and rightly so." He turned to Pris with a smile which was that of the old brother-Richard kind. "How is George Scott these days?"

Pris' flush remained. "Very well, I believe." The words came from between her set teeth flatly.

Perry shook his head. "You are far behind times, Richard. George was given his marching papers some time ago. In the fall, wasn't it, Pris?"

What was Perry trying to do? Caroline forgot all about Althea as she looked from one twin to the other and back again. She could understand Pris, and right now she was surprised at her sister's control, but what made Perry bait her so?

"I did see George the other night," Pris' color remained high, but her voice was forced light. "He escorted Edith Bernard. They seemed much taken with each other's company."

"They did, did they?" Perry stiffened.

"When they waltzed, several people remarked how admirably their steps matched. One would think they had practiced so. I also overheard a remark that they had been partners at at least two other of the assemblies."

Perry's eyes narrowed. "Which assemblies?" His own temper was rising now.

"Oh, those you were too busy elsewhere to attend."
Pris' high color was dropping to normal; she was in control
now and knew it.

Richard laughed. "Your old tricks, eh, you two? Well,
it would seem points are evenly divided. Althea, my
dear," he turned to the figure behind Caroline, "you
must not take alarm at anything these two will say. From
the days they first learned to talk they have been sharp-
ening their tongues on each other. Though it grows less
now that they have grown older."

Had he meant that last as a warning for the two of
them? Pris' color heightened, and Perry's mouth tightened. Then the twins, as if realizing that they might indeed be making spectacles of themselves, smiled. Though
Caroline saw that their lips were grim and that their eyes
never met.

"Althea," Pris swept down the last two steps as Perry,
with a mutter, pushed past to the door of his father's
study, "you must be frozen. These halls in winter—do you
have a shawl? A heavy one? And a fur-lined cloak? You
will need that for church. Though we do have the foot-
warmers, and James is always very careful to see those are
hot—"

Somehow she swept Lady Althea away from Richard and
drew her back up the stairs, chattering of the need for
warm clothing in the chill of winter, commiserating with
the newcomer that she had to see the city first when it was
ice-encased. Caroline would have followed, but Richard
put out a hand and she obediently stopped.

"What is the matter?" he asked. "Pris and Perry—
what started that? Do you know, Carrie—" He had been
studying her, and now his expression changed. "Why,
you've grown up! What had you been doing to yourself,
Pusskins?"

She had to laugh a little as she tossed back the braid which had fallen over her shoulder.

"Not quite grown up, Richard. I haven't put up my hair yet. And I don't go to balls, you know. I don't have beaux to sweep off the doorstep along with the snow."

He echoed her laugh, then sobered as her words brought him back to his first question.

"What is the matter?" he asked again, and his tone was that of equal to equal. But then Richard, Caroline remembered gratefully, had always been aware of her queer forebodings and had often turned to her for answers she was not yet able to give.

"Perry has been unhappy this winter. I do not think that he really enjoys his studies, Richard. Papa has been quite disturbed with him." Should she repeat that gossip about what Perry might be doing with his time? No, Richard was a man, and in a man's world he would soon find out for himself what mistakes Perry might have made.

He was nodding now, understanding as of old. "And when Perry's unhappy he likes company in misery. Preferably Pris. Just as always. Is he truly interested in Edith Barnard? If he is, Pris should keep her tongue out of it; she can make mischief past mending, perhaps. I have seen that happen. You might drop her a word, Carrie." Once more his voice grew lighter. "What do you do beside being half grown up?"

"Oh, there is my music," she could not help making a small face, "though Mama says I am a dullard at that. I don't have many of the proper accomplishments, you see. I fear that I shall be a sad disappointment to Mama when I have my season. Mostly I read and look after the animals. Cook teaches me something of her art when she's in a good mood, and in the summer I go to the farm."

"Beside Pris' occupations that does not sound very exciting.''

"But it is! Why, Mr. Wilson taught me to milk and I have even helped with a horse that had a strained hock. He taught me to drive as well as ride. I love the farm!"

"Pusskins—" Richard looked at her and paused. "Promise me something."

"What, Richard?" She was caught by that odd note in his voice; it was as if what he had to say was very important in some way she did not understand.

"That you'll stay just as you are—underneath—even if they trick you out in ribbon and laces, turn up this hair of yours," he reached out and flicked her braid, "and give you that season."

"I don't know just what you mean, Richard."

He looked very sober. "Just what I say, little sister. Be yourself, don't turn into a fine lady. That is not meant to be your way of life. Now," he looked at his watch, its fob swinging against his hand. "I have to talk to Papa—Even on Sunday a doctor's time may not be his own."

It seemed to Caroline that Richard turned almost reluctantly toward the study. Was it that he did not want to run into Perry? She could not believe that. Again that disturbing disquiet arose in her, but she determined to avoid speculations.

Sunday passed very slowly. Caroline knew that it was wrong to long to put down the improving *Words for Young Females* which was proper Sunday reading and turn to those books she loved—the volumes of Scott which Richard had given her for birthdays, the books of poetry, and those of travel. She could sit with one of those on her lap, shut her eyes, and somehow move into the world of the book, safely away from her own inadequacies. *Words for Young Females* certainly did *not* open any such doors.

It was not until Monday that she was enlightened as to part of the uneasy mystery which haunted the household. Then it was Pris who called her in as she passed along the hall after breakfast, with her sewing basket in her hands and the unhappy knowledge that she must be at her darning—which she had put off far too long—before she would be given a few moments of freedom.

Pris' far more ornate workbox was open on the small table beside her curtained bed; lined up beside it were small bottles filled with glittering beads. Pris was following a pattern of full-blown white and yellow roses on what would become a satin bag suitable for the transportation of dancing slippers.

"Richard, of all people, is in Papa's black book now," Pris announced as she settled a yellow bead into place with a determined stitch.

"Richard!" Caroline sat down on the other and far less comfortable chair. "But why?"

"Oh, he's come home all full of some new medical folly —that's what Perry said Papa calls it. There is a Dr. Liston in London; Richard went to watch him operate. He has this gas or scent, or something of that kind. You smell it and go to sleep; then they can operate and you never know what happens. Richard wants to use it here."

"But—" Caroline had lived too long in a doctor's house not to know that any operation was the very last resort— the pain and shock often killed the patient. "But that is a wonderful thing! Surely Papa knows that. I have heard him say that the extreme pain itself sometimes can kill—"

Pris picked out another bead of a slightly lighter shade. "Papa says that this is not tested fully. That it is something a doctor should not want to try until he was sure of its efficiency. There's something else, too." Now she glanced slyly out of the corner of her eyes at her sister. "You know how Richard's mother died?"

"Of course." Richard's mother had died when he was born. It was sad, but sometimes it happened that way.

Pris ran the tip of her tongue across her lower lip. That sly expression grew stronger. "Well, Richard says that if they use this new gas thing some women who die now when their babies are born might live—that they won't be so weakened by long pain."

No one could live on a farm, mid-wife kittens and puppies into the world, and be ignorant of the process of birth no matter how much a young lady was to be shielded from such things. Caroline stared down at her hands.

"I heard Papa once," she said in a small tight voice, "say it was the Lord's will that females suffer. It says so in the Bible."

"I'll wager you never heard one of the females say that!" Pris selected a green bead this time. "Richard's mother was four days in labor—four *days* in pain—then her heart gave out. *That* I heard Mama tell Mrs. Winston. I was little and I don't think she knew I understood, but I've always remembered." Now her hands were still. "If there is something which could fight pain and I had that pain and they quoted the Bible to me, I—I think I'd scream the house down in their faces!" She was her fierce fighting self now. "Papa—nobody—has any right to say one should suffer when there is a way to help. I hope Richard can prove it in spite of all of Papa's head shaking and warnings."

"Warnings—to Richard?"

"Yes, warnings! Papa told him that he had better not try to teach his elders, who knew a lot more than he did, such untried ways, and said that he might find himself in trouble with all the doctors if he did.''

Caroline's hand went to her mouth. "No! Papa would never make trouble for Richard. He's always been so proud of him, so glad he chose to be a doctor!"

"Papa," said Pris with emphasis, "is master in this house. He is probably the best-known doctor in Montreal. Papa has his own ideas and he won't be talked out of them by anyone—especially by a young man whom he still considers a boy. That's what he thinks of Richard, in spite of all Richard learned overseas. You'll see that I'm right if it ever comes to a test between them. Papa is used to being right, and he will always continue to be so, in his own mind at least." Pris turned back to her beads.

"Papa will come to understand. Richard can show him, tell him—"

Pris laughed. "Carrie, if you believe that Papa—*Papa*—will be talked into trying anything new in medicine which is not his own idea in the first place, you are a little ninny! No, Richard had better keep his mouth shut and watch his step. Perry said so, and this time he is right."

Caroline swallowed once and then again. She did not doubt in the least all Pris had just told her. Though why Perry had passed along such information—unless it was some more of his trouble making. He had always been jealous of Richard, and he perhaps knew that Pris favored her foster brother far above the twin she inevitably quarreled with.

What if Papa did take a stand? Richard in the past had always been unyielding when he believed he was in the right. Suppose, instead of settling comfortably in as Papa's assistant until Perry was qualified, Richard angered Papa so much that he would have to leave, and make his start on his own? Pris was very right in that Papa's word could

make or break a young doctor. He could close doors to
Richard everywhere if he thought it proper. No, Richard
had good sense. He would not anger Papa with new ideas.
There must be ways to make Papa believe in them too,
introduce them with his own approval. If it could be done,
then Richard would discover how to do it.

She said as much now. Pris held two bottles of beads
closer to the light, making sure of their shading.

"Oh, yes," she said as if it did not matter very much,
"Richard will doubtless find a way. He always has had luck
of one kind or another. Carrie, will you ask Mollie if she
has taken in any notes this morning? I am expecting to
hear from Lydia Frazer. She was thinking of a collation
after the reception. And I may be out later—Mama has
calls, and of course she must be at home—everyone will be
coming to meet Althea. It will be quite a sensation when
the news gets around."

Caroline accepted this as dismissal and took her prosaic
darning with her. There were no notes, and she suspected
that had been an excuse to get rid of her. Perhaps Pris was
regretting the disturbing confidence she had passed along
to her younger sister. Caroline was rather used to being
confidante one minute and dismissed like a school-room
miss the next. Pris had to talk to someone, she knew, and
neither of them had ever had close friends outside the
family. Mama believed that such intimacies led to mischievous gossip among girls who should never have heard
its like in the first place.

It was a full week for the household. Mama did keep
Open House in the afternoons, and both matrons and
maidens of the first rank came calling, only too eager to
meet Lady Althea. From two to five each afternoon, sleighs
drew up at the door and their occupants would be ad-

mitted to the formal parlor. The utmost formality followed until Caroline grew so tired of it all she would have cried off from her very small part of it had she dared. Only this was excellent training, according to Mama. Even Pris was subdued into proper manners, though she whispered fiercely to Caroline in the hall as one set of visitors withdrew:

"Did you see Aunt Henrietta just then? She was eyeing Althea's waistline as if she expected her to be in the family way already! If Mama's friends were like Perry's they would be making book on a coming 'little stranger'," she concluded in an affected voice.

Caroline wanted to laugh at Pris' plain speaking, but she tapped her lips with a fingertip and nodded towards the closed parlor door. Sometimes Mama accomplished astonishing feats of hearing, and she would certainly be outraged at such words from any daughter of hers.

"I should think that Althea would just hate it," she returned, "all of them staring at her, even if they pretend not to. It must be very hard to be always on display. One would be afraid of making some wrong move or saying the wrong thing—"

"Not our dear Althea." Pris sounded snappish, but then these At Homes were not her idea of society, and she had been forced into a whole long week of them. "She has doubtless been through much more than this back in London. We're only colonials, after all, and our society must seem very small, in-grown and dull, to one who has been to court and known all the important people we only get to read about, and then months after the balls, and routs and parties are long over. I'm so tired of it. I'll be glad when Althea is thoroughly introduced, Lord Elgin is in his proper place, and we can all settle down to our regular life again.''

She preceded Caroline up the stairs and went into her own room, shutting the door determinedly behind her. Pris might be tired of At Homes—but the reception for the governor was another thing. And the parade. Caroline drew a deep breath. She was certainly looking forward to the parade! To see all the fine uniforms and the horses, to get out of the stuffy parlor into the open—she was looking forward to tomorrow so very much.

And the next day the Warwick family, cloaked, booted, gloved, bonneted, scarfed and hatted against the cold, joined the throng in the street to witness the arrival of Lord Elgin.

''There's Corbie!'' Richard raised a hand with some difficulty to wave to Corbie Hannakar. Although the crowd was getting into quite a press, Mr. Hannakar moved toward them at a serene but steady pace, as if, Caroline thought, he was sure that nobody could stand in his way. And tall and broad-shouldered as he was, few there could.

There was little or no room to bow, but he raised his hat to them and inclined his head especially in Lady Althea's direction.

''I see, my lady, that you do brave the rigors of our snow and ice, as if you were born on these rugged shores.''

She laughed and shook her head at him. ''But, sir, you forget that England is often far from warm.''

''Though I'll warrant it does not have such snow.''

''I never saw so much of that in my life,'' she admitted.

''Your brother continues to find it amazing.''

He was very right about that, Caroline knew. The Honorable Captain Carruthers had made very plain, during his two visits to Warwick house this past week, that he found their land grim and not much to his taste.

There was cheering now, and faint music from the

bands. Then the head of the column came into view. Lord
Elgin rode at a brisk pace (perhaps the climate had gotten
to him also) escorted by detachments of the Rifle Brigade
and the 52nd Light Infantry. Sun glinted from the
polished trappings of both horses and men.

From under the brim of her bonnet, Priscilla glanced
from the marchers to Corbie Hannakar. Caroline caught
that very carefully calculated look. If Priscilla was only in
earnest—if only she really liked Mr. Hannakar—Caroline
pressed her muff-enclosed hands tighter to her breast and
began to hope for the best.

Mr. Hannakar raised his voice a fraction to be heard
above the music. "Miss Priscilla, has your company been
already solicited for the Tandem Club outing tomorrow? If
so, might I then have the pleasure for the following
Saturday?"

Priscilla gave a small, sad shake of her head. "Alas, sir, I
am already engaged for all the club outings." Even Caroline could testify to a note of regret in that answer.

"You leave one quite cast down." His voice was not
quite lazy; there could or could not be regret in it.

Priscilla smiled now. "But, sir, I am not engaged for
Monday afternoon—"

Mrs. Warwick looked about. "Priscilla, afternoon engagements are out of the question for the moment. You
forget we are introducing Lady Althea."

Priscilla looked as if she were about to speak her mind
frankly concerning dull At Homes, and Caroline wondered
if there were any society left in the city which had not already taken tea with Althea.

However, Corbie Hannakar raised his hat again and said
mildly:

"I see I must bide my time then, Miss Priscilla. But it
shall be with impatience, I assure you." Then he was

gone.

Pris looked after him and then swung her head back to watch the parade.

Caroline tugged at her arm. "Lord Elgin," she mouthed through the din.

He did present an impressive figure as he rode along. Just behind him were his two aide-de-camps—Captain Carruthers and another straight-backed figure who had more presence, broader shoulders, and far more well-cut features. If there was a puffiness under red-veined eyes it was not so clear with the sun on the snow, so one could not be sure of that slight defect in what was otherwise the very embodiment of all an officer and a gentleman could be in the dreams of any maiden. Caroline blinked a little at this second newcomer. He quite threw Althea's brother into the shade. She wondered who he was.

Then Richard's hand closed about her arm and he drew her along with Althea, leaving Pris and Perry to come together. "That's all; we had better move before we are caught in the crowd."

"I wish we could see them return to Monkland," Caroline said a little wistfully. "There is going to be an inspection of the guards—"

"It's very cold, Caroline. I hardly think it fitting." Mrs. Warwick and the doctor had caught up to the others.

"Mollie's at the carriage waiting. She'd go with me. And I'm so bundled up I feel quite toasty—"

"Very well. But be careful, and do not stay if there is a large crowd."

Caroline was surprised. Maybe Mama, too, had been influenced by all the brave music, the bright uniforms, and the feeling that this was a one-in-the-time day.

Richard had turned to Papa. "Father, if I can leave Althea in your care, I do have a most important engagement."

"What engagement?" Papa sounded short, almost suspicious.

Richard smiled a little. "One I think you will approve, sir. It is with Dr. Nelson." Then, before Papa could say anything, he was gone.

Papa snorted, "Young fool," but he allowed Mama to steer him toward the waiting carriage while Caroline and Maggie scuffed through the trampled snow on a shortcut toward their own objective.

5

Caroline caught up her skirts with both hands and prepared to dig in her boots. A pile of snow had been shoveled high in an effort to clear the walk; its top of that would be the best place of all from which to view the arrival of the governor's cavalcade. Mollie valiantly followed behind, but not without voicing a misgiving or two.

"Nonsense!" Caroline reached the pinnacle, and reached down to tug at the mittened hand Mollie was waving in the air, as if to regain her balance. "Let me help you—they're coming!"

Only the mounted troops were in escort now. Against the background of the snow the sleek horses and their brilliantly arrayed riders made a brave sight.

Then Caroline let out a cry which was not a cheer for Lord Elgin. The snow moved most treacherously under her feet and she was sliding forward, straight into the road. She let out a second cry.

The small avalanche carried her on out into the road; the foremost riders attempted to rein in their plunging and snorting horses. Suddenly there was someone there, arms about her, steadying her. Caroline, shaking as those pawing hooves barely missed raking down her from shoulder to foot, looked up into Corbie Hannakar's face.

One of the officers pulled his excited horse to a halt beside the two of them. This was the handsome, dark-faced man she had remarked earlier. Only now his face was blackly angry, as he demanded of Mr. Hannakar, "What the devil is this fool girl doing, sliding down like that! Might have been killed! Oh, hello, Hannakar—didn't recognize you. You know this stupid little fool?"

Caroline shrank back against her companion. There was such black anger in the officer's voice as made her shiver.

"Yes, I know her," Mr. Hannakar's tone was nearly hard enough to match the other's anger. "I would advise you, sir, to be a little less free with your language."

Startled, Caroline glanced from the mounted man looming over her to Mr. Hannakar, who still had his arms around her as if he expected the officer to attack. Her supporter's face was hard in a strange way she had never seen before. His eyes were like blue sparks of fire.

"No discourtesy intended, Hannakar," the officer said stiffly. "It might have been a nasty accident, though, that you must admit. Your servant, Miss—" He spoke as if he really did not see her at all, then nodded again to Mr. Hannakar and was gone.

"Miss Caroline! Is it hurt you are?" Mollie, who had found her way down the mound in a more decorous fashion, slithered to a stop beside them on the slippery snow.

Caroline found her tongue. "No. Everything is all right, Mollie." She forced herself to stop shaking and drew out of Mr. Hannakar's arms.

"Indeed, sir," she said over Mollie's bent shoulder as the maid brushed away at her snow-covered cloak. "I do thank you. It is true; I was very foolish, and there might have been a much worse accident."

"Are you sure you are all right?" He was watching her as intently as if he thought she was concealing a sprain or broken bone.

Caroline nodded vehemently. "This isn't the first tumble into a snow bank I ever took. But I confess that never before did I seem about to land under horses' hooves. I must admit *that* was frightening."

"And it was this gentleman as saved you from that! Sir, it is my deep thanks you have. If anything had happened to Miss Caroline, now—what would cook have done? Had me bones and meat entire, maybe!"

Mr. Hannakar laughed. "Now, that is a fate well worth escaping! It would never do to get on the wrong side of cook, I can see."

Caroline managed a smile, though she still felt queer and wobbly inside.

"No, indeed," Mollie agreed, with a freedom Caroline had never heard her use with any other Warwick visitor. "Best be going back, Miss Caroline. You will be wet through by this here dratted snow." She brushed vigorously.

"You will permit me to escort you—" Mr. Hannakar began, but Caroline was enough herself now to decline. To arrive home so accompanied would bring the whole story out, and, since there had been no harm done, it was better that some facts remain discreetly in the background. She could already hear what Mama would say of such an escapade. The fact that she had been so childish would be held against her in the future. Young ladies did *not* go climbing up on snow mounds just to see a parade.

"Please, it is not at all necessary. Mollie and I can manage splendidly. We really can. But you have been so kind—" She hesitated and then held out one hand, its glove stiff with snow. He took it into his much larger one and bowed as if she were a lady and not the hoyden Pris often declared.

"I hope I can again serve you." He said that seriously, and he was not smiling at all. Nor did Caroline believe that he was making fun of her in the teasing fashion Perry so often employed.

She smiled and oddly enough discovered that words came readily. "Not by helping me out of a snowdrift, sir. I assure you that I am now firmly cured of such follies. I thank you again, sincerely."

Mr. Hannakar bowed a second time, and allowed her hand to slip out of his grasp. With a last nod and smile Caroline went on with Mollie, nor did she look back, though she wanted to. She was not quite sure why.

Mollie broke into speech as they hurried along. "My, that was a black-faced man as nearly rode you down, Miss Caroline. He was that angry—only when Mr. Hannakar spoke up, then he pulled back his horns. I wouldn't want to cross that one, no, I wouldn't. Who is he, Miss Caroline?"

Caroline shook her head. "He's one of the governor's aides. He was riding with Captain Carruthers earlier, and must have come ahead for some reason. But he's not one of the garrison officers."

"A handsome kind of black devil he is. He'll set hearts beating, that one will."

"Mollie!" Caroline had never known the maid to be so free with her tongue before, and now regarded her in surprise. "You shouldn't speak like that—"

But Mollie had reached out and laid her hand on Caroline's arm. There was nothing in her face now of the polite, well-trained servant. No, Mollie was apparently shaken out of the shell she had schooled herself to wear.

"I've seen his like, Miss Caroline. 'Tis because of that I let my tongue wag free. There was one like him back in Turleroo. Not an officer all brave in a scarlet coat, mind you, but he was a foreign man from England, come to look at land he heired. There were them as he looked upon and beckoned. And, the fools, they listened and looked—and they were all the worse for it! He was a black devil and left ruin all behind him when he took it in his mind to go back to whatever evil place he came from. There was weeping and heart's sorrow, and even a death he left with us. Two at least who could never hold up their heads again as honest maids. It was a game with him. He did not care— only that he could show his power over wom—"

She stopped in mid-word. "Oh, Miss Caroline, you are right. I should not be speaking so, and to a young maid such as you. But when I looked upon the bold dark face of that one, it all came back in me mind so plain, and I could hear Peg weeping. Broke of heart she was, for he willed her away from Denny. Then Denny he went overseas with the shame of it and Peg— No!" Mollie wiped her snow-caked mitten across her face. "'Tis all done and gone and I shall think of it no more! Save I hope in my heart that there is none in this town who will be the worse for the comin' of that one!"

"We'll never see him." Caroline was shaken by Mollie's hot outburst which was mixed up now in her mind with that dark angry face. Like Mollie, she wanted only to shove the whole incident out of her mind. No, not all of it. She wanted to remember Corbie Hannakar. He had undoubtedly saved her life, and afterward he had not taken her to task for her stupidity, only treated her kindly as a lady.

It was at the dinner table that night that Mama announced placidly (in the voice she used to mention ordinary events) that she had invited Archie and Agatha for dinner the next day. Caroline waited apprehensively for some sharp word from Papa. However, he went on cutting his slice of beef into neat bites as he always did. Caroline guessed that the quarrel with the missing younger Warwicks had been resolved—probably by Mama, who was very clever at such things.

Still, her words were followed by a dead silence. Then Priscilla spoke flatly:

"I will not be here, Mama. I am engaged to drive out with Lieutenant Langely for the Tandem Club outing."

"Yes, my dear. But it is not at all necessary that you be present. It is very proper that your brother and his wife meet dear Althea as soon as possible."

"I won't be here, either," Perry said quickly.

Mama looked at him with her usual unruffled calmness; it was a calm which was well known to her children. "I was not aware that *you* had a previous engagement, Perry."

Perry twirled the slender stem of his wine glass between his fingers, not looking quite directly at Mama. "I hadn't, but I'll attend to turning one up."

Dr. Warwick raised his head. "Peregrine, you will mind your manners and oblige your mother's wishes."

"We expect you to be present, Perry," Mama agreed.

He agreed, but looked mutinous, glaring sullenly at Pris when he was sure his parents were not looking. Caroline's toes tried to curl within her slippers. If Perry were in one of his moods tomorrow— Oh, no, Althea should not have to face unpleasantness just because Perry might be in one of his bad moods.

However, Perry greeted Agatha and Archie with a decent show of family feeling. Far too much of a display,

Caroline was well aware. As usual when he was irritated, Perry was playing a role which ridiculed what had been asked of him.

If Agatha Warwick, now seated on the sofa with the complacency of a well-bred and established matron, had ever possessed any claim to fair looks, she had suppressed it. Her eyes were small slits above puffy cheeks; the latter were dominated by a beak nose above narrow lips set in a constant straight line of disapproval.

That quantity of dun hair she did possess was pulled as firmly back as nature would permit, trussed up in a bun secured by bone hairpins which knew their duty and never released a wisp. Her clothes, though of rich material as was suitable to her station (Agatha was very conscious of station) were drab and without ornament to break the general appearance of dead and dried sameness.

Even now she sat uncomprisingly upright, her back as ramrod stiff as if she drilled each day with the garrison. But those small eyes were never still. The narrow slyness of her mind, Caroline saw now (perhaps because she was so close to all that was light, delicate and fine in Althea) was fully ready to accept all evil of the world and see no good in anything. And those eyes were now turned on Althea. She sniffed, so that those who knew her were well aware of her general disapprobation of this newcomer.

In contrast to his wife, Archie was inclined to be gracious in his usual condescending manner, congratulating Richard in a smugly jovial fashion for his leaving the ranks of benedicks, a comment which brought a second and louder sniff from his life partner and raised a grin from Richard.

"I have found it to be a very pleasant status, Archie, even as you have."

The warmth of Richard's comment brought a little

blush to Althea, and a twist of lips to Agatha.

Perry chuckled. "I will admit that even I now see more in favor of the state." Not even Agatha could not miss the look Perry swept from Agatha to Althea and lingered longer on the English girl.

Agatha bridled, and Archie reddened. Stolid as he always seemed, he had enough of the Warwick quickness to catch Perry at his tricks, Caroline knew. It was Richard who came into the covert battle.

"I hear your affairs are progressing admirably, Archie. I confess I am not surprised; your success in business was assured from the first. You must be one of the city's up-and-coming young men now."

Archie's full cheeks pinked with satisfaction. "I have always endeavored to render satisfaction."

"You are modest, Archie, from what I have been told. In truth, Agatha, you have all reason to be proud of your husband."

She inclined her head solemnly, as if she were the Queen herself.

"You had better watch out," Perry was not yet defeated. "Richard is going to do some shining himself. After his experiment with Nelson yesterday—"

Richard shot Perry a quick frown, but Archie looked interested.

"Nelson? You mean Dr. Nelson? I have heard of him— a young fellow with some rather hare-brained beliefs, or at least it is reported so." Once more his pompousness rose to the surface. "I trust that you will not concern yourself with anything which is not accepted in your profession, Richard. You have been away perhaps too long to remember how circumspect a doctor must be. Take Papa for your example always."

"As an example for what, Archie?" Papa himself had

come in on cue. "In what road is Richard to follow me now? Agatha," he gave his daughter-in-law a slight bow and a token smile, "I see you well, I trust."

Before his wife could answer, Archie's round tones bore her down. "Richard has been visiting Dr. Nelson. I hear that—"

However, Richard himself did not let him finish. "Yes. I went to Nelson's by appointment yesterday. We made a test of the new pain reliever which I had mentioned to you, sir. The results were amazing. I would not have believed it, even though I had seen it used in London, had I not offered myself for the experiment this time."

"Richard!" Althea's soft voice carried, even though she had not raised it. One of her slender hands rose from her lap. He turned and smiled at her.

"Nothing is wrong, my dear. I assure you it was all very interesting and caused no harm."

Papa uttered a sound which was near a grunt and spoke directly to Mama. "I have taken the liberty, my dear, of speaking to James. Dinner has been set forward a few minutes since I have a visitor due later. You will pardon my interference?"

If Perry meant mischief and Archie was ready to lend his weight to the embroilment, nothing came of their efforts. The family settled with dull surface harmony to dinner. There was the second-best linen, gleaming white and, of course, creaseless; and the second-best china, though each piece was lovingly polished. Though Mama had never ordered it so, Caroline was sure, she had long ago tactily accepted the judgment of the lower quarters of the house —the Archie Warwicks were entitled to superlative service, to reflect credit on the family, but only the second best otherwise.

However, Agatha could always find some point of dispute. She eyed the gas jets now with high disfavor and declared, with the heaviness of a bishop discussing a ritual, that candlelight was certainly much safer and better.

"I have discovered that the new brightness is less tiring to the eyes," Mama returned.

"Candlelight is much preferable. If the good Lord had intended to turn night into day, He would have made it so from the beginning."

"Then ain't it going against the Lord to use candles, too?" Perry wanted to know.

If it were possible, Agatha actually stiffened the more. "Do not refer to Our Father so blasphemously," she snapped. "To use the Sacred Name in frivolous conversation is decidedly irreligious. But—" She looked about and stopped short.

Caroline could finish that sentence for her sister-in-law: In this house it was what she expected. However, even Agatha lacked the courage to utter that.

She was growing almost dangerously red though, a color which heightened as Perry continued:

"But, Aggie, I wasn't being blasphemous. All I said was that candles gave light, too. And you had just said that if the Lord wanted light at night, He would have provided it —then where would the candles be?"

To be called Aggie, which she loathed, to have her words questioned, fired Agatha to real heights. Caroline was alarmed at the blaze of her sister-in-law's small eyes and the way her lips were forced into the thinnest of lines. But the doctor spoke.

"I can't recall anything in the Bible objecting to the use of artificial light. Lamps are certainly mentioned there many times. The Lord has left such things to the common sense of men. He did not intend us to starve, and still He does not have grain growing untended or unplanted. No, Agatha, I do not think that the Lord would object to the new discoveries which have given us light for this table.''

''He enables men to make many new discoveries,'' Richard cut in. But perhaps only Caroline and Althea heard him. Althea moved her head in the faintest of negative signals, and he settled back a little in his chair as his foster father sent the sliced roast in the direction of Archie and Agatha. His son helped himself bountifully, but Agatha, true to her disdain for the needs of the body, chose only the thinnest of slivers and toyed with that as one who performed a most distasteful duty. She was not yet defeated.

''I would have thought that Priscilla would be with us. Young girls today do not appear to have much sensibility or true family feeling.''

''Priscilla had an engagement of long standing to drive out with the Tandem Club,'' Mama answered.

''I would *not* have thought you would permit her to accept such engagements. I cannot conceive of this modern laxity which allows young girls to drive alone in a sleigh with a man, even if their equipage is a part of a larger party.''

''What would you expect would happen?'' Perry's eyes were bland, but small devils danced in them.

''One can never tell,'' she replied darkly and finally transferred an infinitesimal bite of the roast to her mouth.

''The outings are very well chaperoned. I, myself, have had that duty several times this season,'' Mama observed. She would never show any sight of temper with Agatha, Caroline knew. Sometimes Mama's control seemed more than anyone could ever think of learning.

"A young girl, alone in a sleigh with a light-minded young man. I cannot imagine the permitting of such a thing."

"Agatha." The doctor had not raised his voice, but none around that table mistook his mood now. "Mrs. Warwick is fully capable of deciding what her daughter may or may not do. A young lady who has been raised with the right principles has no fears of doing wrong. I cannot conceive that your comments upon the subject have any point or value."

Even Agatha's neck and what could be seen of her ears were red now. She glared, not at the doctor but at Perry. She had wit enough to know that not only had Perry enjoyed his father's rebuke fully, but he would doubtless share it with Priscilla.

Once more Richard strove for peace. "Has there been more snow than usual this year, or is it just that I have forgotten how it was? You have no idea how good it is to come back when one can still sleigh. In spite of the cold overseas, there seems to be no real recognition of how to meet it. One night I wore my snowshoe coat—it was bitterly cold—and I do believe that half the urchins of Edinburgh trailed me along. I dared not attempt that comfort for the rest of my stay. Have you gone snowshoeing these past months, Archie?"

"No," Archie's voice was as cold as the snow Richard spoke of. "I have had more important affairs to see to, no longer being a boy."

Richard shook his head. "Healthful exercise *is* important. You've put on weight, Archie, and you're far too pale. Get out, man, it will do you a world of good, no matter what your age."

"I was out 'shoing the other night," Perry said. "Good

footing all the way. You would have enjoyed it, Richard.''

The smooth conversation Richard had begun flowed on. Caroline shifted uncomfortably in her chair, trying to view this through Althea's eyes. This—this squabbling (which it sank to as far as Perry was concerned) was near a total lack of manners. What impression of the Warwicks was Althea getting from this confrontation?

She was glad when Mama gave the signal for the ladies to rise, and even gladder when, having set her lips unhappily to Agatha's cold cheek in a dutiful family acknowledgment, she was able to slip down the backstairs and visit Boots. The kitten was certainly not allowing his splinted leg to cut down on his general activities, cook told her with some pride. That morning he had presented her with a mouse as a sample of his night's hunting in the kitchen. The girl held the purring kitten on her lap, scratching behind his ears and under the chin he raised to accommodate her fingers, and wished that her life was as uncomplicated as Boots'.

She reluctantly left the warmth and good fellowship of the kitchen, and returned to the upper hall just in time to see Agatha, bonneted, booted, cloaked, waiting by the door with Richard, stating stiffly that it was time they were home with young Letty and Edward.

''You have a good nurse, I understand, fully to be trusted,'' Richard said.

Agatha delivered one of her quelling sniffs. ''I prefer to supervise my children closely. Servants are always too lax.'' She placed her hand firmly and with true authority on Archie's arm as he came along from Papa's study. ''Mr. Warwick, it is well time for us to be home.''

As the door closed behind them, Richard let out what could only be a sigh of relief. Then he saw Caroline and grinned.

"It is admittedly a strain to deal with Agatha."

"Yes, but she's family," Caroline stood at the foot of the stairs. "You were good, Richard—keeping Perry from being so outrageous that Papa might have lost his temper. We need you—"

"As a counterirritant to Perry, Archie, and Agatha?" His eyebrow raised a trifle in the way she had always found both amusing and reassuring, as if he could read her thoughts and small fears, and was ready to help.

"Just as yourself," she told him.

Richard swept her a low bow. "Thank you, my lady. I take that as a very great compliment." He had half turned away when Caroline asked:

"What was the experiment you took part in, Richard?" She twisted her hands together then, afraid for an instant that she had presumed too much. "Maybe it was a secret." Of course, she could never tell him all Pris had revealed about the discovery Richard had heard of, and Papa's rejection of it. But she wanted to know more. Think of something so powerful that it would ease pain while a doctor worked!

He did not seem impatient. Instead, he answered her as if she were older, wiser, could well understand what he was saying.

"There is a new chemical, Caroline. Its name is sulphuric ether. It can be given to a patient who needs surgery or is otherwise in too great pain to be safely treated. The effects are to send the patient to sleep or into a state where he does not feel pain at all. Mr. Webster, who has a dental practice, and Dr. Nelson here are very interested in it.

"Yesterday I myself tested this 'anesthesia', as the process is called by Dr. Holmes of Boston. Dr. Nelson had tried it on himself. Now I have done so, under the supervision of both Webster and Nelson. It is very odd. There is a tingling, and then the room seems to just disappear from about one. When one is aware one tries to talk, but the words will not come. You have a feeling of great lightness and happiness—but no pain. While I was in its force Dr. Nelson made a small incision on my chest—''

Caroline could not suppress a gasp at that, and Richard spoke more quickly.

''It was no more than a scratch, but I was not in the least aware of his doing it until he called my attention to the mark. This is a very great discovery, Caroline.'' Now his excitement faded and he looked very sober and unhappy. ''I wish all could see it for what it is. But it is hard to deal with explanations when minds wish to remain closed. Anyway—as Papa Warwick said tonight—the Lord does give knowledge if men are strong enough and have the will-to-purpose to make use of it. I *know* that this will mean an end of much suffering when it is more widely understood and put into practice. I know it!''

It was now as if he spoke not to Caroline but to someone else. She could well guess it was Papa. And surely in time Papa would understand, and at least try it as Richard had done.

''Richard?'' Mama's call came from the slightly open door of the parlor. He waved his hand to Caroline and turned in that direction, leaving her to climb the stairs to bed.

6

Though most of social English Montreal had done their duty at the Warwick At Homes, there were still visitors. And not the least of these arrived on Monday afternoon. Braving the brisk wind and the long drive from Ste. Catherine's came Madam Hannakar herself. Mrs. Warwick was fond of her guest, though she was a little in awe of her. Madam Hannakar was above the usual social rounds, and had, for many years, done exactly as she pleased. It was considered a notable victory to have her appear at a grand tea or a soirée, let alone an At Home. Her visit was an added luster to Althea's welcome.

Her arrival, in state, with her luxurious sleigh, a fine team, and two outriders after the old style, had been announced by Priscilla, who had been at the front window.

"Mama—it's Madam Hannakar!"

"How very pleasant. And how kind of her to come." Mrs. Warwick arose. "Pray compose yourself, my dear. It would not do to be seen staring out of the window."

Pris drew back to a chair, where she seated herself impatiently. Caroline, in her usual seat, was excited; her hand shook a little. If his mother came all the way from St. Catherine's to visit—why, that *must* mean that Corbie

Hannakar was seriously interested in Pris! Mama must think that, too. She was already at the parlor door, ready to receive this very distinguished guest with far more ceremony than she would show to anyone else. Except perhaps the governor's lady, if chance ever brought Lady Elgin to her door.

Their guest was as regal as Lady Elgin could ever hope to be. Though she was not tall, not even as tall as Mama, she dominated the parlor the minute she entered. Friendly, gracious, complimentary, she conversed politely with Althea. However, she did not address Pris very much. Pris did not seem to mind. Lady Althea was charmed, too. Caroline could sense that she found Madam Hannakar, formidable as she might appear, the most pleasant of new acquaintances.

Pris had been so intent on watching their visitor closely that she had not seen Mama's small gesture for her to pass the tea cakes in their silver basket. Caroline, after a moment or two, went to carry out that duty. It was generally hers anyway.

"But you have grown up, child! Have the years sped by as quickly as all that?" Madam's bright eyes were as startlingly blue as her son's. Caroline had the feeling that they could be twice as sharp if some occasion demanded.

"I'm seventeen, Madam Hannakar." Somehow Caroline found her voice.

"And what a great age that is." The answer might have been sarcastic had the inflection been different. As it was, the warm tone seemed to urge Caroline to rejoice that she was exactly the right age. For what, she could not be sure —except that there was something important in everything Madam might say.

"You will be looking forward, of course, to the soirée as

do all the other young ladies?'' Madam continued.

Caroline drew a deep breath and glanced at Mama. There had been no question of her attending. Pris was prepared to shine for all the Warwicks.

Mama came to her rescue. ''Caroline is a little young to take a place in society yet,'' she said, but at the same time she was looking strangely at her younger daughter, as if she saw her in a new way.

''Seventeen too young to come out? Oh, I know that I am sadly unaware of changes which may have taken place since I was active in such affairs. But in my day many girls were wedded at that age. To attend a charity function, one benefiting the institution with which Dr. Warwick is so closely connected—I had thought that both your daughters would indeed be present. Your *three* daughters now,'' she smiled warmly at Althea. ''What a fine sight they would make, all lovely and, in coloring, such contrast to each other! There would be quite a flurry at their appearance. One I was looking forward to seeing.''

''You are thinking of attending, Madam Hannakar?''

''But, of course. Sometimes I feel quite dull, and Corbie has urged me to come. He is always the attentive son, and wishes to relieve my winter tedium. I am so lazy and need a little stirring up now and then.''

''Perhaps you are right.'' Mama looked even more thoughtful. ''Caroline *is* growing up, and for her to attend this affair, it being arranged for the hospital, would be entirely within the bounds of good taste.''

''Such decisions often depend upon the character of the girl herself.''

Caroline suppressed a start. She was used to being discussed as if she had no ears, but what if Madam knew of her slide down the snowpile, that her son had had to rescue her? Certainly Madam would not believe that such a hoyden could be more than a foolish child. But apparently Mr. Hannakar had not mentioned the incident, for Madam continued:

"Of course, care must be expended that early introductions are to the best of company. This is an occasion when one would have no fear of doubtful guests putting in an appearance."

"You are entirely right, Madam," Mama agreed briskly, making up her mind. "To keep a girl in seclusion until she is eighteen and then expose her to society sometimes brings disillusion and unhappiness. Caroline is sensible, and it will be very good for her to attend."

Madam smiled at Caroline, a tiny mischievous quirk at one side of her mouth—as if she had been meddling, Caroline thought. Though why she should think that, she did not know. But she came forward as Madam waved a hand in her direction, setting aside the cake basket to sit down shyly beside the great lady.

It was exciting to be so singled out, although Pris was the one who should be sitting there. It was Pris certainly that Madam Hannakar had really come to inspect—as well as Althea, of course.

"My son tells me," Madam began, "that you admire his horses. That is a good sign of your discernment, my dear. Always compliment a man on his taste in horseflesh. It is so often part of their vanity."

"But the greys are beautiful!" Caroline answered quickly. "They are! No wonder Mr. Hannakar is proud of them."

Madam nodded. "Yes, they make a fine appearance. Corbie is a good judge in truth, like his father before him. You enjoyed your ride?"

"Very much." Caroline was eager.

"Ah, to be young—to be able to brave cold and snow, and to enjoy it!" Madam laughed, and then spoke to Mama about the soirée, Althea and Pris being drawn in to join a conversation concerning ball gowns and the probable weather, and whether the hall would be heated well enough that one might brave it in true formal décolleté. Caroline felt she had very little to add. What kind of dress would she wear? Not one as grand as Pris', of course. But she would have to have a new one. Nothing she had ever owned was fine enough for such an occasion. What might Papa say about that, and about her going at all? Her bedazzlement with the idea was a little shadowed. Then she cheered up. If Mama had decided, it was as good as done. It was Mama who understood about society, and usually she merely informed Papa that this or that was what they had planned.

Before she left them, Madam made one other suggestion which left Mama visibly proud and happy: "As soon as the weather grows better, your three daughters must all come to Ste. Catherine's for a visit." Madam then turned to Caroline herself:

"Since you have such a liking for animals, my dear, you must see those of the Manor. We have several deer which are hand tamed, and there is my beautiful Alexandra. Corbie declares she is the worst-spoiled cat in existence. But that is not so. She is of royal lineage. My dear husband brought her mother and sire back from England, where he bought them from an Indies Captain. She is of a different breed—very long and silky of hair and as grey as Corbie's beloved team."

Caroline had presence of mind enough to express her thanks and her fervent desire to meet Alexandra. Then

Madam was on her way, Mama and the rest of them rising to escort her to the hall. There her maid waited with deeply furred cloak, and James had her small foot stove filled with small coals.

It was as if the Queen had visited them.

"How very gracious," Mama remarked as they returned to the fireside. "She is one of our great ladies, there are few of her kind to be seen any more," she said to Althea, as if proud that this cold provincial city could have an advantage over the richer delights of England.

"She is very pleasant, truly," Althea agreed. "Her son —he is the one we met at the parade, is he not?"

"Yes." There was a shading of satisfaction in Mama's voice. "He has several times taken Priscilla out in his sleigh, and has bespoken some dances at the soirées with her. A young man of character and high standing in the community." Now she smiled at Pris. "I can believe that he may make himself even more agreeable in future."

All knew exactly what she meant. Madam Hannakar would never have displayed such interest in the Warwicks without good reason. And what other reason could there be except the attention her son had been openly paying to Pris these past few weeks? Caroline felt warm inside. If he did marry Pris, then she might go out to the Manor often —Pris would ask her. Ste. Catherine's would provide a whole new world to explore.

However, that was in the future. What lay ahead now was the soirée, when she would learn for herself what Pris' enchanted world was like. She was excited, and a little frightened. Would she be a credit to Mama, or a disappointment as she all to often seemed to be? She longed to ask Pris for advice and help but, when she went to her sister's room a few days later, she found Pris stitching away on her beaded bag so intently that she did not respond to Caroline's first half-question. Rather, she asked abruptly:

"Have you seen Major Vickers?" The question was so sharp, so different from Pris' usual way, that Caroline was startled into forgetting for the moment why she had come.

"Major Vickers?" she repeated, totally at a loss.

"He's Lord Elgin's other aide-de-camp. Oh, I forgot. You weren't here yesterday when Captain Carruthers brought him to call; you went out to match the ribbons for Mama. He is from England, too. I was introduced to him at the Tandem Club sleighing. He—" Pris' busy hands fell to her lap; a bead slid off her needle, but she did not notice. She was staring at the wall as if she were not in the room any more at all, but off somewhere quite different. There was a slow, lazy smile beginning about her lips, a kind of glowing look about her. Like Perry, Pris had her own signs of coming mischief.

"He will be at the soirée, of course," she said. "He has asked me for the first waltz. I am looking forward to watching Amanda Cummings and Gracie Townely when they set eyes on him! He'll be wonderful in dress uniform—"

Caroline remembered the dark angry man of the parade day, the one Mollie had spoken of so strangely. Was that Major Vickers? If so, handsome as he was, how could Pris prefer him to Mr. Hannakar?

"But you promised the waltz to Mr. Hannakar, surely?" she protested.

Pris made a face. "Oh, Corbie—he is too apt to take one for granted. He hasn't called all week."

"But his mother did," Caroline pointed out.

Pris shrugged petulantly. "And so all of you, Mama and the rest, think that she came to look me over, as if I was a doll up for sale, to see if I am good enough for her son! Well, I want you to know, Caroline Warwick, that I am not going to sit around waiting for any man to make up his mind.'' Her lips straightened into a line and there was a dangerous glint in her eyes. Pris might have golden hair, but her temper was far more fitted to Caroline's thick, burnished locks. ''If you wait,'' and now there was a bleak note in her voice, ''perhaps you get nothing at all. I'll be married, all right, and I'll marry well enough to suit Mama —and Papa. However, who I marry will be my choice! Corbie takes too much for granted—far too much! Oh, Carrie, do run along! I've got to finish this leaf while the light is still strong—it's no good trying to match these colors by lamplight and I'll never get this done in time!''

Caroline went soberly down the hall. *You wait and you'll get nothing at all.* Pris—and Richard. Pris had been so gay lately that she had hoped her first guess had been wrong. *Had* Pris been waiting for Richard? Was that why she had flirted but not made any real choice this past year?

But she did have such a good choice—Corbie Hannakar. Only, it was true that if you tried to push Pris in any way, she immediately bolted in the opposite direction. Perhaps now, because everyone believed that she was interested in Corbie, she wanted none of him. She did not want Mama or Papa to think they had made the match for her. Only— Pris and this Major Vickers—if she did flout Corbie Hannakar too openly, Pris might bring all sorts of trouble down on herself. Too often had she done just that.

''Caroline?'' Althea stood in the door of her own chamber; her voice broke through the whirl of Caroline's unhappy thoughts. ''Come in a minute, dear.''

A smell of perfume always seemed to be in the air. It was a little odd that Richard, who had lived before in a room which was so dark and full of books, shared this very feminine place now. The scent came from one of Althea's trinkets which Caroline loved—a small china cottage in which perfumed oil burned, giving forth such a pleasant and soothing odor. Althea had so many pretty and un-usual things; visiting in her room revealed small wonders which Caroline had never before imagined.

"Will that be all you wish pressed, m'lady?" Skinner stood waiting, a froth of white ruffles and lace over her arm. Skinner, Caroline had gathered from Mollie and cook, kept herself to herself, and was very apt to look down her nose at the Warwick lower establishment. However, she was never meant to stay with Althea—being really maid to one of Lady Elgin's ladies. She was prepared to return to her mistress as soon as possible, her services having been only lent to Althea when she had made the sudden decision to make the winter sailing west. Though Althea did not seem aware of the disapproval which radi-ated from her temporary maid, she kept her busy with such small tasks as would occupy her apart from the house-hold.

With Skinner gone, Caroline stood luxuriously sniffing, then laughed as she caught Althea's puzzled look.

"It's the perfume. Even Pris never had anything which smelled as good. It's like being out at the farm at lilac time, when all the bushes are in bloom, and walking slowly down through the garden, just smelling the wind."

"You like the farm."

"I love it," Caroline declared, as a wave of real longing for that small safe part of her world overcame her. There she was always sure of what she was and what she could do. "Papa lets me stay there most of the summer. Taffy must have had her kittens long ago; they will be nearly grown when I see them. And Robin is due to drop her foal in the spring. There are so many new young things—''

She caught sight of the pink on Althea's cheeks, the odd way the older girl was looking at her, and then she realized.

''You—you think that maybe I should not know about such things. But those are true things, and there is nothing bad about them. I've helped Taffy twice when she had kittens. She always has darlings. I guess—well, I guess I should not talk about that. Some girls—well, I've heard them snicker and whisper. But Mr. Wilson at the farm knows I am very fond of animals, that I want to help. When Taffy had her first kittens I did not know what was the matter. He came and explained. I would have asked Papa if he had been there, but he isn't, much. He's too busy. Mama and Papa never ask me questions and so there is no reason to tell. I don't think it is wrong of me, do you? I wouldn't say anything to most people.''

''No,'' Althea declared, both her eyes and her mouth smiling. ''It is not in the least wrong, but you are wise not to discuss what you know. *I* understand that some girls are very curious, sometimes learning unpleasant things in sly ways. I also lived where there were animals. I had a little greyhound—Tippet. She was not as lucky as your Taffy. When her first puppies came she died, though the kennel man tried to help her. It was very sad for me. And that reminds me—''

She took up a long narrow box from the table. It was made of some dark wood, the lid inlaid with mother-of-pearl to form a spray of flowers. ''I wanted to give you this. It will bring you luck, maybe. It did me. It was a gift from my brother—the one who died in India. When his things were sent home, this was among them with a half-finished letter meant for me. He was a soldier, but he always wanted to be something else. From the time he was little and could get a pencil or pen he always drew. He made me this to carry at my first ball. I did, and when I was thoughtless enough to drop it Richard picked it up. That was really how we first met.''

Caroline opened the box to take out a delicate silk fan, its sticks carved in ivory, the silk of its cover patterned with a long trailing vine of dark ivy leaves which curled in the center to frame a small scene of a strange little house with upturned curling eaves at the roof corners.

Mama had decided Caroline would wear a soft floating tulle to the soirée—not in plain white but in very pale green, and Mrs. Riddle had come for her first fitting. The fan would be perfect with it.

"That was the Folly.'' Althea pointed to the little house. ''My father had it built for my mother to take tea in. Such things were the fashion then. It was copied from a house on a screen in the library, which had come from China many years ago. After Mother died it was our play house. Our own place—''

"But your brother—Captain Carruthers—'' Caroline was puzzled.

"Ronald was my younger brother. There was less than a year between us, really.''

Caroline said slowly, "It must be very precious to you. To give it—''

"It brought me my luck, even as Ronald would have wanted. Now it must do the same for you, Caroline. Indeed, he might really have intended it for someone like you. The ivy is more like you than any fat roses, or tooperfect lilies. Yes, I have had so much luck—'' Her eyes were very bright as for a moment she was silent. Then, as if she had made up her mind on some very important thing, she said in a lower voice, slowly, as if she shaped each word carefully in her mind before she spoke it aloud:

"I am going to tell you something, Caroline. I really do not understand why, except that I think you will keep my secret and I just must share it with someone. Richard knows. But with a man it is different. I am going to have a baby."

Caroline nearly dropped the precious fan in her excitement. She did let the box fall to the carpet, as she reached out and caught Althea's hand and held it tightly. "Oh, Althea—but should you not be very careful?"

Althea laughed. "Oh, it won't be arriving for a long time yet—it takes longer for a baby than kittens, you know. I don't think it will be here before October."

"October? Are you certain?"

"Yes, October."

"Do you want a boy? Most people seem to. I don't know why, unless it is because boys are more important somehow. But a little girl—one as pretty and sweet as you—"

Althea drew Caroline into her arms. The Warwicks were not too demonstrative a family, but the younger girl found this soft and scented embrace heartwarming. She *loved* Althea. Pris was beautiful, and charming, and very, very important, but—she loved Althea.

"Caroline, are you excited about the ball?" Althea asked moments later as they sat side by side on the small settee at the foot of the wide bed. "You don't talk very much about it."

"Somehow I don't think my going is really true, you know. Going to a soirée just like Pris. Then I think of my dress. That's real, and Mama wouldn't have ordered it if it were not to be used." She drew the closed fan lovingly through her fingers. "Now I have this to prove it doubly. But sometimes—" Caroline found it very easy now to spill out those doubts which had sent her seeking counsel from Pris, "I get frightened. I can dance—at least I've had lessons, and Monsieur Gabrineau says that I do very well. But it is the talking to strangers and saying the right thing. I know what *not* to say—at least I think I do—but it is what I *should* say that I'm not sure of."

Althea nodded, as if she understood perfectly.

"Your brother must have friends, and do you not have friends with brothers who will attend? You know all of them and can talk to them about what they are interested in. Luckily, Caroline, not much is expected in the way of sparkling conversation from any young lady. Smiles and an air of listening are all that are required. There will probably be a great crush, for Alexander says now that Lord Elgin has decided to attend. If I know company, most attention will be going his way. But Pris, and I, and your Mama will all be there—you will not be left alone. And I think you will be surprised at how easy it will be."

Caroline was not quite sure about the availability of brothers and friends of brothers. She had mingled so little with other girls, due to Mama's belief in family closeness. And she was already wise enough to know that Pris would have her own pleasure to the forefront of her mind. But, of course, she could sit with Mama. She hoped no one would ask her to dance; then she could just sit quietly and watch it all.

"If the gentlemen were all like Mr. Hannakar, then I would be safe," she blurted.

"Mr. Hannakar?" Althea sounded surprised.

Caroline hesitated. Althea had told her a secret; maybe

she should trade hers in return. Quickly, hoping that she
would not seem a foolish child, she told of her adventure.
When she spoke of the horse near treading her down, she
heard a gasp from Althea.

"Oh, I know," Caroline said hurriedly. "I was childish
and foolish and I am sure I have learned my lesson. But
Corbie—Mr. Hannakar—was so kind. He spoke so sharply
to the black man—that's what Mollie called him, but I
think he is a Major Vickers who is with Lord Elgin. He was
in a rage with me until Mr. Hannakar spoke. But I was
really safe then. Mr. Hannakar treated me as if I were a
lady like Pris. I do hope that he *will* marry Pris. He's like
Richard. And Madam Hannakar is so kind. They would be
family then, and I like them both so very much."

Althea was looking at her a little strangely, and Caroline
had a sudden frightening thought. You were not supposed
to tell ladies anything upsetting when they were—
were—"*enceinte*" was the word she had heard Mama use.
Had she done wrong again?

"I wasn't hurt, truly. And I do hope I did not upset
you, Althea. I just wanted you to know why I like Mr.
Hannakar so much."

"I think," Althea said thoughtfully, "I want very much
to meet Mr. Hannakar myself. No, dear, you have not upset me. I am only very, very glad that he was there to help
you. But in the future you must be much more careful.

"I know. I must be a lady."

Now Althea was laughing. "Do not take it so to heart,
Caroline. I assure you that being a young lady has many
excellent compensations. Are you sure that Priscilla is indeed Mr. Hannakar's present interest?"

"Of course! He takes her sleighing, and he would take
her more often to the Tandem Club, only she makes so

many other promises. And his mother almost never comes into the city in winter, but she came to meet you—and, I am sure, to see Pris. She was so kind in getting Mama to let me go to the soirée, and asking me to come out to Ste. Catherine's. That is a wonderful place. Although she does not entertain very much any more, I have heard stories about it, and it must be almost like one of the Queen's places. Her mother came from France when the Revolution began, but the family was lucky and they were able to bring many of their most beautiful things with them. They came on a ship which belonged to Mr. Hannakar—our Mr. Hannakar's great-grandfather. He had a son with that big estate, who married one of the girls who escaped. She was a countess and had been in waiting on the French Queen. All the lovely things went to her home. And *their* son married his cousin who was also French—that was Madam. The Mr. Hannakar we know has all sorts of interests. He was out west for more than a year to visit the fur trading posts he owns, and he lived with Indians. I wish I could hear more about his adventures. If he marries Pris, then we certainly shall."

"I think," Althea said slowly, "that perhaps anyone who married Corbie Hannakar might be considered fortunate."

Caroline beamed. "Pris will. You just wait and see!"

7

Caroline sat with her back as straight as she could make it, her fingers laced tightly together in her lap, staring into the mirror. She felt as if she had been half-scalped—or at least this was how she imagined that one so mutilated by the Indians might feel. It was Skinner who had been brought in to deal with her mass of unbraided hair in the London fashion. But, however skillful she might be in achieving the effect proper for a very young lady, the maid's impersonal hands had pulled and twisted horribly. Caroline had not dared to utter a single word of protest. It was as if she were indeed a doll, and had been buttoned, laced, dressed, combed, and all the rest with no will, power, or desires of her own to be considered.

"There now, m'lady." Skinner stepped away, having inserted a last pin, addressing not Caroline but Althea, who had come to watch the transformation. "Seeing as it is winter and there is no flowers available—that will have to do."

"But it is very fine, Skinner," Althea commented in her soft voice. "Thank you very much."

Caroline roused enough to add a quavering thanks to Skinner, but continued to stare at this person who could not be Caroline Warwick, aged seventeen. She saw a stranger. The wealth of hair was drawn up and back in some mysterious way which left little curls over her ears, while the heavy mass in the back was confined with a criss-cross of well-anchored ribbons of the same delicate green as her dress.

Though the dress was not near as low cut as any in Pris' fashionable collection, or the one Althea was wearing, Caroline's neck and shoulders showed very white above the ruching of the tulle. Around her throat she had what Papa had presented to her only that morning—a string of small pearls. Just proper for her age, Mama had said. They were the most perfect things Caroline had ever owned, except Althea's lovely fan. She could hardly believe that they were hers to keep, to wear.

"Cinderella ready for the ball, is that what you are thinking?" Althea asked laughingly.

"I do not have glass slippers," Caroline awoke a little out of her daze. "But I never could understand those anyway. Wouldn't they break if one tried to dance in them?"

"Fairy tales are apt to be rather impractical in some things, I suppose," Althea agreed.

"I wonder if she worried about the mice changing back." Caroline was working on the new French kid gloves which smelled of lavender and had to be carefully fitted finger by finger. No wonder ladies sometimes wore their rings and bracelets over gloves; one certainly could not crowd them underneath. "But I suppose she really thought the most about the prince."

"And perhaps the two ugly stepsisters?"

"Well, I don't have those. I have two *good* and *kind* sisters—you and Pris. And we won't be going in a pumpkin coach. But wouldn't it be fun if there really was a prince?'' She turned half-way around on the dressing table bench and beamed at Althea. "I think she," Caroline waved a hand at the mirror, "almost deserves a prince tonight."

"Princes, too, have their faults," Althea smiled. "The fairy tales are inaccurate in more than one thing."

"Althea! Should I warn Richard, do you suppose?"

"No, sometimes the prince turns out to be just what the fairy godmother promised."

"Oh, I'm so glad Richard married you!" Caroline cried out impulsively. "You're the best fairy godmother—or is that Madam Hannakar? She started it all. But you—you're so dear."

Althea had risen to lean forward a little and brush Caroline's cheek with her lips. "So are you, Caroline, so are you."

"Now," Althea added more briskly, "go and show your Mama, Cinderella, and take your cloak with you."

"You'll be warm enough, Althea?" Caroline looked at her anxiously. "This won't be too tiring?"

"Not at all! The Warwick ladies are going to make a grand entrance, and even Lord Elgin will be impressed. Get along with you, now."

They were grand, Caroline was sure, as they gathered in the lower hall, their fur-lined cloaks about them, the wide loose hoods adjusted with care over their hair. Pris sparkled in her new dress, its flounces caught up with clusters of flowers made of seed pearls. Her pearl necklace was longer than Caroline's, and, in addition, she had matching dangling drops in her ears. Lady Althea wore deep rose and diamonds in a lace-like necklace. More diamonds flashed from her ears and from a hair ornament which was a tiny fairy crown. Mama was gowned in deep crimson velvet with her ruby pendant and the matching earrings Papa had given her three years ago.

They were ushered into the carriage sleigh, their slipper bags handed in. Papa, Perry and Richard had already gone, since Papa was the head of the committee and must be there to be sure all was going well.

It was a clear night. The runners of the sleigh slid crisply over the hard-packed snow; the silver bells on the harness sang with every step the horses took. Every window in the Donegaga Hotel blazed with light, while St. Paul's Street was lined with sleighs which had drawn to one side to allow Lord Elgin and his mounted escort free passage. In spite of the cold there were crowds along the street, pressing about the entrance to the hotel. And they were cheering as the Governor General came into view.

Luckily the Warwick sleigh had also been ahead of time, so Mama could make her deep curtsey right beside Papa. Then the long formal round of presentations began. Caroline made her curtsey with a fast-beating heart, afraid at this last moment that she might stumble or otherwise disgrace herself. Then, her ordeal safely over, she dared look straight at the Governor, his aides, and the glitter of uniforms. Althea's brother in his dress uniform was almost handsome, but he seemed too pale, too thin. Major Vickers—it was indeed Mollie's "black man" who stood there. Caroline drew a small quick breath. Had he recognized her?

But how could he? She had not even recognized herself when they had changed into their slippers in the lady's cloak room and she had caught a side reflection in one of the mirrors. She had wondered for a moment who it was who had the hair as red as her own!

There was Madam Hannakar coming in now, her gloved hand on her son's arm. She looked even more like a queen in her rich lavender velvet, more diamonds than Lady Althea's making ice fire in her wide lace collar, and in her small cap of such a cobweb fineness that one wondered how it could be set on her silver hair without tearing. Fairy Godmother—all she needed was a star-tipped wand, Caroline thought, warmly grateful.

The tedious introductions over, the band began to play the first quadrille of the evening, and Lord Elgin was bowing before Mama! Papa beamed as he watched. Captain Carruthers had started toward Pris, but the dark major was before him, and she smiled prettily up at him as he led her out into the forming set. Then Caroline was startled: resplendent figure was saluting *her*. It was Captain Carruthers.

Captain Carruthers had come to the Warwick house often to see Althea—but he had left earlier when Pris had not been at home, and Caroline thought that he had hardly noticed her. But now he appeared more attentive. She said "yes" and "no," but she was totally intent on her steps at first, until she realized that her instructor had been right and she did know how to dance properly. This was no more difficult than when she had danced in his big bare studio!

The band of the Rifle Brigades was far better than the dancing master's tinkling piano, and Captain Carruthers did not seem disposed to talk too much. Caroline became sure that he was really watching Pris where she twirled her skirts around and smiled up at Major Vickers so brightly.

Mr. Hannakar was dancing, too—with Cissy Fox, the daughter of one of Papa's good friends at the medical college. Cissy was two years older than Pris and had been to a

great many balls, but she had never seemed to seriously
attract any gentlemen.

There were so many people on the floor that Caroline
could not catch a glimpse of Perry, or Richard, or Althea.
But Madam Hannakar smiled and nodded to her as they
passed the small gold-painted chairs where the older ladies
sat and where Mama would have pride of place as soon as
the quadrille was over. It was back to Mama's side that
Captain Carruthers led Caroline when the dance finished,
thanking her before he moved away.

Just as well pleased to be allowed to sit quietly, Caroline
settled beside Mama. In spite of it being winter the gas
lights in the room were turned up in such plenty, and she
was so warm from dancing, that Caroline found Althea's
gift could be put to real use. Mama was speaking to
Madam Hannakar, but the music was so loud that Caroline
could hear only a word or two. She was content that so far
Cinderella had weathered the pitfalls of this new world.

Pris had not returned to Mama. As Major Vickers had
bowed, another officer had come up to claim her hand.
But Althea came back on Richard's arm, laughing gently
as she seated herself beside Caroline.

"Did the glass slippers sustain the effort?" she leaned
close to whisper. Richard, having murmured that he saw
Dr. Nelson and wanted a word with him, left them.

Caroline nodded. "Oh, yes! But I do not know how to
engage a gentleman in conversation. I was so frightened at
first that all I could say was 'yes' and 'no'. I fear Captain
Carruthers thinks me a very dull person."

"Alexander?" Althea laughed again. "I will tell you a
secret, Caroline. Sometimes I have found Alexander to be
a very dull person. Your worlds have little in common, but
do not let that worry you. We are certainly not all of the

same pattern. If we were, then the world would be a very dull place indeed. I see Pris is dancing again.''

"Pris always has all the partners she wants," Caroline said proudly. "She is so beautiful, and she knows just what to do and say. Isn't she lovely, tonight?''

"Indeed, yes. But—"

What Althea might have added was never said, because there was a gentleman bowing before them—not before them, Caroline realized, before her! She looked up what seemed a long way into Corbie Hannakar's face.

"Might I have the pleasure, Miss Caroline?''

It was a waltz, the first waltz. Caroline glanced at Mama, inquiring. Sometimes people said that the waltz was "fast," and Mama might think she was too young. But Mama was smiling, just as was Madam Hannakar, so she found herself on her feet and out on the floor, her one hand reaching up to touch Mr. Hannakar's broad shoulder, the other clasped in his hand, and they glided away. Her steps matched his without fault. Only, thought Caroline confusedly, this was wrong—Pris should be here, not her.

Her partner looked down at her with that half-smile she found as warming as Richard's.

"I have to salute a beautiful young lady—"

Caroline shook her head. "No, Pris is the beauty. I'm just being Cinderella for tonight. Only I don't have the stepsisters to worry about. Though I do have the fairy godmother." She was finding it easy to talk now.

"Oh, and where is she?" Mr. Hannakar half turned his head for a moment as if seeking that apparition.

Caroline laughed. "She is sitting beside Mama. It is Madam. Your mother persuaded Mama to let me come. I don't know why, and I was afraid of the idea at first—"

"But you aren't now?" he asked swiftly.

"Well, I think that Captain Carruthers must think me dull. I'd never danced with anyone but Perry and Monsieur, of course, and that does not really count. So I was worried about it. Only it is easy after all, isn't it?"

"For you, Cinderella, it is perfectly easy. Do you have to disappear at midnight? Or has your fairy godmother given you special privileges by enchantment tonight?"

"I hope she has," Caroline said simply. "I never used to understand why Pris loves parties so. Now I think I can, a little. Though if one went to them all the time—" She hesitated.

"And saw the very same people? Yes, the brightness would begin to grow a little dim perhaps. But it never did for Cinderella, I am sure. And how is Boots?"

"Two mice this morning. Cook was so pleased." She did not stop to wonder how he knew about Boots. "Your mother—Madam—she has promised to let me meet Alexandra—"

"Who is abominably spoiled and believes she owns us— not that we have any claim on her," he returned promptly. "She demands the richest cream with her tea and our full attention. But she never repays us as Boots has done."

This was like talking to Richard—or even sharing small gossip with Althea. Caroline was disappointed when the waltz was over; it seemed to be very short indeed. She knew that Mr. Hannakar would be looking for Pris now and stifled her own odd reluctance to return to Mama. But Mama was being claimed by Dr. Howards; for Althea was gone again too, and there was no sign of Pris. Caroline settled herself beside Madam Hannakar.

Mr. Hannakar seemed in no hurry to go looking for Pris.

Instead he stood beside his mother and looked out over the crowded floor as if he had no desire to plunge into the throng.

"You are enjoying yourself, child?" Madam Hannakar asked.

"Oh, yes!" Caroline answered swiftly.

"She's Cinderella, you see, Mama," Mr. Hannakar spoke lazily. For a moment Caroline was hurt. Was he making fun of her? Had he thought her as childish as she had been when she climbed the snow pile? "Cinderella cannot help but enjoy the ball."

"Cinderella?" Madam Hannakar sounded as if she did not quite understand. "Ah, the old tale—"

"You have a part in it, Mama, so you must not act as if you do not know what we are talking about."

"I do?"

Caroline felt the heat of her blush which seemed to begin nearly down at her toes and work its way up. How could he make fun of her so? And she had thought he was so kind—like Richard!

"You are the fairy godmother," Mr. Hannakar stated solemnly. "And that *is* an excellent recognition of your very great talents, Mama. I think I have never heard better."

Caroline, her face aflame, stared down at her fan. She wished wildly that she was home. This was what came of trying to enter Pris' world. She did not belong here at all.

"Corbie!" Madam's voice sounded sharp. A hand almost smaller than her own dropped over Caroline's twisting fingers. "You forget yourself. My dear, your naming of me so is a very charming thing, I am happy that you see me thus. This bad boy has no right to distress you. Corbie, you will fetch us each a glass of punch and think about your ill manners as you do so.''

Caroline looked down at that gloved hand; she still felt so embarrassed.

''My dear,'' Madam Hannakar continued, ''Corbie was not trying to make fun or trifling amusement of anything you might have said to him. He was pleased with your fancy. Sometimes young men may not be aware of what we feel—but that does not mean that they will willfully hurt one. Corbie *is* pleased; I know him well enough to recognize that. He wanted to share your very happy little fancy with me because that is what he does with things which he enjoys. Do you understand?''

Caroline was able to look up at last. ''I—it was so easy to talk to him—as if he was Richard. I guess I forgot that one does not think of fairy tales when one is supposed to be a young lady. But it does seem almost like being in a fairy tale to me, and you did lead Mama to think of my coming.''

''And it has worked out very well indeed!'' Madam Hannakar said firmly. ''Where is Corbie? Oh, I see him talking to your brother. And where is your sister, Miss Priscilla? We have not seen much of her this evening?''

Pris should be here. If Madam Hannakar noticed that she had danced steadily and that her son had not been one of Pris' partners, she might be offended. Caroline looked out at the dancers. There were so many light and frothy gowns, but she could not see a blue one. Where was she? Perhaps she had torn a flounce and had gone to the ladies' cloak room for quick repairs. The maids there kept needles and thread.

''I think she must be in the cloak room. Perhaps her dress was torn; once Lieutenant Morris caught a spur in her lace and ripped it dreadfully,'' Caroline said hurriedly. ''I had better go and see.'' She slipped off her chair before Madam Hannakar could answer and made her way towards the door.

In the outer hall she was a little puzzled for a moment. They had been in such a rush when they came, because Mama had to be there to greet the Governor General. Which way had they come? Oh, yes, it was upstairs and to the right. Gathering up the unaccustomed fullness of her skirt in one hand, Caroline hurried forward.

The upper hall was deserted. Caroline was at the door of the cloak room when she heard a laugh from an alcove down the hall, where some plants, carefully tended through the winter, had been arranged to form a screen. She stopped short. There was no mistaking that laugh. Pris was there! But why? She must return at once to the ball-room. To Corbie.

Caroline, still holding her skirts up a little, swept round that frail barrier of potted plants and stood statue still, staring.

Pris was on a settee, but she was far from alone. Her waist was encircled by an arm in a uniform coat, and she was looking up at a dark handsome face which had just risen from touching hers. Caroline was not a simpleton; she realized that Pris had just been very thoroughly and lingeringly kissed. Nor did she miss the fact that a brown hand rested on her sister's bare shoulder, where the soft silk had been creased down to reveal the swell of breast below.

Pris looked up. Then she pushed away from her companion, but, Caroline thought, as if she did not want to leave his embrace in the least.

''Caroline!'' Her sister's voice was tart. Major Vickers moved away, too, his dark face wearing a queer smile as he glanced from one girl to the other.

What might have the power to move Pris? Caroline said the first thing which came into her head. "Pris, Mama wants you."

The Major remained where he was, but her sister arose. As if she were alone in her own chamber, she pulled up the shoulder of her gown, patting it into place. Then she turned to accept her fan, which the Major had gathered up from the floor.

"My little sister," she said to the Major. Her voice was cool, forbidding. This was Pris at her most dangerous, when she might do or say anything, and Caroline was in sudden fear. "I must be a paragon of virtue for her example, you know. Come, Caroline, if Mama wants me we had better not dawdle." She swept by, leaving the younger girl feeling that any fault was largely hers. The Major's smile grew broader, and in that moment Caroline could readily believe everything Mollie had suggested. She was strangely afraid—more so than she had ever been before in her life.

She turned and hurried after Pris, though her sister ignored her. They were passing the ladies' cloak room when the door opened and Althea came out. Caroline knew an inward sigh of relief. At least Althea had not been the one to find Pris so. It was just Pris' way to try some daring thing because she was unhappy. And that Pris was unhappy, Caroline knew.

As Althea joined them Pris stopped short. The look she gave the English girl was one of anger—as if the last thing she wanted to do at the moment was confront Richard's wife.

"Were you hunting me?" Althea asked. "I am sorry I did not tell Mrs. Warwick, but with the heat and the crowd I felt faint for a little and retired. I did not want to worry anyone."

Caroline forgot Pris for an instant. Her hand was under Althea's arm as she asked anxiously:

"How do you feel now? Should I find Richard?"

"No, it is nothing. I am quite myself now. But I am sorry that you were worried and had to come seeking me."

Pris had given only a nod and was passing on ahead. It would be best, Caroline decided, to let Althea believe that they had been seeking her. She must not—no one must know of how she had found Pris and Major Vickers.

The minute they were within the ballroom again, Pris was claimed by Lieutenant Marston, who complained that he had been looking for her everywhere and that this was their promised dance.

Althea and Caroline made their way back to the chairs. Mama was once more seated there while Mr. Hannakar stood beside his mother, a punch cup in his hand, a worried crease between his eyes which smoothed away as the two girls came up. "Miss Caroline. I thought perhaps you had deserted us." He bowed and held out the cup. "You see? I did my duty, and then, alas, found my efforts were in vain."

"Oh, thank you," Caroline, flustered, accepted the cup with a hand which shook a little.

"You will note that I skimped on the contents—purposefully. I did not spill it on my return, I assure you."

Caroline looked down. The cup was but half full.

"It seems that there was an overzealous hand in the making of this concoction," he continued. "I would advise any of the gentler sex to treat it with respect."

Althea laughed. "What a gentlemanly warning, Mr. Hannakar. No, you need not fetch me one." For he had half turned as if to repeat his errand. "Richard has already introduced me to this overzealously made brew. And I agree to the potency. Sip it, Caroline."

Mama regarded them both with an indulgent smile which Caroline had not expected. She took a sip of the punch. It tasted very nasty, but she was polite in her thanks to Mr. Hannakar, who raised an eyebrow and nodded.

"You found your sister?" asked Madam Hannakar.

Under those keen eyes some of Caroline's fluster returned. What would Madam have thought of that scene in the upper hall? She must never, never know. The punch—that must be it! Nobody had warned Pris, and she had had too much of this awful-tasting stuff and been silly. As Perry had been once or twice when he had come home and she had heard him stumbling along the hall. Drink made people do things that they would never do otherwise. But if Pris was—was drunk, what might she do next?

Mama spoke rather sharply: "Madam Hannakar asked you a question, Caroline. I understand you went off quite suddenly in search of Pris for some reason. Why? And where was she?"

Caroline braced herself. Mama was very hard to lie to. Caroline had never tried it since she had been a very little girl and had wanted to keep Mama from knowing that the stable cat had had kittens, because Mama had said they must be drowned. But even Perry and Pris often said that she could see through most tales. Caroline was about to do her best when Althea stepped in to the breach for her.

"I am afraid that I am really the reason," she smiled at both of the older women. "I found myself a little faint—the heat and the crowd—and I went up to the ladies' cloak room. Pris must have seen me leave and followed to be of service—and then Caroline came, too."

Mama's attention was caught, all right. She looked at Althea in a very searching manner, and Caroline wondered if that Mama was guessing the big secret. Ladies in Althea's condition often felt faint or were sick in the mornings. Though no one ever mentioned the reason.

"You are all right now, my dear?" Mama leaned forward, an anxious look on her face.

"A little tired, perhaps. I think that maybe I am not yet over that great sea tossing we experienced."

"Richard must take you home. I cannot go, since the committee must stay until Lord Elgin leaves. But Caroline," she glanced at her younger daughter, "you are looking tired also. These late hours you are not used to. If you slip out, I shall find Richard and send him—"

Mr. Hannakar stepped forward. "Mrs. Warwick, my mother has already decided that she is ready to withdraw from these festivities. And since Richard is such an able lieutenant for the doctor in his official capacity here, why not let me deputize? Mother and I will escort Lady Althea and Miss Caroline safely home."

Madam nodded. "An excellent suggestion! My friend," she spoke to Mama, "your own duties as co-hostess one might say, are binding on you. No one shall notice us when we slip quietly away, and you need have no fears at all about your daughters."

Mama did look relieved. "Pris will stay, of course, and Perry must. All the medical students are here and are supposed to be at the beck of the committee. Very well. I thank you very much, indeed, Madam Hannakar, and you, sir, for your most kind suggestion. It answers extremely well."

Caroline was just as glad that Pris seemed to be forgotten. Surely after that discovery in the upper hall her sister would not be so foolish as to allow herself to be caught by Major Vickers again. Because, of course, that was what had happened. Pris had drunk too much of the punch, and that "black man" had taken advantage of her foolishness. Pris would never have gone with him to such a scandalous place otherwise.

She trailed Althea and Madam Hannakar back upstairs to gather their cloaks, change their dancing slippers, and perhaps to go home happier again. She was tired. Somehow all the best of the ball seemed to have come and gone before she really knew what had happened.

8

Caroline sat up in bed, gratefully sipping the hot chocolate Mollie had brought. It must be very late, as the sun lay in pale winter patches across the carpet. She put down the cup, stretched, and wriggled from beneath the covers. Mollie had already straightened up. Cinderella's ball gown was hung away, the slippers put off in their bag. Only across the dressing table trailed last night's hair ribbons. When Caroline dressed with some haste, feeling guilty about the time, she considered the small box of hairpins. Mama had let her put her hair up for the ball, and somehow she did not want to return to the old childish braid. It was as if in a single evening she had taken a big step of years. Anyway, it was her birthday next week, and she would be eighteen and surely a young lady, though until this past week she had dreaded that coming of age.

However, she found that she lacked Skinner's skill with hairdressing; she was dissatisfied with the best she was able to achieve. Pris—perhaps Pris could help. Brush, comb, and box of pins in her hands, she started down the hall to her sister's room. The door was a little ajar and she caught Mama's voice:

"You are never to speak to any servant in this house the way you just addressed Jessie. I cannot comprehend your behavior of late, Priscilla. You were far from circumspect last night, and if you do not mend your manners, your various parties and excursions shall be sharply curtailed. Caroline—"

"Caroline!" Pris put into that name such heat that her sister, about to withdraw before she eavesdropped any longer, was frozen where she stood. She had seldom been one of Pris' victims when her sister was in a temper, but—

"Caroline makes me very tired. She is just a child!"

"She is only two years younger than you. I see no reason for this outburst. I was very pleased with her last night; she conducted herself very well indeed. Madam Hannakar commented most favorably on her manners, as did Mrs. Desmond and Mrs. Howards. I had feared she might appear a little shy or awkward, but that was not so. You have no reason to speak so of your sister. I will not have it."

Caroline found herself able to move again and retreated hurriedly to her own room, placed her things on the dressing table and sat looking unhappily into the mirror. Pris was angry . . . . Of course, Mama did not know, must never know about Major Vickers. Did Pris think that *she* would tell? Surely she could not believe that! Slowly Caroline began again to struggle with pins and hair and finally achieved something of a soft coil at the back of her head. The pins had a habit of slipping out, whereas they had stayed in place when Skinner had rammed them in. She was placing one important one for the second time when Mama tapped at the door and then came in. Apprehensively Caroline waited to be told to assume her regular braid. But Mama, though she was looking at her measuringly, did not say so. Instead she came up to Caroline with a smile and her good morning kiss.

"Did you have a pleasant time last night, my dear? You were fast asleep when Papa and I finally came home and I did not disturb you."

"It was lovely, Mama. Like a fairy tale."

"It was a very well arranged ball, my dear. There is nothing fanciful about such things, only a good deal of hard work and planning. But I am very pleased with you. You bore yourself well and looked very nice. Madam Hannakar commented on your manners and your presence. I trust you thanked her and Mr. Hannakar for bringing you home?"

"Yes, Mama. It was very kind of them. And Mollie and Skinner were waiting with hot drinks. I guess that is why I must have slept so long. I am sorry, Mama—it must be late."

"After a ball a young lady is permitted to sleep, my dear," Mama laughed.

"Am I?" Caroline asked slowly.

"Are you what, child?"

"A young lady?"

Mama nodded briskly. "Of course, Caroline. I have really been remiss in not noting it sooner. It was good that Madam Hannakar spoke. One sometimes does not realize that the years pass so quickly and a child grows with them. I shall have Mollie take instructions from Skinner, and then she will do your hair properly. But as you have it will suffice for this morning. Papa, Perry, and Richard have all gone, but there is some breakfast saved, and you will find Althea in the dining room."

She had half turned to the door and then she asked, slowly, as if this was something which she found difficult,

"Caroline, my dear, have you noticed any change in Priscilla these past weeks? Sometimes it appears that she is far too sharp of tongue, and that used to mean that she was unhappy. Perhaps you have been aware of something?"

Caroline tried to look directly at Mama. But she couldn't tell the truth, and one did not lie to Mama. She was truly not sure what was the matter with Pris; she only guessed. And she had no right to share a guess with mama. Pris had never been free with confidences. She seemed to pride herself on never telling when she was really hurt; it all turned into anger, and then would come some outburst which put her even more in the wrong.

"She never says anything, Mama. I do not know, truly."

Mrs. Warwick sighed. "Yes, that is Pris' way and an unhappy one. There is something wrong, but unless we know, how can we help her? Just—just be yourself, Caroline. Do not resent it if she is sharp in tongue."

"I never do, Mama."

"I know. Well, I must see to the linen counting."

She was gone as if she had had no tiring ordeal of cohostessing a ball behind her. Mama was nearly always active and did not give in to any claims for rest she did not think proper. Caroline anchored the last hairpin as firmly as she could and then surveyed herself searchingly in the glass.

Richard—and Pris. She shook her head. No matter how much Pris might encourage people like Major Vickers, Caroline was sure that it was Richard who interested her. If she would only look at Corbie Hannakar. He was as good as Richard, and he was miles beyond any bright-coated officer. He was interested in Pris, and he was—

Caroline shook her head. Pris must forget Richard as

being any more than the big brother he had always been. There was Althea, and she must not be disturbed by Pris' queer moods now. Althea was so sweet, and she loved Richard so very much it was like a light coming into her face every time she looked at him. No, Corbie Hannakar—

Even as she thought of him there was the sound of sleigh bells in the air. They were loud, as if the sleigh was coming directly to their own door. Caroline stepped to the window, scratched off a little of the gathered frost from the pane to look down. The Hannakar sleigh! Corbie Hannaker had given the reins to his coachman and was coming up the front steps. Pris—Pris should be on hand to meet him!

She whirled away down the hall again, rapping on her sister's door, hardly waiting to hear muffled words before she entered.

Pris was sitting before her dressing table, her combing cape about her shoulders, her elbows planted among the litter, her fingers laced together to support her chin. She did not look around, but said petulantly:

"What is it, Carrie? Must you bound about like a child? I thought you were to act the lady now."

Caroline shrugged off this attack of ill temper. "Pris, you must hurry and dress. Mr. Hannakar has just come. Perhaps he—"

Pris yawned. "Corbie Hannakar? Why should I concern myself with a visit from him? He certainly did not make himself too visible last night! It seems that he preferred to rob the nursery then." The look in her eyes when they met Caroline's was bleak and hostile.

"But, Pris, you were never there when he looked for you. And he left early because his mother was tired. You mustn't blame him for not asking you to dance when he could not find you."

Flame arose in Pris' cheeks. She swung around to face her sister, her eyes now as blazing hot as her face:

"You forget what you saw last night! You just forget!"

Caroline fell back a step. She had seen Pris in many tempers, but their full blast had seldom been turned in her direction. Before she could answer, her sister continued: "Don't start to give yourself airs because you danced with Corbie Hannakar. He's years too old for you. Mama should not let you put yourself forward the way you did."

This was the old game Pris had played for years: answer some guilt of her own by attacking another. Caroline knew this; still, it hurt. Oh, if Pris was only more like Althea —kind and gentle, and ready to like others. But Pris was Pris, and she had to relieve unhappiness in her own way. Perhaps she really believed that Caroline had done something purposeful to attract Corbie Hannakar—not that she ever would—but she knew that there was no use offering explanations while her sister was in this mood.

"He's waiting downstairs," she said quietly. "I am sure he has come to see you, Pris." Then she went out and closed the door behind her, though she felt weak and trembling inside as she always did when confronted by Pris' temper.

She went slowly down the stairs. There were no voices sounding from the parlor, but Mr. Hannakar's hat and furlined coat were in evidence. Maybe he had come to see Papa about something. Caroline went on to the dining room where Althea sat, a plate bearing toast crumbs before her and a cup of tea at her hand. She looked pale and there were dark smudges under her eyes, but she smiled at Caroline as the girl took her accustomed place across the table.

"You had better ring for fresh tea. This is quite tepid. How do you feel this morning, dear?"

"How do *you* feel?" Caroline countered.

"Tired. It seems I do not quite have the energy I thought I possessed. Do you know, my dear, we have a quite pleasant invitation. Mr. Hannakar arrived this morning, in fact just a few moments ago, bearing this." She indicated a note which lay open on the table. "It is from Madam, and she would like to have us, you and me, come visiting on Monday. She will send her closed sleigh so we shall not get chilled. I confess that I quite forgot about being tired when I read it. Richard has talked so much about Mr. Hannakar and Ste. Catherine's, and I do so much enjoy Madam's company. Is this not a treat?"

"You and me—and Pris?" Caroline asked slowly.

Lady Althea looked a little confused. "No, Priscilla was not mentioned. But then, did she not say yesterday that she had an invitation to drive out with her friends that day? Perhaps she had already mentioned that to Mr. Hannakar."

"Pris should go." Caroline unrolled her napkin unhappily, after ringing, as Althea had suggested, for more tea. "I—I don't think that she will be happy about it if I go—and she does not." She looked across the table, troubled and still feeliing a little sick from her interview with her sister.

"My dear," Althea answered, "you have been invited, and Pris has not. If Pris has another engagement, she would have to refuse this in any case. I heard Madam Hannakar speak to you of coming to Ste. Catherine's. Now she has issued the invitation. This may have nothing to do with Mr. Hannakar's wishes at all, rather those of his mother."

"But—but she should want to see Pris, to know her better—"

"Madam Hannaker makes her own choices. I have not had to know her long to realize that."

"I must ask Mama," Caroline said, as Mollie brought in a new pot of tea, and a covered dish full of cook's lightest biscuits. Only Caroline had somehow lost her appetite since she had first awakened, and found it difficult to manage the biscuits which, for all their lightness, stuck in her throat.

"Of course," Althea nodded. "Mr. Hannakar asked to see Dr. Warwick. I imagine that he is explaining it all to him and assuring him, and your Mama in turn, that we shall be very carefully looked after."

She said nothing more, nor was Caroline even aware, as she kept her own eyes on her plate and tried to eat, that Althea watched her now and then speculatively.

Mama came into the dining room just then, and sat down abruptly at the end of the table. As Caroline looked up inquiringly, she saw Mama staring as if she had been totally surprised in some manner.

"You have an invitation, Caroline," she said in an odd tone which was not Mama's usual voice at all. "Madam Hannakar has asked you with Althea out to St. Catherine's. It is most gracious of her, and you have your father's and my permission to accept."

Caroline opened her mouth and closed it again. If Mama was not thinking of Pris, then it would be an impertinence for her to speak of her sister first. But the whole matter seemed very strange to Caroline. A moment or two later, they heard the front door open and close. Mama sat up a little straighter in her chair, as if she were bracing herself against something.

"Mr. Hannakar has just left. He assured me that his mother's closed sleigh would provide the maximum of comfort even on a chill day, and it will call for you at nine Monday morning. I am sure you will both have a most enjoyable time.''

But the small uncertain worry was still in Caroline's mind.

Pris did not come downstairs until lunch time, when the three women of the household met together over a small meal. Luckily, by that time she appeared to have worked out her unhappiness, or at least buried it deeply. Caroline felt some ease as her sister chattered gayly about the ball and mentioned that the officers were planning various outings to introduce the newcomers on Lord Elgin's staff to some of the sports and pastimes of the country. She never mentioned Corbie Hannakar's visit, and, when Althea spoke of their intended trip to Ste. Catherine's, Pris appeared to accept it as perfectly natural and talked of her own expedition planned for Monday. Caroline noted that, though her sister spoke several times of Captain Carruthers and what he might think of this or that, she never mentioned Major Vickers at all.

Had Pris really forgotten, because of the punch, the liberties the Major had taken? Caroline hoped that that was so, and that it would never happen again.

Caroline sat quietly with Althea and Mama in the afternoon, working on a woolwork picture. Althea told her it had been copied from a well-known portrait by Landseer, who was the Queen's own favorite artist. She had had a comfortable time with Boots in the kitchen, only she had been a little surprised to find cook, Jessie, and Mollie with their heads together when she had entered; they had broken apart guiltily when she came in. Remembering her mother's rebuke to Pris about her treatment of the maid, Caroline thought that perhaps they had been engaged in talk about that episode, and she carefully ignored their confusion.

Skinner had done her hair both for church and again on Monday morning, with Mollie standing by to watch and to insert some of the pins under Skinner's eagle eye. It still bothered Caroline a little to catch a sudden glimpse of herself in the mirror.

"Happy birthday!" Pris had pushed open the door and came up behind them. She reached over and laid a tissue-wrapped package on Caroline's dressing table. When Caroline tore off the wrappings eagerly, she found a small book bound in cream leather, but she opened it to blank pages.

Pris laughed. "Every young lady," she emphasized the last two words, "should have a keepsake book to hold her secret thoughts. I don't know how many such thoughts you may have, Carrie, but here is the place to inscribe them. I decided to give you this before evening so that it could indeed be a secret if you so wish it."

Evening parties for the family were the birthday cele-brations at the Warwicks, and Caroline had expected nothing but good wishes until then. She held the book close to her. She had read of diaries in which one wrote about all the wonderful—and not so wonderful—happen-ings of their lives, but she had never thought of owning one. Pris' gift was indeed a surprise and one which she would treasure, not only for what it might contain—which would be her doing—but because Pris had even thought of such an unusual and exciting gift.

But Pris shrugged off her quick thanks as she so often did. It was almost as if Pris found it difficult to accept thanks for anything, or from anyone. Though she was always sweet and dear when she received her own gifts, seldom as tongue-tied as Caroline was apt to be—especially if the gift were something which she had long wanted and hardly expected to have.

The coach-like sleigh drawn by the beautifully matched blacks which were Madam's own team was prompt in arrival at the Warwick's, but Althea and Caroline were ready in fur cloaks, hoods and boots when James opened the door. They were ushered out and well be-rugged into place by the coachman, who attended them as he might his mistress. Caroline looked about her in a little awe. When they had ridden home with Madam it had been dark, and her concern for Althea had been such that she had not been really interested in the fine appointments of the vehicle. The blankets, the foot stoves, the furred-over robes, were sheer comfort. Both of them relaxed as the team pounded on, harness bells ringing.

In what seemed a very short time the equipage swept between wrought-iron gates and up the curve of a carriage drive, to come to a smooth halt under a wide porte-cochère. The footman descended from the box, as the coachman held the reins, to assist them out with care. At the door Mr. Hannakar welcomed them before handing them over to a fine figure of a housekeeper who requested them to come with her to remove their cloaks, as Madam did not descend the stairs frequently any more.

Having shed their outdoor clothing, they found Madam seated by the fire in her own small drawing room on the second floor. She arose quickly as they entered.

"My dear Lady Althea—and Caroline—come closer to the fire, I beg you. Did you find the drive frosty?"

Her son had followed them in, standing behind his mother's chair as she seated them by the fire.

"One could never be cold in your wonderful sleigh,"

Althea said. "It is a haven of comfort for any traveler."

Caroline tried hard to curb her curiosity and not look about too much, though the impression that she had wandered into a small and exquisite treasure house tempted her to stare rudely. She was startled when Mr. Hannakar said:

"When it grows a little more temperate out—as I assure you it does, Lady Althea, nearer midday—I shall be very glad to escort you around our domain."

Madam shook her head almost in warning. "My son, he thinks so much of his animals. But that is a fault which he inherited from his father and one which I had always to face. I fear that I have spoiled him somewhat in not making sure that he remains a more considerate host."

"But I am sure we would enjoy seeing the stables," said Lady Althea, and Caroline added a quick, warm, "Oh, yes!"

Madam Hannakar smiled. "Then so you shall. Tell me, did you enjoy the ball? You have not been tired again, my dear? Corbie," she looked around, "have you not business with Hawkins?"

He smiled ruefully. "Very well, Mama. What has a mere man to say about balls and such enchanting things?"

It was not only the room itself which felt so warm, decided Caroline, it was Madam's pleasant manner, her show of real friendliness. Why, Althea was talking almost eagerly of her English home which she had not done too often before. And she herself was drawn in, her opinion asked, her words listened to with respect, as if she were as important a person as Althea.

Finally Mr. Hannakar was summoned back, and they were ushered, Madam on her son's arm, Althea and Caroline behind, into a small, well-appointed dining room where luncheon was served. When the servants had withdrawn, Mr. Hannakar, too, displayed warm friendliness, and Caroline was wafted back to her beginning mood of the ball night, when she had indeed been caught up in enchantment.

Nor was Alexandra forgotten. The huge cat, a fluff of such blue-grey fur as Caroline had never seen, had entered the dining room with the manner of a queen, one of the footmen opening the door for her, her plume of a tail held high, just the tip of it swaying back and forth.

"Ah, lazy one," Madam Hannakar picked up a blue dish which had been sitting empty to one side and carefully poured into that a small measure of cream, "you are one without manners. Speak to our guests now, politely, as a lady should."

To Caroline's surprise the big cat went first to Althea and then to her, facing each of them round-eyed, her mouth opening in a soundless mew. Then, apparently satisfied that she had done her duty, Alexandra returned to Madam and her waiting cream and proceeded to ignore them all for the delights of the table.

Madam excused herself from the expedition to the stables.

"One of the privileges of age," she commented as their cloaks and bonnets were brought, "is to be able to say that one is no longer agile and these expeditions are beyond one. Such are for the young."

It was not necessary to go out of the house to reach the barn, for there were covered passageways leading from house to stables, and to the other outbuildings. Althea commented on the convenience of the arrangement in bad weather, and Mr. Hannakar smiled.

"My mother, in spite of her affecting not to care, is

much interested in the stock. When she was younger, she enjoyed visits at all times of the year, so my father had these ways constructed for her.''

He led the way past the horse stalls, pausing at each to introduce its inhabitant, handing Caroline sugar lumps to offer on her gloved palm.

''Such beautiful horses.'' Caroline stroked the greying muzzle of a mare, fat and sleek, yet obviously retired.

''That is Mama's mount. She is old and fat, and as lazy as Alexandra, and greedy for sugar.''

Caroline offered the sugar which was graciously received. But when she peered into the next box she uttered an ''Oh'' of sheer delight, and leaned in wide-eyed pleasure over the low door to see the better.

Sprawling about in the straw were tiny puppies of a gorgeous red shade, whose mother had arisen and was gazing at the newcomers with anxious eyes. Mr. Hannakar opened the stall door, quieted the bitch with a gentle hand on her head, and picked up one of her litter, holding the puppy out to Caroline.

''This is Kathleen, and her family. We haven't named them yet; they are only a week old.''

Caroline accepted the puppy and then knelt down in the straw to stroke Kathleen in turn.

''I believe this is a momentous day for you, is it not, Miss Caroline? Not only your first visit to Ste. Catherine's, but also, I have been told, your birthday. Would you let Kathleen give you a present—one of her very own?''

Caroline gasped and turned up a joyous face.

''Pick one out, name it, and it shall come to you when Kathleen thinks it is ready to begin life for itself.'' He grinned down at her just as Richard might.

''I don't know,'' she hesitated. ''Perhaps Madam—''

"But this is Mama's wish—a little surprise," he assured her.

She hesitated no longer. "This one. The one you gave me." She stroked the little bundle of fun which had settled by her knee.

"Very good. You have selected with a knowing eye. If I am not mistaken, that one will be the prize of the litter."

It was hard to go off and leave Kathleen and her family, but Caroline followed Althea. And she was quick to thank Madam for the birthday surprise. Nor did she note the look, quick come and gone, with which Madam received her thanks.

With dark coming so early they had to leave, but not without a most cordial invitation to come again.

"I am an old woman," Madam said, "and in winter I do not stir far from my own fireside, for I am at an age when I dare pamper myself. Sometimes I am also lonely, for the kind of talk which we have had today. You would be doing me a favor if you would visit again."

"We would be pleased to," Althea began.

Caroline added quickly, and with transparent honest happiness, "It has been such a happy day! You are so kind, Madam Hannakar."

"Then I shall send my son with an invitation again very soon."

Althea smiled. "Oh, that would be so kind of you." She blushed suddenly. "I do beg your pardon, I really should not—everyone has been so kind—"

Madam's black-mittened hand patted Althea's arm gently. "I, too, know what it is to be in a land which I do not altogether understand. It was so for me when my husband took me to England for a year; he was buying new stock for this estate. It is good often just to talk of what comes into one's mind without having to think about consequences.''

Caroline looked at Althea. Was the English girl finding it so different that she did not feel at home with the Warwicks? Her life in England must have been much grander, more like that lived at Ste. Catherine's. Did Althea feel more at home with Madam?

Maybe it was Althea whom Madam Hannakar had really wanted to see and Caroline had been just invited as her companion. She felt a queer little sense of loss as that thought crossed her mind.

"A lovely day," Althea said, as they were on their way back to the city in the warm comfort of the sleigh.

"I do like Madam Hannakar, and yes, it was wonderful!" Caroline refused room to any doubts. "I only wish Pris could have come. He likes her, and he would be such a wonderful brother to have." For the first time she spoke freely.

Althea did not answer at once. When she did, it was with a question: "Is that the way you think of Mr. Hannakar, Caroline? As a brother?"

"Of course. He is Pris' friend, and Mama and Papa would be so pleased if they married."

Again that queer twisting feeling moved within her. She could see, not the dimming interior of the sleigh, but Mr. Hannakar handing her the puppy, smiling his lazy smile which had such warmth in it.

"Of course!" Caroline repeated firmly and decidedly.

9

The Monday of their expedition to Ste. Catherine's was the last promising day for some time, for the full force of winter struck hard the very next dawn. With the air so thin and chill, even full breathing was an ordeal, and none of the Warwick ladies ventured out. There were no ships in the harbor now. Though there was talk of a railroad to the sea, nothing yet had been decided. The only communication with the east, south, or west was by stagecoach, and was not available in or out during the worst of the winter storms.

Montreal was completely sealed off, but there were a few good days when the bite of the season did not close so hard, and then festivities broke out with a feverish gaiety. Into them Caroline ventured, usually with Althea, since Pris was fully and completely occupied with such a whirl of invitations, for the bright days and less bitter nights, that she seemed to be away from home during most of their own cozy meetings by the fire, their work at hand and endless things to talk about. Mama seemed now to take pleasure in listening to Althea tell about her home, and Richard's wife became more and more a part of their close-knit circle—to Caroline's delight.

Richard was often away during the day, out with Papa making calls, or at the college, or with, Caroline believed, Dr. Nelson. But he chanced to be at home a week after their pleasant visit to Ste. Catherine's when Mr. Hannakar appeared, his face ruddy from the cold, but bringing them assurances that the weather was on the mend and that they could expect a little more freedom in the outer world.

"Just the time for a picnic, wouldn't you agree, Richard?" he asked.

Althea looked up in open surprise. "A picnic, Mr. Hannakar? In the depths of winter?"

He smiled. "Ah, but we have winter picnics, Lady Althea. Is that not true, Miss Caroline?"

Though she had never been on such an expedition, she knew from Pris just what was meant. "Yes, it is true, Althea."

Mr. Hannakar nodded. "We take to sleighs," he drawled. Althea looked completely bemused.

Richard laughed. "And your destination, Corbie? Some romantic dell completely filled with drafts, no doubt?"

"Such an expedition loses its charm if you are acquainted from the start with your destination." Now he looked directly at Caroline. "What about it, Miss Caroline, would you be ready for a picnic?"

"I have never been on one, Mr. Hannakar. Though of course Pris has, and she says that they are great fun. What do you think, Althea?"

There was a dubious shade across Althea's face; instinctively she had moved a fraction closer to the fire. "I'm sure there must be attractions." Her voice was notable for its lack of enthusiasm.

Richard laughed. "It would seem, Corbie, that the proof of such a party's advantages is now up to you."

"And I shall be delighted to deliver such," Mr. Hannakar answered promptly. "How about next Friday? Oh, no, that is the night of the Scott musical. Thursday, then, with the weather favoring us. Will that be convenient for you ladies?"

"It sounds most pleasant," Althea was polite.

Mr. Hannakar smiled down at her. "Be sure I shall endeavor to see that it is." Then he began to talk of other things, giving amusing sidelights on recent events, while Caroline listened and enjoyed it. He was so like Richard, kind, amusing, gentle. If only Pris were home to see him here, not as a partner in some crowded party, but at ease in the Warwick parlor as if he belonged there.

When Mr. Hannakar had taken his leave and Richard returned from seeing him to the door, Althea demanded: "Please, Richard, just what *is* a winter picnic?"

"What it is named—a picnic in the winter," Richard chuckled.

"Really, that is most unhelpful!" Althea looked a little cross and made several determined stitches in her needlework.

"If Corbie Hannakar plans it," her husband continued, "you may be assured that it is well arranged—also that it will be one of *the* events of the season. He hasn't given himself much time to be sure, but that never defeated Corbie's organizational skills before. No doubt he'll have everything to hand before the end of tomorrow."

The following morning invitations were delivered. Caroline held hers with real pleasure. She had been asked here and there since the ball, but this was the first invitation addressed directly to her.

"Wasn't it nice for him to send an invitation directly to me?" she asked. Papa glanced at her over the top of his paper.

"Most polite," he said. "He is thoughtful."

Pris was not impressed. She sloshed the tea about in her cup and frowned at the biscuits on her plate. "A winter picnic? Corbie must be out of his mind. The last one I went to was cold, and we were thoroughly miserable. I have a mind not to accept!"

Caroline saw that Althea was looking a little distressed.

Papa spoke again. "You have the right to refuse if you do not care for such outdoor amusements."

Pris flushed. "But, Papa—"

"Since when have either you or Caroline been afraid of venturing out in the winter? A little less dancing in heated rooms and a little more good healthful exercise is bound to be beneficial. You are not made of meltable sugar, Priscilla. I can remember when you went snowshoeing with Richard and Perry and seemed to enjoy every minute of it."

Pris' eyes fell once more to her plate. "Yes, Papa."

"I am sure that any outing arranged by Mr. Hannakar will be as comfortable as possible," Mama said. She had her own invitation, as chaperone for the party. "This will be a pleasant new experience for Althea. Do you remember, Doctor, when Mr. Atkins invited us on a winter picnic before we were married, and the second sleigh overturned? What a time that was, but so amusing when one looks back on it!"

Althea appeared more dismayed than ever. But the doctor had taken his leave before she asked Mrs. Warwick: "What sort of clothing does one wear for such a picnic? If I ask Richard, I am sure he will only say something warm. And that," she commented ruefully, "is never very descriptive."

Mama laughed. "Men do tend to consider such questions of little account, don't they? But it is true that warmth is a good way to gauge your clothing. You will be sitting in an open sleigh, so it is well to provide a scarf to protect your face against the wind. However, you will find it comfortable. Mr. Hannakar will not choose a day when there is any hint of threatening storm. Just take care not to get overtired.''

Her calm advice appeared to reassure Althea, and Caroline added to her knowledge by bringing out the snippets of information she had gained from Pris. Thus the following week, as they walked to the Ottawa Hotel on Great St. James Street where the party was to gather, both of them were looking forward to the adventure with excitement.

Pris, in high spirits, was ahead with Perry, who had cut the afternoon lecture at McGill, declaring that since Papa was so sure of the good healthy results of outdoor exercise, he would take a dose of the same medicine himself.

Richard commented that sometimes Perry used very little excuse to take time off. His foster brother grinned. ''Don't you start getting pompous like old Archie. It doesn't become you in the least, old man.''

When they reached the hotel, Mr. Hannakar came forward to welcome them warmly. The rest of the party had already assembled. There were three other older ladies, the chaperones, whom their host handed with deference into three of the four big waiting sleighs. Then he handed Mrs. Warwick into the fourth. As the girls, twittering and laughing, were settled in, the men mounted. Some of the men were from city families; some were officers of the garrison, and some were from the Governor's staff. Among them, Caroline noticed Major Vickers mounted on the same big horse that had nearly ridden her down.

''We are going to Varennes,'' Mr. Hannakar announced before mounting his horse himself.

Wrapped snugly in fur robes, their feet in the deep straw at the bottom of the sleigh, Althea and Caroline sat side by side, looking about. The sleighbells and the jingling of the horses' bridles made cheerful music, and everyone appeared in high spirits.

Two hours later they drew up before the old habitant cottage at Varennes. Since the air had been nippy, the ladies were glad to enter the warmth of that shelter. There were only a few rooms—one with a round potbelly stove going full blast, and another with a huge table against the wall.

"Best take the table into the other room," Mr. Hannaker decided, and willing hands aided in that change.

The officers and other young men carried in baskets of provisions, and a young, bouncing French girl appeared at the door, proceeding to take over the unpacking and serving. There were only tea and coffee to drink. Mama, Caroline knew, would be very pleased at that. She frowned at wine on such occasions.

Pris had settled on one of the benches. Caroline saw Mr. Hannakar go to her with a dish of small meat pies; Pris seemed to linger some time before making her selection. Caroline watched, but Mr. Hannakar did not linger too long. Of course, he could not give all his time to Pris when he was the host.

As the others were moving in, she caught sight of Major Vickers' dark face, and that was troubling. But there was no chance for him to be alone with Pris here, neither was there any punch. So she glanced to see if Mama had noticed and was concerned. However, when she saw the other young men crowding near Pris, whose cheeks were a little flushed and her eyes glinting as she laughed, she decided that there was nothing to fear today.

Then Mr. Hannakar appeared before her and Althea, offering them some sandwiches which, he reported, were especially toothsome. He beckoned the French girl to bring tea; it was served in thickish mugs which seemed proper in these surroundings.

Richard followed and stopped by Althea.

"I haven't deserted my post, my dear," he commented. "I was merely seeing that Mama had her tea to her liking. Excellent idea this, Corbie. We should have ambition enough to do it more often."

As Mr. Hannakar turned away, Richard spoke to Althea, and Caroline could not help but overhear: "I did not know Pris knew Vickers." He was frowning.

Startled, Caroline looked back across the room. The Major was planted firmly by her sister now, and he was bending a little forward as if to listen to something she was saying, that strange smile which Caroline disliked so much (the one she had seen at the ball) curving his thin lips.

"It is rather hard not to know one of the governor's aides," Althea answered. "Alexander brought him on a formal call; he has entrée everywhere."

"Had you better not drop a hint to Pris? His reputation—"

Althea shook her head slowly. "I do not think Priscilla would take any such hint from me. Yes, he has sought her out several times, but so has Alexander, and so have a number of other young men. She is very popular, Richard. Major Vickers does have a reputation, as you point out. But here, as a member of the governor's staff, and where the social circle is so small and intimate he would not have the foolhardiness to cause any gossip. It might be worth his future were Lord Elgin to hear of such. Alexander told me that he was warned before he left England that he must be most circumspect here. You might speak to Mrs. Warwick or the doctor if you have any doubts, Richard.''

He shrugged. ''I confess I don't like the fellow, and what I have heard of him is not good. I may speak to Pris— if I think it necessary.''

After all had shared Mr. Hannakar's generous picnic refreshment, the big table was removed again and two habitant farmers with fiddles came in, all smiles and oiled-down hair. Their tunes set feet tapping, and the company stood up for the old country dances, now half out of style but still learned for such occasions. It was childish fun and far from the formality of a city ball, rather a relaxed and happy time.

When they started back to the city through the coming dusk, there was contentment and some drowsiness among the occupants of the sleighs. Corbie Hannakar was to be congratulated, all agreed, on one of the high successes of the season.

Caroline was quiet on the way home. Major Vickers, and Richard's uneasiness about him, worried her. She was not the only one who wished that Pris would put an end to the acquaintance. How soon before the ever-present gossips might repeat something? Agatha did not go out much in formal society, yet Agatha seemed always to know everything that went on. Let her comment on Pris' apparent encouragement of the governor's aide, and there would be more trouble, Caroline was sure, than her reckless sister had ever had to face before. What might be Papa's answer to any such gossip? Caroline shivered.

Althea beside her asked quickly, ''Are you chilled, Caroline?''

Before she thought, she answered with what was present

in her mind, and then could have bitten her tongue to have the words unsaid: "I don't like Major Vickers."

"Caroline!" Althea lowered her voice to make certain that none of the others could hear. "You listened." There was reproof in Althea's voice which brought the other girl a small stab of unhappiness.

"I couldn't help it," she defended herself. "I had seen Pris with him before—and I just don't like him."

For a long moment Althea was quiet, and the small unhappiness inside Caroline began to grow. She had admitted to eavesdropping. But she had been sitting right beside Althea; they must have both known she could hear. She could not have gotten up and moved away when Richard started to speak.

"Caroline, you are right. Richard spoke without realizing I was not alone. And—Oh, I do not know what is proper!" There was distress in Althea's voice. "As the governor's aide he is accepted. He has to be. But Pris does not understand such men, I am sure. This is not a sophisticated society. There cannot be many such men as Major Vickers known to the circle in which Pris has moved all her life. We must think of some way to warn her in a manner she will not resent. Pris is, I believe, of a nature to do just the opposite of what is suggested if her temper is aroused. I shall think, and you do also, Caroline. I am sorry that you should have this matter known to you. This should be a happy time for you, not one burdened with difficulties which, in truth, should not touch you at all."

"Only they do," Caroline said in a whisper. "Pris is my sister; I do care what happens. She—she isn't very happy somehow. And when she isn't happy she does things which she regrets later. I—I wish Major Vickers had never come!"

"Richard is aware of the problem," Althea reminded her. "And perhaps he can enlist Mr. Hannakar, who seems to have a very level head and a good sense of responsibility. There *will* be something done, please believe that, Caroline!"

She had forgotten Mr. Hannakar as the answer to Pris' problem. Even if her sister was in love with Richard, even if she had been badly hurt, she would certainly see in time that Mr. Hannakar was the answer. He had the same sweetness of temper, when one got to know him well, and he could give Pris what Richard could not—a place in the highest rank of society. The mistress of Ste. Catherine's would, in time, have as much authority as Madam did now; her acquaintance would be eagerly courted. Pris would love to shine at every ball and party. Besides, who could see Major Vickers if Corbie Hannakar was around? She must hold to that thought and hope it would all work out.

She and Althea had no more chance to talk in the sleigh. And Caroline was very tired suddenly as she climbed the stairs at home. Mollie was there to lay out her dress for dinner, bring a can of hot water, and stand ready with brush and comb to do her hair.

"Miss Caroline, you do look so fine in that dress," she commented with her usual freedom.

"But, Mollie, I have had this dress for a year," Caroline was startled.

"Somehow, with your hair up and all, it looks like new. Sure, Miss Caroline, you are a proper young lady entire, cook was saying so only this mornin'. She and Me and Jessie, we peeked out when you all went off. It seems like you growed up all at once in a big hurry. T'won't be long now before the gentlemen will be leavin' their cards for

Miss Caroline as well as Miss Warwick—that's what cook said. But we do miss our Miss Caroline sometimes.''

Caroline thought of Pris. ''Mollie, sometimes I would rather not be a young lady—grown up. It was fun, and—'' She stopped short. Mollie was an old friend, but she could not share all of Caroline's secrets now.

''Now, Miss Caroline, you are going to be one of the happy ones, 'less you let yourself take on all the cares which rightly belong to others. You're only young once. Best make the most of that time. Then you have somethin' all bright and happy to look back on when—''

''You're young, Mollie. Are you laying up some happy memories for yourself?'' Caroline wanted to change the subject.

To her surprise Mollie blushed.

''Mollie!'' Caroline swung about on the bench of the dressing table. ''Are you walking out?''

Mollie's blush grew deeper, if that were possible. ''Walkin' out, is it? Oh, no, Miss Caroline, cook, she would not allow that—she is strict with us girls. Jessie on her month day goes straight to her mother's—''

''And you, Mollie, what do you do on your month half-day?''

''Mostly I sews, or cleans m'room. I haven't any place to go to, m'family all being across the sea.''

''But you have met someone,'' Caroline persisted, knowing well that Mollie wanted her to, that her interest meant much to the other girl denied all the pleasures Caroline and Pris could take for granted.

''There's him, Miss Caroline. He has a civil word and a nice way with him whenever he comes. Cook, she says he's a good lad and well mannered like, and she asks him in for a cup of tea iffen he has the time. He's—well, he's spoken about his mother and how when the weather gets spring-like his mother comes into market sometimes and then he wants to bring her to meet cook—''

''Who *is* he?'' Caroline broke in.

''That Ralph, Miss Caroline, him that is second groom to Mr. Hannakar and comes with messages. The master told him only last month that he likes his work. 'Course, he ain't really said nothing to me 'cept—well, that he liked a girl from the old country. He never would be one to take liberties. Nor would cook let him, did he or anyone else try it. He ain't no gentry with an eye going every which way for a pretty face and a foolish head! He ain't like that Black Man.''

Caroline gave a start.

Mollie was instantly self-reproachful: ''Now—did I give a pull, Miss Caroline? 'Tis most sorry I am. Seems like every time I think of the bold face of that one, a kind of shadow comes in my mind, like there was trouble hanging out like a far cloud over the mountains readying to come in. He never said nothin' to you again, did he, Miss Caroline? The boldness of him, coming here to this house! That Captain Carruthers brought him which—well, it is none of my place to say what I think of that.''

''No, Mollie,'' Caroline said decidedly, ''don't gossip about Major Vickers, please. He may have an unpleasant reputation, but he is received here and he is aide to Lord Elgin. But I do not think I shall ever have to worry about him.''

She was watching Mollie's face carefully. Had any trace of gossip about Pris and the Major been caught in the kitchen? If so—but no. She was as certain as if Mollie had told her to her face that such gossip would never be repeated to Pris' sister. Even the lower floor had their own set of rules.

"You're right, Miss Caroline. 'Tis my tongue wagging out of the wrong side of my mouth once again. I'll keep my teeth tight on it."

"But I am glad about Ralph," Caroline hastened to say unless Mollie's feelings be hurt. "And I do hope that you will see more of him."

Mollie grinned. "If I don't, t'won't be the way I want it, Miss Caroline. They used to say like master, like man. Mr. Hannakar's a proper sort, he is. Ralph talks 'bout him and all he does for his people. Old Madam, she used to run things while Mr. Hannakar was out west with them cruel heathen savages. But now he's taken over just like his father—a proper gentleman, and one as knows the land and how best to use it. 'Tis a brave fine house he has, Miss Caroline."

"It's lovely! And he is a very kind person, Mollie. So is Madam. She has been so sweet to Althea and me."

"Sure and she would be." Mollie slipped in a last hairpin with much less force than Skinner had ever used. "Now then, Miss Caroline, you're all ready. There's a good roast tonight and cook says to tell you she made apple fritters—good and crisp."

Caroline laughed. "Tell cook that that will surely get me to the table on time. Nobody in Montreal can touch her apple fritters! Thank you, Mollie. You have made me look the proper young lady in spite of myself!"

Both Papa and Richard were missing from the table that evening. Mama announced that they had been suddenly summoned to a consultation by Dr. Howards. She looked quite upset about it, though she had long since learned, Caroline knew, to accept such events as part of a doctor's life.

Althea looked tired. She admitted, when pressed, that she had a headache, and yielded to Mama's decree that she must go to bed immediately after dinner. But Pris was in a sparkling mood, restless, as if the picnic had not tired her but had rather made her wish for more excitement. When she and Caroline were in the sitting room, Perry off on some affairs of his own, and Mama upstairs seeing to Althea's comfort, she did not settle down, but pulled back one of the curtains to look out into the darkness of the street, or what she could see of it beyond the frost on the pane.

At length she swung back to face Caroline, her eyes very bright, her cheeks a little flushed.

"It's true, isn't it? And you knew it?"

Caroline was completely uncomprehending. "What do you mean, Pris?"

"Althea's going to have a child!"

When Caroline did not answer, she burst out: "Oh, anyone with a scrap of sense, and knowing what we know living here, can pick it up. She's been coming down late in the mornings, she doesn't fancy anything but weak tea and dry toast. Then Mama's been watching her like a hawk, and even you've been going around asking if she wants a shawl, a footstool, a cup of tea! She's breeding."

Pris stood by the small table, her fingers busily twisting the plushballed fringe of its velvet covering until, with a vicious pinch, she cut loose one of the balls and it flipped across the room to land at Caroline's feet.

"Richard's child," she said in a low voice. There was no longer such heat in her tone, rather a shadow of something else which Caroline was not acute enough to catch.

Then Pris laughed, high and recklessly. "Boy or girl? Well, if it is a boy, Papa will undoubtedly try to make another doctor out of him, I hope with better luck than he is having with Perry. Althea—she's only doing her proper duty. Isn't that what men really marry for? Or at least they tell us so under all the trimmings—a wife to run their house smoothly, a mother for any brats that turn up—the whole to be kept out of their real existence, shut up in another compartment of their lives! Be warned, dear sister, at what they say to win themselves a wife. The promises they may so glibly make—well, that all changes afterward.

"Althea may be an Earl's daughter, but here she's Richard's wife, without even any home of her own to see to. Mama's the head in this household. Now she's going to have a child, and all the old biddies will oh and ah and coo—

"There's really only one way to marry. Make sure that you are going to get something in return. Althea did not do very well for herself, choosing a doctor just getting started. And Papa is not altogether pleased with Richard these days. Perry says it is because of this new idea about sleeping gas. Papa and the Howards are very upset that Richard keeps wanting to try it. If he doesn't look out, he isn't going to establish much of a practice. And Lady Althea did not bring him a dowry. I've heard that the Carruthers family may have an earl's coronet at the top, but they have precious little in the pocket. Perhaps that is why they let one of their daughters marry beneath her. Because that must be what they said when she wed Richard: "Just a doctor, and a colonial to boot."

"No, Richard doesn't have much and may not get ahead very fast. Lady Althea did not do so well for herself." She stood with both fists resting on her hips, her elbows akimbo. "Be sure—be very sure, that when I marry I'll be stepping into a good life. I'll have my own house, and I'll have other things, too.'' Pris nodded her head. Now she smiled in a way Caroline shivered to see.

''Don't be surprised, little sister. Richard chose, and Althea chose—maybe it is up to me to choose, too. But I'm going to get more in the end than either of them, with no brat in the first year to spoil my fun, either!''

Then she was gone, with a flurry of skirts, leaving Caroline hunched in her chair and trying hard not to cry. Pris—her hard words—a good marriage—Mr. Hannakar— it could only be Mr. Hannakar! But Pris sounded as if she did not even think of—of love. And if she really meant what she just said, that would be a bad marriage, a deceitful one, and not fair to Mr. Hannakar. Oh! She wrung her hands together. Let all those words just mean that Pris was in a temper! They could not be her real feelings, surely that was not so!

10

Saturday morning the sky was blue and cloudless, though it was still cold enough for a crust to have formed over yesterday's broken snow. It was an ideal day for sleighing again, and for the weekly outing of the Tandem Club.

"It is indeed pleasant to go driving out after all. I can accept that after yesterday," Althea commented at the breakfast table. She seemed completely restored, with more energy than she had shown for several days. "Mr. Hannakar's picnic reminded me of the outings we had at home in Scotland, though of course we had no sleighs there—just brakes."

"What is a brake?" Caroline asked. She had fallen into the habit of lingering after breakfast to share the meal with Althea, who ate slowly and came down a little later these days. Mama did not show her usual impatience at such unpunctuality in the least.

Richard had lingered this morning also, and Caroline was aware that he watched his wife with concern.

"It is a sort of carriage," he said, "rather like our tallyhos."

"But it is not, Richard, not at all a tally-ho," Althea

protested. "A brake—well, it is just a brake."

"Now do you understand, Caroline?" Richard wanted to know.

"No," she answered flatly.

Althea laughed. "It is a kind of country carriage—that is about the best I can describe it. We use it for outings at home."

"However that may be," Richard cut in, "Corbie's picnic has now made you ambitious to try some of our other delights, such as the Tandem outings. Is that it?"

Althea turned a little pink. "I did not mean to imply that I wished an invitation," she said quickly.

"As a matter of fact," her husband said, "I have been thinking along the same lines. Have you not noticed there is a new arrival in the stable?"

"Stable?" Althea looked blankly from Richard to Caroline, who, she well knew, was alert to any changes in that portion of the Warwick holdings.

"Richard bought Joby-boy from the Collinses, and a new sleigh, too. Joby-boy is a fine pacer."

"A surprise," Richard smiled at his wife. "I have yet some time before the doctor needs me. Finish up your breakfast, get your cloak, then come and see. You, too, Caroline."

They gathered in the stable where Richard introduced Althea to a sleek bay who stretched his head toward Caroline hopefully in a trustful fashion which suggested that the two of them were already friends.

"To tell you the truth," Richard admitted, "it was Corbie who called my attention to the fact that Collins wanted to sell. And I'd take Hannakar's opinion of any horse at once. Now, my lady, here is your transportation."

Proud and gleaming with a new coat of bright red paint,

a small, two-seated sleigh stood in the corner of the carriage house. Warm buffalo robes were piled in its seat and the brass-trimmed, bell-strung harness was on the pegs waiting for use.

Althea gave her husband a delighted smile. "It is beautiful, Richard, so cheery and bright. It will be like part of a dream to ride in it."

He beamed and said with insincere depreciation, "Oh, it is not at all remarkable, but it will contain the prettiest and most charming muffin of them all!"

"Muffin?" repeated his wife, completely at a loss.

Richard made a deep bow, "My lady, I salute you."

"Muffin? What has a muffin to do—"

"A muffin, my dear unknowledgeable wife, is the young lady who shares a two-seater sleigh with the gentleman of her choice."

"Richard! Such a word!"

"On my honor, that will be your title when we ride out."

"But where did such a name come from? One eats a muffin, one is *not* one!"

"Here one is," he said solemnly. "As for the reason for the name, that I can't tell you. It has been in use as long as I remember."

"Very well," Althea laughed. "Then here stands a muffin, willing and ready."

Pris also had an invitation for the afternoon with a lieutenant of the 23rd. It was the opinion of all the garrison that such outings were the only way to survive the tedium of the long winter. These expeditions were the only times that proper young ladies might share a sled with a young man, the usual chaperones at a distance. Most of the officers, once introduced to the custom, set up their stables immediately and vied with each other over the equipment of their light sleighs.

Lieutenant Pell arrived promptly at a quarter to two, and Pris appeared at once, for no right-minded young lady kept her escort waiting in the cold. Althea and Richard followed with Joby-boy and the new equipage. Caroline waved them off from the stable yard and then turned in surprise as James came hurrying to her.

"Miss Caroline, Mr. Hannakar is here."

She hurried around to see the team of greys harnessed to a three-seater sleigh, their breath making small white clouds in the crisp air.

"Pris—Pris had an invitation," Caroline got out quickly. "I am so sorry."

"I was well aware Miss Priscilla must have been long since engaged," he smiled down at her. "I have come to see if you and Lady Althea would honor me with your company. Lady Althea mentioned that she was interested in the drive across the ice to Laprairie, and this is just the day for it—so I thought she might forgive so late an invitation."

Caroline shook her head. "Althea went out with Richard for the club outing. She just left. I know that she will have been sorry to have missed you."

He laughed. "Now, Miss Caroline, do not allow your sense of what is polite lure you into a fib. I have no doubt at all that she is very happy with her company right now. What about you, Miss Carolilne?"

"I was going with Mollie—we were walking to see the procession."

"Would I be permitted to accompany you for that?"

Caroline looked at the greys, tossing their heads and pawing a little at the snow. They were so beautiful. She was startled when Mr. Hannakar broke into her thoughts.

"May I suggest that *you* change your plans for the afternoon? Why should you and Mollie walk, when you have such transportation as this awaiting your wish?" He waved his hand to the sleigh.

"Mr.—Mr. Hannakar! But you—you must have something else more important—"

"Nonsense. What is ever more important than having a young lady smile on one and say 'yes'?" Caroline was puzzled at the way he was looking at her now.

He gave the reins to James and held the door open for her. "Get your scarf and," he glanced at her head, where her hood had slipped back a little, "anchor your bonnet, or whatever you call it, fetch Mollie, and we'll be off."

With a pounding heart (she was so excited at the unexpected invitation) Caroline scurried up the stairs, only vaguely aware that Mama had appeared from somewhere at the back of the house and was greeting Mr. Hannakar in the hall.

Mollie, summoned, was sent flying for her street cloak, hood and boots, while Caroline jerked a scarf out of a drawer and then sought to fasten her hood more tightly. As her fingers wrestled with the thick fur and wool she paused. Mama—what if she did not approve of such an expedition? After all, there were the proprieties. Though with Mr. Hannakar, who was so close a friend of the family, and with Mollie going along, surely Mama would not be anxious about any gossip.

But some of the joyous excitement had ebbed as she left her chamber and walked more slowly down the hall than she had sped up it.

"You are very kind to Caroline."

Long ago the younger Warwicks had learned that, through some trick of the house, conversations sometimes carried oddly from lower to upper hall. Caroline had never paid much attention to it, except on rainy days when they had all been small and Perry and Richard had played "haunted house" and produced blood-chilling groans, to meet delighted screams of protest from Pris and her.

"She is quite young." Mama's voice came, not like one of the boy's shrieks, but in a low yet still distinguishable tone. "I would not like her to be made unhappy."

Unhappy? About what? How could Mr. Hannakar ever make her unhappy? Caroline stopped short. Without knowing it her mittened hand pressed against the fold of her cloak over her breast. She felt—queer . . . .

"I would not care for that either, Mrs. Warwick." Mr. Hannakar sounded so serious, as if he were making a promise. But why would he be promising Mama anything to do with Caroline?

Caroline purposefully stepped hard enough to make her boots heard as she started down the stairs.

Mama's voice came again: "I am sure Caroline and Mollie will have a most enjoyable drive. It is a kind thought to invite them."

"And it is kind of you to allow me the pleasure of their company," Mr. Hannakar returned. "Ah, Miss Caroline, cloaked, booted, and ready to go," he greeted her. Mollie came hurriedly from the back of the house.

James had been walking the team; now he bundled the robes about the girls while Mr. Hannakar took the reins. Caroline snuggled down happily as they drove to the slope of St. Lambert's Hill to watch the glittering procession of sleighs pass along Notre Dame Street, the parade led by senior officers on horseback.

Caroline waved vigorously as Richard and Althea passed.

"Althea is so lovely," she said. "Don't you think so,

Mr. Hannakar?''

"Most," he agreed.

"And Richard—you know, you are like Richard. I think you both smile in almost the same way. Not as if you are just being polite, but because you really like people." Caroline stopped short, horrified at the way her tongue had betrayed her. One did not make personal remarks in this fashion. He would think she was forward.

"Thank you, Miss Caroline." He was still smiling. "It is seldom that compliments come my way these days. I shall plume myself on that one for some time to come."

Caroline felt very hot. He had been kind enough not to show any signs that he thought she was bold. Feverishly she searched for a new topic, and fate provided her with one as another sleigh pulled by.

"There's Pris!" Again she waved vigorously. "I wonder if Lieutenant Pell does know horses very well. He always seems so uncertain when he has the reins." Again her tongue had led her into frankness, but she didn't care so much this time.

Mr. Hannakar laughed. "You can be quite devastating in your judgments, Miss Caroline."

She refused to allow her embarrassment to show. She would *not!* "I wonder if you mean that to be complimentary. But at least he does not wear one of those big mustaches. Captain Roberston makes me think of a walrus at times. Mustaches are silly." She was babbling, but she was almost afraid to stop. This was like running from something behind her, something she did not want to face. "There's Major Vickers. But who is with him? I don't recognize her."

"I do not believe you would know her, Miss Caroline." Mr. Hannakar's sudden slight curtness was again a check.

She sought wildly for something to say, sure that everything she said was exactly the wrong thing. "I don't like him," she burst out. "Sometimes—sometimes he scares me."

Beside her Mollie stirred. Caroline came to her senses enough to dig her elbow into the maid's side. Mollie must not make any comment about her "black man," even if she was forgetful of her place as to try it.

"You need not be afraid of Vickers," Mr. Hannakar began.

Caroline feverishly broke in to change the subject. "There's George Scott, and he has Edith Barnard with him. I wonder what Perry will say? Perry wanted to come, but there's an operation this afternoon and his class is supposed to observe."

"How is Perry enjoying those studies of his?"

That unhappy frankness which had seemed to have taken possession of Caroline against her will brought another admission.

"I don't think very much. But of course he is a Warwick and Papa's son, so he must become a doctor."

The last sleigh of the procession was flying past. Mr. Hannakar looked down at her.

"Now where would you like to drive?" he asked.

For a moment Caroline longed to say "right home," but some deep sense within her insisted that if she did that, her unfortunate babble would seem all the more important. So she took her rags of courage in both hands.

"Would the Priest's Farm be too far? Mollie has never seen the old towers there, and they do look so unusual in winter."

"An excellent suggestion." He set the greys to a good trot out of the city proper, through the Recollect Suburbs, and those of Ste. Antoine, until the open country was before them.

"How would you like to take the reins, Miss Caroline? I understand from Richard that you have driven at the farm."

In a flash Caroline's uneasiness vanished. "May I, truly? It would be such a pleasure with horses so well trained. Mr. Wilson's team is hard-mouthed, and my arms always ache."

Mr. Hannakar drew the team to a standstill and then transferred the reins into Caroline's eager, mittened hands. She accepted and held the leathers with skill.

"Mr. Wilson always insisted I learn correctly. I am doing it properly?" she looked anxiously at her host.

"Entirely so. And I believe you ride also?"

"Oh, yes." She was centering her attention on the reins as the team started up. Then she giggled as years slipped away, her small success giving her confidence. "It is very shocking, I know, but on the farm I used to ride astride. It was much more comfortable, and there was no sidesaddle until just last year when Papa bought me one. I must say that it is much more difficult to ride like a lady. Gentlemen have much the better of it."

He laughed wholeheartedly. "That may be true in several ways, Miss Caroline. Do you hunt?"

"Well, not exactly. I used to ride with Mr. Wilson's sons crossfields, and we jumped the fences."

The twin towers, built for protection against Indian raids, arose in the distance. Mollie was excited, but more than a little alarmed as Mr. Hannakar related the bloody history of raids which had made such protection necessary.

It was dusk when they returned to the Warwick house and Mr. Hannakar followed her in to pay his respects to

Mama. As Caroline held out her hand to Mr. Hannakar, a little of her uneasiness returned.

"I do want to say thank you for the most pleasant afternoon," she said, summoning up those polite phrases which Mama had drilled into her. "To have the privilege of driving the greys—oh, that was wonderful." Now enthusiastic remembrance broke through the formalities of thanking-the-gentleman-for-a-drive. "I am only sorry that you were not able to take Althea across the river. She has spoken of it several times. When they came they were in a closed sleigh, and she missed the real excitement of it."

"If you and Lady Althea have no previous engagements," Mr. Hannakar said, "always supposing the weather remains clement, I would be most proud to show Lady Althea the charms of the river road."

He looked up at Mama, inquiring, and she smiled and nodded.

"Thank you very much for the pleasure you have given Caroline, Mr. Hannakar. I am sure that Lady Althea will be most happy to take advantage of your kind invitation."

As he bowed himself out, Caroline thought happily to herself that perhaps she had not been overly bold after all. Though it was perhaps very good that Mama had not heard her earlier thoughtless remarks.

Dinner began in a festive manner. Althea, delighted with the Tandem Outing, was more talkative than usual, and Pris capped her with excited chatter of her own. Even though Caroline privately thought that Lieutenant Pell could not have been the most attractive of escorts, it would appear that Pris was very pleased with herself and her day. Richard and Papa, on the other hand, were unusually silent. Though Richard smiled now and then when Althea appealed for support in her comments on their ride, his smiles quickly faded. His thoughts seemed to draw him miles away from their table.

Papa was so grave that Caroline guessed he must have some very serious case on his mind. He said hardly anything at all, and Mama glanced now and then down the length of fine linen between them as if she were disturbed. Perry, too, was silent, even when Pris remarked with gusto that Miss Barnard had seemed taken with the newly painted and furbished Scott sleigh and that George Scott had shown her marked attention. Usually Mama would have not allowed such gossip, but she said nothing to silence Pris. And, though Perry glowered darkly at his sister, he did not rise to any of her barbs.

What had seemed at first to be a happy meal after a lovely day was fast becoming an ordeal. There was something wrong, Caroline knew, and Althea was beginning to sense it also, for her light conversation grew slower, her smile a little strained. Caroline was glad when Mama gave the signal for them to rise and leave the three preoccupied men together.

"What a day!" Pris dropped into a chair with an uncharacteristic thud. "And what a dinner!" Mama had not yet come into the parlor, so the three young women were alone. "I wonder what has happened now? Papa hasn't glowered like that since Perry was caught out after that prank on Dr. Howards. But Richard certainly wasn't engaged in anything foolish like that." She looked to Althea as if for explanation. When Althea did not answer, Pris' little smile, which was not in the least a pleasant one, grew more pronounced:

"Was it because Richard took the afternoon off for pleasure?" she prodded. "Papa does have a severe outlook on the duties of a doctor."

Althea flushed, and spoke with more sharpness than Caroline had ever heard from her: "I am sure that Dr. Warwick's devotion to his duties is no greater than Richard's. Since he has established no practice as yet, and Dr. Warwick was well aware of Richard's plans for the afternoon, there could be no possible disturbance resulting from his not being in the house."

"No, of course not," Pris said, but with a note of disbelief in her voice. "We have always known how dedicated Richard is to his profession. Even when he was a boy he used to follow Papa around asking questions—very good ones, too. Papa was proud of him."

"Papa *is* proud of him!" Caroline interrupted with some heat of her own. She did not know what game Pris was playing now, but she was determined that Pris was not going to hurt Althea.

"*Is* proud," Pris conceded. "Well, it is none of our concern. And you, Carrie—you had quite an outing also, didn't you? It was good of Corbie to amuse you. Men of Corbie's years seldom pay such attention to girls just out of pinafores. You had better remember that, sister mine."

It was Caroline's turn to flush, not with confusion but with rising anger such as she had seldom known before. That Pris would accuse her thus indirectly of—of boldness —of doing what common people called "making a set" at Corbie Hannakar! It was Pris' way, but she was getting tired of Pris' "ways". Some day Pris was going to say something really cruel—maybe to Althea—and that would be unforgivable.

"Mr. Hannakar came to invite Althea, and me, to ride the river road."

Pris leaned forward, her unpleasant smile growing. "Oh, did he? When he bought Joby-boy at Richard's

request, and knew all about the sleigh, and also knew that
Richard intended to surprise dear Althea today? Corbie is
not as absent-minded as all that, my dear!''

Caroline was so taken back as she considered these facts
that she could find no words, in spite of her resentment of
moments earlier. She saw Althea's quick frown at Pris as
her sister swept on:

''I think then my little sister is not quite as naïve as she
would have people believe. Though I never expected such
slyness in you, Carrie. It is strange how people change
sometimes. But I would be very, very careful, if I were you.
Gentlemen as wise in the ways of the world as Corbie Hannakar do not go seeking lady loves who still smell of milk
and bread and butter.''

''Priscilla!'' Mama stood in the doorway. Caroline
shrank farther back in her chair, one hand to her mouth,
staring at her sister unbelievingly. ''You will go to your
room at once!''

Pris' smile was a grimace as she got to her feet, giving
Caroline and Althea a raking glance which sent Caroline
shivering. Pris' temper—it must be Pris' temper. Her sister
always spoke before she thought when she was angered,
and hardly ever meant what she said. She couldn't believe
that Caroline was trying to—to attach Mr. Hannakar!
What if he might think something like that, too? Oh,
what had she said? No!

Hardly knowing what she did, Caroline stood up. She
felt sick, so sick she was afraid she would actually begin
retching then and there.

''Mama?'' Somehow she found voice enough to make
that single cry for help.

And Mama came to her. ''Caroline, my dear—it's all
right, child, it's all right!''

Caroline did not know where the tears had come from, but they were spilling down her cheeks so fast that they ran into her mouth so she could taste their saltiness. She felt the softness of Mama's black satin dress and Mama's arms around her.

"Mama? Pris—Pris didn't mean it. She couldn't have? I —I—Mr. Hannakar—please, Mama, I didn't ever think what Pris said! I didn't!"

"I know it, child. Of course you did not! Mr. Hannakar is a friend of the family. It is only natural that he should have offered you a pleasant ride today. You are not to think of what your sister has said. This time Priscilla has gone too far with her temper.

"Child, you have acted with perfect propriety, and you are *not* to think otherwise. You know that I would never allow you to do anything which was not right. You have nothing to reproach yourself with."

"But Pris—Mr. Hannakar likes her, and she knows it. Why should she say I am trying to interest him?" As the first shock wore off, Caroline was beginning to consider a new idea. That Pris could ever be jealous of her had never before crossed her mind. She was too used to be the un-noticed tag-along, overshadowed by Pris' two years' advantage in age and her undeniable beauty.

"She is in a queer mood," Mama said. "I frankly do not know what is the matter with her. Now, Caroline, I want you to sit here quietly with Althea. I am going up to Pris. We shall see once and for all what is at the bottom of this." As Mama left, Lady Althea held out her arms welcomingly and drew Caroline with her to the settee near the fire.

"'What is the bottom of this'," Caroline thought. What if her own suspicions were the truth, and Mama did discover that Pris was upset over Richard's marriage? There was nothing she could do now. Surely Mama would know how to manage.

Althea had handed her a lavender-scented handkerchief, and Caroline mopped at her face. She felt so ashamed, even though Mama said she had done nothing wrong.

"I thought, I believed, truly I did," she said in a small unhappy voice, "that Pris liked him. That she would like him more and marry him. He's like Richard, you know. He's so kind. I'm sure he was kind to me because of Pris. It has to be so. It has to be."

Lady Althea touched Caroline's cheek gently and then drew her face up and around so she could look straight into her eyes.

"My dearest, I already know enough about your sister to realize that in some moods she is apt to use her tongue as a weapon, not meaning what she says at all. We do not know what happened today, but surely you noticed how she strove to irritate Perry during dinner?"

"Yes," Caroline nodded. "Then she talked in that strange way about Richard. But, truly, Althea, I—I did not try to get Mr. Hannakar to—to notice me in the way Pris says."

"Of course you did not. I have never known a girl with less pretense than you, Caroline. There is not a word of truth in what Pris said of you. You have mentioned that Corbie Hannakar is like Richard. Do you think Richard would believe such a thing of you?"

Slowly Caroline shook her head. "No. Richard wouldn't." She sat up a little straighter. Corbie Hannakar *was* like Richard. Perhaps she could believe in him. Perhaps he would think that she had been trying artfully to engage his interest. If he had thought that, he would not have gone on being so kind and thoughtful. She wiped her tears again.

"But I will be careful. I will have to be, won't I? It is too bad—I did enjoy our ride so much."

"What do you mean, Caroline?"

"Why, just that I cannot go again, of course. It's all spoiled now. I would remember what Pris said, and I would maybe do or say something wrong, so he could guess. And he mustn't, ever. You understand that, Althea, don't you?"

"Oh, my dear. Yes, I can understand—for now. But time changes things. Don't make any firm resolves until you are very, very sure."

Caroline was certain that she was very, very sure right now.

11

On Sunday morning, when they met in the upper hall, Caroline was able to accept Pris' apology, which was made in the same off-hand style that her sister always used.

Since Mama was not present, Caroline impulsively answered, "Pris, I know you are unhappy about something. And truly, I—"

Pris, who had half turned away after her small set speech, which had sounded forced from her, faced her sister again with a flurry of skirts.

"I am all right!" She flung up her head. It was true that she looked her usual vivid self. "In fact," she hesitated, "perhaps you will hear something soon, Carrie, which will surprise you. There is more than one fish in the ocean, if one knows the proper bait to dangle. Yes, I think that a great many people may be surprised." She was smiling.

"What?"

Pris' smile grew more brilliant. "Papa may have a visitor soon. Oh, not on Sunday, of course. That would not be proper. I told you, Carrie, that I wanted more than what I have here in Warwick house. Well, it will be coming." She paused and drew a deeper breath. "There was—oh, there is no use speaking of it now. Only—"

Caroline did not know why she shivered, drawing her shawl closer about her shoulders although the feeling of chill was spreading inside her instead of from without.

"Mr. Hannakar? He is coming to see Papa? Oh, Pris, I am so happy for you!" Of course Pris was happy. There was no reason why she should not be! And if Mr. Hannakar was coming to ask for Pris, then it was no wonder her sister had been so upset last night. Pris had always considered that her own property must be kept wholly for herself alone.

Pris laughed. There was a hard, reckless note in the sound.

"Corbie Hannakar? I declare, half this city must have me pushed into his pocket! There are better *parti*'s than Corbie Hannakar. Men who are part of a much larger world than a provincial society as vapid and dull as this one. I do not aspire to a coronet, but even that is a possibility. It is surely even within reason."

"Miss Priscilla? Miss Caroline?" Mollie appeared at the head of the stairs. "The Missus says, will you be comin' down? It is close on the church hour."

Pris already had her cloak over her arm and her prayer-book in one hand. Caroline fled back to her chamber; her head was in a whirl as she huddled on her cloak, making sure her hair was anchored within the hood.

Her bewilderment was such that she could not keep her mind on any of the serious occupations of the day. They drove to church and Caroline, intent on the puzzle Pris had set her, noted that her sister gave special attention to the officers as they entered. Major Vickers was not among them; neither was Captain Carruthers, Caroline noted in some surprise.

It had been Captain Carruthers' habit to await the

Warwick party outside the church and sit beside Althea on
Sundays. Today there was no sign of him, while Pris' face
had become blank and oddly set. The Major—no! Surely
Pris could *not* believe that Major Vickers would offer for
her?

Papa would never allow it. Only who else was there?
Caroline found that she was hearing nothing of the
sermon. What had a coronet to do with it? Who had a
right to coronets?

Still bewildered, she noticed that Pris was even more
bleak of face as they went home to the heavy Sunday
dinner, made heavier by Mama's announcement that
Archie, Agatha, and the children would come for tea.

"Archie?" Perry openly made a face.

And Pris added in a tone of pure disgust, "Agatha—
and the children?"

Mama's serenity remained unruffled. "With the children, yes," she repeated. "It is time Althea met the whole
of the family."

Pris sniffed. "After meeting Agatha and Archie, I
should think she could do without the rest."

"Priscilla!" Papa said quellingly and Pris subsided.
After that flash of her old spirit, she appeared broodingly
dark again.

No visitors dropped in on a Sunday, nor were there ever
many professional calls for Dr. Warwick. Thus Papa was in
his wing chair by the fireplace, ready to spend the afternoon telling stories of his childhood days. Richard joined
in, though Perry, lounging in a corner seat with closed
eyes, seemed bored to the point of sleep. Pris sat very
quietly staring into the fire.

They all started when the bell of the front door pealed.
Mama looked up at the mantel clock.

"Perhaps it is Archie and Agatha a little early. Richard? Doctor?"

But before any could move Mollie came in, a letter salver in her hand, and held it out to Lady Althea.

"For you, M'Lady. T'was a soldier from the garrison as brought it. He said 'no answer.'"

Althea picked up the folded paper, looked at the seal.

"Alexander! But why would he be writing to me?" As she opened the seal and held the page closer to the lamp, Caroline heard a gasp from beside her.

Pris was leaning forward, her eyes on that sheet, looking startled.

Distress crossed Althea's face as she glanced at Richard for reassurance.

"I do not understand. Alexander says that he is being sent back to England with some important documents and must leave immediately. He says he could not come yesterday to say goodbye because Lord Elgin kept him on duty all day. I cannot understand. This is so sudden, so—so strange. Please," she showed a very troubled face, her eyes beginning to brim with tears, "if you will all please excuse me—"

Richard helped her out of her chair, guided her carefully to the door. As it closed behind them, the Warwicks looked from one to another in amazement. Priscilla had sunk well back in her chair, and only the edge of the lamplight touched her.

"How very odd," commented Mama. "Why, he was here on Thursday, when he escorted Priscilla to the Scott musical. He said nothing then of any such mission."

Dr. Warwick tugged at his beard. "Most unusual," he said. "There must be some emergency of which the province is not aware. If so—well, this household must not mention what has happened. This may concern a matter of grave consequences. Otherwise, Lord Elgin would not have given such orders that Captain Carruthers could not even call on his sister for farewells!"

The doorbell sounded again, and, as it did so, the doctor added, "That must be Archie and his family now. We will not discuss this."

Caroline watched Pris. There had been dazed shock on her face at first. Then something else, an odd little smile, as if she had won in some game. Now she was alive, sparkling, as she always was when things were going her way. But why had Alexander Carruthers' message, which had been such a blow to Althea, excited and pleased Pris? Caroline could not begin to understand.

Agatha stalked in, herding two silent children ahead of her and holding the third, who was so wrapped and rewrapped as to resemble nothing so much as a strapped roll of travelers' rugs. Caroline hurried forward to undo the children's coats. They were silent and shy as ever.

Their mother ordered them to make their manners to Grandfather and Grandmother, but not to annoy their elders. Plumping herself down on one of the wider chairs, she set about freeing her youngest from his cocoon, but over the baby she fastened her eyes on Priscilla.

"I hear that you have been passing a most busy season," she remarked.

Pris smiled brightly. "Yes, such fun, dear Aggie. Have you been indisposed often? You haven't even come to the teas. Really, Aggie, for your own sake you should get out more. I am sure that Archie would enjoy it, too. He was quite a fashionable beau before you were married."

Agatha never seemed to learn that it was not wise to stir Pris up. She frowned and pursed her lips. "Mr.

Warwick," she declaimed, "has more suitable ways of passing time than at low places of amusement!"

"Why, Agatha, how misinformed you are. That must be the result of your own keeping so close to home. Was the charity ball low? Lord Elgin attended it. And Mama was one of the co-hostesses!"

Mrs. Warwick gave Pris a most quelling glance.

"Such a beautiful baby, Agatha," she said pacifically. "Babies are so delightful. Do you not find them so?"

"It is a wife's duty to present her husband with a family. I trust that I have and always will do my duty," returned the infuriated Agatha. "It is time for baby's nap. We allow no interference with those hours of rest."

"I have the cradle waiting, Agatha. This way, please." Mama was not to be defeated on her own ground.

Dr. Warwick attempted to talk with Archie. Perry added nothing at all from his corner of the room, and Pris seemed to have fallen back into her deeply thoughtful mood. Caroline was left to watch the fire and struggle with a tangled skein of thoughts which must be unwound and reduced to tidiness.

"And where is Lady Althea today?" Agatha demanded as she reentered the room. "I suppose her ladyship feels that, having met us once, she has done her entire duty."

Dr. Warwick turned a most forbidding look on his daughter-in-law. "Neither my wife nor I inquire into the plans of Richard and his wife. If they wish to join us, then they will do so."

Agatha's face flushed a dark and unbecoming shade. "Richard, at least, should have greeted us. His lack of manners has become even more acute since he returned."

With a muffled exclamation, the Doctor got to his feet. At the door, he paused. "I find I have some important matters to see to, please excuse me." Then he looked back to the two children huddled together on hassocks, rather like two small rabbits when the hounds were barking nearby, Caroline thought. "You two—come along with me. I have something you might like to see." It was plain that Papa felt much the same.

Agatha opened her mouth and then closed it again. With a fearful glance at their mother, the children lingered, but, as she said nothing, they did go, clasping the hands their grandfather held out invitingly, and disappeared with him.

Archie cleared his throat. "How are your studies progressing, Peregrine? I trust you are devoting more time to them, though I have heard disquieting rumors to the contrary."

Perry shrugged. "Do you have to talk like Evans at his stuffiest, Archie? I don't know what you could have heard. Don't you tell us that you never listen to idle gossip?"

"It is common knowledge that you skip classes for frivious outings," Agatha chimed in.

Perry's eyebrows slid up. "How interesting it must be, Agatha, to be able to put the finger on every one's sins."

Mama cut in quickly then and spoke about Dr. Bethune's sermon, and then kept conversation so relentlessly general that there was no more chance of quarrels.

The door opened and Richard entered. Caroline saw the tense line of her mother's shoulders relax a trifle as he greeted Archie and his wife.

"I have just become acquainted with two of your children. Now I am looking forward to seeing William when he wakes. You have a very delightful family, Agatha."

"A wife should waste no time. It is her duty—"

Richard's mouth tightened and then smoothed into the

same courteous smile. "Of course, Agatha. One is aware of your ever-present sense of duty. I pray you will excuse Althea at present. She seems to have developed the symptoms of an aggravated cold. It is better that she keep quiet."

"It is our disappointment then." Archie roused himself. "I suppose you have observed a number of changes since your return."

"A few. Mainly, I feel much older when I observe the charming young ladies who were still in the schoolroom when I departed." He smiled at Caroline. "Indeed, there was one I hardly recognized at first meeting."

"In my day, a girl of Caroline's age was not appearing at public balls, nor was she permitted to drive out with a gentleman accompanied only by a giddy servant girl," proclaimed Agatha.

Caroline flushed.

Richard answered swiftly, "Was it that parents then had good cause not to trust their daughters, Agatha?"

It was so gently said that Caroline was certain Agatha did not at first understand. When she darkened dusky red, he had already turned back to Archie.

After Dr. Warwick returned with the children, who looked far more alive and happy now, Richard excused himself to take tea to Althea while Mama presided at the table in the parlor.

Afterwards, Archie and Agatha made their farewells; they would attend the evening service at the Methodist church. As soon as they were gone, Caroline asked Richard timidly if she could go to Althea.

He immediately nodded. "Perhaps you would be the best thing in the world for her. She is not quite recovered from the shock of Alexander's sudden departure. I cannot understand the fellow," Richard continued thoughtfully. "Surely Lord Elgin would never have sent him off so pell-mell as this! It is a very queer thing."

Caroline tapped on the chamber door and entered at Althea's call. Lying down, well wrapped in soft shawls, Althea held out her hand to the younger girl. Even in the subdued light of the single lamp it was plain she had been crying. But she found a smile for Caroline.

"My dear, I fear that I may have given offense to Mr. and Mrs. Warwick."

Caroline smiled. "You cannot really give offense to Archie or Agatha." She began to laugh. "Pris and Perry have been trying for years! Oh, you can make Agatha go quite red in the face, and Archie will say all manner of pompous things. But they are always right in their own eyes. I do not think even Papa can crack their self-esteem! Archie was always one to think well of himself. However, he has become much worse since he married. Oh!" Her fingers flew to her lips. "There, I am the one who is speaking out of turn now. But you are family, dear Althea, and I fear that among ourselves we are sometimes quite sharp-tongued." A sudden memory of Pris' late outburst made her flush then. "Anyway, you are well away from them. Remember, Papa said it was best not to discuss your news. It must have been quite upsetting to your brother to have to leave in that fashion."

"Yes," Althea said slowly. "I do not understand it in the least. It is so unlike Alexander, and even unlike Lord Elgin as I have known him. I—I am worried!"

Caroline was instantly aware of her mistake. "Oh, you mustn't be, dear. There must be a good explanation. Captain Carruthers will have a chance to write before he sails surely, and then you will know what is behind it all. You have had tea, I see." She took up the delicate cup and was glad to see it was nearly empty. The plate beside it was bare also, except for a few crumbs.

"Richard said that I must," Althea laughed. "I must admit that at times he puts on all the airs of a bully. Caroline dear, bring me that portfolio over there." She waved to a leather case with a small brass lock which glinted in the lamp light, as she sat up and swung her feet to the floor. "I would like to show you Heather House. My brother—the one who made your fan—sketched these the last time he was home on leave."

With Caroline beside her, Althea opened the case and began to bring out the sketches.

"This is the old house—"

"But it is a castle!" Caroline marveled. She had thought the towers of the Priests Farm impressive, but this was far grander than anything she had ever seen.

Althea laughed. "Oh, perhaps a bit of the wall here, and that tower. But those are the oldest parts. My grandfather had much torn down and rebuilt as was fashionable in his time. He tried to turn a rather dour fortified dwelling into something more romantic. When I was little, one of my governesses had a secret store of blood-chilling novels—those by Mrs. Radcliffe. I used to read them in secret, then went about hunting secret passages and rooms. Ronald liked the idea, too. Look at this one."

Althea swept away three of four drawings to find one which indeed brought a gasp from Caroline. It showed a dungeon with chains hanging from the wall, and a full skeleton stretched out on the floor, reaching for a door one surmised was never to open again.

"That was Ronald's best effort." Althea touched the paper lightly. "Usually he liked to draw pleasant things.

He was so talented—and never able to realize his dearest wish." She sighed, and then spoke with a lighter tone. "That is what I love most about Richard's country. No, I must think of it now as my country, too. The barriers which were so strong about us when we were growing up seem very thin in this frosty air—almost gone. Richard dares to be both a doctor and a gentleman."

"But he is!" Caroline protested.

"Of course he is, dear! Only there are those overseas who would never see it that way." Althea sat up straighter, and this time there was a set to her small dainty face, about her usually soft curving lips, which Caroline had never seen before. "I must tell you that I was considered to have made a most shocking marriage. Perhaps I was only allowed to wed Richard—Richard, who is everything any woman would delight to call husband—because my family were in such difficulties that there could be no marriage portion for me. My father was, and is, very deeply in debt. We lived most simply, in far less comfort than you have here, and I was given a season in London only because one of my mother's cousins very grudgingly came forward. When I met Richard—"

She paused. "It is seldom given one, Caroline, to meet one's love so easily and naturally. We knew almost at once how it was for both of us. He hesitated to speak to my father, since he knew that my world saw a great gulf between us. But to tell the truth, my father was very glad to get a daughter off his hands. We were not—are not—a particularly close family. Ronald and I, yes. But I saw little of Alexander. Perhaps that is why he felt so little responsibility to me in this instance. He is, I am afraid, quite imbued with the beliefs of his class in England."

"But if he were under orders of Lord Elgin," began Caroline, perplexed.

"Yes, of course, it must be that he was under orders." Only Althea sounded as if she were not convinced, as if she found something else disquieting about her brother's departure. Then she shook her head, as if to clear it of unwelcome thoughts.

The small French porcelain clock chimed the half hour and Caroline rose. Dinner on Sunday was a simple meal— far closer to what another class would term supper—but it was formally served and she must appear at the table. She thanked Althea and went hurriedly to her own room to change.

Pris' door was fast closed. Caroline hesitated a moment before it. Pris had seemed so much herself before Archie and his family had left. She would have liked to slip in and make sure that all was well between them. But at length she turned away and went to her own room.

There was no mention of Archie and Agatha's visit or of Alexander Carruther's letter that night, nor in the morning. For the first time Althea did not appear at the breakfast table. Richard gave her excuses, saying that she had not fallen asleep until the early morning, and he had thought it best not to disturb her—an opinion in which Mama decidedly concurred.

Pris was busy with a handful of small gilt-edged notes, sorting them out with pleasure. This was the last week in February, and the official social season was fast drawing to a close. March often brought a sudden thaw, the kind which marooned Montrealers within their own houses.

Tonight was the final assembly. On Tuesday there was the Barnards' large whist party with dancing afterwards. Mr. Anderson had announced in the *Gazette* that his last concert and ball would come on Wednesday evening. The tickets were moderately priced. The Soirée in Aid of the Fine Arts would take place at the Gallery of Painting in

Great St. James Street. Then there would be a meeting of the Tandem Club on Saturday.

Caroline did not greet her array of invitations as eagerly as Pris, but Mama suggested that she might attend the final assembly, since Mama and Papa were going to that—also Althea and Richard, should Althea not be too tired.

Still Caroline felt deeply reluctant about that mad rush of a week of "pleasure." Long afterwards she realized that she must have nursed a foreboding from the first.

Pris was alive, happy, sparkling, with nothing about her to suggest bad temper. She had a gentleman ready for every dance, went everywhere without a sign of fatigue, and was quite like the old Pris, calmly sure of herself and a future that held nothing but good for her.

Caroline, in fact, saw little of her sister save when they met at family meals, for Pris was either out, or preparing to go out, most of the day. She was at the height of her beauty that week. Caroline always after tried to remember her so, like some beautiful painting brilliant with color and life.

The night of the assembly Pris had a new gown, just the pink-white of apple blossoms. Wreaths of those blossoms themselves, cunningly fashioned from silk gauze, outlined the puffing about her breast and shoulders, and trailed over the wide skirt of her gown. She wore no jewels at all, rather another band of the blossoms about her throat like a small, tight ruff, and a coronet of them in her sun-bright hair. Caroline caught her breath when she saw Pris coming down the stairs, Jessie carrying her cloak behind her. It was as if the spring had come as a fair promise for the future in the person of her sister.

For the first time Caroline knew envy of Pris. Never in the world could she hope to rival her sister. Her own pale lemon dress looked faded and dull, her hair far too bright beside this vision. Then she told herself quickly that such envy was wicked. Pris was beautiful, and that she made the most of her beauty was only right and natural.

Althea had not felt up to the fatigue of the evening, and so Richard had also chosen to stay home. But Papa and Perry were with them and Mama, and they went on to a supper at the hotel before the ball. The band of 52nd Infantry played, and the hall was thronged with officers in brilliant full dress, adding dark and more dashing colors to the floating gowns of the young ladies.

Caroline was content to sit by Mama, though she did dance with two of the officers—young Ensign Reaves, who seemed to be quite uncertain of his spurs, and who had no idea of conversation in the least, and again with a Lieutenant Wallace, who talked of nothing but hunting. She had watched for Corbie Hannakar, but he had made no appearance. Finally she decided that he had chosen not to come at all. That realization took away much of the fun of the evening.

She watched Pris sail by in her apple-blossom skirts. Her eyes were sparkling, and about her there was an air of reckless mischief which made Caroline a little uneasy. That the ladies in the chaperones' line were very keen of eye was well known. Let any words be said about Pris, and such would be repeated quickly through the whole of their society. She wished so much that Mr. Hannakar had come. Somehow Caroline always felt safe at any party if she could see his tall figure, even if he did not speak to her or ask for a dance. Now—if he were here and with Pris, how much better things would be. Caroline sighed as her sister whirled by, laughing. There were at least two frowns on the faces of watching matrons.

12

Pris came back to Mama, frowning, her gloved hand holding up her skirt to show a ragged little tear.

"No one could be more awkward than that Ensign Reaves," she said sharply. "Look what he had done now! I vow I shall never dance with him again. Mama—"

Mrs. Warwick looked at the damage and pursed her lips. "It would be best for you to have some stitches taken in that at once, my dear. The material is fragile enough, and it will only fray the worse if you let it go. One of the maids in the ladies' withdrawal chamber will be able to take it well in hand."

Caroline got quickly to her feet. "I'll go, too, Mama. The room is so hot, I would like to be quiet for awhile."

"Of course, dear."

Caroline followed Pris, who was already on her way. Dared she say anything at all to her sister about those frowns she had noted among the chaperones? Pris might well turn to more flagrant flirtation if she did, out of sheer contrariness.

However, once within the ladies' room, Pris stood patiently as a maid knelt beside her and took quick stitches. Caroline knew that within the hearing of the seamstress she could not give any advice.

"It is a good assembly," Pris glanced over at her own brilliant reflection in one of the wall mirrors. "I declare that if I do not dance these slippers into holes it will not be for want of invitations. A fine way to end the season. It is a pity Captain Carruthers had to leave so suddenly. He had asked me for the fourth waltz and supper. But then, I have had no trouble in filling such gaps." She touched the wreath of blossoms in her hair, pushed her fingertips into the loose curls on her shoulders as she smiled at her own reflection with open approval.

"The tear is mended, Miss." The maid arose, and Pris lifted her skirt to survey the repairs. It was an excellent bit of work and she said so, thanking the woman with that warmth and sweetness of manner which she could and did use when she was in the best of humors.

Caroline told herself that everything was all right. Of course it was. It was just Pris' way when she was excited and happy to be a little more exuberant than usual. She pushed aside her worries as Pris turned to the door, gave her an open, happy smile and held out her gloved hand.

"Carrie, dear, you have been far too much of the creep-mouse tonight. We must find you a partner so that you, too, can finish off the season in proper style. Come along. I promise that I shall not recommend any young gentleman clumsy with his feet. But there are others who can prove that some men are not awkward on the dance floor."

They had come out of the ladies' chamber and were starting down the hall. Pris pointed ahead to some potted palms, through which the two girls could see the brilliance of dress uniforms.

"There, now. See fortune favor us. I am sure that we

shall find we are awaited."

Only, before they had reached the palm oasis and those who gathered by it, a name brought both girls up short.

"—Carruthers, altogether a stupid move. Silly ass, thought he was in love with the chit, mind you. Who? Why that bit of muslin who is on the go tonight— Priscilla Warwick. The idea was ridiculous, of course. Would have finished his career. When he mentioned he was going to offer for her, the Old Man put his foot down. Couldn't come right out and make it too plain, or Carruthers might have done a bolt and made the matter worse by actually offering. His sister's married to the gal's brother—or stepbrother, something of the sort. A real mésalliance. Still, since the family is near done up she couldn't hope for much.

"But it would have been ruin for Carruthers. Lord Elgin kept him on duty Saturday when he found out what was up—important dispatches—then he shipped him off for the Boston packet and London. Sent him to Grey at the foreign office and wrote Grey under cover the whole story. Grey will tell the Earl, and they'll see to it he stays in England. Carruthers is a born fool. But to marry one of these colonial chits, no dowry, no position, no connections . . . . He'll see it would never do, once he gets home. How's for a drink, Reaves? They water down the punch for the ladies, but there's a bottle or two handy if a man knows who to ask."

Caroline could have cried out, but did not. Pris' fingers had closed about her sister's arm in a grip which near brought tears to her eyes. Worse than the pain of that hold was the other, sharper, anguish which she felt for Pris. To be spoken of in such a way—to be so judged! It was an insult which must burn proud Pris to the very center of her mind and heart. Caroline was hot with the fires of humiliation; how much worse it must be for Pris! The younger girl had to force herself to look at her sister.

All the bright color had drained from the older girl's face. There was a blind look in her eyes, and she swayed. Caroline pulled Pris' clutching fingers from her arm by force and drew her sister to her, supporting her. She looked actually grey. Nor did she resist when Caroline led her, holding one arm tightly about her shoulders, back into the ladies' chamber.

"Miss!" The maid who had repaired Pris' gown was at their side immediately. "What is the matter? Is the young lady ill?" Caroline had steered her sister to a chair and was gently but firmly pressing Pris down into it. That dreadful blank look on her sister's face frightened her more than she let herself admit.

"Some wine, and a vinegarette—" She discovered a competence which she had not realized.

"Of course, Miss. At once."

Caroline stood beside her sister, steadying Pris by the shoulders, waiting for the wine. When it came she made Pris drink. Coughing, shaking her head, and pulling away from the glass the second time it was offered, the other girl sat up straighter.

"I am all right," she said dully, but in a stronger voice than Caroline expected. Then she looked directly at her sister. "Please, Carrie, just give me a minute or two. It was just a spasm. I feel much better."

It was, Caroline thought, as if Pris was drawing strength from deep within her. Her shoulders went back, she sat erect, color was creeping back to her face. In that moment Caroline had never admired her more.

"Just a minute or two," Pris repeated. Then she turned

to the maid. "It is quite all right. A slight giddiness only. If you will leave me with my sister, all will be well now."

"There is no one you want, Miss? I would be most happy to go for you."

"Mama?" Caroline made a question of the word.

Pris shook her head. "No. I shall be fine." She reached out one hand and took the glass the maid still held, sipping its contents slowly. Her color was well back. Only her eyes held the signs of shock and she had lowered her lids over them, regarding the glass she held and now turned around and around in her fingers.

Caroline nodded to the maid, who withdrew to the other side of the room, though she still watched them doubtfully.

"We can go home," she suggested in a very low voice.

"No!" Pris' answer came in a voice hardly above a whisper. "And perhaps have someone guess that—that I know? That it means anything to me? If this story is going the rounds, and it will, you know it will—!" There was a fierceness in her voice now. "No one is going to guess that I care. No one is going to have the power to laugh at me. A colonial chit who had to be shown her sorry place by the all-powerful governor himself! Yes, Alexander Carruthers was going to offer for me. He spoke at the Scotts' party. I expected him to see Papa. But he was just a way out—a way out of this dull, dull town, out of—" She fell silent. Would she ever admit the whole of it, Caroline wondered, with an ache of tears she dare not shed rising in her throat. Would Pris ever admit that she felt she must get away from Richard and his happiness which did not include her?

Pris drew a deep breath and then another. She set the wine glass firmly on a nearby table, and, for the first time, looked directly at Caroline.

"You will not tell." It was not a question but a command. Caroline found herself nodding. Pris deserved that, surely. Her sister's pride had been bitterly assaulted, but at least she had not had her heart touched. Pris could meet the challenge of showing the world that she was what she had always been, Priscilla Warwick, a person of distinction, even if that snobbish world overseas held her to be of no account. This was Pris' city, and she would not be openly shamed in it.

Pris played her part very well indeed for the rest of the evening. Caroline could only marvel at her sister's iron will, her ability to rise—at least on the surface—above the humiliation of what they had overheard. Of course, Althea had hinted that the lines of society were far more sharply drawn in England than here. But to have her marriage with Richard deemed a "real mésalliance"—Caroline's own chin came up and she felt the rise of anger within her which heretofore had been reserved for those who ill treated animals. These soldiers had accepted the best of the hospitality offered—had allowed themselves to be made welcome in the most friendly fashion. That they held such views! That snobbery could extend to downright insolence—for it was insolence she had heard in the voices of Reaves and his friend (whoever that other officer had been)—she would never have believed! She longed to ask Althea, but Althea was the last one who must ever know of Pris' humiliation.

Pris danced and flirted and was herself—save for a certain glint in her eyes. Caroline refused two offers to dance, wanting to sit by Mama, wondering, every time one of the officers passed, whether he also was secretly sneering at this déclassé provincial society, ready to make fun of all the local belles when he was with his own kind. She was very glad indeed when it was time to go and they drove home through the chill of the night.

The week of festivities ended, and with it the season, but the duty of formal calls continued.

Thursday was the Warwicks' own "At Home" day. At two o'clock of the second Thursday following the assembly, Mama had taken her place behind the massive tea service in the formal parlor, looking her most majestic in last year's best dress of deep purple moiré antique with its ecru lace. Her matron's cap of the same lace displayed a softening of frizzled curls about her temples. Her appearance made it easy to remember stories that she had also been a belle and a sought-after beauty in her youth.

Caroline thought that Althea looked a little pale and languid. She had not mentioned her brother, and no letter written from Boston had arrived. Did Althea somehow guess what had happened? There was so much Caroline wanted to know and dared not ask anyone.

Althea and Pris had both chosen to wear blue. Althea's gown was one from her lovely trousseau, a moiré embroidered with feathers in silver thread. The shade matched her eyes. But Pris' choice did little for her. She looked a little tired, and as she often did these days, and seemed withdrawn into some special inner world. She had been avoiding Caroline, and the younger girl, realizing how Pris' pride had been lashed by those overheard words, did not push her company on her sister. She was afraid that her presence would remind Pris of that outrageous rejection which must burn deep every time it crossed Pris' mind.

Gentlemen came calling, too, though one offered them more robust fare—sherry in the proper glasses. Certain officers from the garrison came regularly, duty bound to show their gratitude for past hospitality. Caroline, always choosing to sit a little apart, would watch their bland mustached, or otherwise behaired, faces and wonder just what tales they told among themselves. She had longed so to speak to Mama, to let her know how little respect these supercilious young men gave the Warwicks and their whole circle. Only to do so would be to reveal Pris' secret, and that she would never do. She was glad that today her dress was of last year's wearing, drab and rather childish, so that she would be overlooked, except by older ladies who treated her as the child she appeared.

Pris would flash into gaiety when the gentlemen arrived, Caroline knew. The officers would show their interest—or their pretense of it—by vying to supply her with a cup of tea, a plate of cakes, while she chatted vivaciously of outings to be taken when the weather finally changed.

This afternoon, however, there was a newcomer. At the sight of him Caroline gave a slight start. Major Vickers had come several times with Captain Carruthers in the past, but he did not make many appearances at tea parties. However, his manners were impeccable, his conversation such as would indicate a special effort to be a polite guest. Mama's face had changed a fraction when she had seen him enter, but she accepted his greetings and compliments with outward serenity. He passed on to Lady Althea, and Caroline heard him relay news of her brother which had filtered back to the garrison as part of the official reports. Althea looked up eagerly, and appeared at ease, asking questions which he answered in his drawling voice, but so low as to reach little beyond the two of them.

Pris was watching. There was some fierceness in her eyes and the set of her mouth. She had that same air of girding on her armor against the world which she had worn that night at the ball.

Then the door opened, and Papa came in. He seldom appeared at such functions, and the ladies stirred a little, turning surprised and pleased faces in his direction. Dr. Warwick was a favorite with all of them; they often deplored the fact that his profession kept him so busy that they saw very little of him.

Now Mama poured a cup of tea, adding a dash of milk and three good lumps of sugar, the way Papa liked it best, and as he came to take it from her hand, she smiled.

"Doctor, I am uncertain as to whether you have met Major Vickers. He is serving as Lord Elgin's aide. In fact he must be very tied to his duties now that Captain Carruthers has gone."

The doctor placed his cup back on the tray. Major Vickers was several inches taller than Papa, and he was facing him now with a queer little half smile, a reckless smile as if he dared Papa—Caroline could not tell how these ideas came into her head; somehow they just did. She always found them disconcerting and frightening.

"Mrs. Warwick. Ladies." The Doctor made a stiff little bow, his eyes still fastened upon the lounging major. "If you will be so good as to excuse me, this young man and I have some business to discuss."

The major's smile grew wider, but he inclined his head and spoke to Althea:

"If you will excuse me then, Lady Althea. If there is any fresher news, I shall make every effort to see that it reaches you at once."

There was an insolent note in his drawl, and Althea watched him sharply as he preceded the doctor out of the room.

As the door into the hall was firmly closed by Papa, a

murmur arose from the guests. Mama looked a little flushed.

A Mrs. Ritcher spoke. "There is some difficulty with the hospital's supplies perhaps—something Major Vickers can draw quickly to the governor's attention?" Mrs. Ritcher and Mama had been good friends since they were girls together, sharing a governess.

"The doctor does not discuss his difficulties," Mama said, with her usual serene control, but Caroline knew well enough that she was shaken. Papa's actions had bordered on the rude. But why? Major Vickers was accepted everywhere, despite the gossip about him.

Caroline wished Mr. Hannakar were here, but he had been summoned to Boston himself only two days before that unfortunate assembly, as she had learned through Mollie. Somehow when he was present she had a feeling of safety. Richard was so engrossed now with the practice Papa was introducing him to, with affairs at the hospital, that he was very seldom at home, and they saw less and less of Perry. Anyway, she had never thought to take her brother into any confidence. Of course, she would never, never tell what had happened to Pris, but there was something very secure and comforting about Mr. Hannakar.

"There is no more news of Barbara Wiley?" Mrs. Mostrain selected a puffy, jam-filled tartlet. "Her chill seems to be most serious. I have sent to inquire several times, but the answer is always the same, that she is still seriously indisposed. It is a pity—having no mother, and that aunt of hers such a scatterbrain. I wonder if the poor girl is indeed well cared for."

Mama set Papa's tea cup on the far side of the tray. "She is a patient of the doctor's. He has said this is a difficult case. Lung fever is so often thus, even with the young.

Barbara is very much alone. I have called with the doctor.''
Caroline saw Mama's hands clasp together hard for a
moment. ''They have nurses in now. Perhaps we can only
pray for the poor child. She has not always been discreet,
but, considering that she has lacked a mother's guidance
and that her father is so often from home, I do not think
that the blame for her thoughtless actions should be put
entirely upon her own head.''

Mrs. Richter nodded. ''She is sometimes a little too free
in her manner, but she has a good heart. I have seen her at
the children's hospital playing with the little ones when
our guild has the Christmas and Easter parties. And she is
always most patient and kind. Yes, we must pray that she
will recover from this illness. Though all is within the
Lord's Will.''

Caroline tried to place Barbara Wiley. She was certainly
not one of the girls who joined in the amusements of their
own circle. Mr. Wiley was one of the western traders like
Mr. Hannakar, though on a much smaller scale, and he
was often away from the big house which rivaled the Warwicks. But when she tried to think of Barbara she could not
honestly remember her.

Papa did not return until after the guests had left.
When he did, he was frowning. He stared for a long
moment into the fire, and then he swung around as if he
were about to deliver an extremely important lecture to his
pupils.

''Althea, my dear,'' he said, and there was a softening
in his scowl as he said her name, ''I must make something
clear. I know that that young man approached you with
the story that he had information concerning your brother,
and, with that in mind, it was only right that you accepted
his presence here. But I must tell you all now, and I mean

it very seriously, Major Vickers is not to cross my doorstep again on any excuse whatsoever. Please accept my decision as final. There is an excellent reason for it.''

Richard had followed Papa into the room. Now he went directly to Althea, sat down beside her and took her hand into both of his. If anything, she looked even more pale, her eyes very large and fastened directly on the doctor as if she feared what he might say next.

''There are ways and manners,'' Papa continued, ''which unfortunately are tolerated in some phases of society. But here in Montreal we do not allow the corrupt and the evil to circulate simply because of rank or blood.

''Priscilla,'' now he spoke in a tight voice which Caroline had never heard him use before, ''you have treated this man after the ways of polite society. I understand you have danced with him, accepted him as an acquaintance. This is to stop at once. I have very excellent reasons for saying this. You are never again to recognize Major Vickers in any possible manner. Do you understand me?''

Pris was looking down at her own hands. There was the slightest of pauses, and then she answered: ''It will be as you say, Papa.''

''That is all. We shall not mention this unfortunate incident again. I have been driven this day to look at a very great evil and it has sickened me. Mrs. Warwick,'' he spoke now to Mama, ''I must go out on some arrangements of necessity. Pray do not wait dinner on me. A meal brought to my study when I return will be sufficient.''

Then Papa was gone, leaving a silence behind him.

Richard broke it. ''My dear.'' He leaned closer to Althea. ''You look very tired. I suggest a rest before dinner.''

"Of course." She allowed him to lead her out.

Mama rose to pull the bell rope, a signal for Mollie to come and clear away, saying over her shoulder, "We shall have dinner a little earlier, since Papa will not be with us. I suggest that you change now, girls."

Caroline trailed Pris out of the room, to find her sister had halted in the lower hall, watching Richard and Althea climb the stairs. His arm was protective about his wife's waist, and she leaned on him as if she were exhausted by the events of the afternoon. It was only when they heard the chamber door close behind the two of them, that Pris went forward and Caroline caught up with her.

"What do you think?" she began.

Pris gave a harsh laugh. "Papa has at last caught up with some of the gossip of this talkative town. The Major is a gambler. Perry has seen him at the upper chamber in the Ville Beaufort; they play quite high there. That was his difficulty in England—high stakes and women; 'bits of muslin' I believe they call them over there. He lives on hopes. There's an uncle well into his dotage; should the old man finally give up, Travis will come into a very nice estate, plus an income and a title. He is able to get credit on that, even over here among us provincials."

"Travis?" Caroline had caught one thing out of that speech. "But Pris, surely you do not know him—"

"Well enough to use his name? Why not, pray? Is it not true that we are hoydens, provincial misses, unfit to associate with those of the blue blood?" demanded Pris fiercely. "Vickers is amusing. He can make you forget—a lot of things."

"But you won't see him again? Not now?" Caroline pressed.

Pris smiled. "Dearest Carrie, I understand very well that

when Papa says 'no' in that tone of voice he is not to be gainsaid. I shall play the very dutiful daughter—to the end, I suppose.'' She suddenly looked tired, as if a number of years had dropped her all at once. ''Since this is to be my lot, I shall endeavor to make the very best of it. That is about all a female can do in this world.''

Caroline found Mollie waiting for her, hot water in the tall copper can, her dress of dark green—a two years' old pattern, but warm—ready for the wearing.

''That black man got his comeuppance,'' Mollie said, as she started to brush out Caroline's thick mane of hair. ''Sure, and I would think it would make him grate his teeth together, the way the doctor showed him the door. But never a bit of it! He marched out head as high in the air as ever. Him with murder on him—''

''Murder!'' Caroline stared. ''Mollie, you're letting your tongue run away with you! Major Vickers hasn't murdered anyone, and you know it.''

''Murder it was, as much as if he put one of those big pistols of his to her head and shot!'' Mollie retorted. ''Miss Barbara Wiley—she died this afternoon, and the doctor was there. She told him all before the good Lord eased her out of her sufferings. It was that black man who played a foul game with her. He had what he wanted, and when she learned that there was disgrace to come of it, he laughed and walked away, saying she was a silly girl to think that the likes of him would ever wed with the likes of her. Took to her bed because of his heartlessness, and then she wanted no more to live under the disgrace of it all. So it was her own death wishing which came to her.''

''But, Mollie, how do you know?'' Caroline stared at her own reflection in the mirror.

''Because Elsie, she was maid to Miss Barbara, told cook.

She was that upset upon such goings-on as there were. That old aunt who was supposed to be looking after Miss Barbara was as deaf as a post, and she takes sleeping drops of a night. Sleeps like a log she does, so the young lady might as well be all alone in the house. Then she had company—a good bit of it. Cook wanted to speak to Mrs. Warwick, but Elsie was afraid then, and when she got around to saying 'yes', it was too late—the mischief was well on. Elsie was afraid of the black man, too. He gets what he wants and then he goes. She locked her door of nights and set a chair under the latch she did, 'cause he looked at her good and long a couple of times. The major's kind—they think girls like Elsie belong to them, do they want to put out their hand and take 'em. A bad man he is, the devil's own kin.''

Caroline shivered. The more she learned of this wider world in which she was now expected to move, the less she liked it. She wished now she could travel back in time and be again the Caroline who was a little girl with a braid down her back, whose worries were all so much lighter and easier to bear.

''Does Mama know?''

''Why else did the doctor have her in with him? Though perhaps she didn't know it was the major. Miss Barbara, she wouldn't tell, as long as she kept her senses sharp. But come today when she was dying, then the doctor, he learned. Turned that major out quick and sharp he did. Maybe he'll even take it to the governor hisself, seeing as how this black one is his aide.''

Slowly Caroline shook her head. ''They don't think the same, not over in England where Lord Elgin came from I—I heard some officers talking, Mollie. They believe that we are all beneath them, that any marriage with one of us would be wrong. They said that was what the governor thought, too.''

''Maybe he'll find out that just isn't so over here.'' Mollie set in the last pins with care. ''Mr. Wiley is no poor man. He's important in the city here. When he comes home and learns what has happened, there may be a lot of trouble. And I would like to see that Lord Elgin or anyone else think he was better than Mr. Hannakar, now!''

Caroline found herself agreeing quickly to that. She could not imagine Corbie Hannakar being considered an inferior by those young sprigs of officers. Why, he was a grand gentleman, even if he had no title to wave about.

''I do wish he was here,'' she said wistfully. ''So many bad things are happening. Richard is always thinking about his work and Althea—which is right. But Pris, she needs someone. I think if Mr. Hannakar came back now she would go to him and be safe—really safe!''

Mollie had an odd look on her face, but it was gone so quickly that Caroline could not understand it. Still, the thought of Mr. Hannakar made her feel warm inside, and she longed to know that his sleigh was going to draw up in front, that she would see his fair head, hear his even voice, the very tone of which offered a feeling of security.

13

A dark cloud appeared to gather above the Warwicks, overhanging the high-ceilinged rooms on St. Gabriel Street, bringing a chill which was more than just wind-borne remnants of the winter. This was lightened on a morning when Caroline and Althea found small gilt-edged notes waiting them at the breakfast table. Caroline did not yet receive any shower of invitations such as that Pris idly leafed through. She tore hers open at once and then looked quickly to Mama.

"It is from Mr. Hannakar! He has returned and wants to drive Althea and me across to Laprairie tomorrow afternoon!"

Mama smiled before she glanced at Althea with a tiny wrinkle between her eyes.

"Do you feel that you can brave the chill, my child?" she asked. "Of course, Mr. Hannakar will do all that is possible to make you comfortable.

Althea turned to Richard, who nodded encouragingly, before she said, "I must confess that the idea of driving across a river is—is rather startling. But Richard has said it is safe and an outing much favored. Yes, I agree with what Caroline—" she smiled at the younger girl—"says now

196

with her eyes, if not her lips!''

Papa laughed, and Richard echoed him. "Yes, my dear," Papa beamed at Caroline, "you do possess a face as easy to read as an open book. I do not think that you could keep any secret when it meant much to you. Of course you must go. Hannakar is a most careful driver, and he would not even suggest such an expedition were there the least doubt of its safety.''

An open face? No secrets? Caroline felt warmth in her cheeks now. She must be very different from what Papa thought she was. She looked to Pris. If only Mr. Hannakar had asked Pris instead. Such an outing was what she needed. Though, Caroline had to admit, if the invitation had been laid at Pris' place she would have not been as singingly happy inside as she was now. Pris went on sipping her morning coffee and had not even looked up. It seemed as it had so often these past days, that her thoughts were very much occupied elsewhere.

The next morning Mama had an errand—a matching of silk for the new firescreen she was making. As Caroline left the house with Mollie, Pris was already bonneted and booted, saying that she was going to visit Addie Sims, who had a bad cold and had asked to borrow the new *Ladies Magazine*. Nor did she offer to walk part way with Caroline, but hurried off in the opposite direction. Caroline herself wasted no time, since she wanted to make sure she was safely back before Mr. Hannakar arrived.

Unfortunately, Miss Martin at the first shop did not have the right shade, but suggested that it might be found at Fargoine's. Caroline, impatient, hurried on, Mollie with her. It was when they turned the corner that they saw the sleigh with its high-stepping horses.

Pris—surely that was Pris! Even so well wrapped in the

furred robes, her muff held high to shield her face against the crisp air, Caroline was certain of her sister. There was an officer driving—

She stood still, Mollie bumping into her shoulder. Pris and Major Vickers! But that could not be true! Not after what Papa had said! Oh, why had she not herself told Pris all the sorry story Mollie knew? Now she turned to the maid, her eyes wide and frightened.

"It was Pris! Oh, Mollie, that was Pris. And with *him!*"

"She had a note she slipped into her pocket this morning," Mollie said slowly. "She's had other ones. One was hid in a magazine she borrowed from Miss Sims. She tore that up and burned it—all but the edge. That was in the ashes when I cleaned out the hearth yesterday."

"Oh, Mollie." Caroline twisted her mittened hands together inside her muff. "I've been so wrong. I should have told her what you told me. Only—only Pris hasn't let me talk to her. She keeps to herself all the time now."

"Miss Caroline, Miss Priscilla is one as will always go her own way. She would not listen even if you told her."

Caroline stamped a boot in the snow. "But she promised Papa! Do you think she has some kind of a fever, Mollie, that she does not know what she is doing?" That was a wild idea, of course; Pris had shown no signs of illness. But to do this!

"I can't tell anyone," Caroline continued unhappily. "Pris would never forgive me." If she told now, she would push Pris into deep trouble, perhaps make her sister even more reckless and uncaring.

If she could only ask Richard's help! But he was the very last one Pris would ever want to come to her aid, Caroline sensed that. Mr. Hannakar, then. Only that would mean telling things—perhaps even betraying what Caroline believed to be the very heart of Pris' unhappy secret. But she could do her best to suggest that Mr. Hannakar turn again to Pris with his invitations.

"Miss Caroline." Mollie plucked her sleeve. "We best get the errand done, or you will be late in getting back."

"Yes—yes, of course!" Caroline had to struggle to recall just what Mama had said once she was in the store, impatience rising in her as she took strands of thread close to the small-paned window to make sure that the match was exact.

They hurried back to the house. Caroline left the package on Mama's work table, and then went to Pris' room. Once inside, she stopped, her hands pressed to her face, looking around. There was perfect order, as if Jessie had been there recently to clear away, for Pris was not a tidy person. Caroline did not know exactly what she was looking for, but that there must be some reason for Pris' flagrant disobedience she was sure. There was only Pris' workbox, sitting a little askew on the table by the window, to catch her eye. Resolutely, hating what she was doing, but sure that she must, Caroline went to that. There were three trays. She lifted out the upper two. In the corner of the third, very much creased and recreased, was a paper that might be a pattern. Caroline smoothed it out.

Bold writing, no scrawl of pattern line. It took her a moment to understand:

"Dear girl, I am at your command, as always. Varennes—"

There was no signature, not even an initial. Varennes— the winter picnic—the empty house!

Caroline's breath seemed to catch in her throat. "No! Oh, no!" What had Pris been driven to?

There was a gentle tap at the door. Without thinking,

Caroline called, "Come in!"

Althea stood there. "Pris? Oh. Caroline. I heard some-one come in, and I thought it was Pris. Where is she? Still with Miss Sims? But she forgot the magazine."

Caroline was shaking, the note still in her hand. She looked at Althea, utterly at a loss.

"Is there something wrong?" The English girl's voice sharpened. She took a quick step and took the open note before Caroline could keep it from her.

"Oh, no!" she echoed Caroline's earlier protest. "This is Vickers' writing! Pris could not have—"

"I saw her, in a sleigh," Caroline answered. "What can we do? Somebody has to go after her." She looked at Althea; then, baldly, she told Richard's wife exactly what they had overheard the night of the ball.

"We're not good enough," she said bitterly. "Pris was not good enough to be your brother's wife! That's what your people think about us! I don't understand it. And Pris—they had no right to judge her so! She doesn't care any more, maybe. She was like that when she was little. If she was punished for something and she thought she was right, she would go and do something twice as wrong as that she had been accused of before. And the major—he's bad."

"Caroline," Althea's face had grown paler and paler. "This is an outrage! If I had only known— It is true that there are false standards back home. But this utter, callous snobbery—Yes, it is true, of some people. But not all of us, Caroline. Don't ever believe that. Pris would have made Alexander a very good wife. She has strength of character in some ways which he sadly lacks. If he had only come to me, we could have worked this out better. But to be so lost now, to all prudence—"

"Somebody has to go after her. She can't be left alone with him!"

"You are right. Richard—Perry—"

"We can reach neither of them. Papa is at the hospital. Mr. Hannakar—if we wait for him, it may be too late. Althea, I'll take Mollie and go in your sleigh if you'll give me permission to use it. When Mr. Hannakar comes, give him that note." She pointed to the creased paper Althea was holding. "Tell him where I've gone; ask him to follow."

"Your mother—" Althea began.

Caroline shook her head determinedly. "Mrs. Elvis is here with Mama. She is a very great gossip. If she suspected anything, it would be all over town before night. Don't tell Mama as long as she is here."

"You can drive?" Althea seemed to accept Caroline's decision as one made by an equal in understanding, age, and position.

"Of course!" Caroline was impatient; she already knew what must be done. Mollie was summoned and given orders for the coachman. Caroline knew that questions would arise, but in her present need and drive she swept them all before her.

On the road to Varennes, Caroline made herself give full attention to keeping Joby-boy to an even, ground-covering pace. Mollie had spoken only once after they had driven out of the Warwick stableyard.

"Miss Caroline, what are you going to do?"

At the moment she had not the least idea, beyond the fact that she and Mollie should be there; their presence would stop some of the gossip, if this disastrous outing ever came to the attention of such as Mrs. Elvis.

"Nothing, I suppose." Caroline frowned at the

churned snow of the road ahead. "Just to be there may be enough. I don't see why—"

Mollie shocked her then. "It is because of Lady Althea, really."

"What do you mean?" Caroline demanded sharply. "Lady Althea has nothing at all to do with this."

"She married Mr. Richard."

Those four words fell heavily. Caroline drew a deep breath. She had not been alone in her guess. Had Pris made her unhappiness so plain that even the servants knew?

"Please, Mollie, you must never say that again. Never!"

"Yes, Miss Caroline. Only you know it is true. Not being Mrs. Richard, when that was all Miss Priscilla wanted."

"No, Mollie. Pris was very young when Richard went away. She may have had some romantic dreams, but dreams aren't truth." Caroline was trying to reassure herself. Surely Pris would have grown out of her dreams of Richard, had she had time. But then had come Captain Carruthers and the terrible insult to her pride. Pris, in her usual fashion, had wanted to put on the brave, bold face, to prove to her world that she *was* desirable, that she could attract one of the catches of the season. Pris had needed that reassurance, whether in the end she would have gone through with the engagement or not. Caroline was not sure about that. But to be rejected a second time, and so harshly, for such an ignoble reason—yes, Pris could well turn as reckless as she had today.

"To Miss Priscilla, it *was* true," Mollie declared.

Caroline shook her head determinedly, but did not reply. Joby-boy took the road well, but the way ahead had deep and treacherous ruts. The sun on the snowy fields about them was brilliant, and the bells jingled merrily, in sharp contrast to Caroline's distress of mind.

What if she herself had been in love with someone—someone like Mr. Hannakar? And he had come back to greet her with a bride she knew nothing about? Of course, that was ridiculous. Mr. Hannakar was Pris' friend and always had been. He was a lot older.

But had Richard felt that way about Pris? That she was just a child, not a beautiful and willful young woman? It seemed now, as she strove to look back, that he had never really singled Pris out any in the old days.

Caroline was glad, though, that Mr. Hannakar would be coming after them. She had every confidence, both in Althea's ability to explain the situation, and in him. He could handle anything or anyone.

A house arose out of the snow not too far ahead. "That's where we came for the picnic. I don't know any place else they could have gone."

"If they came this way," Mollie doubted gloomily.

"We'll soon know." Caroline brought Joby-boy from the steady trot to a walk. "Yes, there's signs a sleigh turned in recently. So someone is here. You stay here." She pulled to a stop before the steps and handed the reins to Mollie. She had no wish to add to maid's knowledge if she could help it.

"Please—let me come!"

Caroline shook her head emphatically. "Somebody has to hold Joby-boy. Nothing will happen, Mollie."

Mollie looked completely unconvinced, but Caroline did not linger for any argument.

She knocked, waited. When there came no answer, she lifted the latch, which was free, and entered.

"Hello." Her voice came out in a lower tone than she

had intended.

The room was bare, but the fat stove was blazing hot and the air was warm. She loosened her cloak a little and stood wondering just what to do next. The door at the back of the room was ajar, and Caroline advanced towards it hesitantly. No one there, either. Then she had been wrong. Pris was not here, and she had been stupid and childish in coming to the rescue. Caroline stopped short. There had been a sound from behind the closed door on the right, from the room which had held the big table for their picnic feasting. Still, if someone *was* there, why had they not answered her?

Part of her wanted out of the silent house, into the cold freshness of the air. But another part—that sense of wrongness, of a need—possessed her more firmly. She crossed swiftly, before she could allow herself to think, and set her hand to the latch.

"Is there anyone here?" Then, before she could have any answer, she jerked the door open, fearing her courage might desert her.

There was more furniture here than she had noticed in her first visit. Against the wall was a wide sofa covered with a tumbled buffalo robe. Caroline stood stock still, her eyes widening in shock. This was a kind of ugliness she had not braced herself to meet.

Over Vickers' bare shoulder Priscilla's eyes, half-open, glittering oddly in a deeply flushed face, met hers. There was clothing strewn about the floor. Caroline stepped back and away, her hands going to her mouth to press tight against her lips, sealing as well as she could the awful waves of nausea which shook her.

She heard a man's voice swearing, and then her sister laughed.

"Only Carrie come snooping."

She caught the slurred words as she backed farther and farther, until she was out of the horrible room. Without realizing what she was doing, Caroline reached out a hand, caught wildly at the door and slammed it shut.

Pris—beautiful, quick-tempered Pris, whom she had always admired, looked up to, and lately pitied so! Pris lying there, her white body so bare against the dirty sofa and the smelly rug, her hair tousled, her mouth slack and her eyes so strange, as if she were drunk. Perhaps she was. Perhaps the major had gotten her drunk! Caroline beat one hand against another and looked about her wildly. This was some kind of nightmare. That could not be Pris in there with—allowing—no!

Still she was unable to take her eyes from the door. Her stomach heaved. Someone was moving in there. Caroline wanted to run, to get outside and away, but she was too shaken to move.

Like a small creature caught in a trap, she stood where she was, one shoulder braced against the wall, her hand rubbing weakly along it. She heard a laugh—a deep man's laugh.

Then the door she had slammed was flung open. Major Vickers stood there, his brown body bare to the waist, his breeches undone. He smiled at her slowly, in a way which made Caroline choke as she tried to keep from retching.

"Little sister spying," he said in his slow lazy voice. "Spies get more than they bargain for sometimes, little sister. Every girl needs a little loving. Some kissing wouldn't hurt you. Teach you better manners, maybe."

He came towards her like a big animal on the prowl, an animal very sure of himself. There was a kind of heat which seemed to envelop him, which made Caroline cower even farther, her hands both pressed now to the wall.

Once more he laughed. "A kiss will warm you up, little sister. You have to pay something for breaking into our fun."

He reached for her, and Caroline knew that for all her willing she could not move.

Then the front door was flung wide open as Mollie burst in, the whip from the sleigh in one hand. The lash snaked out, cutting across the major's shoulder and throat. He snarled in rage and turned on Mollie with an infuriated bellow. He grabbed at the whip and caught the lash, jerking it as the girl held fast, drawing her to him. Grabbing Mollie by the shoulder, he struck her an open-handed blow which sent her sprawling into the corner of the room.

Then he turned back to Caroline. That terrible paralysis which had kept her anchored to the wall had broken. The whip was now in her hands, and she faced him with her chin up.

"You brute! I warn you, I know how to use this."

He laughed. "What a battle maid! Don't be a silly chit. If you make it harder, it will be the worse for you."

Caroline used the lash. There was a chill in her now, but it did not freeze her into inaction. Instead, with the care of one about some very necessary task, she laid three red lines across the major's lower face, his throat, and his breast. He snarled and sprang at her, throwing her back against the wall, at the same time slamming his fist against her jaw. He gripped her arms tightly behind her and brought his wealed face brutally down to hers.

She heard, as if from a far distance, the crash of a door. Over the major's shoulder Corbie Hannakar's face seemed to arise, his eyes wide and so icily blue that they seemed like stones. Then Caroline crumpled forward, the pain of Vickers' blow sending her into red fog and darkness.

"Sure—she'll be all right, Mr. Hannakar. Miss Caroline, for the Glory of God, open your eyes. Speak to your Mollie! The beast—he didn't have time to really hurt you. Miss Caroline!"

Mollie's voice sounded thick, as if she were crying. Caroline tried to move her head, open her eyes. Her hair rasped against something rough. She did not like new pillow cases. Mama would let her have an old one if she asked.

"You see, Mr. Hannakar? She's coming to her senses again. Miss Caroline dear, it's Mollie a-holdin' of you, there's nothing to fear now at all."

"Take a sip of this, Caro," something cold and smooth was tight against her lips. There was such authority in that second voice that she did take a swallow. The fiery liquid made her sputter, and burned her throat as it went down. She opened her eyes, and the room spun so dizzily that she could not really see anything in it.

"Another, Caro."

Again she drank, but she did not try to open her eyes.

"I don't like the look of that bruise," said the voice which called her Caro. "She should have something on it —a hot cloth perhaps."

"Best get her home, Mr. Hannakar. If you try anything like that, she might freeze her cheek, with the way to go being what it is."

"You are quite right. I'll see that cad is drummed out of the army!" There was cold purpose in the second voice now. "There's another to think of, too."

"Please hurry, sir, she can't rest easy here."

"I'll take her out to the big sleigh. I think you can fit in there, and I'll have Barney drive back Richard's.''

There was chill air about Caroline. Then she was being settled in a nest of robes while Mollie moved in beside her, holding her in her arms against any jolt of the sleigh. Caroline felt less as though she was caught in a dream, but all at once a terrible tiredness closed in on her and she wanted only to lie still, in the warmth of Mollie's loving arms.

Once or twice she opened her eyes and saw white fields. But most were darker now—the sun was gone. Her head cleared a little, and she was beginning to remember. She stirred within Mollie's hold.

''Pris?'' she whispered.

''She's with us.'' Mollie's voice was as chill as the wind which blew about them. ''Mr. Hannakar is having Barney drive back our sleigh—she's in there, all right.''

''Pris could not—'' Caroline wanted to deny all that she had seen in that dirty room.

''Now don't you fret yourself, Miss Caroline. Mr. Hannakar is taking care of everything. He is doing a good job of it—beginning with the black man himself.''

Caroline nearly jerked out of Mollie's hold, a vivid flash of memory made horrible face come closer and closer, renewed the helplessness she had felt. ''He—''

''Miss Caroline, don't you be a-thinkin' of that man at all. Mr. Hannakar, he gave him such a hiding as you wouldn't believe. He'll be attended to. Mr. Hannakar promised that.''

Caroline sighed. ''Corbie always knows,'' she said softly. ''If Pris and Corbie—''

''Miss Caroline!'' Mollie leaned closer and spoke with such emphasis that the dizziness cleared from Caroline's mind for a few moments. ''T'weren't for any fine feeling for Miss Pris that Mr. Hannakar hammered that black man 'til he lost any sense he had left. Mr. Hannakar has the feeling for you. By the looks of it, he's carried it a good long time. And wasteful of time he has been in not making it plain to you sooner. That's a fine brave man, Miss Caroline, one as has his heart open, ready for you to walk right in. And if you have the good common sense you seem to own, you will do just that. Now take your rest. There will be another day and all will be well. You'll see.''

Only the day seemed to be postponed in coming. For Caroline did not wake to real knowledge of what was about her that evening, or the next day or the next. It seemed to her that she only wanted to sleep, but that her family would not let her rest. She was constantly being roused to drink some concoction, to have liquids spooned into her mouth. First she was so hot that she tried to push the covers away and find the good clean air; then she would shiver as if she lay on the snow-covered ground.

Always there were those dreams. She would walk to a door, knowing that something very dreadful waited behind, but that she must open it just the same. And, though she cried out and tried to get away, the door would open and out would come a huge black figure, while she could not run nor dodge, only stand screaming. Then from somewhere there would come a soft voice with a drawl, and she knew that the black thing would go—

'' 'Tis a wonder you are with her, Mr. Corbie, sir,'' she heard once, far away. ''She don't seem able to hear anyone but you when these bad fits come on her.''

''I am lucky I can help, Mollie.''

Finally there came a morning when she roused to find herself in her own bed, with everything familiar and right and as it had always been. Except that there was a vase of flowers on the table. Daffodils and paper-white narcissus catching and holding the sun. She felt empty and strange, but she did not hurt. She was happy just to lie and look at the flowers.

Mollie came between her and the table, a covered bowl on a tray with napkin and spoon. With an effort which she found surprising, Caroline raised her hand.

"Mollie?"

"Laws! You know me, Miss Caroline!"

Which was an odd thing for Mollie to say. Of course she knew Mollie! But she must be sick, she felt so queer and weak.

"I've been sick, haven't I?" She got out the words slowly.

"You've had the lung fever, Miss Caroline. But you're on the mend. Now you get some of this good broth (cook's made it special—chicken it is, and very strengthening) inside you and you'll feel a lot better."

The maid set down the tray, brought a soft damp cloth and wiped Caroline's face and hands, then proceeded to feed her, Caroline content at the service.

"That was good." She did feel stronger as the spoon scraped the bottom of the bowl. "Tell cook—it was good."

As Mollie arranged her pillows, Caroline kept her face turned towards the flowers.

"It isn't spring yet—no, it can't be. Where did the flowers come from, Mollie?"

Mollie beamed. "Mr. Corbie brought those yesterday. He grows them ahead of season in a warm house his gardener rigged up. Mighty cheerful they are, too, ain't they, Miss?"

"Bright as the sun," Caroline said drowsily.

She slipped again easily into sleep. But she awoke again when the sun had left the window and the flowers. Mama was sitting there, her face very worn and tired looking, her eyes were closed as if she had fallen into a nap. Caroline's memory began to stir, though she tried to fight it. There was something Mama mustn't know. Pris! Where was Pris?

She struggled to pull up higher on the pillows. What had happened to Pris? That nightmare—it had been all true. And Pris had been caught in it. Was she sick, too?

Caroline must have made a sound, for with a rustle of skirts Mama was quickly beside her.

"Caroline, my dear, what is it?" Her hands were very soft and comforting as she settled her daughter back on her pillows.

"Pris?" Caroline had tried to ask a question, but the name alone came out as a wail.

Her mother's tired face showed a shadow. "Priscilla is not here, dear. She has gone to Boston to visit with Aunt Leah. Auntie has long wanted her to come, you know."

"She—she's all right?"

"Yes, dear. Aunt Leah has always loved Priscilla very much; she is glad to have her there with her. You must not worry. Everything is all right now."

There was such certainty in Mama's voice that Caroline gave a sigh, letting go that feeling which she knew had been so long a burden—that in some way she must watch over Pris, make sure that her sister was happy, or at least safe.

She would not ask Mama any questions. Maybe Mama did not even know what happened out at Varennes. Unless Mollie—or Pris—or Corbie had talked. Corbie. As Mama said something about ordering tea, Caroline lay back on her pillows comfortably and thought slowly and carefully about Corbie Hannakar.

It was a new way of thinking and she found that she must explore it carefully, even as she would explore a path she had never traveled before. Corbie's face—she lifted her hand before her, and her fingers moved as if to sketch the lines of that face. It was as plain to her now as the memory of her own. Corbie's face—his bright eyes which looked lazy and then could come so fiercely alive. Corbie, whose flowers sat by the window; who had come to rescue her; who was so kind—kinder even than Richard.

She drew out of her memory the words Mollie had said in the sleigh. Though she couldn't remember much else, she could remember those.

Corbie loved her!

It was so new and so strange an idea that Caroline had to turn it over and over in her mind. But there was a warmth in her every time she thought it. She was so young, so childish, and yet Corbie apparently did not think so. Corbie.

With his face very bright and vivid in her mind, she went to sleep again, this time with a smile on the small face from which the bruises were fading away. Corbie loved her.

14

Caroline, who had never cared much for staying in bed, found that time slipped away very fast now. She slept, awoke, saw Mama or Mollie, or sometimes Papa, exchanged a few words with them and then was content to close her eyes and drift. Nothing seemed to matter too much. After a day or so, she did not even try any longer to think. Once Mollie brought up Boots who ran across the bed to sniff at her cheek, patted her with his paw, and then leaped down and went to the window to sit in a weak shaft of sunlight. Caroline smiled at him sleepily, but Boots was part of another life which had somehow slipped away into a past.

Mama's face appeared to grow thinner; she was often there in the chair now when Caroline aroused. Mollie kept bringing bowls of things she said cook made especially. But Caroline never seemed very hungry now. It was easier just to lie quiet, and she wished dimly that they would leave her alone.

Althea came one day to stand beside the bed. She looked very tired, too, and her skin seemed white and pale. She moved slowly and carefully and held her shawl tightly about her as if she were cold, though the room was warm.

Caroline summoned up strength enough to say, "Althea?"

The other girl smiled. "Oh, my dear!"

Althea reached out and touched Caroline's cheek with her fingertips.

"Do you suppose," Althea asked a moment later, "that if Mollie brought you some good chicken soup you could eat it? Aren't you hungry, dear?"

Caroline found it a vast effort to smile. "So tired." Her words seemed to trail away of themselves.

"Yes. But you need strength, Caroline. Please try."

Caroline was not quite sure how it happened, but Mollie was there handing a bowl and a spoon to Althea and lifting Caroline a little, setting a cushion at her back. Caroline closed her eyes. To be lifted made her dizzy.

"No," she whispered.

"Yes!" There was such a sharp note in Althea's voice that surprise broke through the half sleep which enfolded Caroline. "Now." It was Althea who held the spoon, dipped it into the bowl, and brought it to Caroline's lips. Caroline swallowed.

The only way to slip back into that pleasant and forgetful place was to do as they wished, so that they would let her alone the sooner.

Yet she was not allowed to slip back so now for any length of time. Sometimes there was lamplight in a shadowed room, sometimes the sun, but *they* were always there with food, demanding efforts she strove to avoid.

Caroline ate and drank only because they kept urging her. For the rest, she only wanted to sleep. There were no more nightmares. She just sank into a soft deep sea of grey, disturbed only by a vague stir of thought now and then which something within her pushed away quickly.

Corbie. Even with her eyes shut, she frowned and turned her head from side to side. She did not want memory now. Just sleep.

"I do not like it! This languor is certainly not natural," a voice said.

Caroline did not open her eyes. If they thought she was still asleep, they might let her be.

"A profound shock, sir, coupled with serious illness—"

"Yes, I have had Howards in, and he says time will heal —but I do not know. She does not respond as she did at first. It is as if the Caroline we have always known has gone, leaving a stranger in her place. There are some ills which appear to be of the spirit."

"Hannakar? He seemed to be the only one who could deal with her during those bouts of raving fear."

"She has not asked for him. Though his coming might be a good experiment. Certainly he is at hand; the man haunts the house. Yes, let Althea prepare her; then we shall try what you have suggested, Richard. If I could get my hands on that—that son of the devil!"

"Something we could all like, sir!"

The words slipped in and out of the soft fog which made up Caroline's new world. She let them go and did not try to understand. During one of the lamplit times someone sought her hand under the safe covering of the bed and pressed it, calling softly; "Caroline? Caroline, dear?"

Reluctantly Caroline opened her eyes. Althea, her lovely pale hair becoming a part of the radiance, leaned close, a glass in her hand. Caroline tried to turn her head away, but Althea slipped her arm behind the younger girl's shoulders to raise her head.

"Drink it, dear. There is some one here to see you."

The hot liquid was choking in her throat, making her

cough. She had tasted such before. There was a break in
the fog for a moment, and a dark and threatening shadow
wavered before her. Then there was a face there—blue
eyes, fair hair—

"Caroline!"

"No!" The hair was not fair at all, it was black. A black
man! She tried to pull herself back, away from that
threatening figure. Her hand flailed free of the covers,
beating away what was reaching for her. "No! Make him
go! Oh, please, God, make him go!" Her voice rang high
in a thin shriek. The black figure wavered, became partly
another. But she knew that that was only a trick. He was
here—he was going to put his hands on her, kiss her—he
was horror incarnate!

"Caroline!" Althea's voice was sharp and commanding.
"This is Corbie, not—not that other!"

Caroline caught feverishly at Althea. "No! Don't let
him come! Please. Please—"

The face vanished from the circle of lamplight, but
Caroline's hold on Althea dug nails into the other's flesh.

"It's all right, dear. There is no one here now. Truly."

"He won't come back?" Caroline huddled into her
pillows as Althea eased her down. "Promise—he won't
come back? Papa—Richard—they won't let him come? He
—he and Pris—"

All she had tried to push away, all she had forgotten in
that wonderful restful grey place came flooding back. She
rocked her body from side to side, her hands covering her
face now, afraid that if she looked beyond her fingers she
might see that face which was so horrible, which could be
one and then split into two, and which she dare not look
upon again.

Oddly enough, the return of that terrible fear did shake

her out of her hiding place. She could no longer hope to rest there; instead, she came back hour by hour, day by day, into the real world. Mama came, and Papa and Richard, and once Dr. Howards, who patted her hand and told her briskly that she was doing fine and would soon be up and around. Mollie always seemed to hover just out of sight, but was there at once when Caroline needed her, and Althea often spent an hour or so beside the window, sewing with beautiful even stitches on small very white things.

Then one day Caroline became really restless and demanded her own sewing box. She wanted to try her hand at frilling lace about the edge of a petticoat which seemed hardly large enough to fit the big doll which had been the pride of her nursery years.

It was difficult, she discovered, to make the needle go just where she wanted it to, but she kept doggedly at work until she finished the frill, at the end of several well-spaced hours of diligent labor. Mama and Althea both praised her work, though she knew that she could do better.

Then she, herself, was able to sit up in the chair by the window, well wrapped in shawls and blankets, looking out through a pane which was no longer fretted by frost. There were rivers of slush below, and those who ventured out were well soaked before they had gone a few feet.

Mama sometimes read aloud from the *Ladies Magazine*, and Althea contributed a pleasant book she had brought from overseas. It made them laugh. It was called *Northanger Abbey*; the young heroine had her mind so full of impossible tales about haunted castles and the like that she kept looking for them in the regular world. Mama did not as a rule believe that novels were good reading, but she was so pleased with the story that she had Papa order

the other books by the same author—for Althea said Miss
Austen had written more. It was a quiet time, but Caroline, who had always been so active a person, was very willing that her days would continue so. This was not the grey
world, but it was indeed a safe one.

She obediently drank unpleasant-tasting tonics which
Papa and Richard ordered her to down, and she ate all that
was on the trays Mollie brought up. From wearing her
wrapper under her shawls, she came at last to putting on a
dress and shoes. But she shrank inwardly from leaving her
room, just as she had tried not to leave the grey land.

Sometimes she thought of Pris, but she never asked
about her. To do that, some inner part of Caroline
warned, was to open doors she wanted to remain closed
forever. Perry dropped in at times, but stood by the door
as if he found her company uncomfortable, usually asking
awkwardly if there was anything he could do for her, or
how she felt, and then going quickly.

The promise of spring outside the window did not last;
there was more snow and cold. Caroline, however, was at
last persuaded to venture downstairs, Papa going with her
step by step when she insisted that she was *not* going to be
carried. Once outside her room, some of her old inde-
pendence came trickling back. She had visitors. Several of
Mama's friends dropped in for tea, and one or two
brought their daughters. But it began to appear to
Caroline that their conversation was very dull, and that
some stared at her as if there was something strange about
her.

The only change she had noticed was that while she had
been so ill she seemed to have grown several inches taller.
Mama had to have Miss Riddle in for alterations to her
wardrobe. They talked also of summer clothes, and the

pattern books were passed around and consulted.

Caroline became quite animated when she thought of
the farm and talked of it longingly, trying to make Althea
understand how pleasant Fairlea was. She found herself
sitting with her sewing on her lap, her fingers idle, day-
dreaming about the wide meadows under the sun—the
lambs and the calves and perhaps a new foal or two. Her
stories of Fairlea led Althea to speak more and more of her
own childhood and how, in spite of the rules and regula-
tions of governesses and Old Nurse, she and her brother
Ronald had often gone exploring at their father's English
seat (which, alas, had been swept away by the Earl's losses
at the gaming tables) and also in wilder Scotland, where
the cottagers would give them oatcake and cheese and
Ronald learned to tickle, poacher fashion, for fish. Though
Althea admitted freely that that was one sport she had had
no wish to rival her brother in.

She brought down Ronald's sketchbook and the small
handful of his letters from India and shared them with
Caroline, who loved the new world they opened for her.
She asked Papa to bring home books on that far land so
they could learn more about it.

Very little news from the outside world seemed to pene-
trate this constrained existence. Then, in April, a letter
arrived that broke open the shell of security Caroline had
so long clung to. The mail had been very erratic because of
the bad weather, and thus quite a postbag full had come
all at once—three letters for Althea from England and two
for Mama and Papa from Boston. They were spilled out on
the hall table, covering quite an expanse. Caroline,
coming down the stairs, stopped short when she saw the
writing on one. There was no mistaking Pris' flourishes. It
was addressed to Mama. At that moment, that sleeping

Caroline awakened a fraction more. Why had she not heard from Pris during all the weeks of her illness?

It was true that Pris had left for Boston almost immediately upon their return from the terrible events at Varennes, Richard acting as her escort, since he was deeply interested in some experiments progressing there with his new sleep-against-pain gas. Caroline had for so long been uncaring—but surely it was odd that Pris had not even dropped her a note. Or so it now appeared. She stood frowning, her fingertip on the letter, as Mama came down the hall from a conference with cook, for they were planning a small festive dinner to celebrate Papa's coming birthday.

"A letter from Pris, Mama." Caroline pushed the square a little to one side. With a troubled look she glanced up. "Mama." It was hard somehow to find the words, and she had to force herself to go on. "Was—was Pris all right when she left? Has she been sick, too?"

Mama whisked the letter into the pocket of her finely embroidered silk morning apron. "Priscilla was perfectly well when she left. She has been enjoying Boston with Aunt Leah. It seems that she does not find much time for writing these days. Ah, here is one from Leah, too!" She took up the second letter with the American stamp. "My dear, Althea has three letters, I see. Would you be so kind as to take them up to her? She might like to read them before she comes down this morning."

Althea had been spending more and more of her mornings resting. She wore looser wrappers, looking paler than Caroline liked to see, but was in good spirits. Richard was to make a second trip to Boston at the end of the month, and while he was gone, the house would be largely turned over to workmen for repainting and papering,

ending with the annual earthquake of spring cleaning—an
occasion from which all male members of the family fled as
far as they could.

Caroline took the letters and went upstairs to be greeted
by Althea and shown a sample of satin-like wall covering,
of the same pale blue Althea always favored, garlanded by
clusters of white rosebuds and trailing green vines.
Caroline agreed that it was a perfect choice for their
bedroom. She wondered anew whether Althea would
always be content to share the Warwick house. Of course,
there was plenty of room, and she had fitted so well into
the family that it would be hard if she and Richard chose
to set up their own establishment. They would not do it
anyway, Caroline supposed, until after the baby came.

She left the letters and went into her own room. A vase
of green-veined marble still stood on the table by the
window. There were no spring flowers in it now; there had
not been for a very long time. Caroline ran her finger
down its smooth side. To have flowers in winter was such a
luxury. Madam Hannakar must enjoy such pleasure all
year around. Caroline remembered the day they had spent
at Ste. Catherine's. The puppy must be quite well grown
now. But of course it would be happier by far in the
country. She was glad that it had not come, after all. So
much had changed since she had held it close in that
stable.

Corbie Hannakar knew everything; he must. Of course,
he would not want to be associated with the Warwicks
now. Nor did she want to see him again. He seemed
someone she had read about in one of the magazine tales
—brave, handsome, good, but not of this life at all. Whatever Mollie had told her in the sleigh (if there had been
any truth in it; Mollie could well have imagined it all), it

had come to an end. And she was glad, she did not want to remember.

"Miss Caroline! Oh, Miss Caroline!"

The door had been thrown open without any warning knock. Jessie stood there, both hands twisting her apron, her eyes wide and frightened.

"It's the Missus, Miss Caroline. She went all faint like! She's taken sick!"

Caroline sped across the room. "Where is she?"

"In her sitting room. She's bad taken. James has gone for the doctor."

Caroline ran down the hall. The door was open and, as she came in, she saw her mother leaning back white and limp on the small sofa, her eyes closed, and one of her hands pressed to her breast as if she were in pain.

"Mama!" Caroline was at her side, catching at the other hand hanging so limp. It was cold, and for one terrible moment she was afraid that Mama was dead. Only, at her cry, Mrs. Warwick's head turned a fraction and her eyes opened a little. She did not seem to be aware of Caroline's presence at all.

"Jessie, help me!" the girl commanded. Together they lifted Mama's feet up on the sofa, pulled over her the heavy shawl Mama always kept there. "Now—bring brandy at once! And—" Caroline tried to remember. Yes. "Then tell Cook tea with a lot of sugar—or honey. Hurry!"

Jessie, sniffling, went, while Caroline drew up a hassock and sat down close to her mother, holding that free hand between her own and trying to warm it. "Mama!" she repeated.

Mrs. Warwick made a small sound but no recognizable word. Then Jessie was back, the tray shaking in her hands so that a glass clinked against the decanter. Caroline had to pour the brandy herself. She got the glass to her mother's lips, which looked oddly grey, even as her face had taken on the same shade.

Some of the liquid dribbled down on Mama's lace collar, but Caroline managed to get her to swallow near all she had poured. Mama coughed and then opened her eyes widely.

"Caroline?"

"Yes, Mama. James has gone for Papa. He will be here and then you will feel better."

Mama's other hand came away from her breast. She reached out and caught Caroline's arm, and there was surely fear in her eyes.

"Letter—letter!" Her head fell back against the pillow Caroline had hastily put behind her, and, from beneath closed eyelids, tears began to run down her plump cheeks.

Letter? Caroline looked around and saw a piece of paper next to her which might well have been crumpled in a moment of shock. It was clearly Aunt Leah's handwriting. The girl smoothed the page out to read. Aunt Leah was given to crossing in her writing, and any letter from her was a puzzle. Also, this one had been so creased that she had the greatest difficulty in making out the words. The girl had only deciphered perhaps half the page when her own shock set her hands to shaking.

"Caroline? What has happened?"

She looked up. Althea stood in the doorway, holding her fleecy wrapper about her.

"Pris," Caroline answered dazedly. "Pris has gone— gone off. Aunt Leah does not know where. It is so hard to read her writing, and she must have been distraught when she wrote. But Pris—where could she go?"

Jessie returned, this time with a brimming cup of

steaming tea. Cramming the letter into the pocket of her skirt, Caroline carefully steadied her mother as she got her to sip. Color was banishing that frightening gray in Mama's face. She looked at Caroline now as if she really saw and knew her.

"Just some hot tea, Mama," Caroline encouraged and was pleased when, after a sip or two, Mama reached out to take the cup herself and drink it slowly.

"That will do, Jessie," Caroline said quite firmly. "If you will wait for Doctor Warwick below and send him up as soon as he comes. And thank you."

Althea closed the door behind the maid, and Caroline said, as soon as Jessie was gone, "I have the letter, Mama. It is in my pocket."

Mama nodded. She finished the tea, her eyes lowered to the cup. Caroline was doubly shaken, for never in her life had she seen Mama lose command in this fashion. It was as if one of the secure supports of the world had been snatched completely away.

"There was a second letter. I had not opened that," Mama said slowly. Her voice was low, very shaken, as if she could hardly find the words she needed. She pushed at the shawl Caroline had thrown over her. "Must find it."

"Yes, Mama," Caroline had already sighted a corner of pale yellow paper which had half slid under the settee. She stooped to snatch it up. Pris' writing ran across it. "Do you want me to open it?"

For a long moment she thought that Mama was going to say no. Then, instead, she was answered by a weak gesture. The tough paper was hard to worry open, but she had it free at last.

"Read it," Mama said.

Pris had not crossed her sheet, and there was only half a page in her small, rather cramped writing:

Dear Mama:

When this reaches you, you will doubtless also already know that I have made my choice. Though in truth I *had* no choice. When Corbie Hannakar and Richard took a hand in my affairs they forced this on me. I will marry Vickers. He has of course been hounded out of his profession by Corbie. But luckily his position at home has bettered and he need no longer depend upon the army. Since this is so he has come to me with an offer which I have no other recourse now than to accept. I know that this step on my part may anger you and Papa greatly. But you know that it is true that I have lost all reputation I had in Montreal. When I received Agatha's letter three weeks ago this was made plain to me, even though, in your kindness, you did not tell me that gossip had so spread.

I am truly sorry that I have brought you such trouble and it is better that you forget me. Major Vickers tells me that we shall deal very well together, and perhaps we shall. Lord Elgin threatened to cashier him, but his resignation and our marriage shall silence tongues in England, even if the story reaches there, and so he is in no danger of losing the favor of his uncle, who is now said to be on his deathbed.

Do not try to find me now—if things go as he believes that they shall, then I may perhaps ask your full forgiveness and you may find it in your heart to grant me that.

I will not sign myself your daughter for perhaps you do not acknowledge me as that now.

                                              Priscilla

Mama raised herself up a little farther on the pillow. She took the letter from Caroline, but it was towards Althea that she looked.

"I knew that Mr. Hannakar had gone to the governor, and that Major Vickers had suddenly resigned and left." Her voice grew stronger as she talked. "But what is this other matter about Vickers' uncle?"

"I heard from Alexander that Major Vickers is heir to his uncle's title, and there is a small estate. But any money must come by favor alone. He left England because of some highly scandalous affair which was hushed up, not for his benefit, but for that of the lady involved. I believe then that he was given a warning to conduct himself more discreetly, unless he wished to lose the money he so desires and needs. He has many debts. A second scandal over here would ruin him, were it reported at home. It may well be that he has decided to return home a married man, so that the gossip will die down."

"But," Mama interrupted, "you cannot believe that this—this marriage comes from anything but expediency on his part and fear on Pris'? Agatha's letter—I do not know what she means by that. If Agatha has been listening to, or recounting gossip, if her interference in any way has brought about this dreadful decision on Pris' part—" Mama sat up fully now. Her tone was grimmer than Caroline had ever heard, and her mouth was a straight line. "We must of course discover where they have gone. I do not think that they can have sailed as yet—the season is still too bad. Richard—and Doctor Warwick himself, if necessary—must go to Boston. Perhaps by that time Leah will have had more information." She brushed her hand impatiently across her check, wiping away the tears she had earlier shed. "In the meantime, I have had a fainting spell as far as the rest of the household is concerned. Doctor must know, and Richard and Perry, if he comes home." There was an impatient note in her voice as she mentioned

her younger son. "We must have a reckoning with
Agatha. What has she heard, or said, or added to? About
the marriage, we shall say nothing until it has been proven
to have taken place."

Althea leaned forward. "If you wish, Mama Warwick, I
can make some discreet inquiries of relatives and friends at
home. I *shall* indeed be discreet, I assure you. But it will
be some time before we know anything."

"That would be kind; I shall see what the doctor has to
say about it. For the time being, we shall endeavor to go
on as always. Though with Agatha in this matter, who
knows what rumors are not already making the rounds?"
She shook her head slowly. "It is a sorry tangle. I wonder
in what way my management of Pris has been so wrong
that she would be caught up in this sinful ugliness. Please,
girls, leave me alone a little now. I need to steady my spirit
before I break this news to the doctor. He is a very proud
man, and to have this dishonor strike at the very roots of
his family will be a harsh blow!"

Caroline arose reluctantly. "You'll be all right,
Mama?"

It was painful to see the faint smile which Mama
struggled to shape.

"Not all right in all ways, Caroline, dear. But I am in
full command of myself again. We must be prepared to
uphold and sustain each other through the days to come.
You have already shown that you can be trusted. And dear
Althea is a true blessing to our family, one for which I
thank the Heavenly Father every night. You need not
worry about me."

But Caroline still lingered outside the door. She could
not forget how dreadful Mama had looked when Jessie had
summoned her.

Althea took her arm. "She is a strong, proud woman, dear, one who is used to bearing burdens. Now she will try not only to bear her own, but to help your father. We can only stand by and be ready if she needs us; the time may well come when she shall."

Caroline felt the beginning smart of tears in her own eyes. "He is such a dreadful man, Althea. How can Pris go with him? It is as if she is another person, one I never knew at all!"

"Don't judge her, dear. Not now. Never, perhaps—unless you know all that lies behind this action of hers. She may have had some motive which we do not know."

"Aggie and her gossip!" flared Caroline. For the first time in months she felt the rise of real rage. "Whatever Aggie wrote her, it must have been awful. I hope Papa can make Aggie understand, once and for all, how wicked the things she says sometimes are!" She hesitated for a moment and then asked, "Did Corbie—Mr. Hannakar—really force Major Vickers to resign?"

"He went to Lord Elgin, and, I gather, told the governor a few home truths. There had been another incident involving the major earlier, and Mr. Hannakar's position here is such that even Lord Elgin must listen to him. Richard did not tell me all, but Mr. Hannakar saw that Major Vickers was out of Montreal very quickly and with as little gossip as was possible. He was very, very angry. I think he might have killed the major had he not had such control of his temper."

"I see," Caroline said. The anger she had felt towards Agatha seemed to have cleared her thoughts in another way. No, she did not want to see Corbie Hannakar again. In a queer way, she felt both frightened and ashamed, almost as if she had been in Pris' place when Corbie had found her. She never wanted any man to touch her again as the major had—never again. Nor did she want to think of Corbie Hannakar except as a kind, but distant friend —always a distant one now.

15

Richard and Papa did go to Boston, even though the weather and the concerns of their practice were against such journeying. There had been a stormy interview with Agatha and Archie, Caroline learned, though she did not learn what was said. She, herself, grew increasingly restless, no longer contented to sit quietly with Mama and Althea, busy with her needle or reading aloud. She ventured out to the stables to see the horses, to listen to Henry talk knowingly of treatment for a strain or the proper concoction of mash for a horse of finicky appetite.

Once more she took up her ledger of treatment for the animals she had taken in and even began reading here and there in Richard's books.

Perry seemed as restless as she. He spent fewer evenings at home with Papa away, and Mama hardly appeared to notice that he was gone, accepting his hurried excuses without comment.

Two or three days after Papa had left, Mama came to a decision as how best to occupy them all. Perhaps it was her way of helping herself by keeping hands briskly busy. There were consultations with painters and handymen. Then came a vast cleaning of closets, and all the linen was ruthlessly examined. The resulting pile needing careful darning or mending was nearly mountain high. Caroline fetched and carried, stood on stools to see upper shelves where carefully wrapped packages of material, long-unused china, and the like, were stored. All were to be brought down now, washed, and then repacked.

She found that being tired was an excellent sleeping tonic, and also found that working so with Mama was a new experience. There was a constant flow of stories as Mama recalled this or that about each new discovery.

Down from the attic came the old carved cradle which held all the Warwicks in turn for two generations or more. Under Mama's direction, it was polished until it was mirror bright. Then she herself set about furnishing it with new pillows, cover and soft inner bedding. Their days were suddenly very full indeed. The house began, room by room, to take on a new appearance as the workmen, having covered all that could not be moved with sheets, went on spreading paint and putting up paper.

Althea moved into Pris' room temporarily while her chosen blue paper was set across the walls, quite lightening the room. Then Caroline took Richard's old chamber while her own walls also sprouted a new garden of flowers —daisies and small yellow blossoms which reminded her now and then of daffodils. There were fresh curtains to be hemmed, pressed, and hung. A coverlet, which Mama found in one of the top shelves, was most carefully washed. Its quilted wreath of puffy flowers matched the paper even though they were in that cream white that time had brought to the material.

There were very few visitors, as though the Warwick House lay far in the country instead of standing in the heart of the city. As the weather grew better, Mama insisted that Althea and Caroline drive out in the afternoons at least twice a week for the air. By unspoken consent, the girls chose to head away from the fashionable streets where such airings were common, in favor of the country. There the hedges were turning slowly green with a haze of small buds, and patches of violets and "spring beauties" could be sighted.

Often Caroline would alight and gather flowers, to bring back her sweet-scented spoil to Althea. Only occasionally, she began to note, did the English girl attempt to join her. Being shaken farther and farther out of her own self-concern, she wondered about Althea's continued air of listlessness, though she felt she could not pressure her companion to try more.

The apple trees were in bloom one day when Caroline signaled James to draw up the carriage.

"It is like Fairlea," she cried. "Oh, Althea, perhaps Mama would let us go out there for a little while. It would be so wonderful!"

This afternoon there was a delicate flush of color on Althea's face. For the first time she looked about her eagerly.

"That would be good," she said softly. She drew a deep breath. "The smell of the paint does cling so."

"I'll ask. If Papa and Richard are gone much longer— And the house is smelly, that is true." She looked longingly at the apple trees. "Oh, I do hope Mama says yes!"

Mama did, in spite of Caroline's fear that her willing hands, as well as Althea's assistance, would continue to be needed.

So two days later they were off, Mollie sitting with the coachman and guarding the most fragile of their belongings in a bandbox on her lap. Caroline felt a surge of pure

joy as they left the city behind. The last time she had been
this way—she frowned a little—was the day Corbie
Hannakar had driven them to visit Madam. She pushed
aside the memory of that rather stiff little note she had
written to Madam two weeks ago—copying it three times
over to make sure that it was the very best she could do—
refusing another visit to Ste. Catherine's. Corbie Hannakar was not in Montreal, Perry had said, having headed
west for another lengthy visit to the trading posts. It might
be six months or more before he would return. Even
though she would not have had to meet Corbie, she felt
the same queer shyness about Madam. Had Corbie told
her the whole story? Caroline did not want to know nor
guess. It was better that things remained as they were.

Their stay at Fairlea was all Caroline had hoped it would
be. She could be out from sunrise nearly to sunset, following the baliff around, helping with the newly born lambs,
calves, and three frisky foals. Althea put off some of her
languor also. Caroline found her in the garden on their
second day, sitting on an upturned cask, energetically
pulling dead leaves away to give breathing room to the be-
ginning-to-show spears of lilies. There was a streak of mud
across one cheek and she was completely intent on what
she was doing, demanding quite sharply of Caroline where
she could find those small tools which the proficient
gardener needed.

The days passed, and both of the girls found them
good. Caroline took her turn at the dairy churn and Althea
sampled, for the first time, biscuits hot from the oven
served with a saucer of this season's maple syrup. Althea
was beginning to draw plans for expanding the garden,
saying with satisfaction that she had never before been
allowed to do *just* what she wanted with any piece of

ground, that the gardeners at home had been so jealous of
their blooms and their duties that one had had to apolo-
gize if one brushed against a leaf!

She was out on her favorite perch—the cask—her head
bare and her sleeves well rolled up, urging Caroline to be
sure she had brought out all the bulbs that had been
bagged away, when they were interrupted by a newcomer.
A moment later Althea was on her feet and had flung herself into his arms with an exuberance Caroline had never
seen before.

"Richard!"

"In person."

Caroline whisked away quickly, a small lost feeling
suddenly darkening the day a little. Althea and Richard—
to see them so. It was right and good and not— She found
herself shivering as she hurried blindly past the lilac
hedge. Everything was good for them. While for Pris—
what had Richard found out about Pris? She came to a
stop, the knuckles of her right hand pressed against her
teeth. It was an old childish gesture of hers when she was
troubled but determined not to let the world know her
difficulties.

She lifted her face to the wind, which was warm, touching her skin with delicate fingers. There was a warm wind
that came in the northwest; they called it by some strange
name, "chinook" or the like. In a night it could strip ice
and snow from the land and leave it ready for spring.
What was it like out there where the traders' posts were set
far apart? Then there was the rendezvous to which the
trappers and the Indians brought the results of their
winter's work, and it was all like a great fair. She remembered that two years ago, after Corbie Hannakar had come
home, he told them all about it one evening, and it had

sounded so exciting. He had even brought them some souvenirs—a pair of fringed and quilled moccasins for her, and a pocket-like bag or purse for Pris. The moccasins had been too large, she had put them away. But if she could wear them now, it would feel good to have her feet so close to the ground. Caroline wished she could reach across the miles and pluck them out of her bureau drawer.

Corbie must be at the rendezvous this year. She had never seen him in his western clothing. He must look very different—the bright red shirt which most of the trappers wore for festive occasions, a sash with its dangling ends hanging over fringed, hide breeches, moccasins instead of well-polished shoes or boots. No one could take him for an Indian—not with that hair which sun would turn nearly white by the end of the summer, and his very blue eyes. Somehow she could see that strange and different Corbie laughing, going from campfire to campfire to talk with trappers and with Indians, to listen to the tales of the far country. Perhaps he might even stay the full year. He had spoken once of wanting to head on into the mountains, and go even to the Pacific coast, about which there was not too much known. He had the whole world to see if he wanted to.

Caroline leaned her arms on the top rail of the fence. The foals were frisking about their placidly grazing mothers, playing a kick-and-run game of their own, but the girl was not watching them. There would be wrestling matches at the rendezvous, and shooting matches—yes, and fights, too, she suspected. They would race the smaller western horses and trade. It would be wild and wonderful, but it was very far away and no part of the life that was for Caroline Warwick. Though why could not a woman travel west; if she were married and her husband had affairs which took him there? Ladies went to Boston, New York, to England and the continent. But there were the settlers who moved west—their wives went with them.

"Miss Caroline," Mollie's voice shook her out of that world of otherwhere. "Miss Caroline, to be seeing what Mr. Richard has brought to me—a letter!" She waved a dingy square of paper in the air. "Oh, I'm fearing that the news, it may be that bad." As she spoke, her words became more and more laced with the brogue of her homeland. She had been trying hard to lose it, since she thought it not the right speech for one of the doctor's own household. "They have a hard time there, it is said now, what with the potatoes rottin' in the ground before they can be dug and all goin' hungry to bed at night, risin' with empty bellies again in the morn." She turned the letter around and around in her hands, her face one of open distress. "Please, will you be kind as to read it, Miss Caroline? I've been a-learnin' m' letters and printin'. I can read a little —but writin', now, that is somethin' else. An', Oh, pray the good Lord and His Holy Mother, it is well with them."

Tears had begun to spill from her eyes. Caroline quickly took the letter, opening the coarse paper carefully lest it tear. She saw spidery handwriting, crossed to save space.

Dear Mollie:
    I write this at the request of your loving father and mother. It is hoped that you are in good health. Your father and mother wish me to tell you that they are taking ship for Canada this coming summer. Food is very scarce here and so many of our folk must seek new homes overseas. You have a new sister since you left, but alas your dear brother William has been taken home by God's mercy. Your family will come as soon as they can obtain passage. They will

seek you out upon their arrival and they wish you to
know that they pray for you ever and ask God to
keep you safe from all harm.

I also have you in my prayers, dear child,

Father Joseph

"M'father an' mother, Bridgie, and Betty, and Rory—"
Mollie's tears overflowed. "Willie, he never were a strong
one—and he's at rest. I wonder what name they put on the
new little one? But they're a-comin! And here I was
a-thinkin' always in my heart that I had seen the last of
them in this life, with all that ocean of water lyin' between
us! I must burn me some candles for them comin' safe.
Oh, Miss Caroline, it makes my heart sing, so it does!"

Caroline threw her arms around Mollie and hugged her
tight.

"Mollie, that's wonderful news! Oh, I'm so happy for
you."

"I've such happiness in me this hour that I can't tell
it!" Mollie burst out. Then she looked straight into
Caroline's face as she stepped back. "There is only one
wish left in me now, Miss Caroline—that you can pick up
your happiness again. It was pure happiness, that was.
Don't let it be lost from you. Don't, Miss Caroline!"

Caroline stiffened. Mollie had no right—but she did.
Mollie had been there; she had tried to help. She shook
her head slowly.

"We can't tell truly what is best for another person,
Mollie, no matter how much we wish them well. No, let's
think about your family, and how wonderful it will be
when they come. We must tell Papa. He will have one of
the factors check the ships and see them safe ashore.
Perhaps we can find them a place to stay and have it all
ready—"

Mollie had taken back the precious letter and put it into the front of her bodice. "Oh, Miss Caroline, I'll be walkin' right up in the air itself when we do see them comin' ashore!" She shook her head. "Here I am forgetting what I really came for. Mr. Richard has been asking for you."

It was a chill wind settling down around her. Pris! Richard had some news about Pris! Caroline gathered up her skirts and started running back towards the house.

"And that is the way it is," Richard said a few minutes later, striding up and down the small parlor while Althea and Caroline sat side by side on the old sofa. "As far as we have been able to trace, they took a coasting schooner down to New York. There is much sea traffic out of there. Your father has put an inquiry agent on the tracing of them, since neither one of us could be away longer from our practice here."

"They were married?" Althea asked in a low voice.

Richard had halted with his back to them, looking out of the window.

"We found no trace of any such wedding, but in the United States, a marriage is mainly a civil rather than a religious matter. They could have had the necessary ceremony performed by any justice-of-the-peace. That we were unable to find trace of marriage does not mean that it was not done."

Althea said thoughtfully, "If Major Vickers wants to find favor with Sir Robert there will have to be a legal marriage and at least a pretense of reformation. The title and the estate will mean nothing if he does not inherit his uncle's money also, and my brother said it was made very plain to him that any further scandal would mean he would lose all. He has lived beyond his means for years, and he needs that inheritance. Since he is not stupid—''

"He is an unprincipled rake!" Richard exploded. "A generation ago, Corbie or I would have faced him with steel or shot. The beating Corbie gave him was not enough!"

Caroline wished she could clap her hands over her ears. Then she tried to remember that the nightmare his words brought back was in the past, and was now gone. Only not to know where Pris was or what had happened to her—

"I have already written to Mrs. Wilkins. You met her only once, Richard, but she was my dear friend as well as my companion-governess during the two years Mother was abroad. She does not move in the highest circles, but since Sir Robert's manor marched with our Kent estate, she is quite familiar with his household. I believe that she is a good correspondent of Sir Robert's sister, who is a sad invalid. Should there be any news reaching Sir Robert, it will so reach me. I have been very discreet, as I promised Mama Warwick."

Richard had come away from the window. "An excellent idea. Anyway, we have done our best for now. Meanwhile, ladies, I have been dispatched to say that the newly readied house is awaiting you both. Mama wonders if you have had enough of rusticating?"

Caroline sighed inwardly. Naturally, if Mama wanted it so, she should go back. There would be weeks here later in the summer. But it had been such a lovely time, she hated to know that it was over.

Now she broke in with Mollie's news. Richard looked grave.

"They will be lucky to reach Canada. Conditions are very bad. Ireland has but the one real crop—the potato—and since that has been blighted, there is real starvation."

"Starvation!" Althea looked shocked, but Richard nodded. "Yes, and those who can raise the price of a voyage are desperate to get away. The trouble is that they are being taken advantage of. Captains are overloading the ships and then virtually selling them as slaves."

"That mustn't happen to Mollie's family!" protested Caroline.

"No, it won't, Carrie," Richard reassured her. "We'll try and find out what ship they are on and see that they are met."

"I told Mollie—perhaps we could find them a place to stay. I don't know what kind of work her father does, but if he is a farmer, perhaps he can come here."

"We'll see," Richard agreed.

They traveled back to town the next day, to find the house still smelling a little of paint and paper paste but indeed freshened up. Only the door of Pris' room was closed. Caroline ran her hand along its surface as she went by. How she wished time would turn back and all was as it had been before.

"It's deuced dull," Perry observed at the dinner table that night. "Last year was a little more lively."

"You look very spruce for a young gentleman intending to spend a good evening's work at his books," Richard observed, taking in Perry's well-fitting coat and the flash of brocaded vest beneath.

"Oh, I've m' plans, old man," Perry winked. "All work and no play, remember? Fact is that I have an invitation from the Bernards for whist."

Papa frowned. "This is the third night this week, Perry —cards, dinner, a visit with a friend. When I was your age, I kept to my studies."

A sullen shadow fell across Perry's face. "I've kept up

with my classes, sir. You can inquire if you wish."

The doctor sighed. "It seems that you do manage to do that. But there is more than just keeping up with classes, Perry. A doctor has to learn continually—"

"More about things like this gas of Richard's?" Perry muttered. "I thought that there was some dispute about the value of that kind of learning, Papa."

Now Dr. Warwick was really frowning. "We do not discuss such things at the table, Perry, as you well know."

Caroline caught a glimpse of Richard's face. His eyes were turned down as if there was something of greater interest than a nicely rare slice of beef on his plate, but his mouth was set in a manner which in the old days meant that he had been arguing, and had *not* been in any way influenced by the opinion of his opponent. Caroline remembered his enthusiasm about his own experiment with the new painkiller. She only hoped that he and Papa would not go on having differences on the subject.

Mama spoke in her old serene voice from the foot of the table, firmly changing the subject.

"Caroline, my dear, you look quite yourself again. The stay at Fairlea has done you a world of good. But I have a treat you will enjoy—Madam Hannakar has sent an invitation for you to come and visit her at Ste. Catherine's for a few days. She says that with her son away she feels very much the need of young company. Though you said you were not feeling well when she asked you several weeks ago, she trusts that you have recovered."

Caroline's mouth went dry. Surely Mama would not make her go. But what excuse did she have? None that Mama would allow her to use. Though she felt sick inside at the very thought of such a visit, she had no way of saying no this time. A second refusal without any good reason

would be an affront, and one did not deliver such to
Madam Hannakar. It would cause far more discomfort perhaps than her managing to stay some days at Ste. Catherine's. Anyway, Corbie was far away; she would not have to
see him.

But it was with no pleasure at all that Caroline, outwardly docile, allowed herself to be fitted for the two new
dresses Mama had chosen, wrote her thanks for the invitation, and at last embarked for the Hannakar estate.

It was a beautiful morning, and Caroline tried to fasten
her attention on the land through which the carriage
passed. She was alone this time, for Mollie had stayed to
help with the last of the housecleaning. Only too soon they
had drawn up to the great house, and Caroline was
ushered in with the circumstance which had not seemed so
burdensome the other time, when Althea was there to
share her adventure.

Now the housekeeper escorted her directly to a chamber
at least twice the size of her comfortable quarters at home,
overshadowed by a canopied bed of an earlier period, so
that she felt as if she had stepped into an enchanted castle
and would not easily find her way out again. Having laid
aside her bonnet and cloak, she went to Madam's own sitting room where she discovered her hostess in a chair, a
small fire on the hearth, and Alexandra lying at lazy
length nearby across Madam's small, slippered feet.

"My dear." There was such real welcome in Madam's
voice that Caroline lost some of her uneasiness. She went
readily enough across the room to have her hand, already a
little brown from her days at Fairlea, taken in both of the
white and beringed ones of her hostess, who was studying
her so intently that Caroline again began to feel flustered.

"It is good, child to see that you are near yourself again.

To be ill is no easy thing, even when one is young. Sometimes especially *if* one is young. They tell me that you have been in the country to gain strength. You look very much as if that prescription—whether it was one of the good doctor's or not—has thoroughly agreed with you.''

"I love Fairlea, and Althea did, too. She likes to garden, but she said she never had a real chance to do her own planting before. You should have seen the number of bulbs she managed to get in.'' That weight of uneasiness had somehow gone. It was as if Madam had some magic of her own, and need only look at one so and ask the right questions to make all well.

Caroline found herself chatting away as she had not for a long time, not since Althea and she had first become friends, and before Pris— But all memory of Pris she pushed resolutely out of her mind.

They spent a very pleasant time together and then had a light lunch served on a small table drawn up before Madam's chair in the sitting room. She said firmly that she had not yet baked the ice of winter out of her bones, and found that they were too stiff for much trotting about. Afterwards Madam did go away to her chamber for a short nap, leaning partly on her silver-headed cane and partly on the arm of a tall dark-haired maid to whom she spoke in French.

"Now, my dear," she said to Caroline, "across the hall is the library if you have a taste for books. There are some pleasant novels on the shelf by the windowseat. When I have had my rest, I shall be more spry. Then we shall go to see the greenhouse; there are already several orchids in bloom. Have you ever seen one of those, Caroline? No? Well, they are strange-looking things but highly prized by gardeners, perhaps because they are rarities.''

Caroline, obedient, entered the library. She was used to
seeing books about—the doctor's and Richard's, and those
Mama approved of—but she had never seen such an array
of shelves and of volumes handsomely bound in fine
leather with gilt lettering. The windowseat Madam had
spoken of was wide and cushioned and the light there excellent. But first Caroline slowly made her way around the
room. Here and there among the bookcases, shelves displayed carvings, or pieces of what she guessed must be very
rare or unusual porcelain. There was a glass-topped table,
in which lay a number of miniatures, each in a frame that
winked with brilliants or the soft luster of petals. One such
was, she was sure, Madam as a girl. Next to her—Caroline
stood very still—was that Corbie?

She looked closer. Though the face was very much like
Corbie's, there was a slightly different set to the mouth
and the eyes were darker. Between the miniatures were
some pieces of strange old jewelry—two necklets, a small
knife with a gemmed hilt, a tiny bottle encased in filigree
gold and having a single gem for a stopper.

Another such table stood close to the massive desk
which had its back to the window seat. In this were queer
bowls with odd paintings on their sides, and some
elaborate, belt-like lengths of solid beadwork which
Caroline decided were Indian.

The top of the desk was bare except for a very large ink-
stand in the form of a stag facing a horse. It was a very
strange horse, for from the center of its forehead there
sprang a single pointed horn. It was of heavy silver, save
for the stag's antlers and that horn, which were yellow-
white. Caroline thought they might be ivory.

She was so lost in her slow discoveries about the room
that she sometimes forgot just where she was. Madam had

judged very rightly that this was the perfect amusement for a young guest. However, at last Caroline subsided on the windowseat and looked for the promised novels. She hoped they would not be covered with that beautiful leather; she felt she would never dare to draw one of those volumes from the shelves, lest her touch mar its perfection. A nearby shelf, however, held books that had cloth bindings and were rather rubbed, as if they had been familiarly handled many times over.

She picked out one at random and was delighted to find that it was one of those by Miss Austen, the author of *Northanger Abbey*. Moments later Caroline, curled up comfortably, began reading *Pride and Prejudice*, and so dropped into an entirely different and most amusing world.

With a start she was drawn back into the here and now when there came a knock at the door and the French-speaking maid entered to say that Madam was awaiting her. Swiftly Caroline returned the book to its place and hurried to the sitting room.

"You found amusement?" Madam looked up at her.

"The book—Althea had one by the same writer—*Pride And Prejudice*!" Caroline said excitedly. "The story is so funny, though Mama says that much of it—the way they lived, I mean—was true, and that it was so when she was a girl. I do thank you, Madam Hannakar. And I enjoyed looking at all the beautiful things, too. Those beaded things are Indian, are they not?"

"They are very important," Madam told her. "It was the custom of the eastern tribes to bind bargains and treaties with what they termed 'belts.' Those beaded ones you see in the library are in truth the original grants of this very land to our family. An exchange of belts could signal

the end or beginning of a war, as well as the transferral of
territory. We have deeds in plenty for all we own, but
those are probably the most precious ones. So. You like
Pride And Prejudice? So do I, my dear. Those books have
seen me through many weary hours in the past. But now,
let me take your arm and we shall go and view the greenhouse.''

They went slowly. Caroline was amazed at the ranks of
potted plants, even small orange and lemon trees, which
stood along the warm corridor with its glassed walls and
roof. She felt again that this was no ordinary house, rather
a place where enchantment might be found just around
the corner. She stared in astonishment at the orchids,
which appeared so strange to her they could hardly be
termed flowers, and admired the many other pots of brilliant blooms. She met the small, hunchbacked man who,
gnomelike, seemed to live in this place and was fiercely
proud of his domain, though he spoke no English and only
bobbed his head abruptly in Caroline's direction. However, he carried on an animated conversation with Madam
dealing with one pale-flowered plant which was suffering
from some blight.

As twilight gathered in, Madam had candles lighted.
Caroline went to her room and changed swiftly into the
best of her new frocks—a soft cream-yellow. They dined in
the small room where Madam had entertained Althea and
Caroline before.

The candle shine was soft, and the food was very good.
In spite of her relatively inactive day Caroline ate heartily,
and then could only sample a last concoction—a basket of
spun sugar holding four of the largest and reddest straw-
berries she had ever seen—which Madam told her were
also out of the greenhouse.

After dinner she was content to sit quietly by the fire in the other room and listen to Madam's stories about her girlhood and Ste. Catherine's, feeling soothed and comfortable and wondering now why she had ever dreaded this visit at all. And when she went back to her room, though there was no lamp lighted, there was a small night light on the table beside the big bed as well as a double candle holder, well filled, standing by her mirror.

Caroline climbed into bed and stretched her arms wide. The sheets smelt of lavender and some other fragrant herb. She was Cinderella—afterwards, of course, when all the bad things were gone and only the good remained. Her eyes closed.

Cold—she was cold. There was the door before her. She had to open it! No. Never! But the door opened of itself. There was a man there—tall, fair-haired, his eyes hard and blue with no warmth in them. He reached out for her.

She had been dumb but suddenly the power of sound returned. Caroline screamed and screamed again. He must not touch her. If he did she would—No!

16

"My dear child, what is wrong?"

The voice sounded far away. Caroline's eyes were screwed tightly shut. If she opened them, she would see—
She flinched from a touch on her hunched shoulder.

"Caroline!"

The sound of her own name uttered so sharply and imperatively brought her eyes open. A candle was being placed on the bedside table beside the dim night lamp.

Madam Hannakar stood within the limited circle of its radiance, her nightcap tied in a trim bow under her chin, a heavy velvet dressing gown well swathed about her. She leaned forward and gently touched her fingers to Caroline's forehead.

"It is well. It is well," she said softly, her low voice carrying with it soothing security. "You have had a bad dream, is that not so? Now you shall come to keep me company. Here is your dressing gown. Put it on, my dear. Then come. All is going to be very well. You shall see."

With the obedience of a small child Caroline slid out of the tangle of covers and drew on her robe. She was still breathing in small hurried gasps. Her heart pounded so that she felt weak and strange when she stood up. But

Madam's hand was ready and she followed docilely as the other brought her towards the door.

There was still a small fire on the hearth in Madam's chamber. The curtained bed there was much larger than the one Caroline had just left and was actually set above the floor on a single-step platform. Madam brought Caroline to the side of it, then left her for a moment to turn back the bed covers carefully. There was a two-branch candlestick on the table beside the bed, and a book lay open with a marker across the pages.

"Such a huge bed," Madam remarked. "It is that of the mistress of the house. I once told Julius that I felt like a Queen when I came to it, needing only enough ladies and maids curtseying about to make that a fact. Quickly now, before you take a chill. In with you, my dear!"

Caroline was obedient still, climbing up into that soft mountain, lying back on the pillows as her hostess tucked her in. But her body was stiff with tension and she glanced quickly at the door. It had all been a dream—surely it had been a dream! She shuddered. Madam dropped her own robe and was in place also, though a mound of pillows braced her higher.

"Now you can sleep, and there shall be no more evil things out of the shadows. I am here and so you are not alone. That will banish the bad dreams."

Caroline gave a little gasp before tears came, quickly, flooding down her cheeks so swiftly she could not even wipe them away. Madam's hand was on her head, stroking her forehead gently. She asked no questions, did not even speak, but slowly the sense of her gentleness and her comfort reacted on Caroline. The girl's sobs grew farther and farther apart.

"Now you shall try to sleep, my dear. You will not fear,

nor worry, nor shall the dark come again. Good night, my dear little one.''

Caroline's last sob was a sigh, her body was slowly relaxing. She felt empty, as if some barrier held within her for a long time had broken, so that now she had no defenses at all. Still, there was the gentle hand on her forehead and the knowledge that she was not alone. She looked up into Madam's face, saw there concern and in her eyes something more.

Caroline's hands came out from under the covers without her willing. She held them out to Madam and then felt herself caught up in a warm embrace as quieting to her spirit as if she were well sheltered from all evil in the world.

"Oh, please." Her voice was hoarse with sobs. "You won't go away?"

"No, child. I am here; sleep well and without dreams."

Caroline settled back on her pillows again, but one of her hands still lay in the warm grasp of the old lady. And the last thing she saw before she closed her eyes, worn out and exhausted by the storm which had shaken her so, was Madam smiling at her.

When she awoke, it was not to darkness and shadows. The curtains of the bed had been pushed far back, and there was sunlight across the floor of the room. However, the fact that she lay in strange surroundings made it difficult for Caroline to be sure at once that she was not caught in another dream. As she pulled up in the bed where she now lay alone, the tall French maid came to her quickly. Caroline found herself managed into washing, and then, still in her robe, being settled in a chair by that window which gave upon the spring day. A tray was brought in. Steaming chocolate was poured into a very delicate cup, and fresh rolls, a small pot of honey, a pat of butter formed into a wide-petaled flower were put before her.

The girl for a moment looked out into the morning, not quite sure if she were hungry or not, drawing back her memories of the night. That was the first time she had had that dream for a long time, or what seemed a long time now. What had brought it back? Was it because she had come here, to Corbie's house?

Caroline made herself pick up the cup, sit its thick, sweet contents slowly.

"Good morning, Caroline."

The cup shook in her hand, and a dollop of chocolate fell upon the tray. She could feel the warmth of the color arising in her face as she looked up. Madam was lowering herself carefully into the padded chair near the hearth.

"And it is a good morning. See the sun and the garden." Madam gestured to the window. "You have a taste for honey? That is from our own bees. They already gather next year's bounty out in the orchards, where Pierre moves their hives each spring."

Caroline found her tongue at last. "Good morning, Madam."

Her hostess smiled with the same gentleness she remembered from the night's shadows.

"I am so pleased that you have come to me. It is good to have young life in this house once again. I wonder if you will do me the very great favor of prolonging your visit? With my son away I find the days long, and, since I go forth so seldom nowadays, I also discover that I am, what youth never expects to be—lonely."

Caroline felt wary. She broke open one of the rolls, not quite aware of what she was doing, cut into the butter flower, dribbled on a bit of honey.

"Perhaps," Madam said after a slight pause, "you would find it too quiet—an old lady in a big house, with no young life around?"

Caroline drew a deep breath. "About last night." How could she accept Madam's invitation if she were to continue to make a fool of herself here?

"We all have evil dreams at times. I have asked Marie to move you to the little room next to this. There is a door— no, you cannot see it, for the paneling conceals it now— but it can be left open at night. When Corbie was a child and did not feel well, he slept there where I could go to him if needed. If you have the nightmare again, you need only call me. I sleep very lightly. In fact, sleep is hard for me to capture some nights, and I read very late. That, too, is one of the signs of age creeping upon me. You are a good child. I think we will deal most happily together."

"I am very proud that you want me, Madam. But—" The roll was crumpled by her fingers into a sticky mess. How much did Madam know? Of course, with Corbie away Caroline need not fear facing him. Only, staying here this way—even with him gone, would that not be a kind of deceit? She did not realize how haunted and pale she appeared in the sunlight.

"Please." She turned again to Madam, her voice carrying some of the same plea it had held in the night. "Perhaps I am not what you think me."

Madam's smile had faded; there was nothing in her face but concern. Caroline swallowed. She had never dared try to speak to Mama about what had happened at Varennes. She never would be able to, nor to Althea, either. Yet it always lay at the back of her mind, waiting to come to life as it had last night. Caroline pushed the tray a little away and rested her head, which had begun to ache, on her hands, her elbows braced on the small table. If Madam knew, would she want Caroline in her house? Had Corbie told her?

"My dear, what has my son done that you find so frightening?"

Caroline's head jerked up; she was startled out of her own weary thoughts.

"Nothing! But why—"

"You called his name last night in your dream, but it was a cry of fear. You are afraid of Corbie. Can you not tell me why?"

Caroline felt again as if her face must be blazing red with guilt.

"He—he has done nothing, Madam. Nothing wrong. What he did was good. Only—he—he *saw*—"

"Caroline, my child, this fear which brings the nightmares, which makes you so unhappy, will rest a burden on you unless you can share it with someone. It is plain that Corbie has a part in it. He was greatly concerned over your illness. Still, a week after you were taken so, he came from your house with such a look on his face as I had never thought to see him wear. He had been going daily to ask for you, yet he never went again. Corbie *is* a part of this fear you live with, is he not?"

"Yes, though it is not his fault—I know that. I say so to myself over and over. He—he has a right instead to have a disgust of me. He saw—everything."

Caroline started to shake. Somehow she got to her feet, holding onto the back of a chair. Now she felt tears slipping down her cheeks once again and smeared them away with the back of her hand.

For weeks she had pushed it all to the back of her mind, pummeling it into hiding there. Now she could no longer control her tangled emotions. She stumbled away from the window and went down on her knees by Madam, who opened her arms and drew her close.

Mama, thought Caroline dazedly, Mama had somehow never given her the same warm comfort. She was shaking still, and now words spilled from her whether she would or not—words which began incoherently, muffled and strange sounding even in her own ears—and then sorted themselves out into broken phrases. She relived all the hideous scene at Varennes.

Madam did not draw away from her as she half expected, but continued to hold her. Caroline's sobs, as they had in the night, grew less heavy.

"I—I dream about *him*. And then—then he looks like Corbie, and—and I cannot bear to think of how *he* kissed me and—"

Madam's hands patted her. "My child, it is understood now. But there is something you must learn. Yes, there is ugliness in some relationships, an ugliness which *is* a nightmare. There are hungers of the flesh which some know and which, because they are hungers only, with no true bond of love between those who would assuage them, become nightmares indeed. There are men who give way to certain appetites, and women who are beguiled or foolish enough to yield to them. These men are such as Major Vickers. But, because you have seen ugliness in what may be a very happy relationship, you are sickened and confused. You will come to know that what Corbie feels for you is not disgust nor the appetite which you have drawn out of bad dreams, but something very different."

"What Corbie feels for me?" Caroline pushed back a little and looked wonderingly up into the gentle face above hers.

For a moment Madam did not answer and then she said: "My child, I was very happy when I married my Julius, perhaps happier than many girls in my time, for ours was truly a union of hearts and a companionship I came to hold very dear—a bond which grew stronger and stronger. I want nothing better for my dear son than for him also to find the fulfillment and contentment which his father and I knew. I have waited for him to make such a discovery. Not until this past winter has there awakened in him an inner awareness that there was someone who might be the other half of his life.

"He came to me with the story of a dear girl who loved animals even as did he, whom others seemed to see as a child, but whom he saw as a woman. Yet she was very young, and he was afraid that he might alarm her if he addressed himself to her as a suitor. Thus he chose what he thought best, to wait, to allow her to know him. For though she was the one on which he had set his heart, how could he be sure that she would see him in the same light? Thus he did not yield to his inner wishes and go courting; he tried to win her friendship first. He hoped that he might even claim her love in time."

Caroline sat back on the floor, her hands still clasped in Madam's. She watched the other's face as one who was first startled, then very thoughtful.

"It has been ill for him that this happening occurred."

"He—he—" Caroline interrupted in a whisper. "He knows about Pris. He got rid of the Major. I know—if it had not been for his coming then—" She shivered again.

"I have never seen my son in the cold anger which was like a cloak about him then," Madam continued. "I think that he restrained himself mightily lest he give 'way to that anger. When you were ill, my dear, he went daily to your house. Several times you accepted from him in your fever, perhaps unknowingly, the nourishment you would not take when it was offered by others. Then there came the hour when you faced him, were so aroused that they feared you would relapse into your illness. Your father told Corbie it was best that he not come again, unless you asked for him or showed, in some way, that you desired to see him.''

Caroline could no longer meet those kind eyes. ''I—I was afraid.''

''Yes. It would seem that even your father and mother did not realize, I see now, the great shock which had come to you at Varennes. Such a shock may indeed shut within one dark trouble, which then is like infection within a wound—a wound which will never heal while the poison lies within. But Corbie waited, until at last he told me that he could not stay here in peace of mind, that it would be better by far that he take himself away for awhile.''

Caroline bit her lip. ''He went west—''

''Yes, he went west. He said little. As you did, my dear, he kept locked within him that which would not let him rest. But he will find the peace which he seeks, in time. Just as you shall, my dear. Now—we shall say no more of this matter. Shut the door of your mind upon it, for it is finished and gone. We must let the future take care of itself. You and I shall have our visit and enjoy it—is that not so? I have been lonely, and I am selfish enough to expect you to banish that loneliness. No longer can I get about easily, but you shall be my deputy and bring me news about what is doing in the stables and the garden, and on the home farm. Thus I can see through your eyes and enjoy that part of life again!''

So Caroline, feeling weak and empty, as if indeed something which had been a heavy burden for a long time had been drawn out of her, became Madam's messenger and deputy. Even as her week at Fairlea had healed her, so more did this time of quiet and peace refresh and soothe her. There were no more nightmares, and she learned to listen calmly as Madam talked of Corbie's ways, his interests, and what he planned for the future of Ste. Catherine's and his many business interests—the shipping line, the proposed railroad, the opening up of the west. Caroline listened and felt that she was learning to know Corbie better at a distance than she had when he was close to hand. She left reluctantly at the end of the month, and Madam let her go with some show of unhappiness, winning from her a promise that she would return before the close of summer.

However, once more at home Caroline found that further misfortune, and such as to hurt her father deeply, had struck at the family. Perry had failed his year at medical school. Not only that, but having gone on a round of consolation visits to various places of refreshment, aided by his more successful classmates, he had ended with a bad fall and a broken arm.

It had been Richard who had brought Perry home and set the arm. He had also used his new sleeping gas, and Perry still swore vehemently that he had felt nothing at all through the setting. But in Dr. Warwick's eyes that had been no victory for Richard's fond hopes. A second attempt to use the gas, at an amputation in the medical school, had not been too successful. The unfortunate patient had roused and had had to be knocked out before Richard could proceed with the surgery. Dr. Warwick remained, Caroline heard from Althea, entirely convinced that that was little or no merit in the discovery. While

Richard grew edgier whenever the doctor referred to the failure of the second demonstration, continuing to insist that Perry's imagination itself had provided much of the success the first time.

Whether Perry would make a second try for medical school was still undecided in the family. Perry himself was very subdued these days and, when with the family, was like a small boy who had been severely chastened.

Caroline slipped back into her old place at home. Even though Pris was no longer there with all her social arts, Caroline still felt the outshone sister and was content to live quietly. She said nothing of any of the undertone of her visit at Ste. Catherine's, enlarging rather on the pleasant time Madam had given her and of the charms of the estate itself. But she was quieter and felt much, much older than the girl she had been when Madam, in the parlor of this very house, had first centered attention on her.

She had claimed Mama's attention, and thus eventually Papa's, in planning for the arrival of Mollie's family. Ships were already coming up river, and the Immigrant Sheds near the Wellington Bridge were in use. Dr. Warwick spoke of the flow of Germans, in exile from their own country because of their liberal beliefs, which was said to be on its way. While the news of the famine in Ireland, and the horrible situation there was already well known. The Countess of Elgin was coming at last, which suggested another social round for those in favor at the government house.

Newspapers and books began to arrive from London itself. Althea had a fat bundle of letters, but the one from her old governess brought no news of Pris. However, Althea shared tidbits with the Warwick ladies—including

the information that the first Drawing Room of the Season
had been held at St. James in London, and the Queen's
dress had been most magnificent, with a train of green
poplin figured in gold shamrocks, a petticoat of white
satin trimmed with gold lace and ivy, and ornamented
with diamonds.

Having listened to that report of overseas magnificence,
Mama turned to her own correspondence. There was a
letter from Boston, from Aunt Leah, noting in a round-
about way that certain friends of hers, the Horners, were
on their way to Sherbrooke to visit with Mrs. Horner's
parents.

Mama, who usually read Aunt Leah's letters aloud, had
sat for a moment or two in silence over that one.

"The Horners are old friends," she said slowly. "Leah
has mentioned them many times. They might well think it
odd if we did not call upon them, or ask them here—"

There was no note of welcome in her voice. Caroline
could guess why. If the Horners were such old friends of
Aunt Leah's, doubtless they knew Pris and also knew or
guessed the circumstances of her sister's elopement from
Boston. At least there was one solution which she herself
could suggest now:

"Mama, you must be very tired after all the overseeing
of the house alterations. Why don't you and Althea go to
Fairlea?"

Her oblique suggestion about what to do concerning the
Horners seemed to be a correct one. That line of frown
which had deepened between Mama's eyes these past
months even smoothed out a little.

"Of course." She sounded eager. "I will tell the
Horners that we will be away. And there must be some
painting done at Fairlea also. The house has doubtless

gotten far too shabby.''

Caroline dared to wink at Althea, who made a comical if fleeting face in return, and heartened Caroline with a small nod of approval.

Caroline offered to stay behind this time for the running of the household. Of course, cook and Jessie were well able to keep the menfolk in comfort, but, by Mama's idea of proper management, there must always be a firm hand at the helm. For a moment that offer seemed to surprise Mama, and then she nodded in agreement.

"Very well, Caroline. It is certainly time you learn to run a household, and this will be excellent practice for you. Althea, my dear, would you find such a trip too fatiguing? The country air is certainly pleasing, and you have often spoken of your desire to see the garden again. We shall hire a boy to put it in order so you need only direct him as to what you want done.''

There was a storm of such torrential proportions that it put off Mama's proposed trip. But when that cleared, she and Althea were safely off, leaving Caroline to feel very much the responsibility of the key basket which Mama had passed over to her as temporary ruler of the household. She took her duties seriously, going over menus with cook, seeing to the linens, the washing of the finest china, keeping the house to Mama's most exacting standards as well as she could.

Perry drifted around the house for a day or two, but then she noted that he was spending more and more of his time in Richard's old room, and that the books he had hardly looked into during the past winter were now often open before him. Though he said little to his father, still she could hear him often at night talking eagerly with Richard. Had Perry, who had always professed to be bored with his classes, and had resented his father's constant urging to work, suddenly decided to apply himself?

They saw nothing of Archie and his family. Caroline believed that whatever mischief Agatha had worked in her letter to Pris had so angered her parents that relations were strained to the breaking point, if not beyond, and that the elder Warwick son would not be seen very often now in his old home. In fact, Mama's social life had dwindled a great deal. Though she had not commented on the fact, she had discontinued her At Homes during Caroline's illness and had never really resumed them again, and she received very few invitations these days. Perhaps she could not help but feel the burden of the cloud of scandal which hung over them, even if no one knew the whole truth of the matter.

That Pris did not return from Boston must have caused a new wave of rumor and gossip. Caroline felt sorry for Mama. For Papa, too. He had taken two hard blows, first Pris and then Perry, and, though he roused himself now and then to discuss something of interest, it was a sorry attempt. There was a feeling of strain between him and Richard of which Caroline was very aware. But there was nothing she could do, save try to make their home as pleasant and run the house as smoothly as possible.

Richard sat down to the table with a sigh one evening, and Caroline, still feeling odd in Mama's seat of rulership, asked, "Tired?"

"Devilishly so, Puss. There are a lot of fever cases coming in. Liddell down at the wharf says that they are holding a lot in quarantine there. The ship that docked this morning had over a hundred sick on board. They pack them in, and there's not enough food. The immigrants are supposed to provide their own, but most of them can't furnish much, and if a ship is delayed by a storm—'' He waved his hands expressively.

"Well, Liddell is a good man," Dr. Warwick said heavily. "He's had enough experience with such fevers through the years."

"I told him I'd lend a hand if he got in a tight place," Richard said.

Perry had raised his eyes from his plate. Caroline saw his lips move as if he wanted to say something, then tighten after a quick glance in his father's direction. But there was a change in his face as if he had come to some decision of his own.

There continued to be heavy rains which kept all housebound except those with very necessary errands. Caroline attended carefully to her household duties. She had refused to bring the dog Corbie had given her back from Ste. Catherine's, saying that the city was not the place for the now half-grown setter who loved to run so much. Boots was a very portly gentleman, plump with good living. But he apparently had not forgotten his leaner days, for he had turned up in the stable yard one night this past week encouraging a very timid young female, who was also manifestly quite pregnant. Susan, as Caroline had named her, had been made comfortable in a straw-lined basket in the coachhouse and had promptly presented Boots, if Boots *was* the proud father, with four kittens the next morning. Caroline had just taken an evening pan of scraps and a bowl of milk out to the new mother, to come scurrying back as a very loud clap of thunder echoed overhead.

Just as she shook out her wet shawl in the hall, there came an insistent peal at the door. Mollie scurried by her to answer, and Caroline heard the message even before the maid had gone to knock on the surgery door where Papa was wont to retire now in the evenings.

Richard had come out and was talking with the man. Trouble at the docks, the man was saying. Could the doctor come right away? Two more ships had come in, and there were many sick with no place to put them. Richard had already reached for his outer coat. Catching sight of Caroline, he called:

"Can you see Cook gives this man something hot to drink? Let him dry out by the fire; he's wet through! Ask Harry to harness Joby-boy to the light carriage. He can bring him back—"

Dr. Warwick came out of his office, with Mollie looking pale and scared behind him.

"I'm going, sir," Richard said. "Good thing I have these oilskins to hand. You stay here. I'll let you know how matters are going."

"Perhaps I should join you," Papa was heading toward where his long coat hung.

"Now now, sir. After all, it may be exaggeration. And I *had* promised Liddell, so he feels free to call on me. I'll send word if matters are bad."

"Wait for me!" Perry came down the steps two at a time, his own oilskins on. "I may not be a doctor, but I can be of some use."

Though he spoke to Richard, he looked at his father. Caroline saw that Richard glanced from father to son. Then he nodded sharply. "Well enough. A second pair of hands—or even one—might be helpful, Perry."

After that glance at his father, Perry pushed past Richard and went out. The older doctor watched him go, a very odd look on his face now. Richard gave a nod of farewell and followed after. Caroline touched Papa's arm.

"Papa, is there something we can do? Suppose Cook made up some kettles of soup—could we get them down there? If the sick people are right off the boat, they may be hungry. Didn't Richard say that a lot of them did not get enough to eat and that made them sick?''

Mollie had come back after taking the messenger to the kitchen at Richard's orders. Her face was very white, and her eyes looked big and dark with fear.

''A good idea, my dear,'' Papa seemed pleased to have that to think of. ''And if we have extra blankets, it might be well to sort them out. I am going to look through my drug store—''

''Miss Caroline,'' Mollie came forward as the doctor shut himself once more into his office. ''Please, do you think maybe m' family, they might be down there? It's been a long time since the good father wrote they was comin', and we never did get no letter after sayin' which boat they would be on. Oh, Miss Caroline—them lying sick in the rain, and perhaps empty in their bellies—'' She twisted her hands together.

''Now, Mollie, don't go hunting bad things,'' Caroline said sharply to break through that growing fear. She took a key from Mama's basket, which she had put down on the hall table when she went out to feed Susan. ''You go up to the big trunks of the winter things and get out the grey blankets. All of them. Bring them down here to the hall. I'll go and see what Cook can do.''

She found the messenger, who in the better light of the kitchen looked hardly more than a boy, a mug of steaming tea in one hand, his shivering body as close to the fire as he could get without scorching. At her questions he seemed to be very vague, or else so overcome by his soaked condition that he was not aware of much about him. He repeated that they were bringing the sick ashore by the boatload, and many were lying out on the bank in the rain because there was no room inside.

"Women, miss, and little children, too. It is a bad business. The doctor there, he is half rushed to death. No one seems to be able to give any orders but him, and he can't be everyplace at once."

Caroline spoke to Cook, who speedily arose to the challenge. She set aside one large kettle for tea and began to assemble, from her larder, the ingredients for a soup "as was a meal of itself and good enough to put life back into a scarecrow, or my name isn't Jenkins."

They had their supplies assembled by ten of the Doctor's watch. He met Caroline in the hall as she was counting blankets and seeing them tied into a bundle compact enough to handle.

"There's been no message," her father told her, "I have had James harness Peter to my own carriage. He'll be in to load these and whatever cook has—after he takes out my drug chest." Papa was well wrapped in his own coat. "I am going to see for myself. Don't wait up, my dear."

Caroline wanted to protest. The storm was shrieking around the house and her father did not have the oilskins the younger men had produced. But she knew that nothing was going to keep Papa from what he considered his duty. She watched him go, but she had no intention of going up to bed. Instead she went back to the kitchen where she found Mollie in Cook's arms, the girl sobbing.

" 'Tis bad luck, it is, and my people comin' into it—"

"Mollie," Caroline said quietly, "don't think the worst before you know the truth. Go to bed now and rest. If there is any news at all, I shall let you know at once."

"Sleep I cannot—" Mollie was beginning when Cook gave her a little shake.

"Take hold of yourself now, m'girl. 'Tis the good truth Miss Caroline is telling you. There is no need for tears until the right time comes. Up to bed with you, and quick about it. 'Tis already wasted near a night's sleep, you have.''

Caroline watched Mollie disappear reluctantly up the back stairs.

"I'll be in my room. If there is any news—"

"Sure, I've told Harry he's to keep himself awake and listening out in the stable. Does anyone come he'll know it, Miss Caroline. You'll be told."

17

However the morning had come before any of the men returned. Caroline, unable to give orders for breakfast, was in the lower hall when the door opened. Richard came in, his face looking strangely gaunt, a dark shadow of beard along his jaw, and his eyes so tired it seemed he had to fight to keep them open. His arm was supporting Dr. Warwick, who looked so grey of face and exhausted that Caroline cried out and hurried forward.

"Hot water," Richard said quickly. "Fresh clothing. Do not touch us now; we must wash immediately."

Caroline gasped one small word—a haunting one she had heard as a threat in the past.

"Cholera?"

Richard shook his head. "No, we think some kind of ship fever. Many are stricken and there were more taken off at Grosse Isle. All the sheds were full. It is a nightmare."

Caroline turned and struck the gong, bringing out not only Mollie and Jessie to answer that unusual summons, but also James.

"Water, hot—and clean clothing, James. Help Dr. Warwick and Dr. Richard and do as exactly as they tell

you. Mollie, Jessie—tellCook, water and then to get breakfast—Richard, where is Perry?''

"Still down there. There are so few—Liddell collapsed.
A priest came last night and sent for some nursing sisters. I
must not waste time. Let me bathe, eat, and get back.
Sir,'' he spoke now to Dr. Warwick, who was already
leaning on James' ready arm and making his way slowly to
the stairs, "you must rest. You have given me your word.''

The doctor's drooping head came up. "As you will do
so also, Richard. What good will you do those poor souls if
you fall among them as Liddell did? I have sent a messenger to the college, and there will be more volunteers.
There have been epidemics before, and those who allow
their own strength to be too greatly drained do themselves
a grave injustice and their patients a greater one.''

"Where are your oilskins?'' Caroline could see how
Richard's drenched clothing clung to his body and he was
shivering.

"Those?'' he said as if he could hardly remember. "Oh,
I put them over some children—they were too awkward to
work in.''

Caroline saw that breakfast trays were taken to their
rooms. She dared visit them later, gathering their
discarded and well-soaked clothing into a special basket.
She ordered James to set it aside for the special washing and
cleaning which might prevent any contagion. Richard was
already asleep. He had fallen crooked across the bed, and
she twitched the cover higher about him. Her father was
propped against a pillow, sipping slowly a second cup of
coffee from the pot Mollie had brough up. He looked
flushed yet he smiled at her.

"My dear, how like your mother. Thank you for the
thought of the blankets and the soup. If Cook can manage

to provide more of tnat—it will be a boon for those suffering down there. They promise us more nursing sisters today. And, Perry—Caroline, I would not have thought that the lad had had it in him. Even one-armed he was such a help. Please, send James down with the carriage and see that Perry is brought home. He is a doctor—he will be a doctor! You will see."

Putting aside his cup, he settled himself against his pillows. "Let Richard have at least a morning's sleep, my dear. He is a good boy, a fine physician. I have never seen any man fight so hard to save lives as he has this night."

But it was only starting. Steamer after steamer came into Grosse Point to disgorge passengers transhipped from the sailing vessels in which they had made the perilous Atlantic crossing. There was word from the Point that a new shed was needed for a hospital—a few days after that, even more room was needed.

Tents were requisitioned from the army, and then soldiers summoned as aides. Grosse Point could not hold the inflow. Any person who could keep on his feet was herded aboard one of the river steamers and sent on. Churches were pressed into service as hospitals. Richard was asked to accompany two other doctors to the Point and report conditions there back to the government.

Nine hundred deaths had already been recorded, and there were reports that over eleven hundred had died at sea. Eleven ships at anchor had not even been boarded by the health officers, but there were rumors of illness aboard.

Upon his return to Montreal, Richard reported directly to the Mayor and the Council, bringing home with forceful language the need for trained assistance. Four more doctors, six medical students, and as many of the

nursing sisters as could be found, were sent to help. The
overflow of the first sheds had spread to a nearby rope
walk.

Dr. Warwick organized a medical board to deal with
complaints and suggestions, but he also insisted on taking
tours of duty in the sheds, in spite of all his family could
say. Hearing the rumors of the plague, Mama had come
back from Fairlea, leaving Althea behind, to take command of the household, and organized the other doctors'
wives into a service of supplies for the sheds.

Twenty-four of the nursing sisters sickened, their places
quickly taken by new volunteers. Then the doctors themselves became ill. One died, as did eight of the sisters.

The dead lay beside the living, to be taken out and
stacked ready for interment in the crude coffins, piles of
which stood boldly in sight. The weather was no help.
Blazing, constant heat turned the sheds into ovens—the
odor was overpowering.

It was that which struck Caroline and Mollie. Unable
any longer to keep Mollie from searching for her family,
whom she was sure was caught up in the horrors of the
sheds, Caroline had taken the carriage and slipped away
with the maid whose haunted face she could no longer
endure.

Blindly, near overcome with horror, she could not
believe in what she saw lying about her as she stumbled
into that dreadful building, her arm about Mollie who was
weaving from side to side, so wracked with tears and her
own fears that she might have been one of the victims
herself.

Mollie broke from Caroline's hold, bent over this moan-
ing or silent woman or child, peering into the flushed
faces. Then she cried out.

"Miss Caroline, 'tis Bridget! Oh, Bridget, m' darlin'!"
The maid was on her knees in the straw beside a little girl
who had reached up and caught at Mollie's hand.

"Your mother—the others?" Caroline forced herself to
look around.

The child continued to cling to Mollie. "Don' go," she
moaned. "Mollie, don' go an' leave me."

"I've got to hunt for Mother. But I'll be right back, and
that I promise you, by Our Lady Herself, I promise it,
Bridget."

Mollie, her tears forgotten, pushed forward with purpose now, peering into faces as she went. They were in a
second shed before Mollie again cried out and dropped on
her knees beside a woman who lay with a baby sleeping
within the crook of her arm, and two children huddled
against her.

The woman did not open her eyes at Mollie's urgent
call, but the children cried feebly and the baby moved.
Caroline gripped her hands tightly together and then knelt
beside Mollie, trying to soothe one of the children who was
crying feebly, though without opening its eyes or respond-
ing to Mollie's voice.

"Miss Caroline—m'mother—" Mollie's fear was hoarse
in her voice.

There was a sharp voice behind Caroline: "What the
devil! Caroline, what are you doing here!" Richard stood
looking down at her with something close to fury in his
face.

"It's Mollie's mother." She gestured. "Please, Richard
—how is she?"

He knelt and raised a bone-thin arm, felt for the pulse.
Then gently he moved the baby away. Mollie watched him
dully:

"'M' mother?''

Richard's voice was very gentle. "She is all right now, Mollie.''

For a long moment she did not understand, then her round face seemed to crumple. She dropped closer to the woman, catching up the thin body and holding it to her, rocking back and forth and sobbing. Richard broke her hold on the dead, lifted her bodily, and then led her to the door as Caroline hurried after.

He looked back over his shoulder. "Did someone tell you the O'Shanes were here?''

She shook her head. "No, but somehow Mollie was sure. She said she had to come. Her sister Bridget—we found her first—is in that shed over there. Do you suppose her father is here, too?''

"I'll find out. And I'll have her sister put with the other children. Mollie, you can help me." He shook her by the shoulder gently, as she seemed dazed and unhearing. "Show me where Bridget is.''

When Caroline would have followed, Richard shook his head at her impatiently.

"Stay where you are. This is no place for you, Caroline.''

She remained where she was, and it seemed to her that, like the terrible stench from the sheds, the waves of misery which spread around her were nearly real enough to see and hear. She wanted to put her hands over her ears, close her eyes and run. This was like nothing she had even guessed might exist.

Mollie came back, still with that queer dazed look on her face, Richard's arm about her shoulders as if he needed to support her.

"We'll look for your father, I promise it, Mollie.''

"Yes, Dr. Richard." But the life had gone out of her voice.

Caroline hurried forward and caught at her hand. "We'll come again, Mollie. We'll make sure Bridget and the others are taken care of."

It was like leaving a world of horror to return home. Mama made both Caroline and Mollie scrub themselves from head to foot and wash their hair, and ordered that the clothing they had worn be washed at once. She was tightlipped, and Caroline well expected swift punishment for her own part in the affair, but Mama did not scold. Instead she was gentle with Mollie, and ordered cook to make her tea then send her off to bed.

Though the fever was a blot on the lower town, the upper town largely dismissed it as an unpleasant happening which had little or no connection with their own life— except for those ladies who worked with Mama. When Lady Elgin arrived in June, and so signaled the beginning of what would be a very brilliant social season, even those began to fall away from the committee meetings.

There was a Drawing Room held at Monklands on the twenty-second of June. An invitation had arrived for the Warwicks; Mama fingered it for a while, set it up on the parlor mantel, and said no more about it. Althea, by Richard's orders, remained at Fairlea and Caroline had not the least desire to attend such an affair. The Warwicks' position in society might still be ambiguous. Besides, she was worried about Mollie. The baby had died, and one of the older children was seriously ill. Richard had been unable to find Patrick O'Shane, and Bridget had only been able to report that Da had gone away—"a long time ago."

The three other children seemed to have passed the crisis, but Mollie went daily to the sheds, taking with her a

basket with extra food, and, against orders, Caroline
would slip away to go with her. There were so many things
one could do, even if one were not a nurse. She saw Perry
now and then, his arm now out of its sling, working under
one of the doctors' orders. He was so unlike the Perry she
had known—the other Perry he slipped into when he came
home—that it was like meeting a stranger.

Now the contagion was spreading up into the town.
There was no wall to keep the city safe from this festering
sore which grew ever larger and more threatening in the
blaze of summer. Caroline heard that Archie's was one of
the loudest voices now raised against the immigrants and
the sheds. There was a growing demand that they be
moved away from the city, yet no practical suggestion of
how this might be done. An idea advanced by the doctors
was that new sheds might be readied at Port St. Charles.
But the merchants who were loud-voiced in the council
wanted all removed to the Boucherville Islands.

"An impossibility!" Richard, hollow-eyed and much
too thin, burst out at the dinner table the evening he had
himself gone to argue before the council. "Archie—" He
closed his mouth firmly, as if he dared not voice his
opinion of Archie.

Perry stirred in his chair. He looked in his way near as
beaten as Richard, and these days he seldom spoke at all,
dragging himself upstairs in a quiet way new to him. Not
always to sleep, Caroline knew, for twice she had seen him
in Richard's old room, sitting staring down at the medical
books, such an exhausted slump to his shoulders that the
second time she had caught him so she had gone downstairs and talked cook into making fresh coffee, which she
had carried up again herself. Perry had smiled at her and
attempted some of his old banter, but he no longer
sounded as if he meant it.

Now he spoke with a little of his old tone: "Archie becomes a bigger ass every day of his life. 'Concern for the precious lives of our beloved wives and children'!" Perry was obviously quoting. "What Archie needs is two days on the clean-up detail down at the sheds. Though I don't think even that would make any impression on his thick head!"

Dr. Warwick sipped his port slowly. "I suppose, by his reckoning, he thinks he has the right of it. What will be the answer, Richard? I cannot see how that Boucherville move can possibly be accomplished."

"With a thousand or more sick and flat on their backs?" Richard shook his head. "Impossible is the only word, sir. It remains what the commission will decide. There are strong forces backing the Point St. Charles plan —Hannakar for one."

Caroline started. Corbie? But Corbie was out west, far away from Montreal and all its troubles.

"Hannakar—yes, I heard that he returned last week, saying he had news of the difficulties we were in and thought that he might be needed at home. Well," Dr. Warwick continued, "he has influence enough to lend a great deal of weight to any argument."

"And he has been for Point St. Charles from the start," Richard said.

The council settled on Point St. Charles, and work began on the sheds, but there seemed no end to the plague. All the Gray Nuns who had been the first to come in as nurses were sick, and now the Sisters of Charity were succumbing in turn. Five doctors, eight medical students—the toll mounted. The Reverend Mister Williams who organized the first Protestant relief party died, and with him Father Richards of St. Patrick and Father Morgan. The Immigration agent and his assistant

were gone. Then Lt. Lloyd of the Royal Navy, who
managed the care of the orphaned children, also. It was
not until the last week in July that the task of evacuating
the immigrants to the newly completed buildings at the
Point was begun.

Then the problem of Mollie's surviving sisters and
brother arose, and Caroline made her own suggestion. A
stream of letters and messages had been coming from
Althea, who was near frantic with Richard's constant
danger of infection. She had begged to return to her husband, only to have him adamantly refuse to have her ex-
posed to contagion. It was plain that her constant fretting
was doing her no good. Thus Caroline proposed that she
take Mollie, the orphans who were now pronounced free of
the disease and able to leave their present quarters, and go
to Fairlea.

She had hoped, foolishly she now believed, that Corbie,
having returned to the city and apparently being on con-
sulting terms over the new station, might appear at the
Warwicks'. Though what she might do if he so came, she
had not the faintest idea. Perhaps his trip to the west had
given him the peace which he had told his mother he was
seeking—a peace which did not include her. At that
thought she always experienced a queer sense of loss. But,
she told herself, she need expect no better. Even yet, she
was not sure of her own feelings and flinched from exploring them too fully.

More letters passed between her and Madam Hannakar,
Caroline describing the dangers of the plague and the conditions in the city. From Ste. Catherine's there had come
hampers of food for the sheds, generous donations of
money and promises of any help possible. Madam had not
mentioned Corbie though, and Caroline had shrunk from
any questions in return.

Richard himself escorted Caroline, Mollie, and three children out to Fairlea, where Althea, looking almost as drawn and worn as her husband, was plainly overjoyed to see Richard and hardly aware that anyone else had come with him.

The threat of the plague withdrew with the removal of the sick, and there had been one surprising event before they left the Warwick house. The Horners, whom Mama had so tried to avoid, had called while passing through the city. There had been no mention of Pris' elopement, of course. But what was stranger, the daughter, Dominica, had spoken so of Pris that one thought them the dearest of friends. Apparently there had been no shadow of scandal in Boston to cloud any relationship they might have had. Perry, at last released from his self-imposed duty at the sheds, and at home on the day they had come, had plainly been struck by Dominica. She was a dark-haired girl, not in any way a beauty, but there was a pert prettiness to her face, and she sparkled so with good humor and joy in life that she was far more attractive than any beauty.

The Horners, choosing to stay on in Montreal for some of the attractions now beginning to be offered with the shadow of the plague gone, became frequent visitors. Mrs. Horner was a comfortable, placid person of ever-smiling good humor, and Mama seemed to find her more soothing company than older acquaintances, who now brought her more uneasiness than pleasure if she was long in their company. Caroline liked both Mrs. Horner and Dominica, but was always so uncertain as to what they knew or surmised about Pris, that she kept a little distance with Minnie, even though it was plain that the American girl was eager to know her better.

In a way this was another reason for seeking the peace of Fairlea, where the past could be so well shoved to the back of one's mind.

Mollie's sisters and brother loved the farm and ran wild in the pastures, following the hands about and watching the animals. They browned under the sun, and day by day Mollie's mouth lost its droop and she was at last heard to laugh. With Caroline she took a picnic basket and swept the children off on a day's venturing into the small wood, or went exploring up the creek. Caroline, too, felt happier than she had for months.

Richard only stayed for three days, and Caroline did not intrude on him and Althea. After he had gone, and she was closer to the English girl, Caroline could not help but be concerned. When she had last seen Althea she had been a little pale, yes, but now her skin seemed almost transparent. Nor did she come out in the garden any more, even though it held two new benches which Caroline guessed had been placed there for her pleasure.

Instead she spoke now and then of being tired. She rose late, and spent the evenings largely lying on the sofa, her sewing basket to hand but seldom used. Caroline had taken to reading aloud, mainly because she was now so uneasy and dared not ask questions. The books by Miss Austen had come, and they went through them with quiet pleasure.

More and more, though, Caroline found Althea with her old scrapbook nearby, and often it was open to the page where there was a drawing of Ronald. Caroline coaxed her with what she hoped were artful questions to talk about the past. But that, too, apparently, Althea wanted no more to share. She seemed to be enclosed in some world of her own from which only Richard's presence could draw her.

He returned the following week, but he was not alone.

When he got out of the carriage he waited until a gaunt man, whose dark hair was streaked with grey, followed, to stand looking around him. His clothing, obviously new, was coarse, and the coat hung loosely on him.

"Oh!" There was a sharp cry as Mollie came running out of the kitchen door at the far end of the house. Her eyes were big and she repeated her first call over and over again until she was in the arms of the stranger.

"You found him—her father!" Caroline clutched Richard's sleeve. They had so long given up any hope that O'Shane had survived that they had ceased to ask questions or search.

"You can thank Corbie," Richard told her. "He came across O'Shane trying to discover what had happened to his family and took him home. The poor fellow was still weak and had to rest up. He was near out of his mind thinking he had lost all of them!" He nodded to where O'Shane stood, Mollie in his arms, the other three children about him, tugging at his coat, crying and laughing altogether.

Caroline's own eyes were moist. She watched Richard hurry up the walk to where Althea stood in the doorway, and then looked to Mollie, who was dragging her father forward by one hand. New life had come into the girl; some of the old perky Mollie had returned.

"Miss Caroline, 'tis my da—not dead and away from us after all! Praise be to God and all His Blessed Saints! Oh, Miss, this is a day of shinin' joy!"

"Indeed it is," Caroline agreed swiftly and welcomed the man. Mr. O'Shane still looked dazed and a little unbelieving at the children and held on to Mollie she noted, with a fierce strength. Though if the pressure of that grasp was painful, Mollie showed no sign of it.

After telling Mollie to see that her father was rested, and to let the cook know of the extra place at dinner, Caroline walked into the garden.

Sitting down on one of the benches Althea so seldom used, Caroline stared at flowers she did not really see and allowed some of her tightly controlled thoughts to stray. She was very glad for Mollie. The future of the children, though Caroline had been trying to formulate plans for them herself, had been much on her mind. Many of the immigrant orphans had been adopted, she knew, but she was also aware that Mollie was bitterly opposed to breaking up what was left of her family and allowing them to go into other homes. Still, the maid would have had no way of caring for them in the city. Nor was there room in the Warwick house to accommodate them, even if Caroline's parents might consent to their staying on with Mollie.

Now, with their father alive, perhaps a new home could be established. She must discover what was for rent in the lower town, where they could be close to a church of their faith, just as she and Mollie had agreed before the terrible plague had blotted out all their hopes. Corbie would perhaps—

Caroline was startled that it was toward Corbie her first thought of help had turned, rather than to Richard, or Papa. But after all, it was Corbie, Richard had said, who had found O'Shane, sheltered him until he could rejoin his family. Corbie seemed always to be at hand when he was needed most.

She closed her eyes and allowed herself to drift back into memories of that very pleasant time with Madam. They had not been able to repeat it and, of course, she could not go now when Corbie was at home. She might almost wish that he had stayed safely in the west just a little while longer—

Caroline, quite deliberately, let the picture of Corbie grow in her mind until it was vivid. Then she waited for her old fear, that queer feeling of sickness to rise in her. Something stirred—but then there was nothing of the old shadow left. She was almost surprised that it was gone. Time, Madam's soothing talk, something, perhaps everything, had made things different. Now her thoughts of Corbie were confused. He was not an easy man, Caroline decided, to really know. Oh, on the surface he was friendly and pleasant; still she had an idea that that was not the real Corbie. There was the Corbie who visited Indian fires at the rendezvous—that Corbie she was sure she did not know at all. There was the Corbie who had faced Major Vickers—Caroline set her mouth firmly as she forced herself to view that memory and set aside the fear and horror. That Corbie—his face with the blaze of blue eyes —was strange also. But no longer frightening. No, no longer frightening.

Also there was the Corbie who had emerged from his mother's easy talk of him—the man of many affairs, interested in new things—not like Archie who was so set in his ways. Caroline's eyes flew open in surprise. Archie and Papa *both* had this mistrust of anything new or different! It was as if any change threatened them. Papa was a very good doctor; everyone knew that. But look how he and Richard no longer even tried to talk about Richard's pain-killing gas, because Papa had set his mind so against it.

Corbie was one, she was certain of that, to keep an open mind and use it. And—she flinched away from the idea— if Madam was to be believed, Corbie was interested in her.

What did she think about Corbie? She could not honestly say. Perhaps if she could see him again, perhaps if Madam did renew her invitation for late summer and Caroline accepted it, she might discover for herself. But it

was all ifs and buts, and she might not be invited again.
Not if Corbie had found his peace of mind and it did not
include her. Caroline gave herself a mental shake. She
must never allow herself to build air castles; that was what
Pris had done, and it had ruined her life.

They had heard nothing at all from the agent in New
York, except that he had been unsuccessful in locating any
passenger of the name Vickers who had taken ship out of
that city for England. And Althea's first discreet inquiries
had borne no fruit. She could only hope that somehow life
had worked out for Pris. Her sister was, she knew now, a
much stronger person inwardly than she had seemed.
Strongheaded as Pris had often been in the past, she also
possessed a vast determination and an iron will. And she
usually won out. The scandal might have been the final
goad needed to set Pris on the way.

''Caroline!''

She was startled out of her thoughts and got swiftly to
her feet as Richard, with Althea on his arm, came down
the walk in the late afternoon sunlight. Their faces might
bear the signs of past strain, but there was a new glow to
both of them. Some of the uneasiness she herself had felt
about Althea lifted from her.

''I was just telling Althea, Papa has decided that it is
time for the Picnic!''

The Picnic was a grand family affair. Perry had once
said, jokingly, that it would summon even long-sleeping
Warwicks from the family cemetery to enjoy it, if they
could be entranced away from whatever staid Heaven they
had gone to grace. Once Papa proclaimed the Picnic, it
became the full center of all family bustle until it was over.

They were to all drive, Richard explained, to the Maple
Grove at Point aux Trembles. Since it was Althea's first

Picnic it was perfectly proper that she appear, even in her condition. Mama was making all the preparations, and they need only be ready to ride in from the opposite direction two days from now.

It seemed that Papa might have ordered the weather, so perfect did the selected day dawn. There had been a rain the day before, which had somewhat dampened Caroline's hopes, but this morning was fresh, cool and fair. They had been packing a hamper of their own—fresh berries, hard-boiled eggs personally selected by Mollie, and pats of fresh butter set within cool, damp cloths. Most of the viands would be prepared by Cook in Montreal, who tried each year to outdo herself. Mollie, her father, and the children followed the carriage in the farm wagon in charge of the Fairlea contributions, for the Picnic included always the entire household.

There was a goodly gathering at the Grove when the Fairlea carriage drew in. All the Warwick household had already arrived and with them were the Horners. There were the Archie Warwicks, it seemed in spite of strained relations. And there were Uncle Henry and Aunt Henrietta, who seldom stirred out of their tall town house any more. But Caroline was surprised at a last carriage.

Madam Hannakar! She was already seated by Mama on a well-cushioned bench. And coming towards their own carriage was a tall man with the wind ruffling his fair hair, bleached even more by the sun. He spoke to Richard and to Althea, bowing as Richard handed her down very carefully. Then he turned and held out his hand to Caroline.

She found that something within her did not hesitate at all. Somehow she had put out her hand to turn without even knowing that she had done so.

Then he swung her out and down, though even when

she put her feet firmly on the ground and needed no support, he still held her hand.

"Caroline," he bowed.

She found her voice deep inside her, and it sounded almost natural.

"Welcome home, Corbie." Then she wondered wildly why she had used just those words.

18

Caroline discovered after the first awkward moment or two that she had not been uneasy with Corbie Hannakar. Instead, it was rather as if the time immediately behind them had been erased and they were on the same friendly footing as they had been before Varennes. Only it was the friendly footing of those who did not really know each other too well. This, Caroline told herself repeatedly, was what she had wanted. To see Corbie as another Richard or Perry—as Perry was beginning to be. Corbie was pleasant and helpful, agreeing at once to help her locate a place for Mollie's family in the lower town and discover some work for Patrick O'Shane.

Caroline found herself during the following days with a growing restlessness. Corbie rode over to Fairlea and brought new magazines from overseas for Althea, as well as fruit more exotic than any growing about them, plucked from that wonderful forcing house Madam had shown Caroline. But never did he suggest—nor did Madam now —that Caroline pay a second visit to Ste. Catherine's.

Her growing restlessness became a little ache, a nagging pain which was always with her and which she could neither entirely forget nor argue herself out of nursing. He had been right, then. The western trip had indeed banished any closer attachment which might have grown between them. Now she knew the loss, and she only hoped her sense of it would not grow. Determinedly she kept up her own façade of friendship, working very hard to present to Corbie the same general air she used with Richard.

As September closed in upon them and Caroline and Althea moved back into town, she expected to see less and less of him, hardening herself to the idea that some things were just never meant to be. There were banners of multi-colored leaves against blue skies, and the city, its ordeal by plague forgotten, was beset by cooler winds. Warm clothing was brought out of storage and there were fires lit.

Caroline knew that Corbie was much occupied with the railroad now being constructed to Lachine, but he still called at St. Gabriel Street and sought Althea to drive out, Caroline with them. Althea's strength seemed restored by the cooler weather and Richard's release from the contagion of the plague sheds.

Perry, subdued, had announced almost roughly that he was returning to McGill in November for the new term at medical school. He mentioned sometimes, in a very off-hand voice which Caroline knew of old, that Dominica Horner was pleasant company. If he had fixed his attention in that quarter, Caroline thought perhaps he would not be successful. She still could not understand how the Horners had not known of Pris' elopement, but if it came into general knowledge, they would certainly not welcome Pris' brother having any serious interest in their only daughter.

Late in September the railroad, the first to operate out of Montreal, was finally completed. Patrick O'Shane had been given work laying track once his strength returned, and had become so competent that he had risen to foreman. The three children were boarded in the lower town with the Widow O'Grady, an old neighbor from Ireland. Mollie went down on her afternoons off, and Caroline often accompanied her. The children were strong and apparently happy, and Mollie was content.

With Corbie as their host, Mama, Caroline and the rest of the Warwicks went to the terminus of the new railway to view the beginning of the first run. The satin hangings and upholstered seats, the shining glass of the carriage windows amazed them. Even the second-class carriages had comfortable seats and blinds. Caroline smoothed one of the seats and wondered how it would feel to travel behind an engine instead of swiftly pacing horses. She was sorry that Althea had waited in Corbie's carriage, rather than joining them in their tour of inspection.

Lord Elgin and his staff appeared. Then the smokestack of the engine emitted heavy puffs, there was the loud squeal of a whistle, the train gave a sharp lurch, and was off, leaving the station filled with billow of the smoke.

Dr. Warwick coughed and rubbed his smarting eyes. "At least it did get off as promised. But we'll all be the better for some fresh air."

"Where's Hannakar's carriage?" he added as he shepherded his family out.

"Over there—" Caroline started and then was puzzled. No carriage stood waiting.

A poorly dressed young man pushed his way through the crowd to touch Richard's arm.

"Begging your honor's pardon, you do be Dr. Harvey?"

Richard nodded, but he hardly looked around; instead, he was searching for a sight of Althea and the carriage.

''The coachman, he said as how I should tell you. He had to be taking the young lady home. The horses, they took fright they did. It was the engine what made 'em rear up.''

Richard flipped him a coin. ''Thank you.'' Then he spoke over his shoulder as he plowed into the crowd himself. ''I'll see to a cab; Althea must need me.''

Caroline, on an impulse she did not at the moment understand, pushed just as vigorously to follow him. ''Wait for me, Richard!'' she called out.

By some miracle Richard found a cab and, though the ride through the crowded streets seemed unending, they got home at last. Mollie was in the lower hall, hovering close to the door.

''Praise be, sir, that you've come!''

''What happened?'' Richard flung at her, already mounting the stairs.

''The horses, they reared up. And your lady, sir, she was thrown from her seat. I got her to bed, me and Jessie—''

Richard was already at the top of the stairs, Caroline speeding after him. Althea lay in bed, her lips colorless in her always pale face, her teeth plainly clenched against waves of pain.

''Please,'' she reached out her hand to catch Richard's. ''Not Barney's fault. Horses—frightened—I—I wasn't expecting it, so I slipped off the seat. Richard—oh, it hurts —it hurts so!''

Richard looked around at Caroline. ''Carrie, you'd better leave. Ask Mama to come up as soon as she gets back.''

''No!'' It was as sharp as a second cry of pain. ''Caroline, please!'' Now the hand went out to her.

Caroline pushed past Richard, caught at that hand. ''I won't leave you. Of course, I won't.''

There was a rustle at the door. Mama came in, shedding bonnet and shawl and letting them drop on the nearest chair. She moved purposefully to the bed. ''Tell Cook she's wanted,'' she commanded.

Althea's grip tightened on Caroline's hand as Mama added: ''Caroline, this is no place for you.''

But her daughter shook her head, and, when she answered, there was some of the same firmness in her voice. ''No, Mama, Althea needs me.''

''Nonsense, this is no place for you.'' Mama smiled at Althea. ''You are going to be all right, my dear.''

''Caroline.'' The name was only a gasp now.

It was Richard who took command. ''All right, darling. Caroline will stay with you. Now, let us see if our son is in so much of a hurry to enter this world that he is on his way a little ahead of time.'' His smile was confident.

A little of the white strain of fear faded from Althea's face. Mrs. Warwick was still frowning at Caroline, but she did not suggest again that the girl leave.

Althea's fingers tightened convulsively as Richard made his examination. He was still smiling. Only Caroline knew somehow that he was no longer as confident as he wished to appear.

''It will be some time. He is not as impatient as we thought.''

The hours dragged on. Richard's smile was strained, then disappeared entirely when he was out of Althea's sight. Mrs. Warwick had an anxious look. Papa came and examined Althea, patted her hand, and said all was well if slow. But his face slipped into lines of worry, Caroline noticed, when he turned to go.

Althea clung to Caroline, looking to her with great eyes full of pain. The younger girl kept her seat as the night wore on. Her hand grew numb from Althea's hold, but she was there and ready to meet Althea's gaze whenever it was turned towards her. That young body under the covers would grow taut, writhe, and utter first small moans and then sharp cries. Dawn came, but with the morning light came no relief.

Caroline could tell from Richard's expression that all was not going well. She kept her place even though her eyes blurred now and then and her body ached. All this was as nothing to what Althea suffered, and she determined that she would continue to stand by.

As the morning hours crept torturously by, Richard, hollow-eyed, the beard shadow dark on his face, moved suddenly to bend over his wife.

"Althea." His voice sounded hoarse, almost harsh. "Will you allow me to use the new gas and try to take the baby?"

Althea's sunken eyes seemed to have trouble focusing on him. "Help me! Please, oh, Lord in Heaven, help me, Richard!"

"Yes. I am going to!" He left the room. Then he was back, a small inhaler in one hand, a bottle of liquid in the other.

"You'll have to help me, Caroline." He spoke quickly, pouring the liquid, explaining what must be done, showing her how to work the valve.

Then he came back to the bed, regarding Althea searchingly for a moment before putting the inhaler to her mouth. Quickly he pinched her nostrils together.

"Breathe in, darling. Now out. Do not fight it. In—out—" His voice was soothing; Althea began to relax. When her body lay quiet Richard turned to Caroline, handed her the inhaler.

"Watch closely. Keep your other hand on her pulse, so. Tell me if that changes—at once!"

His hands were on his wife's body now, intent on the contractions. Althea moaned and stirred.

"Give her the inhaler," Richard ordered curtly. He had forceps in his hands. "Keep her unconscious if you can."

Caroline was only vaguely aware that Mama had come in, gone, and come back with Papa. Without a word Dr. Warwick took Althea's other hand in his, his fingers on her pulse.

Slowly, so slowly, the baby came into view. Richard's face glistened with sweat. "It's here."

Caroline removed the inhaler from Althea's mouth, put it on the small table. She swayed, her head swimming, the room itself twirling about her, and then she slipped to the floor.

There was no cradle waiting in Althea's room when Caroline came in the next morning. Althea herself lay so quiet that Caroline caught at one of the posts of the bed, a cold fear rising in her to see that face, near as white as the pillow against which it rested, unmoving, eyes closed.

Then the blue eyes opened slowly, as if a return to consciousness was more painful than the sleeper could bear. They looked at Caroline. Faint recognition shone in them and then the tears began, slipping down those hollowed cheeks. Caroline crossed to her swiftly.

"It—he—" Althea's lips moved with an effort. "Dead."

"I know, dearest," Caroline stooped, taking out her handkerchief to wipe away those tears. "Do not try to talk. Rest."

Slowly Althea's head turned from one side to the other on the pillow.

"No—son. Richard—no son."

"Dearest, you are much more to Richard. What if he had lost you?" Caroline thought she would never forget the look on Richard's face as he had worked frantically to save his wife, if not the child which she carried.

She settled herself on the bed beside Althea, took both those cold flaccid hands in hers.

"No son," Althea repeated in a thin whisper.

During the days that followed it seemed that Althea might slip away, too. Though she was no longer in the agony which had convulsed her slender body, she seemed to have become so weak and tired that nothing mattered. Caroline stayed with her as much as possible; Richard came to kneel by the bed and talked to her when Caroline slipped away. But it seemed that the loss of the baby had taken all the desire for life from her.

It was when she saw Richard come out of the chamber one morning, his hand over his eyes, his mouth twisted with pain, that Caroline knew something must be done to reach Althea. If the will to live could be poured into a person, then a way of doing so must be found!

She went in with more resolution than she had ever summoned before.

"Althea!" She made that name an insistent call, repeated it until the girl in the bed turned her head a little and opened her eyes. "Althea, what will you do about Richard?"

For a long moment it was as if Althea had either not heard the question or else did not understand it. Then her lips parted slowly and she asked: "Richard?"

Caroline remained exactly where she was.

"Yes, Richard. He needs you very badly, Althea. You make up much of his world." She made herself keep her tone level, even a little sharp. "You must take care of Richard, Althea. You are truly his only family. If he loses you, then he will have no one. Oh, he is like a brother, a son, here, but we are not his—not the way you are,

Althea. Never the way you are.''

She held those eyes which were brimming with tears again.

''I—I lost his son.''

''Althea, that your baby never lived was not your choice.'' Caroline could only hope that she was choosing her words with care, that she was not doing harm now. ''You fought for him, very, very hard. I know. I was here; I watched you fight. We do not choose who lives or dies—unless we will ourselves into something which is a sin—a sin, Althea! I am not going to let you commit that sin!''

Now she came forward and took both of Althea's hands, held them tightly, kept their eyes locked.

''I am not going to let you do this to Richard! He cannot sleep—I have heard him walking the floor at nights. He does not eat. Do you want Richard to be like this—when he loves you so much? That your baby is gone does not mean that your life together is over. Richard is grieving, too—and you are shutting him out—pushing him away when he needs you the very most. Althea, you must stop this! Yes, you will always remember, and you will have an empty place in your heart, but do not leave Richard with a heart which is truly empty. He loves you so much that if you do not fight to stay with him he will only be half a man. I don't want that for Richard, and I do not believe that you want it either.

''Now,'' she gently pressed the hands which she held and then laid them back on the coverlet. ''Mollie is going to bring up the tray which cook has fixed. There is some of her very good soup, and one of her custards. You are going to eat, so that when Richard comes home we shall say to him that you had a meal, and that will hearten him to do the same.''

There was the slightest tinge of color in Althea's cheeks.

She was watching Caroline almost wonderingly, as if the younger girl had suddenly put on an entirely new face.

Caroline went briskly to the nearest window. She loosened the curtain, drew it aside to let in the sunlight. It streamed across the room to touch the end of the bed. Then she came back and smiled down at Althea.

"I won't promise you that it will be easy," she said. "But you will try, and trying counts. It counts a great deal, Althea. I remember when I was so ill that I hardly knew what was going on around me, and you came in and made me drink this or that—you were quite sharp with me. So now you are going to discover that I can also be quite stern. But you are going to get well, Althea. You'll see."

It was a long process, but the Althea who seemed about to slip away from them did slowly gain strength. She sat up against pillows, she moved to a chair by the window, she began to talk, and chiefly she led Richard to talk when he came to her tired and worn. So that Richard, though he was more quiet nowadays, no longer paced the floor at nights.

Caroline arranged for him to share Althea's dinner on the table in their room. Mama seemed willing to leave such matters to her now.

Mama herself was far less bustling and energetic than she had been. Though she appeared happy over Althea's improvement, and Perry's new soberness of manner, Caroline had found her once standing in Pris' old room, looking about her like a sleepwalker suddenly coming to herself in a strange place, and totally bewildered.

For Mama to be this way was frightening. She had turned a tear-stained face in Caroline's direction and asked in a half whisper, "Where is she, Carrie? Where is our Pris?"

Caroline did what she had never ventured to do before. She went to her mother and put her arms about the woman who had always seemed so sure, such a rock of security in the midst of family troubles.

"She'll come back to us, Mama. Someday she surely will."

Mama had never begun her afternoon At Homes again. She seemed more content to spend time each day in Althea's room, sewing and talking quietly now and then. Their only regular visitor, except for Aunt Henrietta who came faithfully each week to urge Mama out for a ride or shopping, was Corbie.

Fruit and flowers flowed in regular abundance from Ste. Catherine's. Twice Madam made the journey into town, though Caroline was distressed to see that her dear friend was finding it more and more difficult to manage, even with her cane for support.

Corbie would talk with Richard and urge him also to go out and about. When Althea was at last able to come downstairs they had a small celebration, and Corbie arrived with a beautiful fur robe—such a wonder as Caroline had never seen. It was all of fine squirrel skins, specially selected to make a coverlet soft and beautiful enough for the Queen herself. With that draped about her, Althea said she felt not the slightest touch of cold.

Snow came before the first of November. Caroline, after her long duties with the invalid, found it good to be going out on short errands. Once a week she and Mollie would visit the lower town with a basket of good things for Mollie's younger sisters and brother. O'Shane had a steady job now with the new railroad, maintaining the tracks, and his son Rory talked of nothing but his ambition to some-day drive the engine itself. Fair mad about the railroad he was, Mollie often said.

But there was another change in the air for the O'Shane family. The Widow O'Grady—she whom they had known for all their lives—was making special dinners more and more for O'Shane. Mollie was a bit sharp about such for a space, and then she relented.

"M' da wants him a true home again. And that he has a right to, the poor man. Ellen O'Grady, she has a heart as big as the world. Even m' mother said that o' her. If they wish to wed, they should have what happiness the Lord sends. M' da and m' mother, they had their time together, good and bad, and they were lovin' of each other. But when a man needs a hearth to set his boots beside, no one should hold it against him when he marries again. The children will have a good woman to see to them." She wiped her hand across the back of her eyes. "Life does not stand around waitin' for a man—nor a woman neither." Now she shot a glance at Caroline. "Maybe you had better be a-thinking of that a little, Miss Caroline."

Caroline had been standing with Corbie's latest offering in her hands—a bowl of flowers, fragrant and beautiful. She flushed, understanding very well Mollie's meaning. But what could she do when Corbie, for all his warm outer friendliness, remained so aloof?

It was that same day that Althea received a letter from England. Flattening out the crossed sheets, Althea had read first to herself and then to Caroline the news of Sir Robert Vickers' heir. Sitting with it on her lap, Caroline looked up, the old fear striking once again at her. She moistened her lips with tongue tip.

"Dead! The major dead! But Pris—where is Pris?"

The news was bad indeed. Sir Robert was still holding on to life, but news had come from America that his heir, the major, had been thrown from a horse in an outlandish overseas place called Louisiana and instantly killed. There was no news of any marriage.

"Papa—Richard—" Caroline drew her shawl about her shoulders. "They will have to know. There must be some way to find Pris." She did not know until that moment how much she had hoped, had told herself that all was well. But if Pris was adrift somewhere in the United States, if there had never been a marriage—if and if—

"Yes." Althea took matters into her hands with quiet decision. It was she who showed the letter to Mama and then to Papa. There must be inquiries made. Perhaps Papa might go himself to New York—though, with the months passed, who might be able to pick up the trail?

Once more the shadow of trouble was dark and heavy over the St. Gabriel Street house. It might never lift again totally, Caroline thought. She went about her round of tasks remembering only too much of Pris. It seemed that the laughing, gay-hearted girl had become a ghost in these rooms, haunting them so that none could forget her for long.

Papa did make the trip to New York, even though bad weather had delayed the coach service to Boston, and might well hold up communication beyond that city. Mama sat in her room now, letting the reins of the household slip slowly into Caroline's grasp, though Althea, much her old self now in strength, shared many duties. But Mama, with her Bible open on her lap, her lips moving often as if she prayed silently, was a painful sight.

Caroline was glad that she could keep busy. With the coming of the cold season there was need in the lower town, for many of the Irish immigrants had not been as lucky as the O'Shanes. Work such as their menfolk were used to was not steady, and there was hunger and the sickness which came from it. Caroline had formed the habit of depending on Mrs. O'Grady, soon to be Mrs. O'Shane, for knowledge of where that help was most needed.

This afternoon, as their sleigh slid down into the darker and meaner streets, where James had to keep a careful eye on the way, Caroline looked about her with a slightly different point of view. She had long known that there was want and trouble in such sections of the city. She could well believe that New York might have even worse sections than this to house the poor and the outcast. What if Pris were in such a place?

She shivered as she took in the darkness, the despair which seemed to radiate from some of the places they passed. Pris—no, not Pris!

They came to the O'Grady's. Rory had been on the watch for them and rushed out to take the two large baskets Mollie handed down to him. Caroline followed her, ivory note leaves and pencil well to hand in her purse to jot down any cases of need Mrs. O'Grady might have turned up this past week. Richard had cautioned her about going into places of illness—had forbidden her to do so, in fact. Respecting his wishes, knowing well that they were born out of his fear for Althea still, as well as his concern for her, Caroline had promised faithfully to report cases of sickness to him, and leave the nursing to others.

Mrs. O'Grady told her about two needy families with children—one family in which there were symptoms of lung fever—taking note of the address for Richard. He devoted part of his practice to charity cases in the lower town.

Still, her thoughts ranged elsewhere until a sudden word of Mrs. O'Grady's caught her full attention.

" 'Tis a lady she is, and all is not right with her, Miss Warwick. She has her pay for the room right enough, Liza says, but she goes out only at night, creepin' in her cloak. And what she buys at the Frenchman's, 'tis scarcely enough to keep a small bird alive. There is trouble there, I'm a-feelin' it in me."

"Where is this—this lady?"

"In the topmost room of the Depree house—and a nasty dirty place it is, too. That Depree woman, she never put a hand to a scrub brush in her life, I'm saying. You need only to look at her to know she's a slut and a drabtail. That poor lady, she chose herself a bad lodging with that one. Liza moved out of there two days ago when there was better lodging down the street. She said as how she'd take no more of the dirt an' the smells an' the nasty tongue of that woman. Drinks she does, and takes the broom to her man. She is a wild one!"

"But this lodger—you say she is a lady?"

"Liza says so. Talks soft and nice, like you do, Miss Warwick. She keeps to herself. But you being another lady an' all—maybe, miss—" She hesitated. "It's a bad house —more'n just the dirt. An' I wouldn't want anyone to be there with that old witch what owns it. I've been thinkin' about a lot, so I have."

Caroline considered what she had heard. A bad house in more ways than one, and a lady living there? She hesitated. This was the kind of thing she had promised Richard—and Mama—that she would not meddle in. But —she thought of Pris. What if her sister were reduced to such straits somewhere, and no one cared?

"Mrs. O'Grady, tell Rory to go out and take the reins for James; James says he is a good steady boy and can be trusted. Then you and I and Mollie and James will go to see this lady—or I shall, and you wait for me.''

"Now that is just the way to do it, Miss Caroline,''
Mollie broke in. "I'll see to Rory and James me ownself.''
She bustled out.

Caroline made a hasty choice from her baskets. There
was a covered pail of soup, a small loaf of new bread, some
cold ends of roast cook had allowed she could spare. With
this made into a packet, Caroline gathered up her allies
and led them across the street. She was uncertain. Perhaps
she would be rebuffed; but that she would not try was a
matter her conscience would not allow.

19

The smell of the house, as Caroline held her skirts carefully away from the foully stained walls, was near as bad as the dreadful odors she remembered of the plague sheds down by the river, and the damp chill was all enveloping. There was shouting and cursing from a back room, but the door was shut. Caroline signaled to James to take up a place at the foot of the rickety staircase, while she, with Mollie and Mrs. O'Grady behind her, made a cautious way up. There were two flights of stairs, and in the gloom of this windowless way they took great care with each step, fearing one of the rotten boards might give way beneath them.

Mrs. O'Grady started puffing, so that Caroline suggested that she and Mollie remain together at the foot of the second flight. The clamor from below was muffled now, and the doors along the landing were all shut. There was an evil atmosphere in this house, more than just that born of decay and foul living. It also held in it a sense of old trouble and despair added to through years of hopelessness.

Caroline came to the final door at the top.

She stood for a long moment, listening for some sound

from within, and then she knocked. There was no imme-
diate answer; perhaps the "lady" was out. Perhaps she
had, like Liza, passed on to other and better lodgings.
Caroline knocked for the second time, more demandingly.

There was a sound. It was not a call to enter, rather—
Caroline's breath caught for an instant—a cry of pain! She
fumbled with the latch, but the door did not yield. Was it
bolted from the other side?

"Please!" She kept her hands on the latch as she called.
"I am a friend. I want to help you. Truly, this is so." How
could one make one's good intentions plain to a stranger
through a closed and bolted door?

She wondered if she dared summon James, allow him to
force the crazy, warped panels before her. She had no
more than a suspicion that something was wrong. But that
suspicion was growing so much stronger that she had
turned to summon the servant when there was a dragging
sound from within, as if something heavy was crossing the
floor, also small whimpers. Then she heard fumbling, the
click of what was certainly a bolt being freed.

Caroline gave a push and the stained door swung
inward. She was facing a square space so gloomy that she
could hardly make out a weaving figure clinging to the
back of a chair, white face turned towards the door.
Caroline took a step forward.

"Carrie! Oh, dear God—Carrie!"

Caroline stumbled. Then she was holding out her arms
to that other who was shrinking away from her, staggering.

"Pris—Pris?" She caught up with the feeble figure still
so masked by the gloom, held it to her. "Pris!"

There was a sour smell arising from the clothing of the
girl she embraced. Pris went limp in Caroline's arms,
nearly dragging her down to the floor with the sudden

weight she had not been braced to take.

"Pris!" Caroline was frightened. It was plain that her sister had fainted or was too weak to stand.

"Mollie!" She raised her voice in a cry which she hoped would carry down to where the maid waited. Now that her eyes were adjusting to the very dim light, she saw a cot-like bed with a tangle of what looked like rotting blankets heaped on it. There was only a single small window, its pane so grimed over that it kept out more light than it emitted, high in the wall.

Somehow she got Pris to the cot, was able to lower her onto it. Her sister stirred and moaned as Caroline looked around to see Mollie in the doorway.

"Get a candle—a lamp—light!" she ordered sharply.

Mollie vanished, and Caroline turned back to Pris. Though she could see only dimly, she suddenly had to steel herself as she tried to settle Pris more straightly on the bed. Pris was going to have a child. And, because of her experience with Althea, Caroline suspected that her sister had already begun labor.

They must get her home—but how could they manage? If James could carry her down to the carriage— Yes. A doctor— Richard— Pris must have help.

"Carrie?"

Caroline bent over her sister. "I am here, Pris. You will be safe now. I have James and the sleigh, and we shall soon have you home."

A hand caught at her arm with a painful grip.

"No!"

"Yes! Pris, of course we shall take you home. You can't stay here."

"No. Swear it to me, Carrie! Swear you won't move me. You can't, anyway. I could not leave this room, not now."

Pris' words were broken by small gasps, and Caroline could guess that pain brought those.

"Then I'll send for Richard." If only Papa was not away!

Again that jerk at her own arm, this time even more demanding and hard.

"I—will—not—have—Richard! Swear it, Carrie! You will not bring Richard! Not him!"

"But you must have help, Pris." Caroline tried to use reason.

Pris laughed then. Not the old laughter which was light and gay—this was such a bitter sound that Caroline wanted to close her eyes to it.

"Not him, Carrie. Get—get Perry."

"Perry!" Caroline repeated.

"Perry. Not—Richard." Pris' body writhed on the noisome bed, her breath caught.

Then the wavering light of a lantern flashed across the room as Mollie came hurrying in. As the beams reached the bed, Caroline flinched; it was very plain indeed that Pris was in labor.

Her sister's face, drawn, greyish, was shining with sweat, her hair, in a dank straggle of unwashed tangles, was plastered to her forehead and cheeks. Even as Caroline tried to brush those strands away from Pris' eyes, the elder girl's body arched and she clenched her teeth, a small trickle of blood coming from the corner of the lip she had bitten in her pain.

Caroline turned to Mollie. "Tell James to go and get Mr. Perry. He will be coming home from classes now. Get him and bring him here. He's not to let any one else know."

"Yes!" The word came as part of the harsh panting from Pris. "No one to know—"

"Ask Mrs. O'Grady for clean blankets—and sheets, if she has them." Caroline stood up from her crouch beside Pris and unfastened her cloak, dropping it on a broken-backed chair. "We shall need water—hot water if she can bring it to us and—"

"Carrie!" It was not really her name but a shriek of pain which brought Caroline back to her sister's side.

"Hurry, Mollie!"

"Yes, Miss." Mollie set the lantern on the floor and was gone again. Then there came the sound of more ponderous steps on the stairs. Mrs. O'Grady reached the door, took one experienced look at the scene, and came briskly forward.

"So this is the way it is. I'll be back, Miss, with what I have that is needful. Don't you fret now. 'Tis a many a little one as has come into the world with my helpin' back in the old country."

From somewhere another lantern and then a lamp appeared. Caroline wondered fleetingly if they might have been borrowed up and down the street. With Mrs. O'Grady and Mollie's help, Caroline got her sister settled on clean bedding, her body sponged with water which was only warm after its transport to this room. Pris' hollow eyes followed Caroline, but she said nothing. She seemed to fight the pain with a tigerish determination which was very different from Althea's pitiful surrender to it. Mrs. O'Grady fastened a towel to the rotting remnants of the headboard, and Pris clutched it with that same fierce look about her that she had worn as a child when she was determined not to yield to any other's will. As Caroline watched the battle, her wonder at Pris' courage grew ever stronger.

There sounded the clatter of boots on the stair, Caroline looked up to see Perry.

"Pris!" he cried out as if he could not believe his eyes.

Then he was by his twin's side.

Pris looked up at him, all her beauty gone, someone who had endured until the only thing left in life was that endurance.

"Perry—help me!"

"I—" For a moment his face had the old softness, the rather indecisive look it had once worn. Then he shook his head as if he were ridding himself of some doubt. "I'll do what I can." Caroline saw his jaw set with the same determination as showed on Pris' agonized face.

Caroline stood back to give him room and caught Mollie's sleeve. How long they had been here, she did not know, but she and Mollie would have been expected back long since, she was sure. With Papa away Richard would be dispatched to hunt them. And if he came when Pris was so opposed, Caroline feared the effect on her sister.

"Mollie, take James and try to think up some story for those at home—" She looked around a little wildly, realizing that at the moment she could not think clearly, that there was probably *no* story to be told. They could not keep this a secret long; she was sure of that, in spite of Pris' wishes. "I don't know what you can do, Mollie, but try."

"Miss Caroline, they won't believe me."

"You'll just have to do your best, Mollie."

The maid went, reluctantly, as Mrs. O'Grady came in, her arms full of more bedding.

"There's more water being brought, Miss. I set Rory to heating up the big kettle. But that old besom down the stairs is ripe to make trouble. She's right behind me now— tried to push me out of the house she did!"

Caroline felt in her side pocket for her purse. There was not much in it—a few coins she had meant to leave with Mrs. O'Grady for the children, because Bridgie's birthday was near. Perhaps those might appease this Depree woman. She went out on the small landing just as there came charging up a harridan with matted hair, a bottle in one clawed hand, shouting words Caroline could not even guess the meaning of.

Catching sight of Caroline, she launched into an even louder tirade and then spat. Raising the bottle like a club, she waved it at the girl, to frighten her out of the way so that she might go on into the room. Caroline stood her ground. She had her purse out, and two of the coins were between her fingers. The rolling eyes of the woman centered on those and she was suddenly silent, her tongue moving out to lick the spittle from her lips.

"Take these," Caroline said with all the firmness she could summon. "Get out!" She would not touch the clutching hand which flailed forward to take the coins; instead she dropped them to the top step, saw the woman scrabble for them quickly, then bite each in turn to assure herself by her straggled, blackened teeth that they were real. She scowled fiercely up at Caroline and waved her bottle, but as the girl stood still, the woman, still muttering, finally turned and went below. Though she stopped again at the foot of the flight of the stairs, shook her fist and screamed a last imprecation.

Caroline edged back into the upper room. Perry looked up; his face seemed almost as haggard and drawn as Pris' as he stepped away from the bed.

"There may be something wrong. I wish Richard was here. Lord, I don't know enough."

"She won't have him—" Caroline began.

Perry looked grim. "She may have to."

Then a scream which was near to a shriek sent him hurrying back to Pris. She had raised her head, was straining with both hands on the towel at the head of the bed, while Mrs. O'Grady urged, "A deep breath now, girl. Bear down. You'll have to help. Aye, now that's a good lass. Try again."

Pris gasped and shuddered. Mrs. O'Grady looked to Perry. "If it's a true doctor you are, man, get to your work. I have seen this aforetimes. The babe needs turning."

Perry's hands as he reached out were shaking. "I'm not a doctor, not yet. Pris—we'll have to get Richard."

Her eyes flew open and there was a rush of dark blood into her cheeks.

"No! You can do it, Perry. You have to—you have to!"

If they only had some of that vapor, Caroline thought wildly. But even if Perry could find it among Richard's supplies, there was no time to go to the St. Gabriel house and back. Pris needed help right now.

"There is no time to get Richard." She was not sure of that, but she *was* sure that Perry had to be pushed into action. Althea had borne her ordeal differently. But Pris was strong, and Caroline sensed that time was running short.

Perry drew a deep breath, thrust his hands into the kettle of water which Rory had fetched only moments previous. He snatched up a threadbare but clean linen towel which lay nearby and turned back to Pris.

There was another shriek from the bed, the agony of which made Caroline fight a rise of sickness into her throat. Then Pris writhed under Perry's hands. A lump of red flesh, bloodstained and limp, slid into her brother's hold. Mrs. O'Grady gathered it into a second towel. She gave it a shake, and there sounded a thin, wailing cry.

Caroline's hands, which had been balled into fists, uncoiled. Somehow she had been sure that there would be no new life this time either. Mrs. O'Grady thrust the feebly crying bundle in her direction, and Caroline took it into her arms as the woman busied herself with Pris. Perry had staggered back, his shoulders supported by the wall, his chest rising and falling under his stained shirt as if he had run a hard race.

There came a screeching cry from the landing. Caroline whirled to see the Depree woman, her bottle upraised, snarling as she lunged in. Perry moved towards her, but she was too quick for him, raking her talons of nails across his face.

"Out—out with th' lot of you!" She had found her English now. "Take that drab and git you out!"

She eluded Perry's grasp and struck Caroline on the shoulder with such force as to send the girl spinning into her brother, striving to keep the baby from being harmed.

Mrs. O'Grady moved between the harridan and the bed, her own fist raised.

"Be off with you—you dirty whore!" the Irishwoman shouted. "She is mad in her cups, sir."

Perry moved in, more carefully this time, caught the woman's shoulders from behind and swiftly swung her around, half throwing her out, to slam the door behind her. Though he swiftly set the bolt into place, that did not deter the Depree woman. She remained outside, battering at the door until Caroline was sure that the ancient planks would give way under the fury of her attack.

"We've got to get Pris out of here," Perry said, looking about as if he expected the dirty walls to suddenly display another exit.

There was a second roar of sound.

Mrs. O'Grady shook her head. "That'll be her man. She holds the reins over him and they are both well out of

their wits with drink. We shall have to wait until they get
tired of the play, sir. He has a knife, does that Georges, sir,
and he can be well nasty when he takes a mind to it.''

Perry gave a small lopsided smile. ''Well,'' he looked at
Caroline, ''there's James.''

She shook her head. ''I sent him and Mollie back. We
had to have some kind of a story—though they'll probably
get the household roused no matter what they say.''

''And the quicker the better.'' He swept Caroline's
cloak from the rickety chair, grabbed up one of the stained
towels; and, standing on the unsteady seat, smeared the
cloth across the window until he could look out.

''There's someone coming—a sleigh.'' Now he
pounded at the window, trying to loosen it. ''Someone
just ran out of the house across the street—''

''Mine,'' Mrs. O'Grady nodded. ''That's Rory, he was
told to watch if there was help needed.''

''Two men out of the sleigh; they're coming in. James
—and another. He must be Richard!''

Caroline glanced at the bed, half expecting to hear a cry
of protest from Pris. But her sister lay with closed eyes, the
blood of her bitten lip still dark against the pallor of her
skin. She might have swooned. With a quick fear, the
baby still mewling weakly in her arms, Caroline moved to
the bedside, bent over Pris. Yes, she was breathing, and
slowly the lines of pain were fading out of her face, leaving
it oddly slack and somehow much older looking.

Even through the walls they could hear now the screaming of the Depree woman, and a deeper roaring which
might mark the presence of her mate. Then those were
muffled, and there came the sound of footsteps on the un-
carpeted stair, coming so swiftly they could not be the
drunken stumbling of the infamous pair from below.

Perry crossed the room quickly, shot the bolt back. "James!"

But the man who came into the lamp light was much taller than the footman, and there was no mistaking that breadth of shoulder, the sun-bronzed face and wide-blue eyes. Caroline felt so faint that she stumbled to the chair where Perry had stood, and fell onto it. A moment later she was snatched up, and found herself steadied, held in a secure arm.

"Please, Corbie. The baby—" she managed, but she did not try in the least to move free of a hold which made her feel as safe as if nothing could ever touch her for harm again.

"The baby?" There was a surprised note in his voice. "To be sure." He had not released her, but he held her off a little, the better to view the fussing bundle she held.

Caroline was not really aware that she was crying until the tears were salty in her mouth as she answered, "Pris—it's Pris' baby. Oh, Corbie." She leaned her head on his shoulder, her cheek against the damp cloth of his overcoat. "I'm so tired—so very tired! But you're here. And now—now it all comes right!"

It did, of course, just as Caroline had in her heart always known that it would when Corbie was there. She was hardly aware of allowing herself to be swathed in her cloak and then half-carried, half-led down the stairs, the baby still in her arms, to be nestled deep into the robes in Corbie's sleigh. There was another sleigh drawing in, and she had a glimpse of James in the driver's box. Mollie tumbled out of that and came running. Caroline roused enough to stop her climbing in with her.

"Pris!" she ordered. "Stay with Pris. Make them bring her home!"

Mollie looked mutinous for a moment, then nodded and returned to that dark and dreadful house.

The baby began to cry, much more forcibly now, as if it were angry at the world in which it found itself. Caroline cuddled it against her, and watched the doorway through which Mollie had gone. It seemed only moments before Corbie's tall figure appeared in the poorly lighted street, James with the lantern before him, Perry and Mollie bringing up the rear.

In his arms Corbie carried Pris who lay limply, still perhaps in a swoon. With Perry steadying her body, they settled her in the other sleigh, her head on Mollie's lap, robes pulled high about her, Perry half crouching beside her to keep her as comfortable as he might. Corbie came lightly back to join Caroline, slipping in beside her, his arm about her shoulders, as he signaled James and his own driver to drive on. Then they were off down the street.

Weariness settled on Caroline like a heavy burden she could not hope to throw off. She found it very right that she should be resting her head against Corbie Hannakar's broad shoulder.

"I knew," she said, speaking her thoughts aloud. "I knew it would be all right if you came. It will always be all right." This was no nightmare but another kind of dream —one which, in spite of the past hours, was of peace and growing quiet happiness—a happiness, she feared now, that was hardly more than a dream.

"It will always be all right, dear," he agreed.

Perhaps Caroline slipped farther into the dream. She did not afterwards ever remember much of the rest of that night. There was a great deal of confusion, during which the baby disappeared from her hold. She had a vague memory of seeing it in Althea's arms, while Mama hurried past her to greet Perry and Corbie coming in the door, carrying Pris between them. Then somehow Caroline was safe in her own bed, a cup of hot tea thick with dissolving honey in her hands while Mollie urged her to drink it all. She could not even remember the cup being taken from her again.

It was at least mid-morning when she awoke, for the sun was bright across her room. There was something—something happy. She searched back into a dream—but it was not a dream. Corbie!

Caroline sat up in bed. She put her hands crosswise over her breast, hugged herself. Corbie's arms around her—Corbie!

For a long and ecstatic moment she allowed herself to remember, to feel. Then other memories crowded in. Pris! The baby!

Slipping out of bed, Caroline washed in a basin which someone must have brought in not too long before, because the water was still warm, though the room itself held chill. She dressed hurriedly, not wanting to ring for Mollie, struggling to get her hair into smooth order before she ventured out in the hall.

Althea stood by the door of Pris' old room. Caroline hurried to her.

"Pris?"

Althea nodded to the closed door. "She is sleeping. They gave her something to make her drowsy. She woke in the night and was hysterical when she found herself here."

"And—and the baby?" She was hesitant about asking that of Althea, though the other girl showed no sign of pain.

"It is a boy, and healthy, Richard says. Pris is not so well, but she is strong and he believes that all will be eventually right with her.''

There was much to be sorted out. Where had Pris been since she left Boston? Why had she come back in hiding to Montreal? What of Major Vickers and his death half the continent away? Caroline began to see that to have Pris safe at home again was merely the beginning of what might be a new time of concern and trouble.

''Perry brought some things from that place,'' Althea said slowly. ''Jessie was going to throw out a cloak, but then she found something sewn into the lining. It is a marriage certificate of sorts, though we do not know whether it is legal. Richard took it this morning to show to Mr. Hannakar. It may be that Pris was married according to some form accepted in America.''

''I wonder where she has been and why.''

Althea shook her head. ''We shall not know until she is well enough and ready to tell us. We must discover whether it was a legal marriage, Caroline. Sir Robert is clearly dying. He may be already dead by now. But any son of the major's would be his direct heir. Richard realized the serious aspect of this at once.''

Caroline began to understand. Pris' homecoming need not be a source of shame to her if the marriage was legal. And a baby who was heir to a title and an estate in England would start life well off; and Pris could hold her head as high as she had always done. This might well be the start of a new and happier life for her.

''Oh. Mrs. O'Grady.'' She remembered that staunch supporter of the night before. ''If it had not been for her —and for Perry—''

Althea smiled. ''Mrs. O'Grady will be amply repaid for her help. Corbie Hannakar has already, I believe, taken steps in that direction. And Perry—well, I think that Perry has proven himself. Papa Warwick will be pleased—''

''Papa?''

Althea understood her. ''A message has been sent to New York. Mr. Hannakar dispatched one of his own men to carry it through.''

''Corbie knows how to do everything!'' Caroline announced, without quite hearing the pride in her voice.

Althea smiled, then kissed her lightly on the cheek. ''I see I am to wish you happy, my dear. And I do—oh, how I do. May you find just what Richard and I have known.''

Caroline's answering smile was a little timid. ''He has never really asked me you know—not really.''

''I think sometimes the actual words, my dear, are not so important as what lies behind them.''

Mollie was coming up the stairs.

''Oh, Miss Caroline, I was wonderin' if you were awake yet. Mr. Hannakar, he is awaitin' downstairs. This is the second time he's come, and I think—''

But what Mollie thought was lost as Caroline ran lightly past her, going down the stairs at the fast pace of her childhood. She threw open the parlor door. He stood before the fireplace watching for her; before she could move, he had taken two long strides and was with her. Once more she was in his arms—not only in his arms, but being kissed as Caroline had never understood one could be kissed.

When she had her breath again, she looked up to meet those blue eyes, which were not in the least cold or glittering.

''You never asked,'' she said.

''I never asked?'' One of his eyebrows slid up in a way she had long ago learned to watch for. ''What is it I have not asked, my darling?''

''If I would—be your darling, I mean,'' Caroline returned with a beginning smile.

"So it is that you want—a formal declaration?" Corbie laughed. "Well, I suppose a gentleman on such occasions does have responsibilities, does he not? Very well, Miss Caroline Warwick, will it please you to become my very dearly beloved wife?"

There was no shadow now, no chance that the nightmares would return. She was so sure of that. Caroline swept a deep and formal curtsey, just as if she were greeting Lord Elgin himself.

"Mr. Corbious Joseph Hannakar, I shall be most deeply honored—"

She did not get to finish before Corbie was upon her again, and she discovered that there was such a thing as true happiness in the world. Even if it might not abide so high and strong in the future, the flow of this would warm her for the rest of her life.

Caroline stood before the long mirror in Pris' room. There was a patch of sun about her as she stared into the glass. For a moment or two she felt odd, as if she were looking at another Caroline, one she did not know. This fine young lady in her green merino with a border of narrow braid was all elegance. The bonnet on her head was of soft gray velvet bordered with ermine.

She reached forth one hand and almost timidly touched the mirror's slick surface as if to assure herself that it was real, so that what it reflected must also be real. Behind her across the low slipper chair lay a cloak lined, collared, bordered with the same ermine, and with it a matching muff. Across the hall, in her old room, were strapped bags —the trunks had already gone.

There was still the scent of orange blossoms in the air, or

at least she felt she could smell them—those orange blossoms and myrtle which dear Madam had sent for her bridal wreath, and which she had worn only an hour or so ago.

Caroline smiled a little timidly at the lady in the mirror —the lady who was no longer Caroline Warwick, but Mrs. Corbius Joseph Hannakar. She repeated the name aloud, trying to get used to the sound of it, as she would hear it all the rest of her life.

She was very glad she had these few last moments alone, a chance to meet Mrs. Corbious Joseph Hannakar for herself, to think back over all that had happened. Althea, Mama, and even Pris—they had guided her, made this day so special and perfect. Only she still felt a little breathless that it had happened at all.

Now she was going to leave the St. Gabriel house and even Montreal, and start a new life which would be more exciting, wider, different from anything she had ever dreamed. But with Corbie—nothing else really mattered. As she stepped back to pick up her cloak, she saw those other bags just inside the door.

Pris' life was about to start over again, too. What would be before *her*? At least she would have their company for her journey. Pris, the new quiet, strange Pris who had become someone so different—so unapproachable. Caroline sighed for just a moment. Pris seemed as old as Mama sometimes now, though since she had regained her health she still was outwardly the Pris who had danced and played and enjoyed life less than a year ago.

"Caroline, we have been waiting for you!"

Mama stood in the doorway, smiling.

Caroline caught up her muff. "I just wanted to see—in a larger mirror—"

Mama laughed softly. "My dear, it is a lovely dress. And you are a lovely bride." She came to take Caroline in her arms and kiss her. "You will be happy, dearest. I do not doubt that in the least. Corbie is a fine young man and he loves you deeply. But it is time to go."

Caroline saw the tears in Mama's eyes.

"I love you!" Now it was her turn to offer a close embrace. "Oh, Mama." For a second or two the strange feeling was back; she was walking away from all she knew, all that had been warm and close about her.

Perhaps Mama guessed her feelings, for she said, "You are a woman now, my dear. You have a husband, a life of your own. But where there is love, there is also trust and security."

As her voice trailed off Caroline knew that Mama was thinking of Pris. How difficult it would be for her. And she would not return later to live close by, to come and spend pleasant times with Althea and Mama. There might be little hope of seeing Pris again.

"She—she wants to go, Mama." Caroline said in a low voice.

"It is her duty, my dear. Since their marriage was legal by the law of the country in which it was made, Pris has a duty to her child—that he inherit what is rightfully his. It is most obliging of Corbie to escort her to England and make sure that her rights are recognized properly. To have you with her on that journey will also be a source of happiness. It—it may be difficult for her, but with you and Corbie at hand to begin with, Pris will be all right. I am sure of that!" Mama's answer came strongly, but Caroline wondered if she was reassuring herself by those words. "Now, my dear, you really must hurry. Pris will join you here in the morning when you return to set off for New

York and then for England. Such a long way.'' Mama drew her hand lovingly down Caroline's shoulder, and gave a little tug to her daughter's cloak as if to make sure it was well fastened.

They went out together and found Althea just coming up the stairs, her blue gown with its wreaths of ribbon rosebuds swirling out about her. There was color in Althea's cheeks now. She appeared stronger, more assured, as if she were looking forward to being Mama's daughter in the singular. She was laughing, too, as she caught sight of Caroline.

''Dearest, I think your new lord and master grows a little impatient. He is becoming so very polite—a warning sign. And Madam is ready to embark in her sleigh. Oh, Caroline—'' Again there were arms about her, and she caught Althea's lovely scent. ''I am so happy for you!''

There was only one left. Caroline had waited, hoping that Pris would come—would wish her well. Though her sister had attended the wedding, she had kept well in the background of the parlor, sitting beside Mama. She had come when they cut the cake to murmur good wishes. But there had been that closed look still in her face, and Caroline had felt a small tinge of hurt. She told herself that Pris must be remembering so much, and those memories must be so ugly—more ugly perhaps than her family would ever understand or know.

No happy wedding for Pris, no smiles and good wishes. She had been alone, listening to a Justice of the Peace (as Corbie had explained) tie her to a man who had already shown his lack of character. He had married her because she was pregnant with his child, because he thought that such a marriage might mean the difference between plenty and failure for him.

Then he had joined in a wild plan to go into South
America, where there was a promise of loot and high pay
for a trained officer who could drill peasants into a raggle-
taggle army. What had made him do that instead of returning to England, to make peace with his kin, Pris could
not or would not say. She had begun to suspect that perhaps he believed their marriage faulty, that the story of his
disgrace had already reached his home. He wanted gold;
he had been promised it by conspirators who talked of an
easy victory in their own land. So he had left her with a
near-empty purse and gone to die, leaving her nothing to
do but to creep back to Montreal. Perhaps, in spite of her
pride, she had hoped that there would be a miracle there
to give her something—

Now there was this new life, well away from all that had
made up the old, in which she would be free of the past. If
Caroline and Corbie could open the door for her, they
would. Corbie himself had wanted to visit England, to
show Caroline some of the wide world in which he loved to
adventure.

Caroline looked down into the hall. No, there was no
Pris. But there was Papa beaming, and Richard, his eyes
kindly and loving for a moment on Caroline and then
going beyond to Althea, Perry standing straight, a new set
to his mouth which became him. Beyond them—

Caroline forgot everyone else.

She took the last steps in a rush and went to Corbie.
Nothing and no one else mattered at this moment. Where
that tall, straight man was—that would always be home!